THE NATURE OF THE GRAVE

A John and Sarah Jarad
Nantucket Island Mystery

Martha Reed

Published by
BUCCANEER/KMA
PITTSBURGH
2005

Permissions
Buccaneer/KMA
reedme@telerama.com

or visit the author's Web site:
www.marthareed.com

Printed in the United States of America.

ISBN 1-59113-638-5

First Buccaneer/KMA edition published 2005

Nantucket Blessing:

"May your joys be as deep as the ocean,
and your troubles as light as the foam."

* * * * * *

Joan and Bill
May 25, 1995

and now, of course,
(since this blasted thing has taken me so long),
C. Reed
and Molly

* * * * * *

EZEKIEL 37:3

"And he said unto me, Son of man, can these bones live?
And I answered, O Lord God, thou knowest."

* * * * * *

Special thanks must go out to my family and friends
who weathered this lengthy creative project
with their unwavering support.

The Writers at 3Rivers
Cynthia Chertos, Jim McCague, Celeste Allen,
Gale McGloin, Betsy Reiling, Michelle Belan

Family & Friends
Joan R. Widdoes & Sarah R. Reed
Christine Hilliard

Chapter One

12 Macy Lane
Wednesday, January 13, 1999

The island was flat, and the cold howled across the moors like a living thing. With no trees for protection, no hills or valleys to channel it away, the wind blasted into the weathered clapboards of the house, shooting icy drafts through the meager insulation, a malevolent banshee trying to force its way in.

Sarah Jarad snuggled deeper under the covers, deciding firmly that nothing had prepared her for winter on Nantucket.

Like all newcomers, Sarah had learned quickly that heating oil was an imported and precious commodity. Each morning she woke with only the tip of her cold nose showing outside the comforter. She slid out of bed, leaving the warmth of her sleeping husband and scrambled into layers of fleece-lined clothing.

The kitchen was the only truly warm room in the house. Her grandfather from Vermont, wise with sixty years of New England winters, had shipped them a wood stove as a wedding present. Back in September, Sarah had scoffed, but now the stove held a place of honor, enthroned on the blue slate hearth. She lit a handful of driftwood sticks, bleached brittle and white like ghostly fingers. Wood was another expensive concern. A cord here cost twice what she had paid for it on the mainland, and since they were saving every dime toward a mortgage, Sarah had taken to the beach, scavenging. John had thrown a fit when he found out what she was doing, until she proved they were saving a third of a month's pay just on fuel. Her husband had given in, grumbling that he had married his mother, whose thrift was legendary.

Overhead in the loft, Sarah heard John stumble out of bed. He bumped down the narrow stairwell, struggling into a rough woolen sweater. Planting himself in a chair, he ran his fingers though his hair, putting it in order. Sarah cheated the coffeemaker and set his mug on the table. As she did, he wrapped his arms around her waist and pulled her, unprotesting, onto his lap.

"I woke up, you were already gone." John worked his face into the folds of Sarah's bathrobe, inhaling deeply.

Sarah lifted his face in her hands and kissed him. "And good morning to you, too."

"Is there a hurry? I don't have to report to the station until nine."

"I want to get to the bank, first thing." She rose, retying her robe and pulling a check from her pocket. "Meredith sent me a commission."

"We're not hurting for money." John sat back in his chair. "The rent's not due for another two weeks."

"I know that, but I like seeing the money in our account. I sleep better, knowing it's there."

John smiled to himself. Getting used to married life was hard enough, without discovering, after the wedding, that your wife had a phobia about bouncing checks. He had tried to explain to Sarah that the town's automatic payroll deposit system had worked without a glitch for years, but she would have none of it. She had been footloose, a gypsy, for too long; Sarah didn't believe the money was real until she held it in her hand. John sighed. There would be no fooling around before work this morning. He had learned to recognize that gleam in his wife's eye. She was on a mission.

Sarah raised the coffeepot. "Touch-up?"

"Just a little," he agreed, pushing his mug across the table. They had been married only four months, and he still found the whole idea of "having a wife" pretty amazing. Sure, there had been girlfriends before, and serious ones, too, but no woman had ever rearranged his life like Sarah had. She blew into town last May, and wham! Everything had changed.

"Must be love," he muttered, pushing back from the table and finishing his coffee over the sink. "Don't run any water for a minute, okay? I'll jump in the shower."

"You got it," Sarah agreed. It amused her they were still working on house rules.

She fixed herself a second cup and went to the window to check on the weather. Another picture perfect January day, clear and crisp. Fresh snow had dusted the bayberry and wild rose bushes that filled their yard, or what passed for a yard on Nantucket, for no one here really had a yard, or even tried growing a lawn. People in town kept brick walkways and clipped boxwood hedges; outside of town they built their homes in the middle of isolated sandy clearings, leaving the remaining property pretty much as they had found it: pitch pine, poverty grass, broom crowberry.

Sarah had asked John why people built their homes this way, and he had given her a one word answer: ticks.

It proved to be another example of misguided human kindness. Passing sailors had rescued a deer swimming across Nantucket Sound and released it to run wild on the island. Years passed, other humans worried the buck might be lonely, so they imported mainland does. The does brought deer ticks as a housewarming present, the ticks carried Lyme disease, and as result, no one on Nantucket ever walked in tall grass anymore.

No matter, Sarah shrugged. I'll take this island as it is. From the moment the ferry had entered the harbor around Brant Point and she had seen the quaint gray palette of a town spreading out before her, she had known this place was home. And it was home for her without apology; home in the corny, old-fashioned sense of the word.

Sarah was the first to admit that her choice made no sense. She certainly had no ancestral claim to this part of the world. One-half of her family had stepped off the boat from Ireland, the other half was eastern Shawnee. Claiming County Cork or the Ohio River valley made a whole lot more sense than loving an isolated elbow of sand thirty miles to sea. But home for Sarah had always been a matter of heart, and her heart had never been ruled by common sense. Nantucket was her home in everything from the way the salt breeze stirred her long hair to the muted colors she discovered in the lapped layers of tidal sand.

Upstairs, she heard John drop the soap, and curse. Husband. Now there was an idea for you. But, just as Sarah had instantly known this place was home, she had also known that this man was her husband, from the first moment she laid eyes on him. Love at first sight was a comic proposition, a bedroom farce, until it happened to you.

Of course, nothing had happened easily. There had been awkward weeks of chance encounter and stammered, blushing reply. The island was only 50 square miles, and patrolling it was a part of John's job description. Sarah had bumped into

John Jarad on a daily basis, either at the Espresso Café first thing in the morning or the Chicken Box after hours, dancing to reggae music. And Sarah's sister Joan hadn't hindered matters either, leading the cheer from the sideline. But somehow, even in the whirling, magical confusion of that time, Sarah had known that everything would work out; that this decision, required of her, would by its very nature have to be a leap of faith, a demonstration of blind trust in her own judgment and in her hopes for the future.

So, one languorous Tuesday afternoon four short months ago, on a sailboat in the middle of Nantucket Sound, she had looked up into John Jarad's hopeful brown eyes, taken a deep breath, and said: 'yes'.

And now, here she was. A wife. Sarah shook her head at the thought and climbed the stairs to their bedroom loft, smiling as she caught the sound of John singing tunefully in the shower. She grabbed her jeans hanging on the footboard of their bed, judged them clean enough, and selected a heather-blue sweater from the dresser. She wasn't planning on taking her coat off in town anyway. Her shower could wait until later.

John hit one last lingering note and shut off the water. Sarah retraced her steps to the kitchen to wait. She finished the coffee, rinsing the pot and setting it in the dish rack to dry. Deciding a grocery list was a good idea, she spent a further five minutes rummaging through the junk drawer looking for some paper and a pen that worked.

"Someday, when we get our own house," she vowed, "I will have a place for everything and everything in its place!"

"I heard that," John called down over the buzz of his electric razor. "And this place isn't so bad. At least it's cheap."

"Twelve hundred a month is not cheap!"

"It is for Nantucket." John clattered down the stairs, straightening his tie. "We could always move in with my mother. You know she offered."

"John, we've been through that already." Sarah tested a pen. "We're too old to be living at home, especially you."

"Seven years is not that much of a difference, and she does have a point. We would be saving more toward our down payment if we didn't pay rent."

"Just because you're right doesn't mean I have to agree." Sarah paused to admire her husband in his police lieutenant's regalia. John in uniform always brought a wickedly evil grin to her face. The uniform made him look so official, so authoritarian, such a contrast to the gentle man she loved. But she had to admit, once John put on his mirrored sunglasses and became The Man with No Eyes, she felt a thrill, a frission, of raw desire.

"Don't look at me like that if you want to get into town this morning," John warned.

She gave herself a shake. "You're right, sorry. Listen, I need to use your truck today, but I'll pick you up after your shift."

"Fine." John grumbled. Married life sometimes involved painful compromise. "But I'm driving."

The distance from their rented house to the South Water Street station was only a short hop, the sole advantage to living in town. John handled his truck with the unconscious skill that follows complete familiarity. Turning the corner on Chestnut, he noticed a pedestrian muffled to the ears in a red-striped scarf and gave him a two-finger salute.

"Who was that?" Sarah asked, idly.

"Mike Hussey. We played league soccer together. Eighth grade."

"Ah." It came as no surprise to Sarah that John knew the man on the street. As a native, and a cop, John seemed to know everyone. It was one of the hardest adjustments she had to make. Her husband could walk into a party full of people and glad-hand every single one of them. Sarah still found herself at a disadvantage, rifling through short-term memory, desperately trying to connect a name to a face. Or even worse, trying to connect an insider childhood nickname to a face. She grew indignant at the thought. How were you supposed to remember the business affiliation for a man introduced as 'Puffy'? Or that your insurance agent's given name was Helen Marie, when everyone called her 'Jinx'?

"What's your game plan for today?" John asked, putting the truck in park.

"First stop the A&P. I'm hungry for roast pork with applesauce. Then lunch with your Mom." Sarah scooted across the seat and took his place behind the wheel. "I'll call you later and let you know how it went."

John leaned back in through the open door. "Honey, my mother likes you, you know."

"I know she does, John. I just can't help it though, sometimes I wonder."

"Wonder what?"

Sarah struggled to explain. "Your Mom's only known me for what? Six, seven months? And all your other girlfriends, well, I mean, they were cousins; I'm sure Jenny knew plenty about them. Sometimes, well, sometimes I think your Mom still wonders who I am."

John zipped his coat. "That is not true. I never dated any of my cousins. They wouldn't go out with me."

"You know what I mean."

"Yes, sweetheart, I do know what you mean." He chose his next words carefully. "I know you've been asked to make a lot of adjustments lately. We both have. And Sarah, I'm counting on you to make them. Just let me know if it gets to be too much; sweetheart, that's why I'm here. And will you please stop worrying about my mother? Consider her side of things. Her thirty-year old son walks in the house one day and announces he's just met a girl in a bar and he's going to get married." He grinned. "Part of this is my fault, I accept that. I did not break 'us' to my mother in the right way. But sweetheart, you'll just have to forgive me, because I wasn't thinking clearly at the time."

Sarah laughed. "Is that really how you told your mother about us?"

"It was worse than that, actually." John scratched his jaw. "I remember telling her you were the only woman in the world for me: my one, true, only. I was probably a complete fruitcake about it. But you have to give Mom some credit; once she sat down, she said if that was how I truly felt then I was not allowed to let anyone or anything stop me. And you can take that to the bank. My mother does not lie. If she says she likes you, she does."

"Well, she'd better, because I'm not leaving."

John relaxed. Somehow, with Sarah, finding the right words came easy. "That's the spirit. I'll call you later. Enjoy your day."

Sarah drove along Main Street, delighting in the brick storefronts with their festive window displays and holiday greenery. The town of Nantucket was deserted this time of year, such a difference from peak season when parking was impossible. As she turned right, the truck's worn tires slipped on the wet cobblestones, and she slowed, crossing a speed bump into the public parking lot.

She was in luck. It was still early, no one was out yet. Sarah pulled a cart from the corral and headed in. Grocery shopping was her least favorite chore, but if she followed her list and kept her focus, she would be home in plenty of time for a shower and lunch with Jenny. Dinner was simple: slice an onion, toss the pork in the crockpot and she would have the whole glorious afternoon free to paint.

She dug the list from her purse and steered through produce. The aisles were narrow and the shelves overstocked, and if there was a floor display, forget it, you could get trapped behind your cart for life. The meat counter ran along the back wall, deserted. Sarah tore a number off the paper roll and waited patiently for some sign of activity. She waited one more minute, and then thought: nuts to this, and rang the bell.

The butcher backed through a swinging door carrying a chrome tray. "Morning. miss. What can I get for you today?"

"A three or four pound pork roast?"

"I've got a nice one in the back. I'll go get it."

Sarah scanned her list one more time, double-checking, because there was nothing worse than getting all the way home and realizing you had forgotten that one thing. And there was always something. It didn't matter how organized you were, how super-efficient, there was always that one thing you forgot . . .

"Gangway!" Sarah heard a woman shout. She had no time to react as a runaway cart smashed into hers, snagging it and carrying it away.

"Oh, lady, I am so sorry! Are you okay?"

Sarah turned to answer and caught herself gaping instead. Standing before her was a middle-aged woman in a worn Navy peacoat. The woman had straggling gray hair, a look of concern in her periwinkle blue eyes, and a curling, almost pubic, blond beard.

Intellectually, Sarah struggled to catalog this last item. More of a goatee, really, she decided.

"Thought I surprised you!" The bearded woman announced, her voice a strong, nasal monotone. "Turned around and my cart was gone! They really need to level this floor!"

"That's alright." Sarah retrieved her cart and wheeled it to one side. "No harm done."

"You're not from around here, are you? You're a coof. I can tell it from your voice."

Coof? Sarah didn't recognize the word, but it sounded dubious. She added it to her 'ask John later' list. "I've been living on Nantucket since May."

"Well, near anything counts, nowadays. Used to be you had to live here years to call yourself a Nantucketer. Now they're letting anyone come over. I saw a yacht pull into the harbor that was bigger than the ferry! And they drive trucks inside the ferry!"

"I saw one like that, too. Last summer, with my sister. It was tremendous."

The older woman lowered her voice. "Who are those people, d'you think? Foreigners from New York, maybe? Or Hollywood movie stars?"

"I'm sure they could be both."

"Let me mend my manners." The woman stuck out her hand. "We're going to be friends. I'm Addie Simpson."

"I'm Sarah Jarad. Nice to meet you, Addie."

"Does Stan know you're here?"

"He's getting a pork roast for me."

"I'm here for corn beef. Mom's making Boston boiled dinner for supper. I love boiled dinner, don't you?"

"Absolutely. Especially the buttered cabbage."

"Well, that's good, but corn beef is the best. With yellow mustard. It's got to be the yellow mustard, too, not the brown."

"Here we go." Stan interrupted, pushing through the door carrying a neat, paper-wrapped package. "One four-pound pork roast. Ah, good morning, Addie. Didn't see you standing there."

"Stan, Mom wants a corn beef for supper."

"And I'll help you pick out a good one, as soon as I'm through with this lady. Will that be all, miss?"

"Yes, thank you."

"Nice to meet you," Addie repeated. "Sorry again I hit you."

Stan glanced between his two customers. "Did something happen while I was in back? Was there an accident?"

"It was nothing, Stan," Addie answered. "Weren't no problem here. We bumped carts, that's all. You don't need to worry about that."

The butcher looked relieved. "Alright, then. Come on, Addie, let's pick you out a corned beef."

As Sarah pushed her cart toward checkout she caught Addie's reply.

"Pick me out a good one, Stan! You know I LOVE corn beef!"

And I LOVE living here, Sarah grinned. Every day is an adventure.

Back out on the sidewalk, Sarah patted the commission check in her pocket and considered: maybe it was time for a splurge. She'd been working hard lately. The splurge didn't have to be big. Something small, but special.

It was a part of Sarah's nature to immediately think of splurging on her husband. But she knew once she bought John a present, he would want to buy her something. He was overly generous that way sometimes, and the last thing she wanted to do was start them on a spending spree. What to do? What to do? Sarah wondered, tapping her fingernails on the steering wheel.

Then she smiled. She had it. The perfect bonus for them both.

She would stop at the packie and pick up a bottle of wine, not too expensive, but festive enough. And then she would take the time to prepare a real meal: set the table, light some candles, pick out some tunes, the works. With a littie effort, she could turn a regular old Wednesday night into a romantic evening they would cherish forever. John was a closet romantic; he would be delighted with her surprise. It was perfect. She was brilliant.

She pulled the wheel around and turned for Nantucket Spirits on Washington Street. Not only did Sarah love the name, but it was as multipurpose a liquor store as you could want. She read their sign as she parked the truck: Beer, Wine &

Cordials. Yes, she agreed, give the girl a little pocket money and she certainly started feeling cordial.

A tinny bell rang as Sarah pushed on the door. She still felt so adult when walking through the racks of wine, admiring the graphics on the labels, glancing peripherally for yellow sale tags. Hand-written note cards announced Wine Selector ratings: this Chilean red had earned a 98, the rioja from Spain an 87. Keeping their budget in mind, Sarah moved toward Domestic.

"Can I help?" A silver-haired saleswoman stood up from a chair behind the counter. "Looking for something special?"

"Yes. I'd like something nice, for dinner. I was thinking about a Merlot."

"We have a very nice selection of Merlot." The saleswoman led the way. "These Californians are some of the best in the world." Surreptitiously, she glanced at Sarah's outfit. "Did you have a price in mind?"

"Less than twenty?"

"I have just the ticket." The saleswoman chose a bottle from the rack and cradled it gently. "This one is nineteen, and you won't find a better wine for that price on the market. It's woodsy, with nice depth, and just a hint of cherry finish."

Sarah dug for her wallet. "Sounds perfect. I'll take it."

"You'll be pleased." The doorbell chimed again. The saleswoman looked up and frowned. "Oh no. Here we go again."

Sarah turned to see who had entered and realized what the saleswoman was up against. Shuffling through the door was a gaunt, elderly man, John's great-uncle, Ethan.

Ethan Jarad ignored their presence, intent on reaching the vodka. Both women watched the elderly man pause before the inventory, drawing himself up to his full, rawboned height and eyeing the display. His fingers trembled past the top shelf, descending toward Kossak on the bottom row. He tipped a plastic bottle off the shelf and caught it with eager hands.

"We go through this every other day," the saleswoman confided sotto voce. "You'd think he'd buy it by the case. It would save him a trip into town."

"I'm sure it would."

"You know," the saleswoman continued. "There is something just plain wrong with that family. Must be tainted blood or something. Every generation one or two of them goes right off the deep-end. I've seen it myself."

She doesn't remember who I am, Sarah realized. Unable to resist the tease, she whispered: "What do you mean?"

"You stay here long enough, miss, and you'll see what I mean. Any trouble on this island, you look close, and you'll find a Jarad somewhere near the middle of it." The older woman drew herself up, shrugging apologetically. "Sorry to trouble you, but I need to see some I.D."

This should be interesting, Sarah grinned, and handed over her driver's license.

"Yes, that's fine. Uhm oh, oh my…" The saleswoman was so mortified she blushed maroon. She returned Sarah's license and retreated into formality. "That'll be nineteen dollars, even."

Sarah handed her a twenty. As she waited for her change, Uncle Ethan shuffled up with his vodka. Even arthritic and bent with age, he still stood a head taller than Sarah's five-foot eight. She waited until he put his bottle on the counter before speaking. "Hello, Uncle Ethan. How are you?"

The elderly man looked over with rheumy, bloodshot eyes. "Ah, Sarah Jarad. Didn't see you standing there."

"Too busy looking at your bottle," the saleswoman muttered.

"Excuse me? What was that?" Ethan Jarad slid his purchase across the counter. "I thought I heard you say something."

"I said that'll be twenty-one fifty."

"Sack that double please. Paper." He turned to Sarah. "John treating you alright?"

"Of course he is. We're very happy together."

"Good. He always was a good boy. A little stubborn, maybe, but I call that grit. Are you going to put that in a sack, or do I have to stand here all day?"

"I said," the saleswoman replied indignantly, one hand on her hip. "I need to see twenty-one fifty, first."

"Got it right here." Ethan Jarad dug into a pocket and retrieved a roll of bills wrapped in a thick rubber band. "There's a ten, and a five, another five, and a one." A handful of coins were dredged up from another pocket and snapped one-by-one against the countertop. "And two quarters makes fifty. There now. Satisfied?"

"We do deliver, you know." The saleswoman's voice squeaked with disapproval. "It's not like it would cost you anything."

"Do you know where I live?"

"I haven't the foggiest idea." She double-sacked the bottle angrily. "And to tell you the truth, I don't really care to know, either."

The old man grinned. "Then how would you deliver?"

"Ethan Jarad, take your bottle and get! And I don't mind saying, if I were the manager here, you'd be taking your business elsewhere! Even if it did mean losing steady custom!"

He slowly gathered his package. "But I like it here. I find service with a smile."

"Get!" The saleswoman pointed at the door, her strident voice following them both out into the cold. "And I feel sorry for you, miss, for marrying into that family! Good luck to you, is all I can say! My mother warned me: marry in haste, repent at leisure!"

The storm door slammed and Uncle Ethan grimaced, shuffling uncomfortably. "Marion didn't upset you with that last remark, did she?"

"It's nothing I haven't heard before. But I'll bet she remembers who I am the next time."

Uncle Ethan chuckled. "Marion's an old battle-axe, but she can't help it. She inherited her Irish temper." His deep cough sounded wet, but he waved it off. "I can remember Marion as a girl. Hair as red as a fresh copper penny." He coughed again, then winked. "Least then she gave some warning."

"I take it you two have been carrying on like this for awhile?"

"Oh, I give Marion something to talk about, true enough. It's one of the reasons I still visit this store. She doesn't know it, but she's going to miss me when I'm gone."

Sarah shook her head. John had warned her this great-uncle of his was a character, but she realized now John might have shaved the truth. Thoughtfully, she paused. It would interfere with her morning, but she knew Uncle Ethan didn't drive, and he was family. "Do you need a lift somewhere?"

The elderly man looked both surprised and pleased. "Why, no, no thank you. My ride will be here soon enough."

"Are you sure? It's no trouble." Sarah pointed. "The truck's right there."

"No, no, Eddie'll be along. He knows I'm waiting."

Sarah paused, feeling unsure. She could sense her precious painting time ticking away, but she couldn't just leave the man standing on the curb, it was freezing out; she could see his lips were turning blue. She had a sudden, inspired idea. "Why don't we wait in the truck until your friend gets here? It'll be warm. I'll blast the heater."

The old man started to protest, then surrendered to the promise of warmth. Uncle Ethan waited patiently as Sarah unlocked the truck, and then climbed stiffly in. "I appreciate the offer. Won't be but a minute before Eddie gets here. Took some training, but he's learned to be prompt."

Sarah started the engine. It was still warm. "No problem. Don't mind the bags."

The elderly man rubbed his rough knuckled hands before the dashboard vent. "Ah, that feel's nice. I don't know why, but I can't seem to get warm today. You'd think, after eighty-seven years, I'd be used to it, but this damp cold cuts right through to my bones."

"Maybe it would help if you put some meat on them," Sarah suggested.

He looked at her wide-eyed. "Young woman, are you usually so outspoken?"

"Pretty much," Sarah admitted.

"Humph. Must be my day to hear from opinionated females." He wheezed. "Well, since we are being so outspoken, let me ask you a question."

"Sure, shoot."

"Are you and John planning on having a family? Any children, I mean?"

Sarah was surprised by the question. Sure, she and John had talked about kids, but they certainly hadn't made any plans. "I'm sure we will, someday, when we're a little more settled. I'd like to be in our own house first, but saving for the down payment is going to take years."

Uncle Ethan shuddered through another deep bronchial cough and groped for his handkerchief. "That's good to hear. There's nothing better than family." He wiped his eyes, and announced: "Job, 15:7: 'For there is hope of a tree, if it be cut down, that it will sprout again, that the tender branch thereof shall not cease.' "

"That's rich, coming from you. If I remember right you never married."

"No, that's true enough, I didn't; but not every man is cut out for family life. Look at King Solomon. He had a thousand wives and he was still unhappy. Perhaps divine Providence saved me from error." He smiled weakly. "Besides, I never lacked for family. My brother Ike put a whole pack of 'em on the ground. I've got more nieces and nephews, and grand-nieces and grand-nephews now than I can count."

"I met most of them at our wedding, but I'm still getting to know everyone."

"That was a fine party you had. It was good to see the whole family together. Some of them I never see anymore, from year to year."

"Maybe we should have a reunion next summer. A picnic or something?"

Uncle Ethan's eyes grew misty and distant. "I can remember a time when the family met up for no reason at all. There'd be a clambake or a taffy-pull, some such foolishness, more for the fun of being together than getting any real work done." The old man sighed. "Those were good times, no doubt about it. And so many kids you couldn't move without stepping on one of them."

"Do you remember John from when he was a boy? What was he like?"

Amused by the question, the old man scratched the stubble on his chin. "Oh, those boys had the devil in them, no doubt about it. But I always said, better a boy with spirit than one without. I'll never forget, one summer Tindy had a picnic and those two boys disappeared. We should have known right then it meant trouble. By the time we went looking they had pulled all Tindy's fancy Japanese carp out of her fishpond! You never saw a prouder pair of fishermen than those two boys with all those dead carp lined up on the patio. Tindy pitched a fit of course, but I mean, how could you get angry? Boys will be boys."

Sarah smiled. "Was John your favorite?"

The elderly man scowled. "What makes you ask such a fool question? My past is none of your business! Job 27:6: 'My righteousness I hold fast, and will not let it go: my heart shall not reproach me so long as I live.' "

"Sorry if I hit a nerve, Uncle Ethan. I didn't mean anything by it." Uh-oh, Sarah realized, Marion was right. Uncle Ethan had a bone to pick, and here she was, stuck with him in the truck. Sarah started hoping for his ride.

He turned to face her. "You remember this, Sarah Jarad. Life is as fragile as the sand we build on and God's implacable hand guides the incoming tide." His quavering voice rose, booming inside the cramped truck. Foam flecked the corners of his mouth and he continued on, blindly: "Job 19:10: 'He hath destroyed me on every side, I am gone: my hope hath he removed like a tree!' "

"Uncle Ethan," Sarah started. "Take it easy…"

The elderly man rattled on, heedless. "Daniel was a judgment! The judgment of God! Job 5:17: 'Happy is the man whom God correcteth! Despiseth not the chastening of the Almighty!' "

As Sarah watched, to her horror, Uncle Ethan's face turned battleship gray. His eyes rolled back into his head and he slumped onto the passenger side door, releasing his purchase. The bag rolled down his leg and thumped against the floorboards, snapping her out of shock. Sarah reined-in her panic, opened her door and raced back inside. "Marion!" she yelled. "911! Call 911!"

The saleswoman looked up, surprised and irritated, from behind a wine rack. "What are you saying? Hey, wait a minute! You can't go back there!"

Sarah grabbed the telephone and started punching numbers. "Uncle Ethan's had a stroke, a heart attack, or something out in the truck. Hello? Hello! Yes, we need a Paramedic. Marion! What's the address here?"

The saleswoman looked stunned. "Number 10 Washington Street. But they'll know that…"

"Did you get that? Number 10. Yes, outside in the parking lot. A white pickup. Yes, yes, I'll wait for you there." Sarah hung up the phone and clawed her way back around the counter.

"Where did you say he was?" Marion followed, buttoning her cabled cardigan. "Ethan's in your truck?"

"Can you help me? I'll try C.P.R." Suddenly, Sarah felt woozy. The adrenaline pounding through her system was leaving her feeling weak and nauseated. She stumbled on the gravel and wondered: maybe I should've taken him straight to the Cottage Hospital; they could have helped, it's only two minutes away... She sucked in a deep, ragged breath. "Marion, we need to stretch him out flat. I'll grab his shoulders. Can you get his feet?"

"I'll try, I'll try..." Perched on the curb, the older woman hesitated. "Dear sweet Lord have mercy. Look at that, the poor dear man." As they drew even nearer, Marion moaned.

It was a nightmare image. Uncle Ethan's sightless white eyes stared at them through the fogged window. Sarah clawed for the handle and the passenger door swung open, propelled by the weight of his body. She grabbed the collar of Uncle Ethan's peacoat. "Marion, are you ready? Grab his feet. I need you to grab his feet."

"I'm right here, I've got him. Oh dear sweet Jesus. Mind his head. Don't drop him."

"I've got it, there, that's good." Sarah staggered as Uncle Ethan's body slid heavily onto the gravel. He hadn't made a sound during the transfer. "Help me stretch him out. We need to get him flat."

Abruptly, Marion let go and stood up, twisting both hands. "Child, why don't you leave him be? Can't you see he's passed?"

Sarah knelt in the wet gravel, fighting the obvious. Marion was right, Sarah knew it, yet she still felt compelled to try to do something. "Maybe we can save him," she argued weakly.

The older woman clutched Sarah's sleeve. "Child, leave him be. Ethan Jarad's been waiting on death longer than you've been alive. You won't be doing him any favor saving him now. This is between himself and God." She drew a string of rosary beads from her cardigan pocket. "Sweet Jesus, have mercy on this poor man's troubled soul."

And as the paramedic van arrived, sirens wailing, Marion closed her eyes and silently began to pray.

CHAPTER TWO

Sunday, January 17, 1999

Unlike the newer wanna-be's scattered across the island, the ancestral Jarad home was no replica. True to Nantucket tradition, the house had been built in sections, room added to carbuncled room as the burgeoning family had grown to need more space. Also true to tradition, any supplies that couldn't be purchased for lack of cash had been salvaged. The timber framing the family's living room had started its pedigree as quarterdeck planking from the old whaler Rachel. Reconstructed for the first time as a fishing shanty on the beach in Codfish Park, downwind the posh village of 'Sconset, the shanty had been placed on a sledge and hauled inland to safety when threatened by the inevitable coastal erosion. There the timber enjoyed its third incarnation, becoming part of a full-blown house.

Standing in the hallway, John smiled, recalling the first time he had brought his artist wife home. Sarah had stopped inside, looking puzzled. She noted that the interior walls formed trapezoids, not squares, and that the mullioned windows, proud with their panes of rippled bulls-eyed glass, staggered along the outer walls at different framing heights. Sarah had taken one look at the odd angles and skewed interior perspectives and announced herself tipsy. He had also warned her repeatedly about the low doorway lintels, notorious for catching tall newcomers smack in the middle of the forehead.

The resultant bump was known locally as a Jarad knot, and his wife had earned her share.

Sarah shrugged off her coat. "It sounds like everyone's here already. Are we late?"

He checked his watch. It was only a quarter-past one. "They probably came straight over after the service."

"Thank God we stopped, I never would have made it. Milestone Road doesn't seem that long until you realize the bathroom is at the far end of it."

"I'm still not convinced this is a good idea. We could have stayed home; you still look a little pale, to me."

Sarah squeezed his arm. "What would the family say if I didn't come to Uncle Ethan's wake?"

"It's not a wake, honey, it's a brunch, and they'd probably say they understand." He tilted his chin and caught jingle of bangle bracelets. "Here comes Mom."

"There you are." Jenny Jarad, a petite, birdlike woman, stood on tip-toe and gave them each a kiss. Her tailored black wool dress, belted and slim, was immaculate. "That's odd, John, I didn't hear your truck pull up?"

"It's in the shop, getting ah, detailed. I borrowed a unit from the pool."

"Oh, of course, I see. You'd have to do that, wouldn't you? Excuse the foolish question." Jenny pointed at the stairs. "Put those coats upstairs, John, in the spare bedroom, if you don't mind."

"What's wrong with this peg right here?"

"Just take them upstairs, will you please? I'd like a word with Sarah privately before we go in. My dear, I'm so glad to see you here today. The Aunties were thinking you might need seclusion to recover from your ordeal – so ridiculous and old-fashioned! But I told them, if you really think about it, Ethan went through the ordeal, not you."

Sarah smiled at her mother-in-law's inescapable logic. "You have a point."

"And you've recovered?"

"Yes, thank you. I was shocky there for awhile, but I feel fine now."

"Good. I'm probably overreacting; the kids tell me I do. I just wanted to warn you that you're going to get grilled for details this afternoon, and I wanted you to prepare yourself, in case you thought you might need to. Don't forget, I know what it's like to marry into this family, I was a mainland bride myself. Although that's such ancient history now no one remembers it."

"Are you two finished?" John stopped halfway down the stairs and gazed at his wife. "Do I even want to know what she said to you?"

"Friendly advice, dear, just friendly advice," Jenny smiled serenely. "Let's go in, shall we? Sarah, mind the steps, they take years getting used to."

In single file, the two women leading, they descended into the living room. Sarah noted an immediate drop in conversational tone and spotted subtly intercepted glances between family members. The scene in front of her flashed like a snapshot straight from a Whistler painting: the women rigid in black, the seated Aunties regal with vintage hats, the men uncomfortable in Sunday suits and stiffly laundered shirts. A beehive of active children wiggled around the buffet table, held in tentative check by John's coltish teenage niece Elsbeth.

"I'll get drinks," John offered. "Honey, what would you like?"

"A bloody Mary sounds great. Thanks."

"Mom? Can I get you something?"

"It's a little early yet for me, dear. I believe I'll hold off for right now."

"Be right back." John stepped away. Sarah watched him stop to greet his older sisters Jackie and Mary Rose who were deep in a commiserative conversation. For the first time since Sarah had met her, Jackie was dressed suitably for the occasion, entirely in black, no surprise there; Sarah had yet to see Jackie wear a color of any kind. Mary Rose looked practical as always in a white cotton turtleneck and a black linen frock. Seeing Sarah observing them from the sidelines, Mary Rose excused herself and worked her way over.

"There you are. I wondered when you'd get here. I know it's a solemn occasion and all that, but you are the guest of honor, in a way."

Sarah relaxed. She knew very little about most of the people in the room, but she had taken an immediate shine to this sister of John's from the beginning. Mary Rose reminded Sarah of her own sister, Joan. Both women were plain-speakers and neither one of them made any apologetic bones about it. Sarah found such honesty refreshing. "I'm glad you're here. At least I'll know someone."

"Are you kidding? I wouldn't have missed this for the world." Mary Rose gestured with her wineglass. "It's the one good thing you can say about our family; when we get together, it draws a crowd." She sipped her wine. "Uncle Ethan got a nice service, don't you think? Father McNimick really pulled out all the stops in the Homily."

"It was a nice sermon. Simple, but nice. Sometimes they get so flowery you don't even recognize who they're talking about."

"You got that right. And listen, I know we heard a sanitized version the other day, but what really happened with him?"

"You tell me first. What did you hear?"

"That you ran into Uncle Ethan at the packie and he had a stroke in John's truck."

"That's pretty much what happened. I called the paramedics but he was gone by the time they got there. It was surreal, now that I think about it. Toward the end he kept quoting Scripture at me."

"He did what?"

"Kept quoting the Bible. The book of Job." Sarah recalled Uncle Ethan's final words. "Something about trees and incoming tides. Oh, and chastisement, he was big on chastisement. I'd have to look it up to be sure."

"What a shame, I left my Bible at home," Mary Rose grinned. "I wouldn't give it too much thought. There's no telling what was going through that old man's mind. He was a strange old coot. Lived all by himself, you know, out past Quammock. It's a shame his house is such a wreck; it might have been worth something."

John returned, balancing drinks, to catch his sister's comment. "Figuring out the inheritance, already, Mary Rose?" He teased, handing Sarah her bloody Mary. "Picked avarice from the family gene pool, did you?"

"Why not?" Mary Rose turned pink and defensive. "Someone has to get his house."

"He wouldn't be doing you any favors leaving it to you. I was out there last Easter, dropping off a ham. The place needs more work than it's worth."

"The land will still be worth something." Mary Rose changed her tack. "Besides, Uncle Ethan wouldn't have left it to me; he never liked me much. But you were close to him there for awhile, John. Maybe he left it to you."

"If we did get the house, we could fix it up," Sarah interrupted hopefully. "It wouldn't have to be perfect right away. Anything would be better than paying rent."

"Watch what you wish for, honey, you just might get it." John took a pull on his beer, his dark eyes thoughtful. "Trust me, that house is no gift. Besides, if anything, Uncle Ethan probably willed it to the Maritime Brotherhood."

Sarah sipped her drink and grimaced. "Yuck. What's in this?"

"What do you mean?" John's concern was immediate. "What's wrong with it?"

"I don't know. It tastes ... soapy."

"Let me try." He took the glass and sipped cautiously. "It tastes alright to me. Let me get you a fresh one."

"Nevermind. I'll switch to gingerale. And it's my turn to fly. Mary Rose, ready for another?"

"I'd better not, I still have things to do today. But thanks for asking."

"Be right back." Sarah headed toward the bar, satisfied now that she had a task to do. That was the secret to family gatherings, she had learned; find a purpose and do it. It didn't even matter what the task was as long as it kept you busy. Gently, Sarah nudged a path through a knot of John's cousins and squeezed between a shield-back armchair and a mahogany piecrust tea-table in her quest for the bar. She took her place in line behind Uncle Tommy Jarad who was complaining about quality of the scotch.

Mary Rose's husband Matthew was acting as bartender and remonstrating patiently, scooping ice cubes from a bucket into a glass. "I don't know what else to tell you, Uncle Tommy, it's the only brand we have. I've got some nice bourbon here."

"Bourbon!" The older man drew himself up to his full five foot four and stood, quivering. "Bourbon? Are you mad?! Bourbon is for women and invalids!"

"Then it's Jack Begg, take it or leave it." Matthew poured a solid shot over some ice and handed the glass to the older man. "There you go. Next!" He glanced up. "Hey, Sarah! What can I get you? Gingerale?" He chopped more ice. "That was quite an experience you went through."

"It sure was. I don't want to repeat that anytime soon."

"I'll bet. You know, for what it's worth, I was talking to Bert Weatherby this morning – he was one of the paramedics you called – and he said there was nothing you could have done. Uncle Ethan went that quick."

Uncle Tommy returned with an interruption and an empty glass. "What scurrilous gossip are you peddling now, Matthew Quigley? Which scrap of familial scandal?"

"Uncle Tommy," Matt stated flatly. "What can I get you this time?"

The older man fingered his bow-tie and replied with some dignity. "It's not for me, it's for Mother. A dry Manhattan, if you please, with two cherries."

"I guess I'll go find John…" Sarah began.

"One moment, my dear," Uncle Tommy accepted the cocktail with a raised pinky. "Mother would like a word."

Sarah obediently trailed the little man toward a pair of upholstered loveseats facing each other in front of a colonial fireplace. Great-Aunt Daisy held court from the loveseat on the left; Great-Aunt Tindy faced her sister from the right. Sarah noticed that although the elderly sisters were well into their eighties, the spines of the two women were as upright as chess pieces. A wicked question flickered through her mind and Sarah wondered: was it dueling righteousness? She stifled her grin.

Great-aunt Daisy spoke first and indicated the cushion beside her. "Sit with us a moment, won't you, dear? There are some questions we'd like to ask."

Sarah seated herself gently, noticing that although Great-aunt Daisy's skin was wrinkled as soft as old parchment, her cocoa brown eyes were clear. There must be something about this sea-air, she decided, these island people live forever.

Great-aunt Tindy leaned forward over her cane. "My girl, I hope you won't mind if I'm direct. It's the only advantage to age. I don't have the time to waste."

"You've always been rude," Great-Aunt Daisy interjected. "Only now you have an excuse for your bad manners."

"It's not rudeness, sister, it's precision. Forty-three years in the teaching profession taught me precision."

"I'd like to suggest that raising a family required precision too, but it didn't teach me to be rude."

Hurriedly, Sarah interrupted. "What can I tell you?"

Great-aunt Daisy settled her arthritic hands in her lap. "I won't pretend to understand the way our brother Ethan lived his life, but we do have a few questions about the way he died. I'm hoping you can provide us with some enlightenment."

"Oh, cut the blather, Daisy. Did Ethan say anything? That's what we want to know," Great-aunt Tindy demanded. "Did he leave us any final words?"

"We only had a few minutes together," Sarah began. "I stopped for a bottle of wine, and I saw him in the store. He was waiting for his ride, but it was really cold out, so I said let's wait in the truck. We talked while we were waiting. Uncle Ethan mentioned his family, and how important the old days were to him. I think he cherished his memories. He mentioned a picnic you'd had, Aunt Tindy, where the boys pulled the fish out of your pond? He really lit up when he told that one."

"I remember that, mother," Uncle Tommy offered. "It was one of Aunt Tindy's Fourth of July picnics."

"Of course," the elderly woman grappled with her cane. "Independence Day, the year Jack's two youngest killed my Japanese koi. I certainly wouldn't forget that! But what has me curious, sister, is why Ethan choose that particular moment to mention those two boys."

"I had asked him about John when he was younger, that's what brought it up," Sarah explained. "But right after that I think Uncle Ethan must have felt something coming on, because that's when he started ranting about redemption and the judgment of God."

Aunt Tindy leaned forward, intent. "Those were his exact words? The judgment of God?"

"Pretty much. To be honest, he scared me. He was really caught up in it."

"Our brother identified with Job, you know," Great-aunt Daisy explained. "The righteous man, wrongly oppressed."

Sarah frowned. "What made him feel oppressed?"

"We don't know why," Great-aunt Daisy answered hastily. "Not for certain. It's true Ethan's nature changed as he got older, but why it changed can only be a matter of speculation, and rumor." She exchanged a knowing glance with her sister. "Tindy, our brother is dead; I think it best if we let the subject rest."

Great-aunt Tindy straightened. "Sister, there is no rest for the wicked."

What is going on here? Sarah wondered. She felt tugged by an undercurrent in the conversation. Never one to be subtle, she decided to give it a push. "I think Uncle Ethan knew what was coming, and he was afraid of it."

"Tommy!" Aunt Daisy raised her empty glass. "Be a good son and fetch me another."

"Mother, don't you think you've had enough?"

"I know how much I've had, my dear. Now be a good son and fetch me another."

"Ladies? Can I get you anything while I'm up?"

"No thank you, Uncle Tommy. I'm all set."

"Nothing for me as well, Tom, thank you. I'm perfectly satisfied." Great-aunt Tindy paused until he stepped away, then leaned forward across the short space separating the two loveseats. "Sarah, now tell us, quickly. Did Ethan mention any names to you?"

"Tindy! Think of what you're doing! What possible good could come from your heedless questions?"

"Because, sister, I want to know the truth if it's available to us. What this girl has to say may be our last opportunity to know."

"Surely there is little virtue in stirring up old trouble! Ethan is dead. I say let the dead bury the dead. Why would you want to cause more discord in the family? Hasn't there been enough already?"

Aunt Tindy paused. "Perhaps you're right. The full truth will only be known when it comes our time to stand before the throne of God."

"And neither of us has that long to wait. I beg you, Tindy, leave it rest. Stirring this up again can do no good..."

"Here you are, Mother," Uncle Tommy returned. "I had Matthew make it a light one."

Great-aunt Daisy reached for her cocktail. "You're such a good son. You take such fine care of me."

Sarah felt the gentle pressure of a pair of hands on her shoulders and looked up into John's smiling eyes. "Where have you been?" she asked.

"Looking for you. Has everyone been behaving themselves?"

"So far, so good. Aunt Daisy and Aunt Tindy are Uncle Ethan's sisters."

"I know that." John gave her an affectionate squeeze and moved behind the couch. Deliberately, he spoke up, knowing that Great-aunt Daisy was hard of hearing. "Hello, Aunt Daisy. I've brought someone to see you."

Reverend McNimick stepped before the fire, warming his long-fingered hands. Although a newcomer to the island, the Reverend was already a formidable presence. Sincere in both his faith and his calling, he held himself to be a true shepherd for his flock. Tall and angular, he was not handsome, with a lantern jaw and a receding hairline, but his compassionate nature had won over the hearts of his congregation. "I hope everyone is well under the circumstances?"

"Yes, Father, quite steady and strong, all things considered," Great-aunt Tindy replied. "That was a lovely service you gave."

"It wasn't difficult. Ethan Jarad was a remarkable man. Perhaps I didn't know him as well as I should have, but I spoke with some of the men who did and they told me amazing things." The Reverend left the fire and sat next to Great-aunt Tindy, who beamed with the honor. "I learned that Ethan Jarad served our country through the entirety of the Second World War. Not many men survived to make that claim."

"He was decorated twice for bravery under fire," Great-Aunt Daisy offered. "When Nemesis was torpedoed by the Japanese, Ethan carried wounded men to the lifeboats. There's no telling how many lives he saved."

"It's his Merchant Marine record that seems incomprehensible to me." Uncle Tommy shook his head. "How many men worked the sea for forty years and only lost their cargo twice?"

Sarah noted that all of the Jarads, even her husband, nodded at this item of information. "That must have been something," she guessed.

"It certainly was," Uncle Tommy agreed. "Even Uncle Ike had to pitch his cargo six times. But then, the Feds were brutally opposed to importing liquor at the time."

"The bastards burned his boat!" Great-aunt Daisy's voice squeaked with indignation. "It's a miracle Ike survived! He had to swim a mile to shore at four in the morning! He barely made it to the beach!"

Sarah did some quick math and hazarded a guess. "Ike Jarad was running liquor during Prohibition?"

"It's the law of the sea, my dear," Great-aunt Tindy reached across and patted Sarah's knee, her fingers dry as mummy. "You have to ship a cargo that pays. Shipping's a business – like any other."

Uncle Tommy held up his hand. "Jarads have shipped cargo since the founding of this country. I don't have to remind everyone here that the tea dumped in Boston Harbor came from the Dartmouth, a Jarad ship. Washington's Continental army fought the British with French guns we shipped through the British blockade, at considerable risk and peril, I might add."

"And they say..." Great-aunt Daisy piped up. "Nehemiah Jarad ran so much salt to the Southerners during the War Between the States he had the shipping lane to Charleston committed to memory."

"One moment," Father McNimick interrupted. "Perhaps I'm misunderstand what's being said, but I'm hearing two different issues in this conversation."

Great-aunt Tindy looked perplexed. "What do you mean, Father?"

"Well, while I applaud your concern for the unfortunate and your pride in performing your patriotic duty, I'm also hearing that this family earned its living on the weakness and suffering of others."

"You don't have to put it that way," Uncle Tommy huffed. "We're not opportunists. Jarads shipped cargo, that's all. It's what we did. It wasn't a moral issue."

"But how we live our daily lives is the greatest moral issue we face." The Reverend earnestly scanned his audience. "If you accept the responsibility for the way you live, it must include the responsibility of how you earn your living. Every decision we make as a free man or woman comes with an underlying moral implication. It's the meaning behind free will. You accept the consequences of your actions and you choose to pursue them anyway."

"I'm sorry, Father," Uncle Tommy bristled. "But I think you're taking what we've said out of context."

"Now, Tommy," his mother warned. "Don't get over-excited. Father's just doing good work."

"No, please. I'd like to hear this." The Reverend placed his hands on his knees. "How so, Tom?"

"Well, Father, when we harvested whales it was because whale oil was a product we could sell, not because we liked killing whales. Now that we have electricity, yes, perhaps killing whales has become a moral issue. But you can't take what we did at that time out of context. Back then, hunting whales meant survival."

"Not to mention civilization," Great-aunt Tindy concurred. "It truly was a dark age, Father, until whale oil lit our lamps."

"I'll grant you that, but I'm hearing the other side of the argument as well." The Reverend pursed his lips. "Perhaps Prohibition was an idealistic experiment, but shipping liquor was illegal until the Act was repealed. Shipping salt during the Civil War supported the southern economy and allowed slavery to continue. You have to see that even at that time these were active moral issues."

"Jarads never shipped slaves!" Great-aunt Tindy replied with spirit. "We were Quaker, some of the first people in the world to advocate emancipation, not to mention the rights of women and children!"

"That's exactly my point, and where I'm finding confusion," the Reverend paused. "I'm hearing the just cause as well as the unjust, and I have to believe that your ancestors understood the difference as well; these were righteous people. They must have known, and accepted, the consequences of their actions."

Uncle Tommy swirled his drink. "Maybe there is no consequence if you don't get caught."

"But you will get caught, Tom," Father McNimick stated flatly. "It may not happen right away, but it will happen. Divine retribution has an unlimited timeline; time is the strongest of God's tools." Father McNimick stood, adding authority to his opinion. "There is nothing easy about making the right moral choice, but that is why God put us here. We are challenged each day to become better than we are, and to help each other become better, in the spirit and brotherhood of Christ."

"Wow." Sarah heard a whisper in her ear. Mary Rose had joined the group. "Two sermons in one day. It's a new personal record."

Great-aunt Tindy rapped her cane. "Pardon me, Father, but I can't support your argument; it's too hard shell for my taste. In my eighty-three years I've seen everything there is to see, and human nature being what it is, people are going to make mistakes. And while I agree that you should strive to do your best, I'm afraid if you spend too much time worrying about every possible consequence, nothing will get done."

"Here, here," Uncle Tommy chorused.

"And I don't need your approval, Tom." She bent for her purse and straightened slowly. "It's getting late. Perhaps we should be going. Where's Jenny? I want to say my goodbye."

Mary Rose gave Sarah a nudge. "I don't know about you, but I'm starving. Let's see if the kids left us anything."

Together, they crossed the room to the buffet table. Sarah's hand hovered over a cheese board. "I don't know why, but I can't seem to get enough cheese lately."

"You're still not eating meat?"

"I can't get my mouth around it. Ever since I ate that bad pork. Even thinking about it now makes me a little queasy."

"You'll get over it." Mary Rose piled thinly-sliced rare roast beef on an onion bun and added a thick dollop of mayonnaise. "Sooner or later, you'll get tired of fish. Let's move over there, the window seat is open."

Sarah followed obediently, balancing her glass and her plate of lobster salad. "Mary Rose, I noticed some tension earlier when Uncle Tommy was talking about the family business. Just so I don't step in it, is that a sore subject?"

"You know it is." Mary Rose returned her sandwich to her plate, dusting crumbs from her fingers. "But you have to understand, Dad was in a tough spot; the banks weren't lending any money and we got pinched. Uncle Tommy, he remembers the glory days, but shipping had changed by the time Dad took over. I'm old enough to remember the arguments, but nobody had an answer." She grinned suddenly. "At least not one that was legal. Uncle Ethan surprised us – he suggested a smuggling operation. Dad told him we wanted to get out of the business, not deeper in."

"So your Dad sold the company?"

"He had to. Jarad Shipping was down to two freighters and they both needed overhauls. I know Dad did what he thought was best. He found a buyer and divv'ied the money out. And listen, for all the squawking, every Jarad got a mortgage button with the balance paid in cash."

"What's a mortgage button?"

Mary Rose grinned around a mouthful of sandwich. "Another island tradition. Once you pay off your mortgage, you're supposed to throw a big party and burn your mortgage papers. Then you drill a hole in the newel post by your staircase, fill it full of the ash and cap the hole with a mortgage button. Mom has one here; I'll show it to you on the way out. In the old days the button was made out of whalebone. I don't know what they use nowadays; probably some kind of plastic."

"So no one in this family owes a mortgage?"

"I'm not saying they haven't taken one out since. But when my Dad sold the business, everyone in that generation was free and clear." She smiled wryly. "Unfortunately, our generation is on our own. And look at Nantucket now! It's taken off! I mean, we're just regular people working jobs and we're up against all this big money pouring in from the mainland. Look at the real estate market. Half a million dollars for a one bedroom house! Mid-island, without a view! I mean, c'mon, it's ridiculous!"

John strolled over, carrying a cup of chowder. He leaned into the window frame. "What's ridiculous?"

"Mary Rose is feeling money pressure, too."

"Not to mention what people are getting for summer rentals. Thirty or forty-thousand dollars a month for July and August! I mean, really! Who are these people? And how do they afford it?"

"We could all move in together and rent out our houses," John suggested. "That would earn us some extra cash."

"You're almost funny," Mary Rose pushed her plate aside. "It's just so insane lately. I heard Foodland is going to start flying their cashiers over from Hyannis because no one on the island can afford to work for minimum wage."

"Why are you worried?" John asked. "You're bills are getting paid."

"Sure they are, but we're not saving anything, and we need to start thinking about college for the boys." Mary Rose dropped her voice to a confidential tone. "Matt's been talking about moving us to New Bedford. I don't even want to consider the idea. Nantucket is my home, not some fancy vacation getaway."

Matt Quigley joined them, carrying his wife's coat. "Sorry to break up the party, but we need to get going. Sam's practice is over at 3 p.m."

John checked his watch. "We should probably get going, too. I need to check in with the station."

As a group they moved toward the hall, surprising Jenny coming out of the kitchen. "Are you leaving? It's early yet."

"Sam needs a ride," Mary Rose explained, zipping her coat. "Mom, you did a great job here. I'm sure everyone appreciated it, especially the Aunties."

"They told me they did, and I was delighted to see them again," Jenny accepted the compliment. "Now, Matthew, remember to watch for deer. I can't forget that dream I had. Hitting that deer caused such a terrible accident."

"But Jenny, you said the accident happened at night. We should be safe now. It's still light out."

"Don't worry about Mom's dreams," John stated. "She dreamt once I hit the lottery, and look at me, I'm poor as ever. Honey, are you ready? I'll get our coats."

The front door opened, admitting a blast of frigid air that tickled their ankles. Two men stepped into the hallway, backlit by bright afternoon sunlight. The shorter, ruddy middle-aged man wore a pea-green rain slicker over a succession of mismatched sweaters. His younger companion swept off his hat and gestured roughly. "I told him this was a bad idea, Mrs. Jarad, but he wouldn't listen. We don't want to grieve the family."

"I knew Ethan Jarad better than any of 'em." The shorter man countered, striking his barrel chest with a closed fist. "Who has more right to be here? Jesus, Rusty! We worked together more'n thirty years."

Rusty took the older man's arm and tried to pull him away. "Pardon us, folks. Eddie's been drinking."

"So I've had a few." Eddie wrenched his arm free. "I'm man enough to admit it. I lost a good friend in Ethan Jarad. We won't see the likes of him again."

John descending the stairs, carrying an armload of coats. "Eddie? What's going on?"

"I came to pay my respects, John, that's all. And maybe have a drink, to honor a real man I was proud to serve with, not one of these gutless wonders you see walking around today."

"I'm sure we appreciate the gesture, but I think you've had enough. Why don't you go home and sleep it off?"

Rusty tugged his friend's sleeve. "C'mon, Eddie. See? It's like I told you. C'mon. I've got a bottle back at t'house."

Eddie's face crumpled and he wiped his eyes with his hand. 'It's a damned shame. The day comes a man wants to pay his respect and's not even welcome at the house. You know what? Ethan Jarad was right. He said he was going to die alone with no one caring and here we are, where a man can't even get a drink at his wake."

"Rusty, take Eddie home and keep him there." John's warning tone was unmistakable. "If I find either of you on the street an hour from now I'm putting you in for drunk and disorderly."

"Alright, John, alright," Rusty nodded. "Come on, Eddie, let's get out of here."

"Ethan Jarad was a fine man, there were none better." Eddie muttered, tugging his coat straight and following Rusty out. "And it's a sad pack of spineless milksops he left behind."

Jenny shut the door firmly. "That Eddie Farrar is the oddest man. I've often wondered how he makes a living scavenging bottles and tin cans off the roadside."

"I've seen him collecting driftwood on the beach," Sarah offered.

"Not to mention," Mary Rose jingled her keys. "Lifting lobsters from other people's pots. Eddie'd better be careful. Someone's going to catch him one of these days and he'll get deep-sixed."

"That would be justice," Matt Quigley grinned, pausing at the door. "Lobster's revenge."

Sarah frowned. "What do you mean?"

"Matt, don't," John warned.

"Lobsters are scavengers, too," Matt continued on, blithely. "They'll eat anything they find dead on the bottom."

"Even something as nasty as Eddie Farrar, if it comes to that," Mary Rose added.

Sarah felt her stomach, full of warm lobster salad and rich mayonnaise, flip. "Oh, great! Now you can cross lobster off my list!"

"Down to cheese?" Mary Rose inquired sweetly.

Chapter Three

Monday, January 18, 1999

When they had first moved into their rental, Sarah had commandeered the one-car garage for use as her studio. She bought raw furniture from Jackson Vance, a local carpenter, and sold the finished pieces through Meredith's store. It was a perfect set-up and she knew it. She kept her own hours, painted at her own speed, and took time off whenever she needed to. And, if the last year's sales were any indication, she was establishing a pretty good reputation around the island for her work. Three of her current pieces were actually pre-paid commissions, and Tish Bennett, the hot new island interior decorator, had left a message on the machine wanting to discuss a lightship mural idea for the dining room of one of her high-end Shawkemo Estate clients.

Sarah picked up her brush and smiled, remembering her first island commission. At least she wasn't being asked to paint floors 'to look like sand' anymore. Today she was set to finish her latest project, a rocking-horse toy chest. All that was needed was to scroll a pink ribbon across the lid and add the name 'Rebecca'. Sarah sipped her bachi tea and savored its heat, knowing from past experience that the next time she reached for her mug it would be stone-cold.

"Sarah? Hello?" A woman's voice called from the kitchen. "You home?"

She thumbed her dry brush. "In here."

"Hi there," Mary Rose poked her head through the doorway. "Am I interrupting?"

"No, I haven't started, yet."

"I can come back," her sister-in-law offered. "Seriously, if you want me to go, just tell me. I know you're busy."

"No, no, Mary Rose, that's fine." Sarah replaced her brush. "Don't mind me, I was thinking about the work. Let's go in the kitchen, it's warmer. I'll make some fresh tea."

"Wait a minute, let me see what you're doing." Mary Rose stood over the unfinished toy chest. "Sarah, this is gorgeous! Becky Macy is going to love this."

"Do you think so? I think it's turned out nice, so far."

"Nice! This is more than just nice! It looks just like a picture." Mary Rose ran her fingers across the glossy painted surface. "You are so lucky to have this talent. Just once, I wish I could paint something."

"It's not impossible, Mary Rose. I could show you how."

"Oh, no. Something like this takes more than just trying; this is a gift, you have to be born with it ... Sarah?" Involuntarily, Mary Rose reached out her hand. "Are you alright?"

Without warning, Sarah found herself struggling with a roiling wave of pea-green nausea. "Oh my God," she gasped.

"Here, sit down." Mary Rose helped her to a chair, grabbing a glass from the dish rack and filling it quickly with tap water. "Drink this. Slowly. There. That's right."

Sarah sipped the tepid water, taking deep, slow breaths, still feeling woozy. "Holy cow. I must have picked up food poisoning again. I bet it was that lobster salad."

"Wait a minute." Mary Rose, standing with one hand on her hip, appeared enlightened. "This isn't food poisoning. What's the chance you're pregnant?"

"Pregnant? I can't be pregnant. We've been really careful."

"I wouldn't be so sure. I know what morning sickness looks like, and trust me, I'm looking right at it."

"I can't be pregnant, Mary Rose. We haven't made any mistakes ..." Even as she spoke, Sarah recalled Thanksgiving dinner at the Jarad house. Roast turkey, stuffing with gravy, a glass too much white wine. When they had returned home, John had been so eager they hadn't even made it upstairs to the bed. And they hadn't used any precautions. 'What can it hurt?' Sarah recalled thinking at the time. Well, she had her answer.

She ran her fingers through her hair. "Oh my God, Mary Rose, you might be right. What am I going to do?"

"That's easy." Mary Rose calmly poured tea. "You're going to have a baby."

"But we can't have a baby here! I mean, look at this place! There's no room to turn around! Where are we supposed to fit a crib?"

"Trust me, you'll adjust. Everyone does. Mom told me she was so unprepared when Jackie was born she kept her in a laundry basket." Mary Rose grinned crookedly. "Which explains a lot about my sister, actually."

"Wait a minute; maybe I was right. Maybe it is food poisoning."

"There's one way to find out; we can run over to Congdon's Pharmacy and buy a pregnancy kit. Then you'll know for sure."

"Wait a minute. I should call John. He needs to know."

"Sarah, hold on. It's early days yet. My advice is to wait until you know for sure. Trust me, those kits are really fast. You could know for sure an hour from now. C'mon, let's go."

Sarah struggled into her coat, moving in slow motion. "I can't believe this is happening. Sure, we wanted kids, but not right away." She followed Mary Rose outside to a vintage silver Volvo sedan, opening the creaking door and sinking deeply into the low passenger seat. Sarah wrapped her parka tight and noted that sitting so low to the ground pretty accurately mirrored the way she felt.

"Don't look so stricken." Mary Rose reached under the floor mat for her keys and manhandled the steering wheel, backing out of the driveway heading for town. "This is a great new stage in your life. You two are going to have a blast."

"But we're not ready to have a baby!" Sarah wailed.

Mary Rose chuckled. "Funny thing about the little buggers; ready or not, here they come. Now it's up to you to adapt. When my friend Caroline Chase found out she was pregnant, she worked up a complete schedule. She even showed it to me, where the baby would fit in, how many hours she would spend doing this and that. Caroline really got annoyed when I started laughing, but I mean, she had no idea. Let me tell you, once you have a baby, everything goes out the window. And I mean everything." Mary Rose angled into a parking space and took a deep breath. "Alrighty then. Ready?"

They crossed the sidewalk and stepped into the pharmacy. "Let's look under Family Planning," Mary Rose suggested, leading the way. "Although from what I gather there wasn't any planning involved. Here. Try this one. I know from personal experience it works."

Sarah grasped the azure-colored cardboard box. While she admired the bold graphics and the simple design, when she considered the contents of the kit and how the answer to this test could alter her life, she felt dizzy.

"Let me pay for that," Mary Rose dug for her wallet. "It can be my first baby gift. Just think. John might be a Dad! He's going to have a heart attack when you tell him!"

As she spoke, a slim brunette standing at the counter turned in evident delight. Desiccated and deeply-tanned, the young woman tossed her embroidered pashmina shawl over one shoulder and stretched out both arms. "Mary Rose! I thought that sounded like you!"

"Ava?!" Mary Rose returned the hug. "I don't believe it. When did you get back from Rome?"

"It was Milan, Mary Rose, and that was eight months ago!"

Mary Rose looked skeptical. "You didn't get that tan here."

"No, no, this was South Beach, in Miami. Just got back. Love that traveling, I have to say, but I ran out of cash. Had to get serious and come back and earn more for my next big adventure. I'm thinking about Capri. Or Mykenos. I can't decide which." The chic young woman glanced at Sarah. "Hi. I don't think we've met. Ava Descartes."

Quickly, Sarah switched the pregnancy kit to her left hand. "Sarah Jarad. Nice to meet you, uhm, Ava."

"Don't tell me, let me guess." Ava placed one hand on her hip, lowered her chin and cut her eyes at Mary Rose. "This would be John's wife?"

"Yes, sorry, should have mentioned that," Mary Rose apologized. "John and Sarah got married last September."

"Well," Ava gestured toward the pregnancy kit. "Don't mind me saying so, but it looks like you two didn't waste any time."

A hot blush flooded Sarah's cheeks. She hated being put on the spot and hearing this remark coming from a virtual stranger made it even worse. "Yes, well," she stammered, "it's a surprise."

Mary Rose had noticed Sarah's heightened color and deliberately changed the subject. "So, Ava, where are you working now?"

"I'm clerking for a lawyer, Molly Witherspoon. Do you know her?"

"Sure. She's in my mother's garden club."

"That's the one. The job's not perfect, but it pays well enough." Ava smiled at Sarah warmly. "John and I used to work together until the Council downsized me out of a job. I took it kind of hard at the time, but in retrospect, it's the best thing that could have happened. I cashed their severance check and never looked back."

"You were a cop?" Sarah remarked, surprised. She couldn't imagine this slim, elegant woman posted on duty anywhere. Well, Sarah thought, Lord and Taylor®, maybe.

"Oh, no. I handled administration. At least I managed to update the filing system before I left. It was truly archaic!" Ava laughed lightly and checked her watch. "Well, that does it for me. Lunchtime's over." She lowered her voice conspiratorially. "Mrs. Witherspoon's a stickler for punctuality. Sarah, it was nice to meet you; I hope I see you around. Tell John I said 'hello'. Ciao, Mary Rose."

"Ciao," Mary Rose echoed and pulled a twenty-dollar bill from her wallet. "Now, Sarah, don't argue. I want to pay. I insist."

The saleswoman covertly glanced at Sarah's wedding ring and smiled as she rang up the purchase. "Will this be all for you ladies today?"

"Yes, thank you." Sarah turned. "Mary Rose, who was that woman? Should I know her?"

Mary Rose accepted her change and handed Sarah the package. "Ava was one of John's old girlfriends. One of the more serious ones, I might add."

"Oh." Sarah nodded and followed Mary Rose back outside. She waited patiently for Mary Rose to unlock the car and then sat, placing the small package thoughtfully in her lap. Of course she had known that John had dated other woman, after all he was thirty years old; a history of previous girlfriends was only to be expected. There would be something wrong if he hadn't had a history. But, Sarah admitted, feeling a spangle of jealousy, she hadn't expected any of John's ex-girlfriends to be so, well, stylish. "Did John have a lot of serious old girlfriends?"

"A couple." Mary Rose put the car in gear. "A few Christmas's back there was even some talk John and Ava might get engaged. Personally, I think Ava started the rumor herself to try and force the issue. But John wasn't sure about it and when he told Ava he had doubts, well, she walked." Mary Rose glanced sideways. "Ava's high maintenance, you can see that. I think that's what scared John off; he's never wanted a fast-track lifestyle. And not for nothing, but I notice my brother didn't have any trouble making a commitment when it came to you."

"That works both ways." Sarah felt a tiny prickle of doubt. "I don't know, Mary Rose. I really wanted to be living in our own house before we started our family."

"You know what, Sarah? You worry too much." Mary Rose pulled back into the driveway and parked, resting her hands on the steering wheel. "Look around; you'll manage. Everyone does. And you're not in this alone, you know. You have a lot of family here on Nantucket, and we'll help every way we can. Car pooling. Free babysitting. Mothers-Day-Out. Come on, relax. It'll be fun."

"It's just that I like to plan things ahead of time," Sarah admitted, fumbling with her house keys. She unlocked the door and the two women hung up their coats. "I'm not great with surprises." She drew the pregnancy kit from the paper bag and turned the box over in her hands. "How do I do this?"

"It's simple." Mary Rose pushed her toward the bathroom. "Just follow the directions. What's it say? Twenty minutes? Do you have a timer?"

"There's one on the stove."

"I'll get it. You go ahead."

Ten minutes later Sarah reopened the bathroom door. She had brushed her hair and was feeling much calmer. "I was so nervous my hands were shaking."

"Why don't you make us some of that tea you like?"

Sarah smiled at the transparent ploy. "Mary Rose, you don't even like bachi tea."

"It's not for me, it's for you. It'll keep you busy, to pass the time."

Sarah worked slowly, filling the kettle with fresh cold water. The telephone rang and she glanced at caller I.D. "Oh my God. It's John." She looked to Mary Rose as the phone rang a second time. "What do I say?"

"Don't tell him anything until you know for sure. Act normal."

"Normal? I wouldn't know how to begin." Sarah drew a deep breath and picked up the phone. "Uhm, hello, honey."

"I've got news," John announced, his voice thin over the phone. "Uncle Ethan's attorney wants to see me this afternoon. Evidently, there's some kind of bequest. I can swing by and pick you up, if you want to go. Can you be ready by three?"

"A bequest? Oh, John, do you think maybe he left you something?"

"Don't even go there; you saw the way my uncle lived. We buried him in the only suit he owned. Besides, this is all speculation until we talk to the lawyer. It's two o'clock now. Can you be ready in half an hour?"

"Sure I can." Sarah began, "John…"

"Great," he interrupted. "I'll see you then. Got to go. Love you."

"Love you too." Sarah replied slowly, hanging up the phone. A bequest? Now that was an intriguing idea. Everyone knew these old guys squirreled their money away. Hid their fortune under their mattress or buried it in a jar out in their yard. What if Uncle Ethan had left John enough for a down payment! Why not? This could be the answer to her worries.

Mary Rose raised an eyebrow, curious. "What's up?"

"Uncle Ethan's attorney wants to see John; he said there was a bequest." Sarah frowned. "Mary Rose, I know this is a terrible question, but did Uncle Ethan have any money?"

"I hate to burst your bubble, but Uncle Ethan was a pauper. Any bequest of his is probably some old photographs or something."

"But why did he ask for John? Uncle Ethan told me he still had nieces and nephews running around. Shouldn't he have asked one of them to do this?"

"Ask who? The generation you're talking about is down in Florida right now, and I'm sure the estate isn't worth the trouble of coming back for. Uncle Tommy is still here of course, but Uncle Ethan couldn't stand him. Called him a lubber. Actually, now that I think of it, the feeling may go back further than that. I know Uncle Ethan disliked Aunt Daisy's choice of a husband. That feeling may have passed down to their son."

The timer rattled and both women jumped. "Oh my God, I forgot!" Mary Rose laughed nervously. "Time's up!"

Butterflies fluttered in Sarah's stomach. "Has it been twenty minutes?"

"Don't be a chicken." Mary Rose gave her a prod. "Don't you want to know?"

Sarah climbed the stairs again and both women paused at the bathroom door. Sarah pushed the door open as Mary Rose peered over her shoulder. The plastic indicator stick waited for them with a vibrant indigo dot.

"Congratulations!" Mary Rose whooped, dancing down the hallway. "I'm an aunt!"

Sarah stepped inside, took a deep breath and looked at herself in the bathroom mirror. She certainly looked calm enough. It was her eyes that surprised her. Her pupils were dilated and when she looked deeper into them she smiled. For all her fear there was an equal amount of … what was that in there? Anticipation? She released her breath and decided then and there that they were, in fact, going to be fine. Sure, they hadn't planned on having a baby this soon, but here it was; and Sarah liked holding firm to bedrock reality. It had been her strength all through her life, and she wasn't going to lose it now. She loved John, she loved her life, and now she was going to love their baby. She took a deep breath and shouldered the possibilities of her new world. "This is going to be great." She stated, descending the staircase to the kitchen. "And John is going to have a heart attack."

"I am so excited! How are you going to tell him?"

"I'm not sure yet. One part of me wants to tell him sweetly, and the other part wants to yank his chain."

"Oh, yank his chain. Definitely. Yank his chain." Mary Rose enveloped Sarah in a hug. "Sarah, I'm so happy for you both; you have no idea. I know he's my brother, but John is such a nice guy, and he was too stubborn to ever say he was lonely until he met you, and now he has all this. It's just so great I don't even have words for it."

Sarah returned the hug. "It sounds to me like you have plenty of words."

"I know I rattle on; everyone tells me I do. It's only because I'm so excited." Mary Rose stepped back. "Now, listen, John's on his way home and I don't want to be here when he arrives. This moment should be just between the two of you. But promise me you'll call as soon as you can and let me know how it went; I want to hear all the juicy details, and I promise I won't tell a living soul until you say I can." She dug in her purse for her keys. "But it's going to be hard. Okay, I'm out of here." Mary Rose stopped at the door, turned, and hugged Sarah again. "Okay, that's it. Bye."

Sarah watched as Mary Rose trotted out to her car. Her sister-in-law turned to wave one last time before pulling out of the driveway in a cloud of steel-blue oil smoke. Sarah closed the door, returned to the kitchen table and picked up her tea. It was stone cold.

She discovered how difficult it was to sit with one ear listening for the sound of John's truck while her mind raced over how to break the news. She was sure he would be delighted; they had talked about this day and here it was. Now, the question was, how should she go about it? She rehearsed the scene in her mind: John would walk in, she would ask him to sit and take his hand and tell him the news. They would laugh together, they might even cry a little, and then they would begin making plans for the future.

Sarah was rinsing her cup when she heard John pull up and tap the horn. She glanced at the clock; it was two-forty. He was running late. No time for the slow, sweet scene now. Wasn't that the way it always worked? She grabbed her coat and keys and pulled the door shut, puffing through the cold toward the truck.

"Sorry I'm late," John apologized. "We got a call just as I was leaving. We'll get there on time, but it'll be close. Or," he smiled, mischief written large in his dark eyes. "I could call ahead and ask Mrs. Witherspoon to reschedule."

"Are you kidding? Don't you want to hear what she has to say?"

"Not really." He pulled onto Hooper Farm road. "Never had good news from a lawyer yet."

"But you said this was a bequest. That means you're supposed to inherit something." Sarah straightened her hat.

"You never know, Uncle Ethan might have left you something fabulous."

"Honey, my uncle didn't own anything fabulous. And even if he did leave me something, it's probably a family Bible."

"Fine." Sarah could contain her secret no longer. "But you have to admit some money would help us out right now, with a baby coming."

The truck wobbled onto the road's graveled shoulder. "What?" John yelled. "What?"

"Hey, take it easy." Sarah patted her stomach. "I'm carrying precious cargo."

John pulled off the road and stood on the brake. He was staring at Sarah so wide-eyed, and went pale so quickly, that for a moment she thought he was going to pass out.

She pointed at the gear shift. "Park," she suggested gently. "Put it in park."

"What did you say?"

"We're going to have a baby, sometime in August. I took a pregnancy test. It was positive."

"Are you sure?"

"As sure as the little blue dot will let me be. I should have guessed sooner. My jeans have been a little tight but I thought it was the way you did laundry."

"Oh my God." John pulled Sarah close. His heart felt expansive, limitless. He was washed by a wave of gratitude. All the previous busyness and concerns of his day became inconsequential. This new knowledge, this bright new future, this profound new fear, was breathtaking. Sitting on the side of the road, inhaling Sarah's warm scent, John realized he had never been happier. Or more afraid.

He drew back and brushed the hair out of her eyes. Sarah was blushing and her eyes sparkled with amusement at his reaction to her news. "Sarah, you are the most beautiful woman I've ever known. I can't believe you're my wife, and I can't believe you're having a baby."

"We're having a baby," she corrected, gently.

"Sar-aaah." He sighed her name, drawing her hands up and kissing her palms. She giggled and wrapped both arms around his neck. He knew he would always remember their first kiss, that warm, golden day last September, but to his delight this one was even sweeter. That first kiss had been about surrender; but this, this was about triumph! He felt like a king! John squeezed Sarah tight, his blood dancing in his veins. "You you're the best thing that's ever happened to me; it's almost too much to take in. Jesus! Look at all that's happened to us, in less than a year."

"I know, it blows me away, too. But it's going to be okay. We're going to adapt." Sarah glanced at her watch and sat up straight. "Yikes! John, we're late. It's almost three."

"Never enough time for romance…" He grinned, squaring himself back behind the wheel, putting the truck into gear and pulling back onto the road. "Hold that thought for later."

Sarah untangled her seatbelt. "When you called this morning I didn't know how to tell you. I had just found out about it myself. That's why I got so excited when you mentioned the bequest. Maybe Uncle Ethan left you something and we can finally get our own place in time for the baby!"

"That's a great idea, honey, but don't count on it. Uncle Ethan had no reason to single me out for anything special. We weren't that close."

"But John, think about it. He did single you out. No one else was invited to this meeting."

"True, but that's another reason I don't believe Uncle Ethan had anything valuable to leave. He knew better than anyone it doesn't take much to start a punitive war in our family."

Sarah turned in her seat. "Now who's exaggerating?"

"It's no joke. When my grandfather Ike Jarad died and they settled his estate, two of his sisters went to war over a pair of brass andirons. That was thirty years ago, and both women went to their graves still not speaking to the other."

"So who kept the andirons?"

John grinned. "From what I remember, they each took one."

"Get out of here," Sarah scoffed. "What good is one andiron?"

"You tell me. All I know is, my Aunt Meribah ordered hers placed in her coffin so Aunt Keziah couldn't get it after she died and remake the set. We had to tip the pallbearers extra because of the weight."

Sarah crossed her arms. "Just so you know this, I'm not believing a word you say. It's taken me awhile, but I've learned to know when you're pulling my leg."

"Okay, so maybe we didn't tip the pallbearers, but the rest of it is true. Honey, I can't help myself." He tapped the steering wheel. "I'm so happy it's bubbling out of me. I'm going to be a Dad!"

"I know how you feel. When I think about it my breath catches right here." She tapped the base of her throat with her hand. "I feel excited, and scared, and wonderful, all at the same time."

"It's pretty powerful, isn't it?"

"Yes, it is." Sarah agreed, glancing out the windshield. She was distracted from her happy thoughts by the vision of a single coal-black raven struggling to perch on the barren tip of a blasted sea-pine. The bird flapped its wings to settle in, cawed repeatedly, smoothed its feathers and left her with a perfectly dismal image. "You know, John, I can't help thinking Uncle Ethan's life was such a contrast to what we have. He was so alone, he didn't have anyone. I can't help thinking if he really was that bad off, maybe we should have done something to help him."

"That's a nice thought, honey, but we've been trying to do something for him for years. He wouldn't have it. He even avoided my mother, and when she's on a crusade, that takes some doing."

"What made him such a recluse?"

John shrugged. "He always been strange. I used to get nightmares when I was a kid and I had to go visit."

"I can't imagine you being afraid of anything."

"Oh, I was afraid of him, alright. Gave me the heebie-jeebies, all alone with him in that spooky old house. I'd pretend to be asleep and he'd stand there in the doorway, watching me, in the dark."

Sarah glanced sideways. "Are you saying he tried something with you?"

"No, nothing like that. He was just a strange old man and I'm not hoping for any inheritance from that direction, and you shouldn't, either."

"Well, you can't blame me for trying. It's fun to imagine hitting a jackpot."

"And imagine all you want, as long as you don't think it's going to happen. Money doesn't just fall out of the sky. There's only one way to build a secure future, and that's one slow step at a time, just like we're doing."

"Wow. You sound exactly like your mother."

"That's because she's been there, and she's right," John chuckled. "I wish you'd stop worrying."

"I can't help it. Babies are expensive."

"So are wives." John raised his shoulder to block the incoming punch and pulled into a parking space. "It'll be different once the baby gets here. We'll both be too tired to worry about anything."

The law office of Hussey, Witherspoon & Silvia was located on the second floor of the Nantucket Island Bank building, a two-story brick structure so vital to island business that the cobblestone streets of town radiated from it like spokes from a hub. The banks' porticoed main entrance faced the Old South Wharf down in the harbor, and since island fortunes were based entirely on shipments of cargo, the early Quaker bankers had gone to great lengths to ensure the most expedient transfer of profit from ship to shore. Eventually they even paved the way, using private funds, and christened the approach Easy Street.

"It must have been tough waiting for your ship to come in," Sarah noted, skating across the icy sidewalk.

"Would you mind being more careful? You're making me nervous." John's strong fingers grasped her waist. "Besides, not every ship made it back. That's why they call them widow's walks."

He opened the glass-front door and together they crossed the lobby, climbing carpeted stairs, rising slowly past paddle fans clinging to the stamped tin ceiling like giant dragonflies dormant for the winter. Sarah teased her fear of heights by glancing over the railing at the marble lobby below. "You don't seem very excited about this."

"Yes, I am – but it's probably for nothing."

"Don't be such a pessimist."

"And don't you get started again. I've said it before. Let's wait to hear what Mrs. Witherspoon has to say."

"Mrs. Witherspoon?" Sarah stopped. "Your lawyer is Molly Witherspoon?"

"Yes, why? She's been my family's attorney for years."

"Then you're in for another surprise. I met one of your old girlfriends this morning, and she works for Molly Witherspoon."

"Really? An old girlfriend?" John teased, holding the door and pausing to let his wife enter first. "Which one?"

Noticing their minuet, Ava Descartes rose from her desk, smoothing her suit and extending a thin hand. "John! There you are! And you've brought your wife. It's nice to see you again, Sarah."

"Ava, how're you?" John shrugged out of his coat and then helped Sarah out of hers. "You look great. I hear you two have already met."

"We met this morning." Ava cocked one eyebrow. "Can I add my congratulations?"

"Yes, yes, you can," Sarah stammered, determined not to blush. "Thank you."

"She knew before I did?" John glanced between the two women. "That's not right."

"Nantucket holds no secrets, John, you know that." Ava swept her hair back. "How's the new station?"

"Busy as usual, but we have settled in. Oh, and you'll like this. They put Joe Curly in charge of your filing system."

"Better him than Jim Parsons! I can still remember what that man's dashboard looked like!" Ava laughed. "Well, I'd better pass you in, it's after three." She crossed the room and tapped on the mahogany door. "Mrs. Witherspoon? Excuse me, but John Jarad, and his wife, are here."

"Send them in," an unseen elderly female voice commanded. "John Jarad! Come in here, young man, and let me take a look at you."

John guided Sarah into a room, opulently paneled in wide chestnut boards. "Mrs. Witherspoon, how're you?"

"Never better, I'm pleased to report." The elderly lawyer indicated a pair of crimson leather chairs. "Please sit down. And you brought your wife; I hoped you would. How do you do, young lady? I've been wanting to meet you."

"Sarah Jarad, Mrs. Witherspoon. Pleased to meet you."

"Delighted. Please, make yourselves comfortable. Ava, don't go far. I'll need you to notarize a document for me in a moment."

"I'll get my stamp ready, Mrs. Witherspoon."

"Very good." The lawyer waited for the door to close before continuing. "So, John, how is police business these days?"

"Mostly domestic disputes, now that everyone is stuck inside for the winter."

"I suspect we have a lot in common, you and I." Mrs. Witherspoon chuckled. "Yes, well, perhaps we should get down to business, we have a lot of ground to cover." She adjusted her bifocals and opened a manila folder. "Now, John, Ethan Jarad directed me in his Will to act as Executor for his estate; I have already filed a bond as such with the Probate Court. Under the General Laws of the State of Massachusetts, I have three months to file an inventory of Ethan's real and personal property; even so, I can see no reason not to inform you now that he named you, John Fitzhugh Jarad, Jr. as his sole beneficiary."

"I'm surprised by that," John admitted. "We weren't that close."

"I warned Ethan his decision might engender hard feelings. After all, he had a large pool of nominees to choose from, and family feelings bruise easily. But, whatever his reason, Ethan was adamant on the subject. He insisted that you be named sole heir, and no one else."

"If you were named the Executor, Mrs. Witherspoon, what's left for me to do?"

"I suppose the first order of business would be to dispose of his remains."

Sarah felt a wiggle of unease. "Wasn't he cremated?"

"Yes, but Ethan requested that his ashes be, and I quote, 'pitched from Sankaty Head'. I'm afraid he left that task for his heir. When you're ready, Stevenson's Mortuary has them. I trust you to know what type of permit you'll need."

"Are you sure?" John leaned forward. "I know he's entitled to a plot in the cemetery. We all have one."

"Evidently, Ethan wanted it both ways; his letter of intent was very specific. It directs you to scatter his ashes; I'm to arrange for a headstone for the cemetery. I've ordered the stone; it's granite, imported from Maine. I'm afraid the shipping cost more than the engraving."

"Which verse did he choose?"

"I have it here." Mrs. Witherspoon consulted an index card. "Let me see now. He ordered his name, and the dates, and the Biblical inscription Job 14:13."

"I'll have to look it up," John pulled his ear. "I'm not up on my Scripture like I should be."

"I've already done that." Mrs. Witherspoon blushed. "Oh, don't act so surprised. We lawyers are only human too. It reads: 'Oh, that thou wouldst appoint a set time, and remember me!' "

Sarah glanced between the lawyer and her husband. "What's all that about?"

"It's a family tradition," John explained. "We choose biblical references for our headstones. That way, a descendant can look it up later and gain some insight into your life."

Sarah felt it her duty to protest. "What's so insightful about a grave without a body in it?"

"Honey, I don't have an answer for you." He sat back. "Did Uncle Ethan mention why he picked me to be his beneficiary?"

"No, John, Ethan never offered an explanation, and I never pushed for one." Mrs. Witherspoon steepled her fingers. "Your great-uncle was an extremely private man, and our relationship was strictly professional. I believe I offered Ethan opportunity for disclosure, but he never took advantage of it." She shook her head. "Some people are like that. They never need much in the way of human companionship and they never do. In the fifty-odd years I knew him, Ethan Jarad never once mentioned a desire for a wife, or a family of his own. Although, come to think of it, he did joke once that marriage was something he couldn't afford."

"I'm beginning to agree with him," John stated.

"You'll pay for that later," Sarah warned.

"Yes, well," Mrs. Witherspoon coughed, unsure of their humor. "John, your great-uncle was a remarkable man. It's a shame you didn't get to know him better."

"He was away most of the time I was growing up, working the sea."

"Yes, Ethan Jarad certainly traveled the globe. I can still remember the day he joined the Merchant Marine. Fresh out of school and as handsome as the devil himself. Your family threw him quite a bon voyage party." The elderly woman sighed. "And then we didn't see him again for more than forty years."

"You were there? At the party?" Sarah wondered.

"My girl, the whole island was there. It's one of my favorite memories." Mrs. Witherspoon relaxed into her tufted leather chair. "Everyone brought a hamper, and the Firehall brass band played all afternoon. John, your great-grandfather gave quite a speech, and then, together, we presented Ethan with a gold St. Nicholas' medal to keep him safe at sea. Ethan even got a laugh out of the gift, saying he'd rather have had a gold earring to wear like a buccaneer, but that he would have had to fight his sisters for it." Mrs. Witherspoon's eyes softened. "Oh, there's no doubt about it, Ethan Jarad was ready to go. To this day, I've never seen a man go after a goal with more determination."

"What goal was that?" Sarah asked.

Mrs. Witherspoon leaned forward. "Apparently, Ethan's only desire was to pursue the security of a large estate. It cost him any semblance of a normal life, but pursue it he did, and when he retired to Nantucket, he brought back with him a full pension and nearly every penny he had ever earned."

"But every time I saw him he was broke," John protested.

"Oh, it's true Ethan made some poor business decisions toward the end. There's very little left in the way of cash, and I had to use what money there was to pay a few private debts before I closed his account at the bank. And he canceled his life insurance policy, such a mistake after all those years of premiums, but I couldn't talk him out of it. And his pension won't help you either, it was an annuity and ceased at his time of death."

"So what's left?"

Mrs. Witherspoon smiled gently. "There are two items. The first is Ethan's house, of course, but you've seen it; I'm afraid it's a complete teardown. The site itself has eroded to the point I don't think it would pass inspection even if you did find a buyer."

"This just gets better and better."

"Now, John," the lawyer scolded, resting her elbows on her desk. "The second item should prove to be of more interest. You see, when Ethan first retired, he bought an additional piece of land out near Sesachacha Pond. It's a prime piece of real estate, although he never developed it."

"Sesachacha Pond? I don't recall anything looking undeveloped, out that way."

"Looks can be deceiving. I've driven by it, and I admit, from the road, it does look like another Conservancy holding."

"I've never noticed it," John admitted.

"You'll notice it now, because Ethan left you the entire sixty acre parcel."

"Excuse me," John blinked. "Did you say sixty acres?"

"I have the deed right here." The lawyer detached a sheaf of onion-skin paper. "I've already instituted a title search on behalf of the estate, and I can assure you that both properties are clear of any liens or conservatorial restrictions. The acreage also contains the only remaining stand of virgin timber on Nantucket. Ethan liked to call it the Lost Forest." Mrs. Witherspoon pressed an intercom button and Ava reentered, carrying her chrome notary stamp like a votive offering. "Ava, witness John's signature on this letter of instruction for me, if you please."

"I have everything ready, Mrs. Witherspoon."

"Fine. Now, John, if you'll sign right there, I'll register the title transfer this afternoon and you can take possession. Thank you. Ava, make this official for us, will you, please? Thank you. Now, John, it's my privilege to tell you that, with Ethan's foresight and today's booming real estate market, your property is currently appraised in the vicinity of eighteen million dollars."

John deflated into his chair. "Excuse me? What did you say?"

"You heard me correctly," the lawyer repeated, smiling broadly. "I said eighteen million dollars. And every penny of it is yours." Mrs. Witherspoon leaned back into her chair, triumphant. "Not bad for an old sea-dog, was it? Of course, Ethan had a lifetime of expert legal and investment advice, when he chose to take it."

"Are you sure that's right?" John stammered. "And he left it all for me?"

"For you and you alone. His estate is yours, to do with as you see fit."

"Jesus, John," Sarah found her voice. "That's one hell of a family bible."

"Jesus is right." He ran his fingers through his hair. "There's no other way to put it. I have had one hell of a day."

Chapter Four

"I don't feel like the same man I was, this time yesterday," John remarked the following morning.

Sarah ruffled his dark hair. "How does it feel to wake up both a Dad and a millionaire?"

"It's hard to believe it really happened. Yesterday seems like a dream."

"Trust me, I was there. I saw it. It happened."

John smiled and stretched. "What's your workload like today?"

"I could take some time off. Why? What have you got in mind?"

"What do you say we spend the whole day together?"

Sarah raised herself on one elbow and carefully studied her husband. Recent experience had taught her to be cautious around this offer of his, it could be treacherous. The first time John had suggested 'let's spend the day together' she spent three hours fine-sanding the teak trim on his cousin Eli's boat; the last time he had asked she had spent the afternoon up to her elbows in gutted bluefish.

John read her expression and chuckled. "I promise this has nothing to do with fish. What do you say we go explore the Lost Forest?"

The freshness of the suggestion appealed to Sarah immediately. "I'd love to do that."

"I thought you might. And while we're there, we should look around and get some ideas. I've been thinking. Sixty acres is a lot of land. What do you say we subdivide it, sell off a few parcels, and use the money to build a new house?"

"Oh, John! Do you mean it? Do you think we could?"

"I don't see why not. The property is ours 'to do with as we see fit.' Give me a kiss and I'll build you a house before the baby gets here."

With a warning yell, Sarah leapt.

"Hold on," John caught her up, delighted. "Be careful, will you? You might not hurt the baby, but you might hurt me!"

Sarah covered him with kisses, then drew back, taking his face in both hands and staring intently into his eyes. "You better mean this, John Jarad, because I'm going to hold you to it."

"I mean it, I mean it. Now get dressed and let's go see my property."

Polpis Road meandered northeast from town, a strip of asphalt cutting a level swath through stands of thick-needled sea-pine and scrubby pin oak. Along the sandy shoulder of the road, dried vetch the color of caramel competed with auburn bayberry for territory. In the distance, a gray, weatherworn cottage stood solitary and defiant, its access road hidden somewhere in a maze of lichen-barked corkscrew cedar.

"I don't get it. This all looks so familiar, so flat," Sarah noted. "It's hard to imagine a real forest anywhere around here."

John tapped a scrap of paper on the dashboard. "I'm following the directions Mrs. Witherspoon gave me. Keep an eye out for Hoicks Crossing. It should be coming up. We'll need to make a left."

"I think that's it right there."

As they made the turn, an expansive stretch of Sesachacha Pond slid into view. Sunlight sparkled across the sapphire blue water as a chorus line of small whitecaps danced toward the narrow strip of beach separating the brackish pond from the sea. Overhead, black-banded gulls swooped and hovered, ruffling their stiff white feathers in the breeze, searching the dun-colored sand for a meal.

John peered through the windshield. "Do you suppose that's the barn we're looking for?"

Sarah laughed. "That's some barn alright."

True to Nantucket tradition, any timber worth saving had been salvaged. The roof had collapsed into a sinkhole of broken, splintered shingles; the three remaining walls listed ominously. An ancient fence line was anchored to a corner of the crumbling fieldstone foundation. A homemade gate matched the barn, a wobbly concoction of barbed wire and twisted tree limbs. Two hand-painted signs, faded gray with age, warned the unwary: Don't Even THINK About Trespassing and Mind Your Own Damn Business.

"That sounds like Uncle Ethan," John parked. "Hold on, I'll get the gate."

"No, wait, I'll get it." Sarah opened her door and slid to the ground.

"Are you sure?"

"That's sweet of you, John, but I'm pregnant, not crippled." She crunched through the dried weeds and paused before the gate, trying to decipher its secret. She freed a pivotal twist of baling wire and the gate sagged to the ground. After dragging it off to one side, Sarah returned to the truck, dusting rust flakes from her gloves.

"Nice job," John admitted.

"Thank you very much."

They jolted across the rough meadow with the truck in low gear. All around them, the acreage lay fallow, showcasing a wild mounded crop of heather, purple-stemmed bramble and silvered thistle. An ancient apple orchard ran parallel to the road, bowing its neglected branches to the pressures of winter.

"So where is this Lost Forest?" Sarah expressed her doubt. "I still don't see any real trees."

"I think I know what's going on." John parked. "But we'll have to walk in from here."

"Walk into where?" Sarah gestured, raising both hands to the sky. "What are you talking about?"

"Follow me." John smiled enigmatically, moving toward a metal t-bar planted near the ragged line of scrub cedar. Sarah followed hesitantly, unsure of exactly where it was they were going. As she watched, John lost his footing and scrambled to regain his balance. He stooped to investigate.

"What is this supposed to be?" John wondered, and flipped over a rusting metal rectangle.

'EXTREME HAZARD!' Neon orange lettering warned. 'TICK INFESTED AREA! EXERCISE CAUTION!'

"Ticks!" Sarah froze instinctively, arms outstretched. "John! I didn't think about ticks!"

"Don't worry, honey, we're safe. It's January." He propped the sign against the t-bar. "If this were July, it would be another story, but there's nothing to worry about now. We've had a heavy frost."

"Are you sure, absolutely sure? I don't want anything to hurt the baby."

"I'm sure. I would never take that kind of chance, with you or with the baby. But I have to give Uncle Ethan some credit for this sign. Who's going to hike through here after reading this?"

"I still don't get you. Hike through where?"

John scanned the cedar, searching for a gap. He pushed aside a large overgrown holly and stepped through its branches, disappearing from sight. Sarah heard his delighted laugh. "Honey? You'd better come in here. You're not going to believe this."

Sarah closed her eyes, braced her gloves to protect her face, and followed. "Just don't let me fall."

"You're not going to fall." He took her arm and drew her through the brush. "Open your eyes and take a look. Isn't this incredible?"

Sarah reopened her eyes and gasped. The ground in front of them gradually sloped away to create a deep protected hollow. Overhead, thick branches wove a massed and tangled canopy, a stark silhouette against a wiggle of pale blue winter sky. The east wind picked up, and the trees whispered. It was a sound Sarah had half-forgotten. The wind in the bare treetops was like the rushing of great waters. "Oh, John, it's beautiful!"

"See? Here are the trees. They grew wide, instead of tall." His enthusiasm was infectious. He took Sarah's hand and led her down the slope. "Isn't this amazing?"

Paired and single, perfect of form, the trees possessed the hollow. Not scrubby pine, or town-coddled elm, but oak, royal oak, the king of trees, the heart of ships.

Sarah pushed her hair behind her ears. "I can't believe what I'm seeing! You'd never know these were here from the road!"

"The wind warped them to grow protected in the hollow. I've heard of groves like this before, but I've never seen one."

"Seen one?" Sarah laughed. "John, you own one."

Realization lit John's eyes. "You know what? For a moment, I forgot about that. This is ours!"

They moved toward the brook, their boots squelching soggy footholds across the boggy, peaty ground. The sound of the water enchanted them, but it was the trees that overwhelmed. Choosing the smaller of a pair, Sarah dug her gloves into its deeply channeled bark and wrapped her arms around its massive trunk. She tried to reach her hands all the way around and had to give up, no matter how she tried, it was too wide. "I've never even seen trees this big before. They must be two hundred years old."

"Older than that." John scooped a handful of acorns and rolled them between his gloves. "Nantucket was harvested clean before 1700. How on earth did these monsters get away?"

"Maybe they couldn't haul them up that slope?"

"No, I don't think so." John shook his head thoughtfully. "The old-time sailors were masters of the block and tackle. If they wanted this timber, they could have got it. No, I think it must have been more than that. I think that someone, a long time ago, wanted to keep this place private, and they did."

"Well, your Uncle Ethan certainly did his part. He kept it a secret for forty years." The sun disappeared behind a cloud, and Sarah shivered. "You know what? Without the sun it's kind of spooky down here. It reminds me of those trees in the Wizard of Oz. I wouldn't be surprised to hear them talk."

John pitched the acorns into the shallow stream and stepped off paces around a majestic patriarch. "I'd like to hear what they'd have to say. Think about it, Sarah. These trees are part of our history. They were growing here even before we arrived."

"Uh-oh, here we go," Sarah teased. The sun returned, and a sunbeam as warm as amber patterned the trunk of a fallen giant. Taking it for a sign, she sat. "Jarad family history, lesson thirty-six."

John grinned sheepishly. "You knew when you married me you married my family, too."

"And I love you for it. It just trips me out that you have so much history. Most people remember their grandparents or maybe even their great-grandparents, but yours go all the way back."

John crossed his arms and rested his chin on his chest. "And that's the heritage I'll be passing on to our baby. I'm proud to do it. It's hard to explain to someone who never had it, it doesn't really translate, but I have such stories to tell our kids, the way they were told to me. Inheriting this property, and having the baby, has really brought home to me lately that I'm not the end of the line. I'm just one link in a long, long chain. How I live my life, or how I screw it up, is just another story to tell, and I don't know how that story ends yet. And honey, you're part of my story, the best part, and our baby is going to be a part of my story, too." He sat down next to Sarah. "I don't know. Maybe I'm finally growing up, to realize all this. I don't feel like I'm at the beginning anymore. I feel like I'm in the middle of something, and whatever it is, it's pretty wonderful."

They kissed and the east wind picked up again, whirling a dance of fallen oak leaves around them. Sunlight speckled the forest floor, highlighting frosted lichen, moss, and fern. Snugly protected in their hollow, the oak trees sighed a rustling chorus as the wind swept through the taller branches.

John pulled Sarah tight, and leaned into the fallen tree. His voice was soft with wonder. "How do I thank you for what you've given me?"

She snuggled, warm in his arms. "That's the greatest thing, John. You don't have to. It's not a gift. It's sharing."

"We'll be sharing all this with our baby soon." He brushed back Sarah's bangs with his glove. "When did my life get so rich?"

"No pun intended?"

"Ha." John smiled gently, shifting his position. "Here's an idea. When we design our new house, let's build a nursery and a studio, a real studio, for you. With that northern light you always talk about."

"And a spare bedroom, for when your sisters-in-law come to visit?"

"I was just going to suggest that."

"I'll bet you were." Sarah sat up, suspicious. "Wait a minute. What are you getting out of this?"

"A three-car garage? With a slot for my boat?"

"So now you have a boat?"

"The one I'm going to buy, once we get the money."

Sarah bowed to the inevitable. It was John's inheritance. He was entitled to his splurge. She snuggled back into his embrace. "Will subdividing the property be a problem? You know how strict the Zoning Commission is."

"My guess is they'll suggest a cluster development, but that's too close quarters for me." John pointed to the surrounding grove. "I was thinking; if we offer to donate the valley for conservation they may favor our single-lot application. Besides, I think we should keep this place as we found it. There's some kind of magic down here. Don't you feel it? Not every square inch of Nantucket needs to be developed. We'll develop the meadow and leave this valley alone. That's should be enough."

"I can see you've given this a lot of thought."

"I had trouble sleeping last night, I had so many different ideas rolling around in my head."

"So I noticed. Is that the only thing bothering you?"

"No," he smiled, surprised by Sarah's perception. "You know, honey, people joke about striking it rich, but I never in my life thought it would happen to me. Think of what this property actually represents. Eighteen million dollars! I can't get my mind around that number! I mean, how do I manage this? What am I supposed to do next? Do I need an accountant? A tax lawyer? What?"

Sarah laughed. "Don't get bent out of shape! Most people wish they had your problem."

"It's more than that," he confessed. "Up 'til now, I had my life pretty well mapped out. And now, in the space of two days, everything has changed. Everything. I don't even have to report to work on Monday unless I want to."

Sarah sat up. "Would you want to do that? Stop being a cop?"

"No, not really. I can't even imagine doing anything else, it's all I ever wanted to be. I love my job, and I'm good at it."

Sarah feigned exasperation. "So you'll be Nantucket's first millionaire police officer. What's the problem? Have you told anyone at the station about your inheritance yet?"

"I won't have to. They'll read about the title transfer in the Inky Mirror. Once the paper hits the street, it'll be common knowledge." He sighed. "I've also been wondering how this is going to affect my family."

"In a good way, I hope."

"I hope so, too. But honey, I've got to figure out how to do this right. Some of my family is living on Social Security. A little something extra would really help them out. But how do I help one, or some, and not all? And that takes care of the older generation, but what about my first cousins? I've got seventeen of them, and they're all going to want something too."

"I'm amazed you got any sleep at all. John, you're anticipating problems you don't even have yet. Yes, everything has changed, but that doesn't mean it has to be bad. You've been given a chance to help a lot of people. I know you'll make the right decisions. You're going to do fine."

He looked up at the dark branches blocking the sky. "I wish I had your confidence."

"You will. Give it time, you'll see I'm right." Ever practical, Sarah kept her focus on their primary goal. "First things first, you need to sell the land." She stood. "Let's go back to the truck and warm up. And then we can pick out our new home site."

Hand-in-hand, they climbed the slope and returned to the meadow. Sarah took a seat on the still-warm hood of the truck as John began mapping out suggested parcels. The air was fresh and crisp, and Sarah could feel her cheeks turning pink with the cold as she watched John stride this way and that, stamping paths through the weeds to indicate potential boundaries. Three different times she made a suggestion, and held a firm line between avarice and privacy. After forty-five minutes, they had decided to try for zoning approval on a five-acre parcel for themselves with eight additional five-acre parcels for development. That would keep the valley safe. Satisfied, they retreated to the cab of the truck where John made another suggestion.

"What do you say, since we're out and about already, that we use the rest of the day to bid farewell to Uncle Ethan?"

Sarah stopped fiddling with the dashboard vents. "You want to scatter his ashes? Now?"

"Why not? I can't think of a reason to keep them. Unless you want them for the garden."

"That's disgusting! I don't even want them in the house."

"So why don't we run over to Sankaty Head?" He leaned on the steering wheel. "Or I could do it later, alone, if you prefer."

"No, we're out, let's get it done." Sarah reached for her purse and dug for her lip gloss. "Wait a minute, it's Sunday. Stevenson's will be closed."

John pulled a big circle across the snow-dusted meadow and turned for the gate before answering. He parked the truck next to the barn and replied through his open door. "I've already picked them up."

"You did? When? Where are they?"

"Under your seat. Hey! Don't put your feet up there, you'll scratch my dashboard!" He turned and sprinted for the gate, taking his time wiring it shut and making frequent glances toward the truck while sniggering into his coat.

Sarah rolled down her window. "That's not funny!" she yelled and rolled the window back up. She stretched her legs across the bench seat, waiting for him to finish. She had the truck. She had his keys. He was outside in the cold and she was inside toasty and warm. It was only a matter of time. She reached over and turned the heater on full.

John approached the truck cautiously. "Honey, are you mad? I had to do it. It was a very funny joke."

"I can see that. And I do have a sense of humor."

"I'm counting on it." He opened the door, and as Sarah drew her legs up, returned to his place behind the wheel.

"Just don't drive too fast, that's all I ask," Sarah requested tightly. "They might spill."

"Nothing's going to spill. Stevenson's made sure the urn was secure. They put it in a box and tied it with string." The truck bounced out of the meadow, up onto the asphalt paving and they continued northeast.

They followed Hollow Road in silence through a stately residential neighborhood. The Sankaty Head lighthouse kept its lone vigil on a slight elevation, standing as the proud terminus of a crumbling asphalt road. The light-keeper's house that had partnered it had been demolished years ago, leaving the white tower with its wide horizontal red-stripe a solitary neighborhood landmark. From its base stretched miles of rolling heathered moor and the manicured fifth hole fairway of the exclusive Sankaty Golf Club.

Sarah used her sleeve to rub the fog off her window. "I can't believe Uncle Ethan asked you to do this."

"It's the only thing he did ask, and considering the compensation, I don't think it was too big a favor."

"Just because you're right doesn't mean I have to like it."

"I can't believe you're still mad at me."

"I am not mad." Sarah tucked her chin in her parka. "I just hate practical jokes, that's all. They're mean-spirited. I didn't know you had them in you."

Sarah's revelation surprised John. Usually, he behaved with what he felt was complete maturity. The only time he felt like clowning was in her presence. "I didn't know they bothered you. I apologize. I won't do it again."

"Really?"

"Of course. And I'll make you a promise. That was the first and only practical joke I will ever play on you. Am I forgiven?"

"Yes," she smiled shyly. "Thank you for understanding."

"Live and learn." He shrugged, pulling into the small circular graveled lot. At this heightened elevation the gusty wind snapped at any immovable object and the truck's antenna hummed a low, persistent note. John reached back under the seat, and Sarah scrambled from her side of the truck, watching nervously as he removed a cardboard box, carrying it gently by its string like a bakery pie.

"Where are you going with that? Down to the water?"

"No." He shook his head. The stiff ocean breeze ruffled his hair. "Uncle Ethan specifically asked to be 'pitched from Sankaty Head'. I think he meant from up here. And I'll tell you another thing, I'm pitching the whole urn too, not just his ashes. I mean, what are we supposed to do with the urn when we're finished? Save it for recycling?"

"Won't it wash ashore?" Sarah protested, following him along a narrow, uneven track toward the sandy bluff. "That would be a lovely thing for someone to find."

"I don't think so. It's pretty stout." John hefted the urn. "It should go straight to the bottom. But I'll have to get right to the edge if I want to make the water. The tide's further out than I thought."

"Please be careful." Sarah hesitated. "I have a bad feeling about this. That bluff might be undercut. I don't want you to fall over."

"Don't worry." He eyed the distant water. "I'll be careful."

"John, wait a minute. I know this is going to sound weird, but before you throw the urn, could I take a look?"

"Look at what? The ashes?"

"I know it sounds gruesome, but I've never seen ashes before. This might be my only chance."

"I'm learning all kinds of things today. I never knew you had a morbid curiosity." He untied the string and lifted the urn from the box. "But I'll humor you since I did the same thing myself before Stevenson's packaged it up."

"You did? What did they look like?"

He turned his back to the wind and carefully unscrewed the fitted bronze lid. "See for yourself."

Sarah peered inside. "That's not so bad. That just looks like sand, gray sand."

"What were you expecting?"

"Oh, I don't know. Something horrible, like teeth."

"Big molars," John chuckled, replacing the lid. "No, there's nothing in there for nightmares. But it is time to say goodbye. And now, if you're ready, I'll give Uncle Ethan my best shot."

He turned his face into the wind and assumed a classic pose, extending the urn in his right hand and swinging it to and fro like a discus. "What do you think?" He winked. "Do I have a chance at the summer Olympics?"

"I think you'd better be careful." Sarah wagged her finger. "Some people would call what you're doing sacrilegious."

"Oh, that's right, I forgot. We're supposed to be all serious. Alright then. Thank you, Uncle Ethan," John intoned solemnly. "We will think of you every time we visit the bank. And a one, and a two, and a three!"

It was a beautiful high spiraling toss. The urn sped across the flat tidal sand toward the distant breakers, glinting a metallic farewell in the low afternoon sun.

Sarah clapped politely. "Nice shot. Not bad, not bad at all, for an amateur."

"And I...call that...a ten." John turned, waving to an imaginary arena full of fans. "Even if I do say so myself."

At the height of its arc, tumbling toward the sea, they stared in disbelief as the urn separated from its lid, spilling its crystalline contents directly into the headwind.

"Hit the deck!" John yelled.

Sarah buried her face in the sand, frantically stuffing her hair into the hood of her parka. The ash cloud drifted with the wind and pelted the backs of their coats with a dry, melodic rain. Once the ash had settled, she lifted one elbow cautiously to check on her husband, and found John laughing – hysterically – face down in the sand.

"John Jarad," Sarah sputtered. "That's not funny! You just scattered Uncle Ethan across the Sankaty Golf Club!"

"Fore!" he howled.

CHAPTER FIVE

The road to Quammock was narrow, full of blind curves and steep scrub-covered banks, but since John was driving Sarah ignored the hazards and turned to study the landscape instead, catching glimpses of distant cranberry bogs through breaks in the wall of roadside pitch pine.

Ethan Jarad had lived a hermit's life and, in choosing a home, he had found a hermit's location. Quammock had no commercial center to it, no general store, no gas station, no post office. It was a small cluster of homes high above the dunes and nothing more. Even the sandy rutted track called East Quammock Road petered out and was best traveled using four-wheeled drive. The community was small and private and preferred to keep it that way. As they jolted toward Ethan's isolated house, a neighboring dog ran up, barking and snapping as they passed. Scraping ice from his windshield, the dog's owner looked up, but did not wave.

"Friendly place," Sarah remarked.

"Sorry about the ride," John pulled the steering wheel hard left, then right, trying to avoid the muddy ruts. "But I don't want to get stuck. They'd have a hard time pulling us out of here."

"No kidding." Sarah agreed, clutching the dashboard for support. "I can't believe Uncle Ethan lived way out here. He really worked hard at avoiding company."

"He only went into town to get groceries or, as you saw, visit the liquor store."

The tires spun for traction as the truck crossed a sandy headland curling out to sea like a flattened question mark. On this side of Nantucket, where the Gulf Stream current was strongest, shoreline erosion was an unbeatable fact of life. As they neared Ethan's house, it was obvious to them both that the sea was winning. John slowed to navigate around a large recent sand fall, and Sarah scooted closer to his side of the truck, since there was nothing between her door and seawater but thirty vertical feet of air.

"Don't worry," John smiled, grimly. "I'm not about to put us in it."

"I don't get it." Sarah scanned the empty headland. "What did he do out here?"

"He was an old man, honey. He didn't have to do anything."

"But how did he spend his time? Just sit and watch the ocean all day?"

"I know he liked to read. He had some books of the Bible memorized."

"He sure knew Job." Sarah rummaged through her purse for an elastic, pulling her hair into a ponytail. "I wish he was still here. I'd like to ask him some questions."

"Think of what you're saying. If Uncle Ethan were still here, we wouldn't be." John gestured as the truck rolled to a stop. "I should have warned you. He wasn't big on renovation."

"No kidding."

Ramshackle was too nice a word for the condition of Uncle Ethan's home. Once a graceful Victorian cottage, the house now sagged in forlorn disrepair. Second-floor dormer windows were blocked by sheets of plywood, and the roof was a hodgepodge of odd-lot shingles and oil cans, flattened for use. Half-hidden in the weeds of the neglected side yard, a white Kelvinator refrigerator lay on its side like a dead cow, uptilted legs splayed and ridiculous.

John sighed. "At least when I was a kid he kept it painted."

"You're showing your age. This house hasn't seen a coat of paint in twenty years."

"Still want to live here?"

"I'm having second thoughts," Sarah admitted.

They left the truck and walked toward the front door, treading carefully, on the lookout for nails. The wrap-around porch had warped and buckled, splintering its supports under the strain. One of the porch pillars was missing altogether, and Uncle Ethan had replaced it with a thick driftwood log, salt-slick and twisted like an angry ogre.

Sarah hesitated at the base of the steps. "He wouldn't have set any booby-traps or anything, would he? Hermits do things like that, you know, to scare thieves."

"No," John chuckled. "I'm sure he didn't set any booby-traps, but he was an old man. It's probably a mess inside. Do you want to wait out here while I take a look?"

"No, I'd rather stay with you."

"Alright, but don't lean on anything. Habit is the only thing holding this place up."

The central hallway was dark and smelled of mildew, damp wood, and old fires. Pale winter sunlight striped the floor, catching the dust they disturbed and highlighting it like tiny spinning flecks of gold. Sarah crossed to the front parlor and felt a ripple of disappointment. She had been warned but there wasn't much here: an old rush-bottomed chair, a spindly cast-iron lamp, a Victorian horsehair couch, its original maroon upholstery long since faded to beige. Her eyes fell on the most pathetic sight of all: a white enamel hospital bed, its unwashed sheets grimy with dirt. Sarah voiced her disbelief. "He slept down here?"

"Look at those stairs. Would you have trusted them?" John replied, his voice hollow with echo. "If he'd fallen, it would have been awhile before anyone noticed."

"No wonder he was a hermit. What woman's going to put up with this kind of nonsense?"

"It's just a guess, but I think Mrs. Witherspoon might have, if she'd been asked." John stooped to investigate the chimney. "Why don't I make a fire? At least he left plenty of wood." He poked through the trash on the mantle. "Oops. I should have checked before I offered. Do you have any matches on you?"

"No, but I can look in the kitchen. There might be some in there."

"Okay, just be careful. Don't trust anything."

Sarah waded toward the back of the house, using her knees to push aside bundles of newspaper. The back of the house smelled like pee and the linoleum was cracked with age. The kitchen was dim with shadow and Sarah clicked an old-fashioned light switch to discover why: the single window was blocked by a stack of cardboard boxes. She lifted one lid and peered inside, knowing even as she did what she would find. Like the logo said, it was Kossack Vodka, and all the bottles were empty.

"I should've guessed," she chided herself. "At least that's no surprise."

She opened the door to a corner cupboard and made her first happy discovery: a stack of Grandma's china, all hand-painted flowers and gilded rims, each plate lovingly protected by a dusty circle of mauve felt. Sarah lifted the top plate to check the maker's mark and smiled. She was right. It was Haviland.

"Honey?" John called from the front room. "Any luck?"

Sarah ran her fingers along the delicate floral design. "I found some china in here."

"Great! But did you find any matches?"

Sarah replaced the plate and grabbed the box of Blue Cross matches from the top of the gas stove. Returning to the front room she found John kneeling on the hearth, dusting his hands and looking satisfied with his work. Sarah handed him the matchbox. "Here you go. Try these."

"Shouldn't be a minute." He struck the first one, snapping the wooden match in half. The second strike spit sulfur and John cupped his hand to protect the flame. "You were saying something about china?"

"I found a set in the kitchen. We should take it with us when we go tonight. It's worth some money, and it might walk off, now that people know the house is vacant."

"You're right." John chuckled, using a small hearth broom to sweep ash into the fire. "My first case was just like that."

Sarah stretched her fingers before the crackling tinder. "Why? What happened?"

"Do you really want to hear this?"

"You know I do. I love your stories. They're why I married you."

"I thought you married me for my looks."

"Hello." Sarah snapped her fingers. "Wake up, you're dreaming. Come on, spill."

He patted the hearth beside him and Sarah made herself comfortable. "Okay. Well, way back when I was a rookie, there was a local man named Tom Weston. He owned Island Mercantile, over on Main? Well, one birthday Tom turned fifty, took up jogging, and it killed him."

"Heart attack?" Sarah guessed.

"Nope. Tripped on a curb and fell in front of an Island Tour bus. Bang, it was over, just like that. Never knew what hit him." John added a log to the fire. "Now that's no crime, but Tom had no immediate family on island, so his lawyers had to send to Chicago for a cousin to come over and close up his house. Tom lived in Squantum, are you familiar with that area yet?"

"The development where you look out your kitchen window into your neighbor's bathroom?"

"That's the one. Well, it turned out Tom's cousin was a busy man, and it was six weeks before he could fly over. Meanwhile, in those six weeks, someone went into Tom's house and stole all the interior doors and most of the custom pegged-pine flooring. The cousin was furious when he found out, and I don't blame him, I would have been, too."

Sarah was entranced. "So who stole the doors?"

"I never found out." John frowned. "You would think, in a neighborhood that tight, someone would see doors walking out of a house. But I never found a witness, so I never found my thief."

"So, you're telling me you never solved your first case."

"It's not closed yet." He tugged his ear. "To this day, every time I enter a house I check their floor. I'm going to find that pegged-pine board someday, and those spoon-molded doors, too. And then I'll have my answer."

"That's your secret, isn't it? You never give up."

"You're my proof of that." He smiled and stood, reaching down a hand to help her up. "Story time's over. We should get started. We won't get anything done this way."

"Alright." Sarah dusted her hands. "What looks promising?"

"Pick any spot you like. I'll get the boxes from the truck."

Left to her own devices, Sarah started to investigate. Evidently, if Uncle Ethan was in the house, he either sat or slept on the bed, since there was no other furniture in the room. Holding her breath against the dust, she stripped the sheets and discarded them to the floor. The embroidered linen, once so fine, was simply ruined with dirt. The lumpy, buttoned mattress had its own sad story to tell, but at least it was clean enough to pile things on while they packed.

Sarah took another look around and felt sadness wash over her. Even knowing as little about Uncle Ethan as she did, she imagined how lonely he must have been out here, how isolated. She could see no items of comfort anywhere; no family pictures, no souvenirs, and this was a man who had traveled the world. The room was bare except for the bed, a nightstand and a lamp, one dirty water glass and an ancient Bible, its tooled leather binding decaying to a soft ochre brown. Using both hands, Sarah gently lifted its fragile cover.

"Find something?" John startled her, returning from the truck.

"You weren't kidding about Uncle Ethan leaving you a Bible." She traced a genealogy penciled on the flyleaf. "This one has your family written all over it."

"Let me see." He peered over her shoulder. "Obiah Jarad, 1864. This one's not that old. There's a family Bible at the Atheneum that dates to 1659."

"Look." Sarah pointed. "Here's your Mom and Dad. John FitzHugh Jarad, deceased, married Genevieve Louisa Hamilton. I didn't know your mother's name was Genevieve!"

"She prefers Jenny. Wouldn't you?"

"You know it." Suddenly, as Sarah watched, the humor drained from her husband's eyes. "John, what is it? What's the matter?"

"Goddammit!" His voice was so low it barely registered. "I should've know he'd pull something like this."

"Pull what? John, what are you talking about?"

"Look. Right there." He lowered himself onto the mattress and pointed at the Bible. "Read the names."

"Alright. Jacqueline Winifred Jarad, spinster. Oh, Jackie would love that all right."

"That's not what I meant. Keep reading."

"Mary Rose Jarad, married Matthew Beachum Quigley?"

No response. Sarah tried the next line.

"Wheatley James Jarad, married Anne Marissa Schyler. That's your brother Pete, right?"

"That's right. Keep going." John's voice sounded lifeless.

"Micah Fulsom Jarad." No response. "John FitzHugh Jarad, Junior married Sarah Elizabeth Hawthorne. That's us. And Daniel Carrick Jarad, deceased." Sarah looked into his eyes. "John, I don't understand. What's the problem?"

"Danny didn't die," he insisted, blindly. "And Uncle Ethan had no right to put that in here."

"But you told me yourself that you lost a brother when you were little. Don't you remember? The night we talked about family? On the beach?"

"I did lose a brother. But I only told you half the truth that night. My brother Danny didn't die, he disappeared."

"Disappeared? What do you mean disappeared?" She turned to look at him. "And why haven't you told me this before?"

"It's not something I like to discuss." John stood abruptly, leaving Sarah to catch the Bible. "And I had only just met you, and it's not a subject I talk about with strangers."

"I am not a stranger," Sarah stated. Her brain was spinning. "John, we live on an island. Where did Danny go?"

He stopped pacing and stood before the fire. "That's just it. We don't know where Danny went. He just vanished."

She returned the Bible to the nightstand. "So what happened?"

"We called the police, of course, my God, and they searched everywhere. They even climbed into the church steeples and the lighthouses. Then they found Danny's bike on the beach road near Tom Nevers and brought in the F.B.I. The Feds thought it might have been a kidnapping, but in the end they couldn't help us either."

"They gave up?"

"Honey, they had to. There was nothing left to investigate." Sparks leapt as John prodded the fire. "The Medical Examiner ruled it "death by misadventure". He suggested Danny washed to sea. We never recovered his body."

"John, I'm so sorry," Sarah paused. She knew John well enough to recognize his tone and it still sounded off. "But you don't think that's what happened, do you? I can hear the doubt in your voice."

John turned away from the fire, his dark eyes blazing. "I only know Danny would never have gone in that water. That's what they said but I know it's not true. He was only seven, but

Danny was smart. Besides, it was May – who goes swimming in May? You know how cold the water is that time of year. And Tom Nevers is a shelving beach, he couldn't have just fallen in." He ran his fingers through his hair. "That's what got to me. Nothing about losing Danny ever made sense."

Sarah tried to imagine having someone just disappear from your life. "How old were you when this happened?"

"Twelve," he stared into the fire. "Twelve and a half."

Sarah waited patiently with the still talents of a good listener. John dusted his hands and walked over to the bed. The box springs creaked as he sat next to her. Gently, she took his hand. "Do you blame yourself for what happened to him?"

"Maybe I do." He whispered. "He was my little brother; I was supposed to watch out for him. We shared a room back at the house. Me, I liked to sleep in, but Danny? He loved the morning. He loved getting up early. He'd hear Dad get up at four to go fishing and he'd get up, too. Mom would send him back to bed because it would still be dark out. Sometimes he'd fix himself some cereal and watch cartoons and wait for the rest of us to get up. If I woke up and Danny wasn't in his bed, it was no big deal." A log split, collapsing into a shower of sparks. "When I woke up that morning he was already gone. It was a miserable day too, cold wind, slashing rain. He had no reason to go outside. We sat down to breakfast and Mom ran a head count. That's when she noticed Danny's slicker and his boots were gone, and she sent me outside to check the clams, but he wasn't there."

Sarah blinked. "Sorry, you lost me. Check the clams?"

"Dad kept a fifty-gallon drum of seawater in the garage and when he came back from clamming he'd put the clams in the drum and Mom could get them when she needed to. Clams will stay alive for weeks if you feed them cornmeal, and that was Danny's job. That's where I thought he was. I went outside to check but he wasn't there. And his bike was gone. We had a fort built near the water tower, so I went to check that too, but he wasn't there, either." He rubbed his eyes. "It was pouring rain. By the time I got home I was soaked. And no one there had found him, either. That's when I knew something was wrong. Everyone tried to pretend it was okay, but I knew better. Mom called all the neighbors and Dad bolted out of the house and I just sat there, dripping wet, leaving a puddle on the floor, and I knew. Sarah, I can't explain it. I just knew he was gone."

"John, I'm so sorry. It tears me up to see you hurt like this."

"It hurts," he admitted. "Sometimes I forget about him for a little while; I can go for months and then we get a report about a missing child, or I see a boy who looks like him walking down the street and it snaps right back at me." He released a long, slow breath. "You can't know what that's like unless it happens to you. When you say goodnight to someone, you expect to see them in the morning."

"I do know what you mean." Sarah gently stroked his palm. "It's kind of like what happened with my Mom."

"Oh God, Sarah. I didn't mean to bring that up. That's not what I meant."

"I know it wasn't." She squeezed his hand. "But do you see where I'm coming from? I do understand a little bit of what you went through. The last time I said 'good night' to my mother, she was fine. We had no warning. When something like that happens it leaves a scar; of course it does. You're never the same person you were before it happened. There'd be something wrong if you were."

"Maybe that's the price we pay for living." John tried to smile and failed miserably. "I have horrible old memories like Danny, and wonderful new ones, like you and the baby. Maybe in the end, if I'm lucky, I'll find some kind of balance."

"I hope so. I have to think the good will outweigh the bad. I have to believe it, John, because I'm here with you and that's where my heart has led me, and I cannot believe that what I feel for you is wrong."

John crooked his finger to lift her chin. "You are my strength. You are my rock."

"You got that right and don't you forget it." Sarah stood and pulled him to his feet. "Come on now. I'll tell you what. You get the tape out of the truck, and I'll start packing the china."

"That's a deal. I'll be right back."

Sarah slowly gathered a cardboard carton and some fresh newspaper. For the first time in her young marriage, she fully realized the extent of the gap that existed between her world and John's. It was more than their seven-year age difference; that they could weather. This was a gap in their shared background and experience. Only time would tell if they could bridge the gap, and until that time she would have to find strength in blind trust, never one of her stronger suits. "Ethan Jarad," she remarked to the air. "Marion was right. You were a troublemaker."

She opened a corner cupboard and discovered a matching china serving set. The gravy boat had a chip in it, but the soup tureen was worth a month's rent from any island antique store. She wrapped it in newspaper and carefully lowered it into a box, returning to the parlor for the strapping tape only to realize John was still outside. She used her cuff to wipe a clean spot in the dingy windowpane and saw her husband talking to the owner of a hunter-green Suburban. The Suburban's door panel logo read Robey Island Development, Ltd.

"Come in, George." She heard John say. "We've got a fire going."

"Are you sure it's safe?" The stranger's voice carried honeyed Ivy League overtones. Sarah watched him cast a dubious eye across the facade. "Place looks more like a firetrap, to me."

"If you're serious, George, come inside. I want my wife to hear this."

The Suburban chirped an alert as the two men climbed the porch. Although Sarah had never seen the stranger before, she knew she would recognize him the next time she did. 'George' was not only darkly handsome, he possessed an urbane quality that seemed vaguely European. Or, she smiled, it could just be his well-cut camel-hair coat, which to her eye looked like Armani, a surprisingly sophisticated choice for an island businessman, even one from Nantucket.

John opened the door and called. "Sarah? Oh, there you are. Honey, come meet George Robey."

"Hello, George." Sarah extended her hand and, glancing down, pulled it back, realizing in time that her fingers were covered with black newsprint. "Oh, I'm sorry. Don't let me get this on you."

George graced her with a warm, broad smile. "No, no, quite right. Thank you. Delighted."

"Honey, George is a developer. He wants to discuss the Lost Forest property with us."

"I have a few ideas." The developer took a quick inventory of the room. "Excuse me for mentioning this, but it looks like Hurricane Edouard blew through here."

"If you think this is bad, you should see the kitchen," Sarah replied.

"I'll take your word for it. Have you found anything interesting yet?"

John toyed with the roll of tape. "Sarah found some china. But we literally just got started. There's no telling what we'll find once we get upstairs."

"I don't envy you your chore." George drew off his pigskin gloves. "Is there somewhere we could sit?"

"Furniture is a weak point in this house," John apologized. "What you see is what we've got."

"Very well then, why don't you two sit on the bed." The developer took charge, reaching for the rush-bottomed chair. "And I'll place my…faith…on this wobbly creature. Now, John and Sarah, I'm not going to waste your time repeating what you probably already know. Sesachacha Pond means a two-acre lot minimum, and two-acre lots carry million-dollar homes. It's going to take a lot of time and money to develop that acreage properly. And zoning will be a nightmare, it always is."

"I've heard stories," John agreed.

"Yes. Well, some brave souls have tried to develop their own property, and God love them, a few have actually done quite well. But if you asked them about it right now, I believe every one of them would tell you to leave real estate development to the professionals. It's not worth the headache. They'd tell you to accept my offer and run."

John glanced at his wife. "George, we're willing to listen to what you have to say."

"Why not?" Sarah agreed.

"Sensible people," George purred. "Now, my offer may seem a little low, but remember, I'm offering to pay you cash. No mortgage to carry, no promissory notes. That, in and of itself, should be worth something. To be fair, I'm quite sure the LandBank is trying to reach you even now with another offer. And John, you can wait for their offer, but I guarantee it will not match mine."

"You want to buy the entire parcel?" John asked.

"Yes; the development I have in mind is going to require it."

"We had talked about keeping a few acres for ourselves and building a new house on it."

"That's a fine idea." The developer nodded. "But I'm afraid the property isn't divisible."

"We were there yesterday," John countered. "It looked divisible to us."

"That hollow will do you in." George delicately plucked the crease in his trousers. "If I know the zoning board, and I do, they'll label that a watershed, and watersheds are a red flag to any regular developer."

It was Sarah's turn to wonder. "So what makes you so interested?"

"Because I can turn a handicap into good business. If Robey Island Development donates that portion of the property to the Conservancy, we'll get a nice tax write-off for our books, not to mention the free publicity. But I'm afraid that leaves me with only forty-five acres to develop, and to meet my proposal, I'm going to need every inch of it."

Sarah leaned forward, her elbows on her knees. "What are your plans for the property, George?"

The developer waved off her question. "Everything's purely tentative, at this point. But it doesn't make sense to invest my time and effort into anything smaller. I'm afraid my offer covers all the property, or none of it."

John crossed his arms. "What's your offer, George?"

"Twelve million dollars. Cash. One lump sum."

John showed his surprise. "You've done very well for yourself."

"Which only proves I know what I'm doing." George relaxed against his chair. "And John, my offer is bona fide. I guarantee that within forty-eight hours of our signing a sales agreement the money will be in your bank account. John, think of it. Twelve million dollars, in your bank account the day after tomorrow."

John studied the developer. "You must want this property pretty badly, George."

"I'm not going to pretend otherwise. And you should consider my offer seriously. You want a new house? Well, here it is. Say 'yes' to my proposal and you two could be living in decent, permanent housing before this next summer."

John rose. "Thank you, George. We'll talk it over and let you know."

"Don't wait too long, John. We need to get a jump on this." The developer stood, buttoning his coat. He reached into his pocket and withdrew a stainless steel card case, passing one card to John and another to Sarah. "All my numbers are right there. Call me anytime, day or night. I have to say, this is a tremendous opportunity for us all."

"Thank you again, George. We'll let you know," John repeated.

"Sarah," the developer bowed politely. "Delighted to meet you. You take care."

"Thank you, George, I will. Nice to meet you, too."

Standing at the window arm in arm, John and Sarah watched the developer pull on his leather gloves as he strolled toward his Suburban. As George pulled away, he tooted the horn and waved confidently.

Sarah toyed with George's business card, flicking it with her thumbnail. "Are we really considering his offer?"

"I think we should."

"That 'living in decent, permanent housing before this next summer' was a nice touch, don't you think?"

"George always had a reputation as a smooth talker."

"He's earned it. And he really is charming. Did you notice that, too?"

"You know," John scowled. "I never did like that guy."

CHAPTER SIX

In spite of recent redecorating efforts, Jenny Jarad had kept an ancestral portrait over the mantel, a study in oils of a sea-captain smoking an amber pipe. Jarad family resemblance was obvious in the dark eyes, so familiar to her, and as Sarah studied the portrait, the dark eyes steadfastly studied her back.

"Oh, don't mind him." Jenny hesitated over the three short steps, holding a platter high. Peering over her bifocals, she tested the stairs for her footing. Safely standing on the floor, she relaxed, and smiled graciously. "That's Lemuel Abad Jarad, and he's always grumpy this time of day."

Sarah stepped back, interpreting the work. "He almost looks upset about something."

"Oh, he is. He objects to the way I've redecorated." Jenny placed the platter on a low table and removed the linen napkin with a flourish. "He thinks old roses are too feminine for a public room, and he absolutely loathes salmon as a wall color."

"But I love what you've done in here, Jenny. It's so bright."

"Thank you, Sarah, so do I." Jenny poured out mint tea and handed Sarah a cup. "And if you think about it, his opinion shouldn't count for much anymore. I mean, he has been dead for over one hundred and sixty years, and all he does anymore, really, is scare the cat."

Sarah smiled behind her cup, reminding herself she should know by now where John gets it from. His mother had to be pulling her leg. "Are you saying this house is haunted?"

"Oh, no. I'd hate to call it haunted. Well, not maliciously, anyway. But I do think any house with character would have to have some spirit in it, don't you agree?"

"Yes, I do," Sarah answered. Hesitantly, she selected half a sandwich and relaxed. She was safe. It was cheese. Jenny had remembered the lobster salad fiasco.

"So let's talk happy news. You saw Dr. Reynolds this morning?"

"Um-hum. John took me in for my checkup. Everything is fine. My due date is September 30th."

Jenny beamed. "September 30th! That is so wonderful and exciting! You know, I really don't care which the baby is as long as you both are healthy, but I would so love another girl. Now don't take me wrong, I love my grandsons more than life, but there is just something about a baby girl. It's been years since we had one in the family."

"It's the dresses," Sarah suggested. "John caught me looking at some baby catalogs yesterday. He says I am not allowed to buy anything that has smocking or poodles on it."

"I used to sew, back when my girls were little," Jenny tapped her lips with her index finger. "I may still have a few of their things up in the attic. I know there's a crib up there, if you're interested. Mary Rose didn't need it, she used one from Matthew's side of the family, but you might like it."

"Thank you, Jenny. That's very generous."

"While we're up there you should look at some of the furniture we have in storage, too. I'd be delighted to find a new home for some of those old things." Jenny replaced her teaspoon on her saucer with an audible click. "So, my dear, now tell me. I never did hear the full story. What did Molly Witherspoon have to say?"

"Well, we went in not expecting much of anything, really. John kept warning me how poor Uncle Ethan was, how he wouldn't have anything to leave. And at first I thought that was what Mrs. Witherspoon was telling us, too. Then, right when I thought she was asking us to pay for the funeral or something, she dropped the bomb about how Uncle Ethan left his house and the Lost Forest property all for John."

"That surprised me, too. I had no idea Ethan owned anything valuable, least of all a sizable piece of land. What has me curious is why Ethan picked John to be his beneficiary. Did Molly mention a reason?"

"No. She just said Uncle Ethan insisted on it. 'Adamant' was the word she used."

"Adamant!" Jenny laughed. "Adamant runs deeply in this family. Even John has a streak of it, have you noticed? He's just like his father; once he makes up his mind he will not be shifted." She shook her head. "I just pray everything works out for the best. I'm worried in the long run this inheritance may do John more harm than good."

"What makes you say that?"

"Because, my dear, I've survived situations like this before. Disproportionate inheritance so often brings out the worst in people. When Jack inherited the controlling interest in Jarad Shipping, I saw a similar thing happen." Jenny refilled her cup. "I know this decision is between you and John, but I suggest that you consider somehow 'gifting' the other family members. Perhaps setting up college scholarships for their children?" She sipped her tea and added a teaspoonful of sugar. "And I suspect you are about to be inundated by every trickster and shaky relative there is."

"I appreciate your honesty, Jenny. When John and I have some time, we'll talk about it. I promise."

"That's all I can ask." Jenny smiled graciously. "Now, let's put this inheritance down to Ethan's normally erratic behavior and leave it at that."

"You know," Sarah paused. "John said Uncle Ethan was erratic, too, but Mrs. Witherspoon said he really knew what he was doing. He almost sounds like two different men."

"In a way, I suppose he was. Ethan changed after he retired. I don't know why, perhaps he lost his mooring when he lost his structure after so many years. I've seen it happen to other retired men I've known." Jenny dusted crumbs from her fingers. "It was the oddest thing, really, but something was just not right with him."

"What do you mean?"

"Well, he went actively out of his way to alienate every single person he knew. If Ethan saw you walking down the street, he would duck down an alley. We'd invite him over for cocktails or for dinner and he would make some poor excuse. Eventually, we gave up on him. We had to. The man was obviously uncomfortable whenever he was around."

Sarah reconsidered Marion's remark about the Jarad family. Maybe she had been right. Maybe Uncle Ethan did just go off the deep-end. Marion had certainly seen enough of the family to know.

Jenny folded her napkin. "Would you like to see the crib?"

"I'd love to."

"I apologize in advance for the state of my attic. It's a disgrace." Jenny rose and made her way to the kitchen. She left the empty platter on the countertop and continued deeper into the kitchen. "I've been meaning to get to it for years."

Where was Jenny going? Sarah wondered. The staircase was back in the hall.

Jenny intercepted her look and smiled. "I have another surprise for you. I don't believe you've seen this yet." She reached for a black wrought-iron ring to the left of the open brick fireplace and gave it a hearty tug. To Sarah's delight, what she had assumed to be a small paneled cupboard swung open to reveal a full-sized door.

Jenny started up the staircase briskly, offering an explanation over her shoulder. "This passage is original to the house. I know it pre-dates the Civil War, and I was told it was part of the Underground Railroad. You can still find names penciled on the walls." She paused and pointed to a name scratched into the old plaster. " 'Frederick Douglas'. I'm not convinced that particular signature is authentic. It's my understanding Frederick Douglass the Abolitionist was a literate man, and spelled his last name with a double 's'. However, believe what you will."

They climbed the stairway to a small landing, made a tight turn around the chimney stack and continued without a break to the third floor. The atmosphere in the attic was stale, the air tasting of tarry parched pine. At either end of the roof under the eaves, narrow mullioned windows admitted shafts of sunlight. Jenny paused at the top of the stairs and flicked a switch, and a series of naked bulbs lit the center beam.

"I warned you." Jenny turned back an old sheet and fell onto an overstuffed chair which released a puff of dust. "Honestly, I don't think the Jarad's have thrown anything out since this house was built. And with this family, that's saying something. Let me know if you see anything you like."

"Are you kidding me?" Sarah had a hard time believing the treasure trove that met her eyes. "Jenny, this is fantastic."

A row of leather-strapped steamer trunks ran along the left side of the attic, many of them monogrammed in a formal, archaic script. Sarah ran her fingers covetously over an inlaid Sheraton sideboard standing tip-toe on tapered legs, and nudged a hard-rock maple rocker with its seat worn smooth from use. Propped in one corner, a beveled mirror with a Chinese-red lacquered frame reflected her image and her delight. She looked like a kid on Christmas morning.

Jenny plumped a needlepoint pillow. "Take your time; there's more here than you could go through in a month. It's the only virtue in staying in one location for three hundred years. The Jarads kept everything."

Sarah next discovered a spidery, hinged contraption carved from ivory, or bone. Curious, she picked it up and the unknown object suddenly expanded in her hands. Afraid to drop it, and afraid of getting pinched, she did the only thing she could think of: she clutched it away from her body and looked to her mother-in-law for an explanation. "What is this thing? Is it a parasol? Or a corset?"

Jenny laughed, sharing in Sarah's obvious delight. "That my dear, is a swift, a yarn-spinner. It's whalebone, carved by some idle Jarad male to pass the time during a tedious voyage. Most of our scrimshaw is downstairs on display, but I never could find room for that particular piece. Isn't it splendid?"

"It certainly is." Sarah next spied an ornate gilt frame peeking from behind a wicker chair and drew it out, expecting to find another ancestral portrait only to discover an elaborate heart-shaped pattern fabricated entirely of tiny pink and white shells instead. "Wow. Look at the work somebody did on this."

"It's a sailor's valentine." Jenny stood, moving slowly toward a distant corner, turning back another dust sheet. "Here's the crib I mentioned. I know it's old-fashioned, but do you think you'll be able to use it?"

Sarah joined her mother-in-law as Jenny ran a hand across the headboard, lost in memory. The crib was sturdy, and clean of line, displaying the mellow patinated grain of quarter-sawn oak. The crib would need some modern updating, but Sarah knew a carpenter who could do the trick. "We'll have to adapt it a little, Jenny. Do you mind?"

"Of course not. I'd like to see it used again." Jenny's voice was almost breathless. She caressed the railing. "I used this crib for all six of my babies. It's fitting that you and John should use it for yours."

With a chill, Sarah noted the number. Six. Jenny used this crib for all six of her babies. It dawned on her what the number implied. The last baby to use this crib had been Jenny's missing son Daniel. "John told me a little about what happened to his brother, but he doesn't remember much."

"I'm not surprised. He was so young at the time, himself." Jenny looked up, meeting Sarah's eye. "Actually, I've been wanting to talk to you about Danny ever since you and John first got serious, but the timing never seemed right. It's not a subject you can just drop on someone." Jenny retraced her steps to the soft chair, gripping the arms and lowering herself slowly. "And we had only known you for such a short while. I meant to get to it, I really did, but I could never find the right moment." Jenny pulled a tissue from her pocket and blotted her eyes. "Do you like irony, my dear? Saturday, May 12, 1979, was the day my little boy vanished. I will never forget that date; it was the day before Mother's Day. That's why I never celebrate it. But you don't know that about me yet, do you? Well, that's the reason."

Jenny suddenly looked frail and Sarah questioned the wisdom in this painful pursuit. "We don't have to talk about this if it's upsetting you."

"No, no, I do want to talk about it. You should know about Danny. You are a part of this family." Jenny took a deep, shuddering breath and composed herself. "You have to understand Jack and I had five children living in this house the day Danny disappeared. Jackie had already moved into her own place, but it was still easy to overlook one in the crowd, especially first thing in the morning with everyone rummaging around for breakfast. I didn't even notice he was missing until everyone sat down at the table, and even then that wasn't unusual. Danny was usually up and out before the rest of us, especially on a Saturday."

"John said he liked getting up early."

"Oh, he did. Danny was an active little boy, and it gets light here so early. Even then I didn't think anything was wrong. We live on Nantucket, bad things don't happen here. So I just kept dishing out the eggs and sent John out to find him. I didn't think Danny had gone far. But when John came back in tears because he couldn't find Danny anywhere, that's when I started to worry."

"So that's when you called the police?"

"No, not right away. I don't know. Maybe we should have." Jenny smoothed her skirt. "Jack went out looking while I made some calls. I tried Ethan's first, thinking Danny might have run over there, but I couldn't get an answer. Then I called a few of the neighbors to find out if anyone had seen him. 'Sconset was a real neighborhood then, everyone was so helpful, they all dropped their weekend plans and came right over." She rubbed her temples. "The weather that morning didn't help either. First it was fog, and then it poured rain. After an hour of not finding Danny, that's when we called the police."

"What did they say?"

"They thought he had found somewhere dry and was sitting it out. But as the day wore on, you could see, their attitude changed. One of the men called me 'the boy's mother' and his tone told me all I needed to know." She rested her head on the back of the chair. "Later that afternoon they found Danny's bicycle on the beach at Tom Nevers. And then the police moved in to search the water. I will never forget the look on Jack's face when they told him they were going to do that. I can see his face before me now. It was black with fear and rage." She sighed. "In some ways I lost my husband that day too. Once Danny disappeared, Jack shut up tight like a clam. I loved Jack more than I can say, but there was a place inside of him where he could go and I couldn't follow. We had six children together, and that tight, private place was always there." Jenny twisted her wedding band. "I think it had something to do with his sense of pride. Or responsibility. Whatever it was, losing Danny cut Jack to the quick." She adjusted her bifocals and glanced at her daughter-in-law. "John is a lot like his father in that way. Have you noticed that?"

"No, he's always been very open with me."

"Good, good, I'm glad. Perhaps I'm wrong about him. I hope so." Slowly, Jenny stood and moved to one of the trunks lining the wall. She ran her hand across the top, then knelt and lifted the latch. The lid sighed open. "I've kept some of Danny's things all this time. Do you think that's strange?"

"Not at all." Sarah moved to Jenny's side. The trunk was three-quarters full and heartbreaking in its contents. Sarah noticed a faded blue silk baby book stuffed fat with photographs, a much abused Kermit the Frog® and a snarled wreckage of ubiquitous Star Wars® figurines.

Jenny reached in and withdrew some snapshots. "Here's my baby boy. My little caboose." She passed Sarah a photo, blinking back tears. "I think he looked very much like Micah did at that age. It's the Jarad stamp. You can spot it a mile away."

Sarah accepted the ragged photograph, cupping it in both hands. Taken on an anonymous beach, the amateur photographer's shadow had fallen diagonally across the sandy foreground. But the image had captured a slim, laughing boy in dark swim trunks racing toward the camera. Hello, Danny Jarad, Sarah silently introduced herself. Pleased to finally make your acquaintance.

Jenny studied the next picture for a moment before passing it across. "He's with John in this one."

The image had faded from poor developer but there could be no doubt about its subject. Two boys clowned for the camera, the taller one obviously John at ten or eleven years of age. John had one long arm draped around his younger brother's neck and both boys were wearing cut-off shorts. Additionally, Danny was sporting a ragged palm-frond hat that screened half his face with shadow. He was holding two fingers up behind John's head to make horns.

Jenny pried another curling picture loose, running her fingers across its faded surface. "This one is Danny and Jack. I'm not sure, Sarah, how much John had told you, but losing

Danny was a double tragedy. You see, losing my son also cost me my husband."

Sarah nodded as another piece clicked into the puzzle. "I knew John's father had a stroke, but I didn't know this was the reason."

"Jack was strong, but losing Danny was too much for him. You see, he never stopped searching. He only came home for dry clothes or more coffee. I tried to help Jack, I did. I tried to get him to slow down, but he couldn't. He couldn't stop himself. And to be perfectly honest, I'm not sure I really wanted him to." She folded her hands in her lap. "The insanity continued on for little over a month. Then I came down one morning and found Jack asleep on the couch. At least I thought he was asleep; he looked that peaceful to me. I went to get him a blanket, and when I came back, that's when I realized he was gone." She cradled the photographs gently, her eyes soft and distant. "He was so young. Jack was only forty-two when he died." She bit her lower lip and ran her thumb across the back of one hand, wrinkling her age-spotted skin. "If he saw me now he wouldn't know who I was."

"How did you deal with it, Jenny? How did you deal with so much pain?"

"Thank God, I had the other children to keep me busy. I know it was a hard time for us all. I know the kids remember hand-me-downs and pancake suppers. But you have to understand, Sarah, I was not going to let this evil thing destroy my family. No matter what, I was not going to let that happen."

"For what it's worth, I think you did a great job. I've met your family, and they're all very nice people."

"Thank you, my dear. Those are kind words." Jenny patted Sarah's hand and returned the photographs to the trunk. "Now, I would never say this to John, but I've often wondered if that's why he became a policeman. No one else in our family ever chose that profession. But I can't help wondering if, somewhere way down deep, John still wonders what happened to his little brother."

Sarah looked into the older woman's eyes, so clear with unforgotten pain.

"Him and me both, Jenny," she answered.

"You're a sweet girl," Jenny stated, and cocked her head at the sound of footfalls climbing the stairwell. "That's odd. I wonder who that is? I'm not expecting anyone. Hello?"

Mary Rose reached the top of the stairs, clutching the banister, breathless. "Don't worry, it's me. What are you two doing up here?"

"Looking at baby things," Jenny replied. "Sarah's going to use the Jarad crib."

"I bet that made you happy." Mary Rose quirked a thumb in her mother's direction. "She was miffed when I used the Quigley crib. I pointed out that I was married to a Quigley and having a Quigley baby, but that didn't seem to matter."

"I was not miffed." Jenny flattened her collar. "Sometimes, Mary Rose, I don't know where you get your ideas."

"Do you need help bringing it down?"

"Jenny, could we leave it here for now?" Sarah temporized. "We don't have room in our house for one more piece of furniture."

"That's fine with me. Why don't you and John come and get it when you're ready?" Jenny checked her watch. "Now, you're welcome to stay, girls, but I have got to go. I promised

Peggy I would stop by today and help her with her curtains. It's half-past one and I'm going to be late as it is."

"I could give Sarah a ride home, if that would help," Mary Rose volunteered.

"That would be a help. Sarah, do you mind?"

"Not at all." Sarah agreed, and she meant it. Catching a ride with Mary Rose would work out even better. There were some questions she wanted to ask, and she knew she could count on John's sister for some straight answers.

"Alright, then. All aboard the Squeekmobile." Mary Rose announced, following her mother down the stairway into the kitchen. In the hallway, she lifted a black wool coat off the tall peg and courteously held it open for her mother. "Here you go, Mom. Come on, Sarah, grab your gear. On the way home I can tell you about the Quigley bassinet and matching ancestral highchair."

"Mary Rose," Jenny scolded, tugging on her gloves. "Sometimes, daughter, your teasing goes too far."

"Only when you deserve it." She gave her mother a kiss. "I wouldn't tease you if I didn't care. Tell Aunt Peg I said hello. I'll see her in church."

As Mary Rose drove through the peaceful tree-lined streets of 'Sconset, Sarah peeked at the car's odometer. She was not surprised to find it registering over one hundred and thirty thousand miles. Doing a quick calculation, and knowing the island was only twenty-one miles long, Sarah figured that Mary Rose had made almost eleven thousand twelve-mile trips into town. "You sure got your money's worth out of this car."

"I know it looks bad, but the salt rusts everything. Nothing stays new for long. But as long as she's running, Old Reliable's a keeper. She's been paid for years, and she handles well, even in the snow. Those two new tires helped." Mary Rose turned right onto the straightaway of Milestone Road and headed for town. "I ran into my cousin Dorcas this morning. She asked me ten kinds of questions about John's inheritance. Have you two decided anything yet?"

"We're trying not to rush into anything. There's a lot to consider. Your mom thinks college scholarships for the kids is a good idea."

"That's a terrific idea," Mary Rose smiled broadly. "Not that my opinion is prejudiced in any way, with three intelligent boys who happen to be your nephews heading in that direction. So when are you two selling the property? Have you had any nibbles yet?"

"John talked to the LandBank yesterday. They're definitely interested. And that George Robey is something else, isn't he? He calls the house every morning after John has left for work. I think that's his way of making sure I know where I stand with his offer."

"Sounds like George. I knew him in high school. He usually gets what he wants."

"Well, he must want this property pretty bad. He upped his original offer by half a million."

"Five hundred thousand dollars." Mary Rose smacked her lips, tasting the words. "Imagine having access to that kind of money. Wait! What am I saying? That's your money! Hold out for it! Hold out for it!"

"Mary Rose, take it easy." Sarah laughed. "We're not there yet."

"But you will be; that's the great thing about it. I'll tell you what, whatever you may think of him personally, you have to give George credit. No one handed him that development business; he built it from scratch. I know he's a little hard to take, but it might not be a bad idea to sell the property to someone local. Hopefully, he won't abuse the zoning too much."

"That sounds like an endorsement, Mary Rose."

"Trust me, if it was, I'd take the money. You know, for all his success, the Robey's are a hard luck family. Their Dad, Frank, shot himself years ago, and their mom, Althea, took to drinking in a big way."

"The family's from Nantucket, then?"

"Althea was. Frank Robey was an off-islander, but Althea was a Burgess, one of our first families. They lived in one of those big old barns on Cliff Road."

"The gray one?" Sarah teased, knowing that ninety-five percent of the homes on Nantucket fit this description. "With the white trim?"

Mary Rose acknowledged the traditional tourist dig with a grin. "That's the one. But I heard the house got to be too much for her and after Frank died Althea sold it and moved into an apartment in town. Then she really got screwed. The real-estate boom hit and rents went sky-high; when she tried to buy back into a smaller house she couldn't afford anything decent. Eventually she moved to Savannah to live with her sister, and after she died, George had her body shipped back to be buried with the rest of the family in the Burgess cemetery. And George's older brother Richard was in my graduating class but he doesn't live here anymore; Sheriff Toohey caught him in some kind of drug trouble and ran him off the island years ago." Mary Rose slowed the car to watch a private jet approaching Ackerman Field. "So, how's it coming with Uncle Ethan's house?"

"It's a rat's nest. We made a stab at clearing the first floor. At least now you can walk around without tripping over newspapers."

"You be careful with that baby. You don't want to fall."

"Oh, I'm careful alright. John's going to have to bring everything down from the second floor. I'm not going near those stairs, you should see them, Mary Rose, they're more air than stair. Oh, and here's a surprise. Did you know Uncle Ethan liked spy thrillers? We found a closet full of paperbacks."

"I'll be surprised if that's the worst thing you find. Make sure you go through those books before you give them away. He might have hidden money in them."

"Trust me, we're going through everything. We even went through his Bible." As they pulled into the driveway, Sarah paused. She had a question to ask and it was now or never. "Mary Rose, can I ask you something?"

"Ask away."

"What do you remember about your brother Danny?"

Mary Rose looked shocked. "Jesus! It's been a long time since anyone's asked me about Danny."

"Do you mind me asking?"

"Of course not. But if we're going to talk about him, let's go inside. This is going to take awhile." Mary Rose followed Sarah into the house. Still in their coats, they sat at the kitchen table.

"Do you want some tea?" Sarah felt the need to ask. "Or would you like something stronger?"

"No, nothing for me, thanks." Mary Rose waved her off, placing one arm on the back of her chair. "So who's been talking to you about Danny?"

"Your Mom told me what she remembered. I've tried asking John, but he doesn't remember much."

"I'm not surprised. He was only twelve when Danny disappeared. I'm not even sure what he heard. The cops kept some of the information quiet. The other parents were worried their kids would get frightened if they knew."

"Frightened of what?"

"The whole idea of kidnapping. You know, some stranger grabbing them off the street. They didn't want the kids to get upset, which was silly, because we knew enough to know the adults were holding something back and that scared us even more, since kids don't really trust adults anyway. Then the police found Danny's bike and everyone started saying he drowned. It was a strange time. People were acting really weird."

"Weird, how?"

"For one thing my Dad started not coming home at night and he never did that before. Sure, he'd get up at four to go fishing, but he never stayed out all night. And then he started bringing these men home, fishermen mostly, at odd hours. And these guys weren't his usual friends, either. You could tell they didn't give a damn about scallops."

Sarah was puzzled. "What kind of fishermen were they?"

"Sarah," Mary Rose smiled at her ignorance. "They were smugglers."

"Smugglers? What do you mean smugglers?"

"Men who ship illegal cargo? Oh, look, you're shocked. Don't be. Smuggling's been going on from the beginning."

"Come on. Smugglers don't exist anymore, do they? They're a myth, like pirates."

"These guys were no myth, let me tell you. You should have seen them. That was one tough bunch of men. You did not mess around with those guys and I am not kidding."

"What were they smuggling?"

"Pot mostly, I would think, with all the schools in Boston. But Dad wasn't into that. He was such a straight arrow, he wouldn't even let us smoke cigarettes."

"So why was your father hanging out with smugglers?"

"I don't know. I tried to find out one time, but when I walked in the kitchen they all froze. They just sat there, smoking and drinking Dad's brandy, and never said a word. I tried asking Mom about it, but she said nevermind, Dad knew what he was doing. Well, that didn't get me anywhere, so I went upstairs and listened through the heating vent in the bathroom. I heard Dad ask Portuguese Joe to find out who came ashore the night Danny disappeared. Joe said he'd try, but he couldn't make any promises. He said the deep-water men were killers, and they didn't like anyone asking questions."

"Your Dad thought Danny got kidnapped by smugglers?"

"No, I think he thought they might have seen something. Listen, if my Dad had thought anyone was involved with Danny's disappearance he would have gone after them. You didn't know him, Sarah, but once he got focused you couldn't stop him. It was a kind of tunnel-vision; nothing was going to keep him from finding Danny." She grew silent. "Then he had his stroke and died, and that was the end of it."

"Your Mom told me a little about that, too. I'm sorry."

"It's too bad you didn't know our Dad. He was a great guy. When he was with us, our house was a really happy place to be."

"Mary Rose, what do you think happened to Danny? Do you think he drowned, like they say?"

Mary Rose stared out the kitchen window. "There really is no other explanation, is there? I mean, if there was we would have found something. We had the whole island out looking. Uncle Ethan even organized the sea-search. You should have seen Nantucket Sound, it looked like an armada out there. Anyone with a boat, he had them out, looking."

"That's the first thing I've heard that makes Uncle Ethan sound normal."

"It's probably the last normal thing he did. But the strain must have been too much. I heard later he decked Peter Jacoby. Not that Peter didn't deserve it. He is a pig."

"Why did Uncle Ethan deck him?"

"Peter said they were wasting their time searching the Sound. He said if Danny was in the water the Rip would wash him up in Madaket. And he'd been up all night fishing, and he wanted to go home and get some sleep. When Uncle Ethan heard that, he picked Peter up and threw him back into his boat. Uncle Ethan and my Dad, I don't think they slept for three days straight."

"And that was it?"

"Pretty much. Trust me, I saw them. The police checked everywhere. They even searched the cars leaving the island on the ferry." She sighed. "Losing Danny was tough. I don't even think there is an answer, anymore."

"Excuse me one second, Mary Rose, hold that thought. I need to make a pit stop."

"Get used to it, my friend."

When Sarah returned, she found her sister-in-law bending over Uncle Ethan's Bible on the counter. Mary Rose pointed.

"He wrote in here that Danny was 'deceased'. Is that what got you started?"

"Um-hum." Sarah joined her at the counter. "Look at this Bible. It's such a shame. It's really falling apart." Sarah inserted a fingernail at a faded silk bookmark and gently folded back the pages. "Uncle Ethan liked this chapter. It's Job. He used it for his tombstone."

"What's he got underlined?" Mary Rose peered down and read: " 'For now thou numberest my steps: dost thou not watch over my sin?' Is that the verse he used?"

"No, he used something about remembrance. Let me see. 'Surely the mountain falling cometh to nought, and the rock is removed from its place'. No, that's not it, either. Let me see if I can find it…"

"Hold on…" Mary Rose grasped Sarah's hand. "Do you think Uncle Ethan might have hidden some stocks, or deeds or something in his house? And he left John this Bible to tell him where to look?"

"What makes you say that?"

"Because he had a secret hiding place. Uncle Ethan showed it to me once when I was little. There was a loose stone in his chimney. You could pull it out and it left a hollow space behind." Mary Rose pinched her fingers together to illustrate the move. Deliberately, she repeated the quote: 'the rock is removed from its place'."

Sarah laughed. "That's easy enough to check on, Nancy Drew. I have a key, and we're only twenty minutes away. Do you want to go look?"

"What do you say?" Possibility danced in Mary Rose's eyes. "Come on, let's go! We'll have an adventure."

"I'm with you," Sarah agreed. "Let's go."

They returned to the Volvo and headed northeast on Polpis Road. In her excitement, Mary Rose pushed the little car and it responded gamely. "I feel like a teenager again, ditching school!" She laughed as they passed the turn for Shimmo. "You know, Sarah, spending time with you is doing me good. I don't know what Matt's going to say when I tell him what we've done; he thinks I'm too impetuous already. Hey, wait a minute! What if we find something? Do I get a split?"

"Definitely. We'll call it a finder's fee."

"Then I hope it's loot, lots of loot. Spanish gold or jewels maybe." She looked up suddenly, eyeing the rear view mirror. "Holy smoke, where is he going?"

A speeding paramedic passed them with a wave of sound. The SUV wavered along the median stripe and vanished around a tight, dangerous bend in the road. Mary Rose slowed to make the curve. "Jesus, he was taking a chance! Good thing no one else was coming."

The vista ahead opened through a stand of slim larch trees. In the distance, the landscape flattened into the habitual snarl of cedar, shrubby shadblow and cockspur hawthorn. Sarah noted that the skyline so well matched the wintered vegetation that the horizon was virtually invisible.

With a sudden sinking feeling she realized the only visible distinction was a vertical plume of oily black smoke.

"Mary Rose..."

"I see it." Her sister-in-law replied, accelerating the worn car even more.

They sped through Quammock, Sarah clutching the door handle, Mary Rose hunched behind the wheel. The small car swayed from right to left, clawing traction from the sandy road. As they skidded out onto the headland, the full panorama unveiled itself, the volunteer firemen in their yellow and black coats, the hoses fat as anacondas, the flashing crimson and white halogen lights. And in the background, blazing away regardless of their best efforts, the blackened shell of Ethan Jarad's house.

"Sweet Jesus," Mary Rose swore softly. "It's gone. The whole thing is gone."

She's right, Sarah realized numbly. They weren't able to save any of it. She caught herself watching in fascinated horror at the oily smoke boiling up from the red-hot heart of the fire, poisoning the sky. Waves of furious heat flickered overhead, warping her perception. It was mighty, and awful, and beautiful, all at the same time.

Mary Rose drove toward a cluster of parked vehicles. Many were cars and trucks abandoned by the volunteers, but the rest were gawkers, drawn to the fire by the sirens, the fire trucks, and mid-winter doldrums. A fire this size would be the talk of the town for at least two days.

"This is as far as I'm going," Mary Rose announced, parking.

"John has to be here somewhere. That's his truck. He'll know what's going on."

"He's over there. Talking to Mike Prescott."

They left the car and stepped carefully over the hoses, making their way toward the two men. John looked up, surprised. "How did you two hear about this already?"

"We had no idea," Mary Rose replied. "We were coming out here to explore. Mike? What happened?"

"We're not sure, yet. We only just got the call." The fire chief checked his watch. "Thirty-five minutes ago."

Sarah raised her hand to shield her face against the blistering heat. "We won't find anything in that chimney now."

John turned, puzzled. "Why? What's in the chimney?"

"We found a passage marked in Uncle Ethan's Bible. We thought maybe he left you a message about hiding something in there."

"And we came to find out," Mary Rose added. She pointed to the right side of the fieldstone stack. "Don't you remember Uncle Ethan's secret hiding place?"

"I do remember it," John turned slowly. He couldn't see the specific stone; the chimney was wreathed in thick black smoke.

"Nobody goes near that chimney," Matt Prescott ordered. "I don't care if your uncle hid Blackbeard's treasure. Steam's corroded the mortar and there's nothing's holding those stones in place except gravity. If that stack decides to go, it could kill somebody." Mike Prescott tipped back his helmet and rubbed his red-rimmed eyes. "I am sorry about this, folks. The fire was four-alarm before we got here. There wasn't much we could do except contain it."

"You did your best," John stated. "The important thing is that no one got hurt."

"Ayeh. And the road out here didn't help us much, either. We almost stuck the pumper in the sand."

"It was a fire waiting to happen," John stepped on a feathery piece of ash. "We should've been more careful."

Mike removed his helmet. "Why? Are you saying you built a fire here?"

"Yes, we had one going yesterday while Sarah and I were working in the house. I was sure I put it out, but some cinders must have caught the roof after we left."

The fire chief looked up suddenly. "John, I have to ask you something. Don't take it wrong, but is there any reason you wanted this house to burn?"

"What are you saying, Matt?" Mary Rose demanded. "You think John set this fire on purpose?"

"Arson?" Sarah echoed.

"I wouldn't risk anything like that, Mike, and you know it." John crossed his arms and radiated anger. "Maybe I made a stupid mistake, but it wasn't deliberate."

"Take it easy, John. I have my reasons for asking. Thomas!" Mike yelled. "Come over here."

A baby-faced volunteer trotted over, clodhopping in boots at least one size too large. "What's up, Chief?"

"Tell these folks what you noticed when we first got here."

"Accelerant." The young firefighter nodded eagerly. "I smelled accelerant. Too thin for gasoline. More like lighter fluid. But it was there. I'd swear to it in court if I had to."

"I didn't catch it, but then, Thomas here is younger than I am, his nose is better. If he says he smelled accelerant, I'll go with that. Besides, this place went up too quickly, even for an old house. The idea of the roof smoldering a full day and then going up doesn't sit well with me. And what really has me doubtful is that chimney."

John glanced over sharply. "What about it?"

"See that charred line against the stone? It's too low to be the roof. If the roof had gone up first, that line would be higher up along the stones." Mike Prescott frowned. "No. I think the fire started somewhere on the second floor and went from there."

"But we weren't on the second floor yesterday. I swear to you, Mike. Neither one of us went up there yesterday."

"That's right," Sarah agreed. "We only worked on the first floor."

"Can't help what I think. Maybe you two didn't, but someone did." The fire chief spun his helmet in his hands. "Got any idea who?"

Chapter Seven

John turned the defroster on high and waited for the heat to melt the frost field blooming across the windshield. He sipped his coffee and readied himself for a normal 9-5. Only what defined normal anymore? Five days ago he had been a cop, with a cop's job to do. Everything had been spelled out. Now he was a…what? He wondered. What was he now? And what if he decided not to do this job anymore? What else would he do?

He felt the thrill of fresh possibility. It felt very much like fear.

He reversed out of the driveway and followed the curves of Orange Street into town. A few perimeter shops were busily removing their Christmas Stroll decorations, the celebration just over, in preparation for Daffodil Days, the artificial holiday just ahead. Island merchants had recently started marketing winter weekends as catchy new getaways. John recalled the Nantucket of his childhood, the idle summer days, the long, bleak winter months. That's all gone now, he realized. We've been discovered. There is no off-season anymore.

He remembered a story his grandfather Ike Jarad had told, of wise men pointing to the sea, predicting the direction of future growth for Nantucket. That's not true anymore, he admitted ruefully. Nowadays, to be accurate, we'd have to point squarely back at the mainland. Tourism. Our new bottom line.

He pulled into the six-slot station lot and parked, zipping his parka on the way in. Typically, the first person he met was the last one he really wanted to see. Hank Viera was a good rookie, but a better pest. "Morning, Hank."

"Lookie here, it's our millionaire! Sorry I missed your big news yesterday, Lieutenant. Guess you're buying lunch today, eh?"

"I don't have a dime more on me, Hank, than I had yesterday," John grumbled. "But I'll split a pizza with you later, if you like."

"Cheap bastard," the junior officer scoffed. "Christ, John! Live a little! Whip out that credit card! We could have ourselves a good time. I know a couple of girls who like to party."

Tina Bradley spoke up from behind her console. "Always ready to party as long as someone else pays the bill. Ignore him, John. I do."

Hank waved a donut at her. "You're just jealous because I don't ask you."

"Do me a favor. Keep it up," she retorted.

John smiled. The irascible banter between Tina and Hank had started from Day One. He was reasonably sure they didn't know the station pool had them engaged by Christmas. "I'm feeling restless today, Tina. Anything on deck?"

"Not really. It's pretty quiet." She displayed the dispatch log. "Miacomet Water wants us to check their property on Ticcoma Way. One of their meter reader's found a lean-to. They think Underground Bob's been at it again."

"You'd think he'd learn." John poured a cup of coffee. "Sooner or later Bob's going to have to pay rent like the rest of us."

"You try telling him that." Hank chose another donut from the Downey Flake box and continued around a large mouthful.

"I was there the last time they dug him out. He kept yelling he was entitled to live wherever he could, it was one of his inalienable rights as an American citizen."

"It's called criminal trespass," Tina stated flatly. "Anyway, the whole idea is disgusting! How anyone could live underground is beyond me. Think of the bugs, if nothing else."

"It wasn't that bad." Hank licked his fingers. "I saw his last place before Island Electric filled it in. I'll tell you what, Bob had it pretty cozy down there. Running water, a 'frige, the guy even had a shower. He really put a lot of work into it."

"Hank, the guy was sleeping underground," Tina scoffed. "Doesn't that tell you anything?"

"Sure he does, but at least it's free. No rent to pay, no landlord telling him what to do. That doesn't sound completely nuts to me."

Tina crossed her arms. "I worry about you, Hank. I really do."

John poured a second cup. "If it's Miacomet Water, Bob may be trying to run a pipe. Since you're such good friends, Hank, why don't you check it out?"

"I'm there." The rookie wiped his hands and grabbed his jacket. "Tina, I'll keep the radio on, in case you get lonely."

"In your dreams," she replied spiritedly. "Bye-bye."

John checked his desk. "Tina? Did Curly get a chance to pull that file for me?"

"Oh yeah, John, I've got it here. Curly had some fun finding it. He said to tell you 1979 might as well have been 1879 as far as he's concerned and you owe him a beer." Tina crossed the small office carrying an accordion folder. "This is all he found under that file number. There's not much here."

"No. There wouldn't be."

She passed him the folder. "I couldn't help but notice the name, Daniel Jarad. Was he a relation?"

"He was my brother. I want to review his file."

"Is there anything I can do? I could double-check the archive if you want."

"Not right now. Thanks for the offer." John patted his pocket, feeling for his keys and tucking the folder under his arm. "I'm going out for a loop."

He took Unit Three and headed east toward 'Sconset on Milestone Road. It had been an unconscious decision to choose this straight stretch of asphalt. He had always found the trip along Milestone Road soothing and he needed to find some sense of that clear-headed quiet right now. He sat back with the police-band radio turned low and enjoyed the peaceful eight mile ride through the pines.

So much had happened he didn't know where to begin. First there was Uncle Ethan's death, a jolt any way you looked at it. But the recollection was less of a burden once he realized the episode wasn't going to permanently scar Sarah. He had worried about her those first couple of days, but she seemed to be handling the memory of it just fine now. He would know she was completely recovered when she let him crack jokes about it.

"I'm not ready to test that water just yet," he admitted.

Then there was Uncle Ethan's bequest. Although he was certainly grateful for it, the logic behind the old man's inheritance remained a puzzler. He glanced at the accordion folder on the seat beside him, instinctively wondering if the explanation for Uncle Ethan's gift was somehow connected to his missing brother. I wasn't Uncle Ethan's favorite, he recalled, but Danny was. The old man had doted on Danny.

There had been special fishing trips, a silver Sting-Ray bike on Danny's sixth birthday so he wouldn't have to ask for rides anymore when he wanted to visit. John and Danny had been the youngest boys in the Jarad family. What if somewhere in his alcohol-addled brain, late in life, Uncle Ethan had confused the two?

He surprised himself by veering right and heading south on Tom Nevers road, automatically slowing to scan the new developments that seemed to mushroom overnight. Houses here were literally sheathed in gold, their as yet unweathered shingles a public attestation of pricey new construction. Off-island affluence further manifested itself through the traditional name-punning quarterboards that hung over entranceways so elaborate they would have shamed the island's original Quaker inhabitants. Massive new McMansions with titles like Mann-Made, Bull Markette, Dewey Diligence.

Whatever happened, he wondered, to the island spirit behind cottage names like Sea-Sighed and Thistle-Do?

He continued southwest, dodging potholes and following the crumbling road out to the VFW. The low, one-story cinderblock building looked haunted, surrounded by broken sections of chain-link fence and rusting metal dumpsters. He drove to the end of the pavement and parked on the sand and gravel bluff overlooking the beach. Immediately, he experienced déjà vu and realized just what he had done: without conscious thought, he had driven to the exact spot where the police had found Danny's abandoned bicycle twenty years earlier. Involuntarily, he shivered.

Chief Rawlins and his men had done their best, of that John was sure. He could still remember the eagerness from those officers when the call for volunteers went out. He had waited with his family while they had gone out in the pouring rain to search for his brother, and he had not heard one complaint from any of them. The men had known their duty and done it. He would do the same thing now himself, and he knew why. It was a part of the job.

It had taken two decades, but he was ready to continue the investigation.

"Let's get to work," John whispered.

He drew the folder near and slowly unfastened the black cord binding. He felt like an archeologist, researching ancient records. It struck him that everything in the folder was pre-computer. The police report had been typed; hand-written notes were scribbled along the margins in blue ink. There wasn't a single sticky note to be found in the file. All the photographs were black and white. John observed these superficial details, took a deep breath, and forced himself to actually look at the information in front of him.

He turned to the yellowing police report first, scanning the listed items. Stapled to the upper left-hand corner was a picture of Danny, aged seven. The photograph was a typically bungled second-grade school attempt. Some harried photographer's assistant had parted his brother's hair, slicking it over his left ear. Protesting this indignity, Danny had refused to smile, compressing his lips and grimacing toothlessly for the camera. John sighed. He had forgotten about his little brother's rebellious spirit.

"Danny? Where did you go?" John wondered, looking out across the sand at the tide scouring the shoreline. Gulls hovered, swooped and squawked over the incoming rush of water. It was a dull gray day, and the atmosphere mirrored his thoughts. He returned his focus to the file.

The information was skimpy. All told, two official reports, eight sheets of typed notation, a mint-green dental chart and the stack of photographs. The first report recorded a call received at 9:33 AM on Saturday, May 12, 1979. Daniel Jarad was officially reported missing. Seven years old, red plaid jacket, blue jeans, on his bike. John recognized the referenced incoming phone number. It was the Jarad house, the same number his mother still used. She had never had it changed.

A patrol car carrying Officer Lawrence Milburn had been dispatched. Larry Milburn had been cautious and thorough. Once he had realized the enormity of the task at hand, he had radioed for backup. Chief Rawlins had appeared in person on-site. That much John remembered. He had been sitting in the kitchen. Someone had wrapped him in a blanket, but still he shivered. The Chief had appeared, towering over him, then crouching to eye-level and patting his knee. "Don't worry, son," the Chief had said kindly. "It's going to be alright. We'll find your brother."

Only they hadn't. John took a deep breath, recalling the faces of the officers as bafflement turned to frustration. Over their heads, the F.B.I. had been summoned. Federal agents flew in just as the local cops found Danny's bike on the very spot where John now parked.

He studied the photograph of Danny's bike tipped on its side in the muddy gravel. Knowing Danny as he did, the picture made no sense on two levels. First off, Danny had cherished his bike and devoutly employed the kickstand. Even at his young age, Danny had understood the correlation between damp and rust and insisted on protecting his possession as thoroughly as possible.

Secondly, Danny had no reason to ride to this beach. There was no shoreline pier here, no rocks to play on, nothing but a lonely stretch of busy tidal surf. Yet everyone had assumed that Danny had ridden here. Even the F.B.I. had accepted this explanation and flown home. The Medical Examiner's final report was included in the file. Death by Misadventure – Drowning, it proclaimed.

"It doesn't make sense." John shook his head. "It never did."

He examined the photographs. The decade in which they were taken was self-evident. The federal agents sported pin-striped suits with wide lapels and wider ties. Several of the local cops had bushy sideburns. In one photograph the searchers had gathered in front of the Jarad house and been captured on film. John recognized the participants: his father and Chief Rawlins deliberating under the shelter of the porch, his older brother Micah and Jamie Starbuck off to one side, hands deep in their coat pockets as they stared at the ground. A third blurred cluster of men stood next to the picket fence smoking cigarettes. John drew the photograph closer and identified Uncle Ethan, George and Richard Robey, and Eddie Farrar. It was true. The whole island had turned out to help.

He reshuffled the photographs and returned them to the folder. He was surprised to find himself feeling calm about reviewing the investigation. He had expected to be more upset, and had steeled himself for that outcome. But his training as an investigator had held up even in this personal situation. He was able to look at the facts dispassionately, and realized this ability had liberated him from his fear.

John admitted to himself that it was fear that had held him back all these years. Fear had magnified the emotional aspect of Danny's disappearance until it had paralyzed him through inaction. Looking at the situation now from a more rational perspective, his fear seemed ludicrous, almost indulgent. Opening Danny's file had done more than free his mind. It had freed his spirit. He might not ever know the truth of what had happened, but if any new information did come up, he wouldn't be afraid to explore it anymore.

He pushed the folder back across the seat, turned the car around and returned to the paved road. He now possessed as much factual information about his brother's disappearance as anyone ever had. Unfortunately, most of his clues were dust and memory. Even the eye-witnesses from that era were gone: his father from his stroke, Chief Rawlins dead in a commercial airliner crash in the Florida Everglades. Larry Milburn had been surprised by a massive coronary while captaining the helm during the annual Figawi race, his sailboat careening out of control the first and only harbinger of lethal heart trouble.

At the next intersection, John paused. There was one eyewitness left, although never an official member of the force. The Nantucket Police Department handled criminal investigations, as John well knew; Sheriff Toohey had been an independent agent for the Court, processing and transporting prisoners for the state. Retired now and living in a glass-fronted house on Low Beach road, John had heard the sheriff was spending his leisure time hiding from his wife, smoking cigars, and fishing for blues. He tapped the steering wheel and wondered: how much of Danny's case would Sheriff Toohey remember?

There was one way to find out. He turned right and continued into 'Sconset proper, slowing to the posted speed limit and cruising the tree-lined streets. Circling the flag pole rotary he took another right, past the airy, wooden 'Sconset footbridge, following the narrow road that ran parallel to the doll-house cottages of Codfish Park and the flat wide expanse of Atlantic coastal beach.

The houses diminished in size as John continued east. The comfortable Toohey home was the last house on the road; as John parked in the driveway he spotted Rebecca Toohey busily straightening magazines in the glassed-in front room. The sheriff's trim wife straightened and waved, and was lost to sight as she moved toward the front door. John heard her draw back the bolt, and Rebecca Toohey greeted him, holding the door open with one shoulder while drying both hands on a striped dishtowel.

"Why, John, it's good to see you." She smiled, brushing her blonde bangs back with one hand. "Won't you come in?"

"Actually, Mrs. Toohey, I wanted to see the sheriff. Is he around?"

"Out back with the other wharf rats, I'm sure. God knows who he's got out there with him now." She nodded toward the side yard. "Do me a favor if you're going out there. Tell His Highness I'm taking the car into town and he's on his own for lunch today. I promised to love, honor and obey, but I don't remember promising him lunch."

"I'll do that." John grinned as he followed a mossy brick pathway around the garage toward a shed set back on the edge of the property. For all Rebecca Toohey's grumbling, the sheriff and his wife were known to be one of the most devoted couples on the island. As he drew near the shed, he knew the sheriff was 'at home'; a stream of pungent cigar smoke was wafting out the cracked single windowpane. John knocked and waited for permission to enter.

"Rebecca!" The unseen sheriff thundered. "I said I'll come in when I'm ready!"

John tapped again. "Sheriff Toohey? It's John Jarad. Can I talk to you?"

The wooden shed door opened inward and the sheriff's stubbled face appeared. He eyed John suspiciously. "Is she out there with you?"

"No, sir, no, I'm alone."

The door opened wider and John stepped in, surprised by the décor. The shed's interior had been completely converted from any original gardening intent; it now housed two overstuffed recliners (one mended with silver duct tape), a big-screen T.V., a mini-fridge, and a green and black plaid carpet laid over a poured concrete floor. A misappropriated bamboo end table supported a large burled maple humidor and the array of implements necessary for the civilized enjoyment of a quality cigar.

"Welcome to my sanctum sanctorum. Absolutely no females allowed. Take a seat," the sheriff growled companionably. "It's the only place I can find any peace. I love that woman, God knows, been married forty-two years, but she is driving me crazy." He rolled a perfect ring of gray ash off his cigar. "So, John Jarad. What brings you to my hideaway?"

John placed the folder next to his right heel and leaned forward, resting his elbows on his knees. "I wanted to ask you what you remembered about an old case. My brother Danny. I brought his file with me, if you want to review the notes."

"No need to see what I've still got memorized." The sheriff settled into the cozy depths of his chair. "I wondered if I was ever going to see you about this. You've got me curious, John. Your brother's been gone a long time. What got you started?"

"My Uncle Ethan died and left me all his property and I don't know why." John rubbed a knuckle. "I can only wonder if he confused me somehow with Danny. Danny was his favorite."

"I sincerely doubt Ethan Jarad ever confused any one or any thing." Sheriff Toohey stated, wiping the corners of his mouth with his free hand. "A lot of things were going on back then, in the late 'seventies. We were feeling a lot of outside pressure, from the tourists, the developers, that zoning horror in Madaket was a product of those times. There was a lot of intercoastal pressure, too; the drug traffic was thick in these waters."

The sheriff reached for his diet soda and took a sip. "The smugglers were looking for an off-shore site with access to the East Coast markets; and it was new cargo, too, stuff we'd never seen before: cocaine, heroin, PCP. The Feds warned us it was starting to filter through here, but we didn't need to hear from them; we could read the signs. A couple of local overdoses, a deal goes bad, someone got shot; an unregistered boat floats in on the tide. We knew what was going on." He left his cigar to burn and settled his hands across his stomach. "Ted Rawlins figured the way to stop the smuggling was to break the shoreline contact. He worked his men like dogs, too, trying to find out where this shit was coming ashore. We worked up a list of suspects; but Ted could never make an arrest; you see, he could never prove anything. However, we had our suspicions. Smuggling is tough, dangerous work, and the bottom line is, to do it well you need someone who understands the sea like the back of his hand."

"What are you saying?" John blinked as he made the connection. "Uncle Ethan? You thought my uncle was the contact?"

"Like I said, John, we had no proof. But yes, we thought he was. For a while there, anyway."

John sat back. This story was news to him, but considering his family's history, not entirely unbelievable. "Say that he was; what has this got to do with Danny?"

"Remember, John, when your brother disappeared, we were already keeping an eye on your uncle. Oh sure, Ethan helped us search at first, but once we called it off Ethan Jarad sold his boat pretty damn quick and locked himself up in his house. If you want to know what's going on beneath the surface, watch human behavior; it will tell you when something is wrong." Sheriff Toohey returned to his cigar. "Personally? I think Ethan knew something; what else explains the bizarre change in his behavior?"

John felt washed by anger. "Did any of you bother asking him that?"

"Of course we tried. It's in the report. But Ethan wouldn't comment. Chased Ted Rawlins off his property, as a matter-of-fact." The sheriff grimaced. "As for what happened to your brother, in the end Ted and I disagreed. Ted found another suspect; we had a convicted child molester in 'Sconset the day your brother disappeared. Ted's theory was that your brother got kidnapped, and, I'm sorry, son, but there's a lot of deep water out there. Ted interrogated the suspect, it's in the report, too; but the guy had an alibi and we had to let him go." The sheriff dropped his chin to his chest. "For what it's worth, John, we both agreed that if Ethan Jarad was involved in your brother's disappearance, there was nothing we could do to him that was worse than what we knew he would do to himself. And judging from the way he spent his last years, I think we were right. We didn't need to put Ethan in prison; you saw the way he lived; he built his own."

"But you let my family go on not knowing!"

Sheriff Toohey raised his eyes indignantly. "Because we didn't know anything; we still don't know!" He pulled on his lip. "I may be damned for telling you this, but if you're going to reopen this case there is something you should consider."

John still felt the fine edge of anger coursing through his blood. "And what is that?"

Sheriff Toohey sighed. "A smuggling operation is never a one man deal; it takes a crew to pull it off. If Ethan was smuggling, he had a partner, someone on the island to back him up. Truthfully, I thought we were through with this when Ethan died, that everyone involved was dead. But I'm wrong; I know I'm wrong and I'll tell you why. Ethan's partner is still out there. I can still see his handiwork on the island." The sheriff reached for his lighter and flicked its smooth yellow flame. "I know he's out there, because whoever worked with Ethan Jarad was a clever bastard, and if you think about it, arson is a very clever solution, don't you agree?"

"So you think Ethan's partner burned down his house?"

"Ayeh, that's my idea. Unless you think it was just a coincidence or fool kids." Sheriff Toohey carefully steepled his fingers. "Think about it, John. What if Ethan had left you something in his house, a diary, or a confession? Can you think of a better way to destroy all the evidence than to burn the place to the ground?" The sheriff retrieved his cigar. "I'll tell you this, whoever he is, he's one ruthless bastard; and that's just what I would expect from Ethan's shadow partner."

John leaned forward. "Sheriff, you said you had a list of suspects. Give me a name."

"I wish to God I had one for you, John, but I don't. Every man I suspected is dead. Hell, it's been twenty years! Ethan Jarad was the last man standing from that generation."

John reviewed what he knew about Uncle Ethan and considered any possible contact. One name sprang to mind. "What about Eddie Farrar?"

"You know, I've thought about Eddie Farrar. God knows Eddie's been skating the line long enough. But Ethan's partner was no clown; whoever it is, I've never even heard a whisper about him. John, we're talking high caliber intelligence here; Eddie's not in that league."

John stood. "Whoever it is, I'm going to find him. And I'll find out what he knows about my brother."

"Of that I have no doubt." The sheriff chuckled. "You remind me a lot of your father right now, John. Jack Jarad had the same Katie-bar-the-door pig-headedness I see standing in front of me. Don't get mad; I meant it as a compliment. Anyway, keep in touch. Let me know if there's anything more I can do."

John closed the shed door and returned to the patrol car. This new information left him feeling vaguely dissatisfied with the previous investigation. You would think, he wondered, that on an island this size and over a reasonable span of time, a pattern of involvement between two unrelated people would eventually emerge and be noticed by someone. Especially by officers specifically trained to observe! How was it that no one had spotted an odd twenty-year pattern? John shook his head. He would have to study the reports and start from scratch.

He returned to 'Sconset, turning onto Broadway, a misnomer if ever there was one, and followed Sankaty Avenue north toward the familiar red-striped lighthouse. As he drove he recalled a more recent memory. After they had scattered Uncle Ethan's ashes, albeit inaccurately, Sarah had demanded to be taken home immediately. Meekly, he had complied. Sarah had marched directly into the house, stripping on the way to the shower. She had not come back out until the hot water tank was depleted.

John had chanced a remark that this did not seem fair, he needed hot water for his shower, too. He had received a withering glare in reply. Luckily, Sarah had a resilient sense of humor, and after John had howled through a cold shower and she had dried her hair he caught her eye in the mirror. She had started with her infectious laugh, he had caught it, and they had finished their afternoon breathlessly on the bed.

He was smiling again by the time he reached Polpis Road. The Lost Forest was hidden in the scrub to his right, the pewter water of Sesachacha Pond rippling directly ahead. Last July, when they were first dating, they had picnicked near here. Sharing the load and carrying a wicker basket along the path to the beach, Sarah had stopped so suddenly John had been pulled up short. Is something wrong? he had worried. These are shells, she replied, pointing to the ground. We're walking on shells. He had shrugged and explained: they dump them here, the scallopers, after they're done. They want the scallops, not the shells. The shells are just rubbish to them.

This is rubbish? Sarah had protested, releasing the basket and stooping to examine a handful of the ruffled paper-thin shells. But they're so pretty. Can't someone do something with them?

They are doing something, he had answered sensibly. They're using them to pave the path.

Sarah had tip-toed around the shells onto the sand. I can't walk on them, she declared. Stepping on this much beauty is wrong. Besides, it's creepy. It sounds like I'm walking on poker chips, or bones.

Left to carry their lunch, John had followed this interesting girl to the beach. It had never occurred to him before to think of cast-off scallop shells as anything but rubbish, and her keen observation about the sound they made when stepped on was dead on, too. Scallop shells did crunch underfoot like poker chips or bones. He was intrigued by her insight, and realized he felt more aware of the present moment because of her observation. He remembered hoping at the time that Sarah Hawthorne would like him, and consent to go out with him again.

"What was I thinking?" he joked. "If only I had known!"

There was something about the way Sarah had reached out to smile hello, the way her smile quirked up one side of her mouth and lit her eyes with an alert understanding that had stopped his breathing. She had gathered her long hair back with her left hand and extended her right for a greeting. And with her touch, he had known. He hadn't been certain of anything, but he had known. And here he was. A husband.

And now, a Dad. That was an intriguing new complication. John felt pretty sure he would make a good Dad. He would certainly try his best and he felt ready for it. And why not? He had always earned his own living; he loved his wife; he was ready for the next stage of their life together. And now, thanks to his inheritance, it would be relatively painless. The thought brought him back to business. He would have to decide soon on the best approach to selling the Lost Forest property. George Robey's multi-million dollar offer still lead the pack, with the LandBank's more reasonable bid trailing a poor second. George had stated that he wanted the property and he was keeping the pressure on with two phone calls a day, one to John's number at work every morning between ten and ten-thirty, the other message waiting for him when he got home. Sarah was keeping a tally on the kitchen chalkboard, updating the dollar amount daily. Robey Island Development remained in the lead, and yesterday's quote stood at eighteen million, five hundred thousand dollars. John considered the number. It was an amazing amount of money.

At the intersection of East Quammock road John slowed and turned right. If they were going to sell the acreage to George, and it looked that way, they would need to find another home site. They could afford to buy a half-acre lot somewhere else, but before they even investigated that idea he wanted to review Uncle Ethan's property in Quammock. Hauling the debris away would be a filthy chore, but he could hire a professional to do that. His main concern was shoreline erosion. It made no sense to build a fine new house and then have to relocate it inland ten or fifteen years down the road. He wanted to build his family a permanent new home. Or, he admitted, as permanent a home as anything built on a sandbar would allow.

The road had not been improved by the recent heavy traffic. He tried to spare the car's suspension system and took it slowly, avoiding the worst of the ruts and muddy potholes. As he continued out onto the headland, he was surprised to see a pair of men studying the smoldering, gutted ruin. The distance was too great to make out identities, but he recognized the worn-out pickup truck parked nearby and was intrigued. For some reason, Eddie Farrar and a friend were showing an interest in his business.

John parked and the two men sauntered closer. He peered through the windshield and abruptly recognized the stranger with Eddie as Richard Robey, George's brother, the black sheep of the Robey family, banned from the island at least fifteen years ago. Now that's interesting, John thought. What brings Richard Robey back on island?

He unfastened his seat belt and slowly opened the door. Richard Robey hadn't changed. Thin as ever, with light brown hair pulled back into a finger-combed ponytail, Richard looked older, coarser, but essentially the same. John noted that George and Richard's shared resemblance had grown closer with age; but where George's features looked well-bred and well-groomed, his brother's looks had followed a different path. Richard looked like a thug, ill-used and street-wise.

John kept walking, keeping one eye on Richard. He had been trouble when he left, and judging from his present company, there was no reason to suspect a change. "It's Richard, Richard Robey, right? It's been awhile since I've seen you."

Richard nodded, keeping both hands in his jeans pockets. He rolled forward on his toes, a gesture John eerily remembered. "And John Jarad. Look at you. A cop. Who'd've guessed?"

"I'm surprised to see you back here. Is it business?"

"Just a visit." The slim man shrugged. "The island's changed. I hardly recognize it anymore. There's a lot of new things. A lot of new money."

John wondered if this was a dig and decided it was. Money was the first topic Richard and Eddie would have discussed. They might be trouble, but at least they were consistent.

"I stopped by to look at this job." Eddie crooked his thumb at the debris. "You'll need someone to haul this off, John. I could make you a good price."

"Thanks, Eddie. When we're ready, I'll keep you in mind."

"I'd appreciate the work. There's none you'd find who'd work cheaper." Eddie shrugged. "C'mon Richard, let's go."

Richard tapped a cigarette from his pack. "How'd the fire start, John? Something electrical?"

"It's still under investigation."

"Such a shame. Really." Richard lipped his cigarette and patted his pockets. "Dammit, I've lost my lighter. Eddie, you got a match?"

"There's some in my truck. Richard, let's go. I've got work to do."

"That's a first." Richard remarked, spinning his cigarette through his fingers and tucking it behind his right ear. "John, it's good to see you again. Maybe we'll bump into each other. I'm going to be here awhile."

"Working for your brother?"

"No, no, but I'll find something. There's always opportunity, if you know where to look."

The two men strolled back to Eddie's rusted pickup truck. Just before he climbed in, Richard paused and turned, resting one hand on the doorframe. He gazed over his shoulder and grinned. John didn't like Richard's grin; it was canny and unpleasant. He remembered a remark Sheriff Toohey had made to his Dad while they were standing outside Hardy's

Hardware years ago. In case you've ever wondered, the sheriff had said, indicating Richard Robey sauntering by, that's what local trouble looks like. Sooner or later, I'm going to have to deal with that boy. John's father had smiled and the sheriff had remonstrated: Don't laugh at me, Jack. You may not believe me now, but I can see it coming at me like a train.

Eddie's pickup coughed and the two men pulled away. John relaxed and realized he had been holding his breath ever since he had stepped out of the patrol car. That information was interesting, too. Consciously, he hadn't considered Eddie or Richard a threat; evidently his instinct had decided otherwise.

Left alone, John took his time, examining what remained of Uncle Ethan's house. The front yard was a soggy black bog, the damp sand and wood ash developing a reeking, acrid odor that burned his nose and brought tears to his eyes. A long, knobby spiral protruded from the destruction, and John tried to place it, finally realizing that he was staring at the central staircase, its banister collapsing upon itself when the second floor gave out.

He stepped across a row of burnt two-by-twelves, all that remained of a section of roof, and studied the chimney. It was the only part of the house that remained upright. John kept a cautious distance, recalling Mike Prescott's warning about the danger of imminent collapse, and ran his eyes across the rows of stone, the seared limestone blocks, the rounded ballast pebbles, the slim intermittent lines of slate. And then he had it. Five feet up and to the right. The slim blue slate that he knew protected Uncle Ethan's secret hiding place.

John paused, considering the cryptic clue that Sarah and Mary Rose thought they had found in Uncle Ethan's Bible.

What if the old man had hidden something in the chimney? Would the stones have protected whatever it was from the heat of the fire? Was it worth the risk to find out?

He knew even standing this close to the chimney was foolhardy. Mike Prescott's warning had been accurate; the mortar was corroded, honeycombed by steam; the stones were loose. John could see the damage from where he stood. And he had specifically warned his wife and his sister away from this very idea. Was discovering the truth worth getting crushed under a ton of loose stone?

John stepped closer. The wind whistled softly through the flue, a low, tuneless melody, and he made his decision. If he was going to do this stupid, reckless thing, then it was best to just get it done.

He moved quickly toward the stack, the blood pounding in his ears. Imagination or not, the wind picked up and the chimney sang louder. John stepped firmly onto the soot-covered hearth and rewarded himself with a shallow intake of breath. Reaching up, he wiggled the slate. It was still warm, and came away in his hand.

It took all the courage he could muster to put his hand into the cavity behind the stone. As he did, his skin registered ambient heat; the stack was still warm from the fire. He withdrew his hand and pulled on his gloves, and tried again.

About three inches in he felt something. His fingertips tapped across a square of hollow metal. John felt a thin wire handle and fumbled it upright. Lifting gently, he pulled an old tin lockbox from the hole. The metal box was still hot; he could feel the heat through the leather of his gloves. Grasping the box tightly in both hands, John dashed for safety. Clear of any danger, he centered the box on the hood of the car and examined his find.

"Okay, Uncle Ethan." He dusted gritty soot from the tin lid. "What did you want? Talk to me."

The box had no padlock, but the hasp was wedged tight. John retrieved his army knife and decided the screwdriver attachment was his best bet. He wedged the tool under the lid. The fit was tighter than he expected, and the lid stayed sealed shut. He increased his leverage, tightening his grip, and insisted.

He heard a hissing intake of air. With a yelp, John fell back onto the sand.

The tin lid popped open and the box exploded into dancing blue flame.

Chapter Eight

Sarah usually saved her driftwood gathering expeditions for late morning, when what sun there was had warmed the day. Her footsteps, crunching the cold sand, soothed her spirit and freed her mind. She felt she did some of her best thinking during her long walks, and the fresh air definitely helped clear the cobwebs from her brain.

As she entered the dunes of Dionis beach, she considered John's concerns about managing his inheritance. He was right, she agreed, this was the chance of a lifetime. And she was grateful for that chance, but she didn't want to get spoiled by it. They had worked too hard to throw everything away just because of a fat new bank balance. The time was still fresh in her mind when twenty dollars had to stretch until payday, and there was a lesson in there for anyone with smarts.

And Jenny had a valid point, too. They should consider John's relatives. For whatever his reason, Uncle Ethan had passed them over, and there was plenty of room in that for trouble, too. So for now, Sarah decided, we'll play it cool. No sudden displays of wealth. No new his and her cars. No big jewelry. A new house would be more than enough.

Unbidden, the thought of heating oil, unlimited gallons of heating oil, crept into her mind. She imagined a permanent seventy degree setting on the thermostat of their new home. And why not? Sarah wondered. We can certainly afford it now.

With a start, Sarah realized what she was doing. Get thee behind me, Satan, she commanded. Work being an antidote for idle thought, she clapped her gloves together and marched down to the beach.

The retreating tide had left a visible high-water mark: inky clumps of black eel grass punctuated by white plastic soda caps and mint-green styrofoam peanuts. Sarah had learned that scavenging was an art form unto itself. Cradling her left arm and loading with her right, she plucked sticks and twigs and broken two-by-four free of the gritty sand. An occasional golden bubble shell or desiccated crab caught her eye, but she ignored these distractions, intent on completing her task.

Balancing half an armload, she straightened and paused, delighted by the day. The horizon was streaked with pink and peach and baby blue, the flaming sky opalescent. Her cheekbones tingled from the crisp morning air; the exercise kept her blood warm. It was a splendid combination.

Working steadily, Sarah moved toward her favorite stashing place, a small hollow tucked between two large rippled dunes. Reaching deeper dry sand, it was slow going, a real workout, and she was concentrating so intently on her footing that she didn't see Addie Simpson until she almost stepped on her. Startled, Sarah lost her balance, scattering her load and sitting down hard in the sand. "Addie! Addie, I didn't see you there. What are you doing?"

The whiskered woman studied Sarah carefully, chewing the knuckle of her left thumb. "I met you before. You're Sarah Jarad."

"That's right. Remember? We met at the store." Sarah returned to her feet and brushed the sand off her coat. After her initial surprise, she did not feel threatened by the strange older woman. She had shared with John their earlier grocery store encounter, and he had explained Addie's family history and peccadillos, promising her that Addie was an odd but essentially harmless member of the island gene pool.

"Do you want help with that?" Addie offered in her curiously flat voice. Once again Sarah wondered if Addie was tone-deaf. "Father Whittaker says I'm his best helper when it's time for the collection."

"Sure, if you want to. We can split whatever we find and you can take some home, too." Sarah scanned the deserted beach and realized that she had no idea where Addie's 'home' was. "Do you live nearby?"

"Eel Point." Addie pointed northwest. "Sometimes Mom needs quiet so I come here. I can always find something to do on this beach. Like now I can help you." Addie darted forward, tugging a half-buried driftwood branch. "See? Look at this one! This will burn a long time." She pulled the branch free of the sand and gave it a shake. "Have you ever seen wood burn in colors?"

"I've seen blue in the flames, sometimes."

"Oh, I've seen blue. There's green, too, but you have to look really close to see it. Green is much harder to see than blue."

Sarah wrestled a loop of six-pack plastic for a triangle of milled lumber. "Green is one of my favorite colors," she offered.

"You like green?" Addie trotted back, digging deeply into her coat pocket. "Here, then, Sarah, look at this. Look what I found in the water."

"What is it?" Sarah hesitated. Modern beach flotsam was risky. There was no telling what Addie had found in the water.

"No, it's nothing bad. I wouldn't give anything bad to you." Addie chuckled, and opened her glove. "Look, they're jewels. Jewels from the sea."

Sarah admired the woman's cupped handful of opaque sea-glass. The cobalt and teal 'jewels' were exceptional colors, and she spotted a burnt orange fragment that could only have come from an old root beer bottle. "Oh, yes, Addie, those are very pretty. They're very pretty jewels."

"Hold out your hand," Addie ordered. Serious and intent, she selected a concave ribbed square, rubbing it free of lint with her thumb. "This one's for you. It's magic glass. You make a wish and throw it back in the sea. Then your wish comes true."

"Gee, Addie, I don't know." Sarah smiled, adding this new superstition to her archive of island idiosyncrasies. "That sounds like pretty powerful stuff."

The older woman closed her fist and pulled back. "Are you poking fun at me? I'm not kidding about this, you know. I only give magic to my friends, and if you're not my friend, you let me know."

Instantly, Sarah felt contrite. She could see that Addie sincerely believed in the power of her magic, and who was she to doubt that power? She had felt it flowing through her brush often enough. "I'm not making fun of you, Addie. I'm sorry if you thought I was. Can I please see the jewel?"

Addie slowly reopened her chapped hand and toyed with the frosted emerald square. "Now don't waste it," she admonished, placing the jewel in the center of Sarah's palm. "It's not for wasting, you know. You only get one."

Sarah admired her prize. "I don't know what to wish for. I've been very lucky already. I'll tell you what. Can I save this for later? That way I'll be sure my wish is very important."

Addie considered her idea. "Maybe you should save it, if you don't know what you want. You don't want to make a bad wish. That would be worse than wasting, even."

"I'll save it for something very special. I promise." Sarah tucked the glass square deep inside her pocket.

"Waste not, want not, Mother always said." Addie nodded, returning to her driftwood and doodling down to the waterline. "There's a lot of driftwood here today."

The previous tide had done them good service, washing up a surfeit of debris. The two women spent the next forty minutes sorting and piling their finds to be gathered on the return trip. They had worked almost a mile of sand before Sarah felt a sudden chill. She glanced up to check on the sky and found that the day had changed. The sun had disappeared behind a bank of dark clouds and the wind had shifted direction, blowing in from the southeast. The breeze hinted at fresh snow and the ocean was running choppy whitecaps toward the shore. Even the gulls had landed, ruffling their feathers and seeking shelter between the dunes. The morning had lost its promise, and Sarah decided to call it a day. "Addie! Addie! C'mon. Let's head in."

Addie turned and acknowledged Sarah's suggestion with a wave.

Sarah retraced their tracks, retrieving her finds as she went. Because of Addie's assistance, the day's take was going to set a new record. Returning to her cache, she dropped her armload and turned to look for her helper. What she saw staggering toward her was some weird sea-monster, half-human, half-flotsam, the wild-haired mother of the Creature from the Black Lagoon, driftwood with legs.

"Addie, hold on!" Sarah laughed. "You didn't have to carry it all! I was going to make another trip!"

She ran across the sand and peered through the mountain of debris in Addie's arms, searching for the older woman's face. She spotted Addie's eyes through a long twiggy tunnel. Hampered by a driftwood limb wedged beneath her jaw, Addie tried to smile.

"No, Sarah, I got it," she mumbled, staggering between the two dunes and heaving her load on the top of the pile. Dusting her hands, Addie whistled. "Would you look at that. It's like I told you. I'm a good helper."

"You certainly are." Sarah eyed the impressive accumulation. "There's enough here to last for days. Give me a minute to catch my breath and I'll go get the truck. It'll be easier to load if I move it closer."

Addie trudged up a dune and shaded her eyes. "Where did you park? I only see one truck on the road and it looks like John Jarad's truck to me."

"That is John's truck. He's my husband."

Addie slipped back down the dune, taking outsized steps and pin-wheeling her arms for balance. "Oh, I know all about John Jarad. He's a policeman. I don't like policemen. They yell."

Sarah smiled, stretching an elastic between her fingers to reclaim her ponytail. "John only yells when he's afraid. Most of the time he's a nice guy."

"Policemen yell." Addie insisted sullenly. She fingered her gray hair. "They came to my house and they yelled. They made my Mom cry. I never seen her cry before."

"John made your mother cry?" Doubt colored Sarah's voice. "When did he do that?"

"Oh, it wasn't John Jarad, no, no. It was them others. They yelled and called me names." Addie tilted her head to one side, resting it against her shoulder. Crossing her arms, Addie hugged herself, swaying to an unheard, internal rhythm. "They shouldn't have done that. I wasn't bad. I wasn't."

Silence fell, and Sarah grew alarmed as the silence lengthened. Genetics be damned, she decided, John hadn't warned her about anything like this. "Addie? Are you alright?"

The older woman blinked and a thread of spit dribbled from her lower lip. Suddenly, Addie turned and kicked the driftwood pile. Splinters flew. "Tell me where he went!" she demanded. "Tell me where he went, you little bitch. I know you saw him. Tell me where he went. Tell me." Addie stopped kicking and stood, trembling instead. "I hate people who yell! People who yell are mean!"

Sarah struggled to keep her voice even. "People who yell are mean, Addie. Nice people don't yell, and they don't kick, either."

The older woman nodded and dissolved into tears. She drew a handkerchief from her pocket and wiped her eyes and nose. "I'm a nice person. I am. So why did they yell at me?"

Why would the police have questioned Addie? Sarah wondered. John had said she was harmless; evidently he had never heard of any violent episode. Her reaction made no sense. "Addie, did you see an accident? Is that why the police questioned you?"

"They said it was an accident, oh my yes, that's what they said," Addie sniffled. "But I didn't see it happen. I wasn't even on the beach that day. Mom had her headache and we didn't go to work. I was supposed to meet him and I didn't and then the police came to our house and they yelled. But I didn't see anything and they should not have been so mean."

Sarah struggled for a timeframe. "When did the police come to your house, Addie? When did this happen?"

"A long time ago, oh my yes." Addie dug her heel in the sand. "Mom said I was too old to be his girlfriend then, but ha! I'm a lot older now. And he would be all grown up now, too."

A dark possibility wiggled in the depths of Sarah's mind. She considered the idea, chilled by premonition. "Addie, were the police asking you questions about Danny Jarad?"

"Um-hum. They thought I knew where he went. But I didn't." Addie tried to smile. "He wasn't bad, Sarah. He wasn't. He was pretty. He danced with the sea. He loved the sea. I could tell, because I love the sea too."

Addie's information resonated through Sarah to the marrow of her bones. "Danny Jarad was your friend?"

"I know I was too old, but he was friends with me anyway. He was a nice boy. Not like them others. He loved to chase the water. That's what I remember about him the most. He would run all the way down to where the sand turned to pebbles, and then run back, laughing at the wave when it tried to tickle his feet."

Sarah felt a warning prickle of doubt. There was no way Danny could have ridden his bike to Dionis to meet with Addie, and 'Sconset was at the opposite end of the island. It had to be seven or eight miles each way. "Danny met you here? In Dionis?"

"Oh no, we met in Codfish Park." Addie wiped her nose and stuffed the handkerchief back in her pocket. "Mom used to clean house for Mrs. Tucker, and she brought me to help. You know I'm a good helper."

"Yes, I do know that."

"Mrs. Tucker lived in 'Sconset. She was a lady artist just like you. Oh, she had a beautiful house. 'Charm, charm, charm', that's what Mrs. Tucker said. But one bad, bad day I was scrubbing the floor and I bumped the table and I broke her vase." Addie dropped her eyes, ashamed. "It was family rose. Mom said the vase cost a lot of money. Mrs. Tucker said she knew it was an accident but that I couldn't work for her anymore. After that, Mom went to Mrs. Tucker's but I never went back in her house. I went to the beach, and that's where I found Danny. He was on the beach a lot."

"Addie, do you know where Danny went?"

"No. He stopped coming to meet me." She twisted inside her coat. "He was never there anymore. Mom said he got taken by the tide but sometimes, when the ocean is rough, I think he might come back. He was my friend, but he never said goodbye." She turned and cocked her head to listen, and Sarah heard it too: somewhere to their leeward side a bell was tolling. "I have to go," Addie explained hurriedly. "That's Mom. She rings the bell when she needs me."

"What about this wood?" Sarah gestured. "Half of it is yours. Should I bring it to your house?"

"No, Sarah, you keep it." Addie was already trudging up the dune toward home. "I can find more later." Reaching the top Addie turned and smiled shyly. "I'm glad you're my friend. I don't have a lot of friends." Nodding once, she stepped over the crest of the dune and vanished.

Sarah turned to follow the low path through the dunes to the truck. She backed it up carefully, avoiding the soft, deeper sand. John wasn't crazy about her scavenging anyway, and if she planted his truck in a dune he was sure to put a stop to it. Especially now that their budget didn't absolutely warrant her effort. But she loved the excuse to get outside and she was determined to continue with this exercise until her belly got so big she couldn't walk. She figured that gave her six or seven months. What she would do after the baby got here was another thing, but they had all sorts of neat carriers for sale nowadays; she was sure to find something that would work.

The brakes squealed as she parked beneath a bleached red picket barrier, the latest Parks and Recreation attempt to control the shifting movement of the dunes. Sarah smiled. Controlling the dunes was like stemming the tide; you were welcome to try, but sooner or later the dunes would win. She lowered the tailgate and started stacking her load. Longer limbs went in first, then smaller branches with the flat lumber on top. Having a system definitely helped, Sarah admitted, stretching a striped bungee cord from side to side across the truck bed. She dusted her gloves and admired her handiwork. It looked good. She had this down to a science. It would be crime to give it up.

The tires spun a little as she followed the sandy cut out back out to the blacktop and headed back into town. Seeing Addie again had certainly added an interesting element to her day and as for stories, the old woman was batting two-for-two. It was funny, though. Sarah would never have pictured Addie playing on any beach with John's little brother. In her mind she had pictured Addie as always having been middle-aged; it was a perfect example of the distortion of time, and Sarah took it for a lesson: you'll never know what you'll learn until you ask.

And she knew she was in a good spot if she ever needed to ask more questions. When John asked someone something, even off-duty, they remembered he was a cop. She had seen that delicate, initial hesitation herself. But when she asked someone a question, they humored her: she was the off-islander, the outsider, not an in-law but an outlaw. Sarah smiled. There. She had admitted it. Her true nature, revealed. It was just as her sister Joan had always suspected. She was an outlaw.

Sarah pulled up short in the driveway, surprised to find a Nantucket Police patrol car parked there. What was John doing home this time of day? she wondered, her emotions wavering between curiosity and fear. And if it wasn't John and something was wrong, wouldn't they have parked in the street? She grabbed her purse, fighting a small flutter of panic. The front door was unlocked; Sarah pushed her way in shouting: "John?! Are you home?"

"Up here," he replied from the loft. "I had a little accident."

"What happened?" Sarah dropped her purse on the floor and took the stairs two at a time. "Are you alright?"

"I'm fine. I just feel like a fool." He admitted, standing in the small, available square of floor between the bed and the bathroom door, toweling his hair. His uniform, freshly clean that morning, lay heaped in one corner, streaked with gray paint. Sarah blinked. It wasn't paint. It was ash.

"My God!" She threw her arms in the air, gesturing theatrically. "What was left to burn?!"

"Take it easy, Miss Bernhardt. It was paper this time." He tugged on a pair of jeans and struggled into a navy sweatshirt. "Ouch." He turned his arm to try to examine his left elbow. "That hurts."

"Let me see that." Sarah stepped across the bed to examine his arm. "John, you have a huge bruise here."

"I'm sure I do. I landed on it. Trust me to hit the only rock on Nantucket."

"Did you see a doctor about this?"

He clenched his fist and worked his fingers. "That isn't necessary; nothing's broken. I'll put some ice on it. I did take the rest of the day off, though. Tina kidded me about only working part-time now that I have money."

"You never answered my question. What burned?"

"I have a surprise for you. Downstairs, in the kitchen. Come with me, I want to show you something."

Sarah followed him dubiously. "We've been through this before. You know your surprises make me nervous."

"Trust me on this one." He stopped short at the base of the stairs and pulled her close. "Now close your eyes." He snuggled in tight behind her and placed his hands over her eyes. Like an old-time dance duo, they shuffled around the hall corner into their kitchen. "No peeking."

"What's that smell?" Sarah remonstrated. "Is that burnt hair?"

"Those were my eyebrows. Don't worry. They'll grow back." He removed his hands from her eyes with a flourish. "Taa-daa."

The kitchen floor was protected by a swath of Sunday's newspaper. An old tin box was displayed in the center of the paper, reeking distinctly of recent fire. Sarah knelt. "What is this? And where did you find it?"

"It's the box from Uncle Ethan's hiding place. I found it in his chimney this morning." He joined her on the floor. "When I opened it, it popped. That's what earned me my bruise. I was so surprised by the noise I tripped and fell."

Sarah gave him a long questioning look. "And why did it pop?"

"Spontaneous combustion, I think. I should have let the box cool before I opened it, but honestly, it never occurred to me." He freed the latch and opened the lid. The box was lined with a smooth layer of fine gray ash. "In the time it took me to pick myself up and reseal the lid, the papers inside were on fire."

Sarah dipped her fingers into the ash and removed a charred piece of thick vellum, turning it over gently in her hand. "This looks like a letter. And that is Uncle Ethan's handwriting. I recognize it from his Bible."

"I know." John sat back, leaning against the doorway arch. "I can't help thinking it might have been a confession."

Sarah looked up sharply. "A confession of what?"

"About what happened to my brother. I talked to Sheriff Toohey this morning, and he told me he suspected Uncle Ethan of smuggling around the time of the disappearance. He thinks Uncle Ethan might have been involved somehow. And the sheriff's right; I remember Uncle Ethan from around that time and that is when he started acting strangely. He also thinks an arsonist burned down Uncle Ethan's house, and that Uncle Ethan's smuggling partner may be the one responsible for it."

"So who was his partner?"

"That's the big question. Sheriff Toohey didn't know and he wouldn't guess. But he did say he thinks whoever it was is still around. And I'm going to find him."

Sarah wiggled her fingers through the loose, fluffy ash. "There's something else in here, John." She lifted a flat, tooled leather parcel out of the ash and opened a folded leather flap. She inserted her fingers and removed a flattened parchment square. "Here. Hold that end flat," she directed.

He cocked his head. "It's a chart. But north should point the other way."

Working together, they gently shifted the parchment square 180 degrees. A familiar outline sprang into view. Sarah pointed. "Of course! It's Nantucket."

"An older version. Tuckernuck is still marked a peninsula, and there's no channel shown here at all." He smoothed the rough surface. "I know what this is. Uncle Ethan marked his property on it. There's his house in Quammock and that's the Lost Forest: 'X' marks the spot."

"Was there anything else in the chimney besides this box?"

"This was all there was. Once you removed the stone you could see the hole; it wasn't big enough to hide anything else."

"Mary Rose will be disappointed; she was hoping for Spanish treasure."

"Well, we didn't find Captain Kidds' pirate map, but we can make sure she's happy." John blinked. "What do you say we decide right now to accept George Robey's offer?"

"Are you serious? Really?"

He nodded. "I went to Quammock this morning to look at the site. We could build our house there if you like. We'd just have to move it inland a bit. Honey, are you ready for this? Construction is a huge project."

"Are you kidding me? You know I am." Sarah patted her stomach. "And I'm giving us seven months to get it done. What's the next step? Do we need to find an architect?"

"I'd like to see what T.B. May can come up with. And I ran into Eddie Farrar this morning; he offered to clear the debris. For a price, of course."

"And I ran into Addie Simpson." Sarah dusted her hands. "And I don't think she's the simple little soul you make her out to be. She threw a nasty temper tantrum. I was scared there, for a minute."

"What was Addie upset about?"

"She started out upset about you. She put two and two together and finally figured out that we were married. Do you know she has a fear of cops? She was interrogated once and it left a bad impression."

"Addie told you this?"

"After she stopped kicking driftwood all over the sand. She said she used to meet up with Danny in Codfish Park. When he disappeared, the police interviewed her. Evidently, they were pretty brutal about it."

"That could have been the F.B.I." John paused, then stood, brushing his knees. "If we did interview Addie, it'll be in Danny's file. I brought it home with me. It's in the car. I'll go get it."

While John was gone, Sarah carefully lifted the reeking tin box and carried it out to the studio. She paused for a moment in the chilled garage atmosphere and wrapped both arms around herself, relishing the fact that John had accepted things much calmer this time when she had broached the subject of his missing brother. That was certainly an improvement from his initial reaction when they had discussed it in Uncle Ethan's house. Maybe he was coming to grips with it, Sarah hoped. Maybe the wound was healing.

And even better, John was sharing his work with her. Sarah was delighted. Granted, Danny's case wasn't anything current, but it was personal, which had to make it more difficult. She considered his decision as a new level of trust in their relationship, and she rejoiced.

She returned to the kitchen to start a pot of tea, filling the kettle and putting it on to boil as John returned from the car, stomping snow from his boots. He carried a brown folder under his arm, and settled in at the table, untying a length of brown cord. "I probably shouldn't be showing this to you, these are official documents. But honey, I did some thinking this morning. About my brother, and about me and you. Danny was a part of my life and you are a part of my life, and I don't want there to be any walls between us. Any walls, of any kind."

She carefully spooned loose tea. "Thank you for that."

"You've mentioned before that you sometimes still feel like an outsider. I'm sure that's true. I know our circle is a tough one to crack. I also think it's important that I do what I can to help you get past that feeling. So this morning I decided that if going over my brother's case helps you feel more a part of 'us', then by God that's what we're going to do." He removed a sheaf of papers and photographs and fanned them across the tabletop. "Here you go. Besides our individual memories, this is all there is."

Sarah reached across the stack. The photographs were black and white, grainy; most of them were location shots. A tipped bike near a beach, a gathering of men in front of Jenny's house, a grinning schoolboy. "Your Mom was right. He did look like Micah. He didn't have the curl in his hair that you have though."

"You've talked with Mom? About Danny?"

"Yes, the other day. We were in the attic going through some baby stuff. She showed me Danny's things. Pictures, mostly. She keeps them in a trunk. Did you know that?"

"No," John confessed. "We don't talk about Danny much. I don't know why. We never said we wouldn't talk about him. I think at first there was too much pain, and now not talking about him has become a habit."

Sarah scrabbled through the pile and double-checked the paperwork laid across the table. "Shouldn't there be a fingerprint card in here?"

"Honey, no one fingerprinted kids twenty years ago," John answered, half-distracted by a paper-clipped sheaf of notes. "We do have a dental chart. That was standard procedure. It still is."

"Here it is." Sarah rotated the blue cardboard square with its graphic outlines of pointed incisors and pronged molars. "What did you find?"

"An interview with a suspect. 'Albert Franklin Stanton of Bridgeport, Connecticut'. It looks like they pulled him off the Hyannis ferry the day my brother disappeared. An officer spotted him acting 'unduly nervous and suspicious'." John flipped over a stapled page. "And no wonder. Mr. Stanton had a prior. Statutory rape and sodomy. No wonder he was acting nervous. He must have known we'd be looking for someone with this exact profile."

Sarah leaned forward. "What was he doing on Nantucket? Does it say?"

" 'Visiting friends'. In 'Sconset, no less." John continued to read the report. "They had to release him; he had an alibi. Two houseguests swore he was in the house from Friday afternoon until they drove him to the wharf on Saturday morning…" The phone rang and John stood up. "I'll get it. Hello? Jackie? What? Calm down. I can't understand what you're saying."

"What is it? John, what is it?"

He waved her off. "Of course, we'll be right there." John dropped the phone. "Grab your coat. Mom's at the Cottage Hospital, she's had a heart attack."

They ran outside where John, with remarkable presence of mind, decided to take the patrol car in order to utilize both its authority and its siren. The unit was blocked in the driveway by his truck, left where Sarah had parked it. John spun the wheel hard and floored the accelerator, churning a muddy lane across the yard onto the open road.

Sarah fastened her seatbelt. She had to yell to be heard over the siren. "John, slow down! What did Jackie say?"

"She found Mom on the floor, unconscious." He barely slowed for a stop sign and skidded left on Prospect Street. "When Jackie couldn't wake her she called 911 and followed the ambulance in. She was calling us from the hospital." They pulled through the Cottage Hospital emergency entrance and parked next to a late model Wagoneer. "That's her Jeep there."

His sister was waiting for them in the reception area, huddled in a black wool coat. As they pushed through the door, Jackie struggled upright, her face haggard with fear. "Thank God you're here. You should have seen her, John. Her face was gray, all gray. I thought she was dead."

"J.J., take it easy." John wrapped his sister in a hug. "You did just fine."

Jackie pulled back, twisting a kleenex. "She's in intensive care. Oh, John, I didn't know what else to do."

Sarah glanced around for assistance. "I'll try to find out what's going on," she volunteered.

The Admittance desk was vacant until a middle-aged nurse in uniform marched around the corner, silent on thick white sneakers. She set her clipboard down and smiled. "Can I help you?"

"Jarad?" Sarah heard the apologetic tone of hospitals and libraries in her voice. "Jenny Jarad?"

"Mrs. Jarad has been admitted to intensive care. Shall I call her doctor?"

"Yes, thank you. That would be great." Sarah felt sluggish, mechanical. Simple decisions took conscious effort. "Yes, please."

The nurse pressed an intercom. "Dr. Nguyen? To admittance, please. Dr. Nguyen."

"What's wrong with her?"

"I'm sorry, I don't have that information." The nurse kept her eyes glued to a wall chart. "You'll need to speak with her doctor."

Footfalls echoed down the corridor, and as Sarah looked up, perspective played a trick on her eyes. The laws of nature had gone mad. Although she blinked repeatedly, the doctor grew shorter as he approached.

"Jarad?" he inquired gently. Nature reasserted herself. The doctor was Vietnamese, less than five feet tall, and his lab coat hung to his knees.

"I'm Sarah Jarad. The rest of the family is around the corner."

"I am Dr. Nguyen," he bowed slightly, placing his hands deep in his pockets. "Let us join them, so that I can give you what information I have only once."

John stood as Sarah returned. "Doctor? What's wrong with my mother? Was it a heart attack?"

"We are not yet certain." Dr. Nguyen pursed his lips. "Vomiting, unconsciousness, shortness of breath, these symptoms are indicative of many things. However, I believe your mother is suffering from a viral infection."

"Viral infection?" Jackie interrupted, struggling to her feet. "Like the flu?"

"Influenza can be very serious in a person of her age, but I do not believe that to be the case here. I have found evidence of hemolytic anemia, as well as a general inflammation in the heart muscle. I cannot yet be sure, but I believe your mother has viral myocarditis."

Shock made Jackie rude. "What does that mean in English?"

"Her long-term prognosis is good," Dr. Nguyen replied, his eyes dark with sympathy. "I have placed your mother on ACE-inhibitors; her cardiac function has already improved. We will know more after I have seen her test results. Now that she has regained consciousness, I have ordered an electrocardiogram."

"But how did this happen?" Sarah wondered. "She was fine when I saw her yesterday."

"This virus is silent," Dr. Nguyen explained. "It can wait many years to strike. One day, there is a sudden, new strain on the patient. A sickness, a tension, or a release. The immune system is affected, and the virus is released to do its harm."

John noted the odd word choice first. "What do you mean, a release?"

Dr. Nguyen paused. "For example. Two elderly people have been married a long time. One of them dies, the second one dies soon after. There is no medical reason for the second death, only that the heart is broken. I have seen this virus do its damage many times."

"Are you saying my mother wants to die?" Jackie sputtered.

"No." The doctor removed his glasses, polishing them slowly. "What I am saying is, the human will says 'no' to this virus for many years, and then one day it says 'yes'."

"But why now?" Jackie persisted. "Why would this virus hit her now?"

"I do not know that answer. Perhaps your mother can tell us once she regains her strength."

John ran his fingers through his hair, a telling nervous gesture. "So what do we do?"

"All you can do now is wait." Dr. Nguyen smiled gently. "If you would like to leave your telephone numbers, we can call you once there is a change." He checked his watch. "I believe you may hope for the best. Now you will excuse me? I must finish my rounds."

Jackie took a deep breath. "John, are you going to stay?"

"I'd like to. Honey, is that a problem?"

"Of course not, John. We'll stay as long as you want."

Jackie twisted her hands. "I know this sounds terrible, but I need to get home. Murray can't last more than six hours locked in the house, and I need to let her out."

"J.J., go do what you have to do. We'll call you as soon as we know something."

"Are you sure?"

"Of course. We'll let you you know as soon as we have news."

"Okay." Jackie stooped to retrieve her purse. "I'll call everyone and let them know what's happened. But promise me you'll call as soon as you hear something."

"I will," John promised.

John and Sarah took Jackie's place on the couch. The waiting room was painted in primary colors, horizontal stripes, yet the atmosphere was stale and oppressive. Sarah scooted closer to her husband, and he wrapped his arm around her shoulders, rubbing his eyes with his free hand. "It's been some kind of day. Seems like all we have been getting, lately."

"I know. I just hate feeling this helpless. Jenny's going to be alright, John, isn't she?"

"I'm sure she will be. We just have to give her some time. Our doctors here are as good as any on the mainland. I'm sure if Dr. Nguyen thought it was really serious they would have medivac'd her to Boston General."

The nurse reentered the waiting room and smiled. "I have news. Your mother is asking for you, and Dr. Nguyen has given permission for a short visit. Mrs. Jarad is in Room 210. The doctor has asked that you limit your visit to ten minutes."

John struggled upright. "That's great. Thank you very much."

Sarah followed John down the corridor. She hated hospitals. She always had. She glanced at room numbers: 202, 204. The floor tiles stuck to the soles of her shoes like soft death. Huddled in corners, people whispered and moaned, death's sexual parody. 206, 208. Desperation flashed by, room by room, visions glimpsed from a nightmare train. She turned her head, too late; bloodshot eyes beseeched her: pain, pain, pain. A laminate door held a disposable paper name tag. Overlarge chrome handles clicked, and allowed them in.

Jenny lay on the bed, her eyes closed. A plastic oxygen tube branched up her nose, an I.V. was taped to a bruised vein in the back of her hand. Sarah felt her knees go weak and sank into a chair next to the bed.

John noticed her reaction. "Honey, are you OK?"

"I'm fine, John. Go on."

"Rest then, while I check on Mom." He walked to the side of the bed, reaching out to gently stroke his mother's hair. "Mom? Hey, Mom, how are you doing?"

"John?" Jenny slowly opened her eyes, their usual sparkle dulled by painkillers. "John? Oh, John, it hurts."

"Mom, take it easy. The doctor says you're going to be okay. It'll be alright. I promise."

"Promise!" Jenny struggled upright, frantic with effort, clutching the front of John's shirt. "Oh, John, Wednesday? Is't Wednesday? Promise!"

"Mom, please!" He caught himself on the handrails of her bed. "Take it easy!"

"Oh-mi-God, John." Jenny fell back, panting. "Promise you'll meet…the ferry. Danny's coming home. Wednesday. Meet the ferry."

"What did you say?" he whispered. "Mom? What did you say?"

Jenny closed her eyes, gasping for breath. "Danny called. From New York. He's coming home. Wednesday. Find him, John," she insisted, tears pooling along her lower eyelids. "Find your brother. Find Danny. Bring him home."

An unfamiliar nurse trotted in the room and quickly assessed the situation. "I'm afraid you need to leave. She wasn't supposed to be upset. This isn't helping her."

Sarah pulled John out of the room into the hallway. He was stiff with shock. They braced themselves against a tile wall as John shook his head. "It must be the medication. It must be. She doesn't know what she's saying."

"My God, John, could it be possible?"

"I don't know. Honestly, I don't know…"

"So, are you going to meet the ferry?"

He glanced up, haunted. "Do I have a choice?"

Chapter Nine

Jenny's condition had stabilized by the afternoon of the following day. John and Sarah moved to the airport to intercept incoming family members returning to Nantucket because of the news. Sarah recognized several relatives as they stepped off the plane, eerie in their shared resemblance. John welcomed them home, reassured them about his mother's condition and sent them on their way, in borrowed cars, to stay with island cousins.

Micah Jarad, John's second-oldest brother, was the last to arrive, flying in on the red-eye from San Diego. Finding John and Sarah waiting for him at the gate, Micah dropped his naval duffle bag and wrapped them both in a collective bear hug.

"Man, I hate the reason why I'm here, but it's good to see you two! So, what's the update with Mom? It's something with her heart?"

"They think it's a virus," John explained. "She's on medication."

"But she's going to be alright, isn't she?"

"Her doctor seems to think so."

"Good. That's good." Micah shouldered his duffle bag. "Let's get to the hospital. I'll feel better once I've seen her for myself."

"We can't, Micah, not just yet." John hesitated. "We're still waiting on someone."

"Who's not here yet?"

"I don't know how to tell you this other than to just say it – but Mom gave us a message yesterday. She told us to meet the ferry; she said Danny was coming home today on the three o'clock ferry."

"That's…not…possible. Is it?"

"I don't know what's possible." John massaged his temples. "That's what she said."

"Did anyone else hear this call?"

"Who else would? Mom lives by herself. We didn't even know she was sick until Jackie found her on the floor."

"Did you call the Steamship Authority and ask them if Danny was aboard?"

"Of course I did. I asked Betty Cooper to check the manifest. No one named Jarad reserved a slot for a car, but they don't I.D. walk-ons if he left the car parked in Hyannis." John grimaced. "Anyway, all this could be delusion. Mom's on some heavy medication."

"There's one way to find out," Micah clapped both hands together. "Let's go meet the ferry."

They crossed the terminal for the airport parking lot. An island shuttle-hopper flew in overhead as John unlocked the minivan. Sarah claimed the front passenger seat. Micah slid open the large side door, tossed his duffle and followed it in. He sat back heavily. "So what else did Mom say?"

Hampered by her seatbelt, Sarah turned to answer. "We were only in her room for a few minutes, but she did say Danny was coming home today on the ferry. We both heard her say it."

"Chrissakes! I don't know what to believe. You know, I still wonder what happened to him. I guess I bought the story he drowned." Micah ran a hand through his mane of brown hair. "And if it is Danny, where the hell has he been? It's been twenty years!"

John adjusted the rear-view mirror. "That's the first question I'm going to ask, and I have plenty more." He pulled out and drove toward Steamboat Wharf, finding an open space and parking. Leaning forward, John rested both arms on the steering wheel. The ferry hadn't arrived yet, and the wharf held a half-dozen assorted vehicles and three black and yellow taxi-cabs.

Micah leaned forward between the seats. "This whole thing is nuts! Even if he is on the boat, how do we know it's him?"

John tapped the wheel. "Let's take this one step at a time. First, let's see if he's on the boat. Then we'll dig out his dental records. If all else fails, there's DNA testing. Don't worry, Micah. We have plenty of ways to check."

"Something about this is bothering me," Sarah admitted. "Why did he pick right now to come home? I've read about cases like this, John. Con men pretend to be lost children, hoping to get something out of the families."

"That argues the point that he is Danny. Our family has nothing to get."

"Oh, yes, you do. Don't forget, you have the Lost Forest property now."

"Honey, if that's what you think, then why do you want him to stay at Mom's house?"

"Because if he is a con man and he's there, Micah can keep an eye on him."

"Lord help me," John winked at his brother. "I married a policeman's wife."

Micah stretched and made himself comfortable. "Meanwhile, what is the story with that property? I've only heard bits and pieces."

"Uncle Ethan had a secret," John explained. "He wasn't broke. After he died, I got a call from Molly Witherspoon. It turns out Uncle Ethan owned sixty acres near Sesachacha Pond and Micah, for some ungodly reason, he left it to me."

"Sixty acres!" Micah whistled. "That's worth some money!" He reached around the front seat and grappled with his younger brother. "Let me guess. Are you feeling heat from the rest of the family yet?"

John fought back, using his elbow. "You know I am, dammit. And I suppose you want a cut too."

"You bet I do, I'm no fool. I'd retire from the Navy in a heartbeat," Micah chuckled. "C'mon, John. Give me a big old slice of that pie."

"You go to hell," John laughed easily, shoving his brother back into his seat.

Sarah was relieved to hear the banter between the two brothers. The last thirty-six hours had been nothing but stress and she had worried about John's resilience. She should have remembered that she could count on Micah. John's older brother was a natural comedian and as even-keeled as they come. Micah had been one of the three groomsmen at their wedding, and everyone had looked to Micah for entertainment during the reception. He had insisted on dancing with every single one of the old Aunties and had led a conga line of delighted children through the Funky Chicken. Sarah was glad Micah was home to help.

She glanced over and noticed The Eagle steaming around Brant Point. "Hey, you two, cut it out. Here she comes."

The broad-beamed ferry navigated the point, straightening her line and approaching the wharf. Passengers were clustered along the rail in bright colors, braving the January cold for their first frosty glimpse of Nantucket town. The ship's waterline cargo doors groaned open like a huge, gaping maw and displayed segregated rows of passenger cars and flatbed semi-trailers laden with pre-built, modular homes and mustard-yellow construction equipment.

The ferry reversed its engines with a concussive rush of sound and power. Perched on creosote pilings the color of molasses, seagulls squawked and took to the air, hovering over the turgid backwash. An unseen anchor chain dropped, clinking and clattering across the steel deck before making one final punctuative splash.

A slim dreadlocked dockhand clambered up a fixed steel ladder, laughing over his shoulder to another dockhand waiting below. He manipulated a crane that swung an exit ramp toward the ferry's restive deck and, with a dancer's ease, settled the ramp into place, jumping on its corrugated steel surface and sliding home a set of retaining bolts. Giving a thumb's up, the dockland released a barrier chain and slid to ground using the ladder's rail like a fireman's pole.

In the cars around them people began to stir. A black Range Rover disgorged three children who raced across the asphalt toward the departure gate, shouting excitedly and waving to a red-coated passenger positioned along the top rail. The passenger returned their salute and shouted an unintelligible reply. On the ground, a stout uniformed shipping agent used his authority and universal sign language to warn the kids to stay behind a sturdy barrier, while opening it, stepping through, and closing it again before starting his ascension up the steel access ramp.

Sitting quietly in the minivan, John, Sarah and Micah waited nervously for the one family member no one had expected to come home. They were waiting for Daniel Jarad to return from the dead.

Slowly, John zipped his coat. "What do you say we wait at the gate?"

"It'll be cold out there," Sarah noted.

"Yes, but if he is on that boat I want him to see us, first thing."

"I'm with you, 'bro." Micah slid open the minivan's door and stepped out.

They crossed the asphalt and sheltered along the broad side of an idling, mainland-bound truck. Burdened by boots, bulky winter clothing and monogrammed canvas carry-ons, departing passengers clattered down the ramp to exchange hugs, handshakes and kisses with the groups they met. An ecstatic golden retriever wearing a blue bandanna woofed with doggy delight and tugged himself free of his leash, lunging toward his human who dropped everything on the tarmac for a welcome homecoming furry tackle.

Sarah scanned the crowd, stopping and starting with each disembarking passenger. Not a single person looked lost or out of place; each passenger stepped confidently down the ramp toward a waiting car or cab. The stream of passengers gradually dwindled, thinned, and finally trickled to a stop.

Unused to the cold, Micah was hugging himself for warmth. "That looks like it. Damnation! It must've been a hoax."

Anger percolated through Sarah's blood. "Who would do something that cruel?"

"It's no hoax." John's voice stopped them both.

They turned and followed John's sight-line. "Oh my God," Micah exhaled.

Windblown on the deck, a slim, deeply-tanned young man in jeans and a black leather jacket stood at the top of the departure ramp. He scanned the parking lot, hesitant. Sarah watched him search the crowd, his eyes eventually locking onto her, book-ended as she was by the pair of Jarad brothers. Sarah took a deep breath and acknowledged the obvious. Dear, sweet Lord, she admitted. That same dark hair. That familiar chin.

"John?" Micah's voice rose in question. "John? What do you think?"

"It could be," John whispered. "It could be."

The stranger stepped down the ramp, carrying a small nylon duffle bag. As he drew near, all three Jarads were startled by the resemblance. The stranger had the same eyes, the same smile, even his walk looked familiar. The young man paused at the base of the ramp and an expression passed across his face. Sarah recognized in it a mixture of hope and distrust.

He approached Micah first. "You must be a…Jarad?"

"I'm Micah Jarad. This is my brother John, and his wife Sarah. You are?"

Tears puddled in the young man's eyes. He dropped his duffle bag and blinked them back. "I can't believe I'm saying this. I'm your brother, Danny." He scanned the line of parked vehicles. "Did Jenny tell you to meet me? Is she here?"

John raised his hand. "Before we go any further, I need to see some I.D."

"Sure." The young man dug out his wallet and offered a New York State driver's license. "That's all I have. I don't have anything with the name Danny Jarad on it."

John examined the hologrammed I.D. "Kevin Sumners?"

"Uhm-hum. It's the name I got from my foster family. You see, I never had a birth certificate."

John tapped the I.D. between his fingers. "Then how did you get this?"

"Court order," Danny replied easily. "We went to a Judge to establish my identity." He hefted his duffle bag. "I brought the court papers with me if you want to see them."

"I do want to see them..." John nodded.

"Wait a minute," Sarah interrupted, finding a flaw in the logic. "If you didn't know your name was Danny Jarad, then how did you know to come to Nantucket?"

The young man turned, eagerly. "That was pure luck. I was visiting a friend of mine in Florida, and when I watched the video he took on his vacation here I started having these really weird dreams. I mean, they were strange, really twisted. And they didn't really seem like dreams, they were more like visions. A lot of them looked like that." He pointed to a row of trim, shingled waterfront homes. "Then, when I got back, I called my therapist and she tried regression hypnosis on me. In our session the name 'Danny Jarad' came up. I didn't know what that meant but at least I had something to go on."

It was Micah's turn for doubt. "That still doesn't answer the question. How did you know to call us?"

"The island operator helped me. I told her I was looking for some lost relatives and did she know of anyone on Nantucket named Jarad?" The young man grinned. "You should have heard that bitch laugh. When she got done, she asked me which one because there were three pages of Jarads in the book. So I asked her who would be the best person to talk to about the family and she gave me Jenny's number."

"And you called her," John stated.

"Um-hum, yesterday." Danny tapped a cigarette from his pack and cupped both hands to light it. Inhaling deeply, he whistled a stream of smoke through his teeth. "Toughest call I have ever made. I bet I tried a dozen times, picking up the phone and working up my nerve. I think now I was afraid to find out it might not be true. You know what I mean? At least there's some hope when you don't know something for sure."

Sarah nodded sympathetically. She had also once trusted the traitor security that inhabited denial.

"Then yesterday I said 'fuck it' and let the phone ring. Jenny answered. I told her who I thought I was and asked her if it could be true. You should have heard her. She begged me to come here. She even wanted to pay for a plane ticket." He dropped and stepped on his cigarette. "I said 'no thanks', I'm not here to sponge off anybody and I could swing the bus fare on my own." He shrugged inside his jacket. "I know this must sound nuts to you; it sounds nuts to me and I'm living in it."

John frowned. "So what happened to you? Where have you been all this time?"

"Listen." Danny raised both hands. "That is a long fucking story and I'm freezing my ass off out here. Can we go someplace warm and talk about it?"

"Micah, what do you think?"

"It sounds possible, John. I don't see that going somewhere warm can do any harm."

"So where's Jenny?" Danny danced with impatience and cold. "Is she waiting in the car?"

"She couldn't be here," John answered. "She's had a viral attack and she's in the hospital."

"Attack?" Danny went pale. "But they'll let me see her, won't they? They have to!"

"I suppose so," Micah frowned uncertainly. "She's expecting you anyway."

"Then let's go! I've come a long fucking way and I'm not stopping now."

John led the group back to the minivan. Unlocking the hatchback, he reached for Danny's duffle and Danny passed it over.

"I packed light. I didn't know how long I was staying."

The bald statement struck John hard. The instinctive side of his nature wanted to reach out and hug this stranger and believe every word of his story, to be done with all the questions and doubts, just like that. This overwhelming impulse was at war with what John felt like was the left frontal lobe of his brain, which struggled for rationality and proof. Never before in his life had he felt so divided within himself.

Sarah opened the passenger door and paused. "Danny, uhm, well, first off, should we even call you Danny? Or Kevin?"

"Whatever you feel comfortable with. I'd prefer Danny, if that's alright with you."

"Well, okay then, Danny, why don't you sit up front? You'll see more that way. I'll sit in back with Micah."

"Thanks. I'd like that." Danny smiled gratefully and with his smile, Sarah realized just how good-looking he was. He wasn't as tall as either of his brothers, but there was no mistaking the Jarad stamp. Jenny was right; you could spot it a mile away.

"Some of these buildings look familiar." Danny pointed to the golden dome of the Unitarian Church. "That one there, for instance."

"Classic New England architecture," John agreed, offering his hand to Sarah and helping her into the middle seat. He waited until everyone had fastened their seatbelts before climbing into the driver's seat, putting the minivan in gear and following Easy Street back to Main, heading toward Prospect and the Cottage Hospital.

"Is there a motel somewhere? Near the hospital?" Danny wondered. "Some place I could get a room?"

"You're staying at the house," Micah stated. "With me."

Danny squirmed uncomfortably. "Thank you, uhm, Micah, but if I do, I'd want to pay for my room. Like I said, I'm not here to sponge off anybody. I brought my own money."

"I'll tell you what," Micah leaned forward. "You feed Mom's cat and water her plants and we'll call it even."

"That's a deal." Danny smiled excitedly, pointing. "Jesus! This is some neighborhood. Look at these houses!"

"The whole island is pretty much like this," John explained patiently. "Don't you remember it?"

"No. No, I don't." Danny dropped his head. "The truth is I don't remember much. And what I do remember is choppy. Not much of it is clear."

"What do you remember?" Sarah asked softly.

"I remember I got grabbed." Danny drew a ragged breath. "I can remember that like it happened yesterday. That part is so clear, I'll never forget it." He looked out his window. "I can remember riding my bike and a man stopped his car to ask directions. He said he was lost and he needed help. Then he grabbed me. I tried to run away but he was strong, and he locked me in his trunk. Later, when he opened the trunk I tried to fight, but he had a towel ready and he pressed it over my face; there was some kind of chemical on it. I don't know what it was but it blistered my skin for a long time after. My therapist says I have traumatic shock syndrome; she says I may never get my memory back, and you know what? I'm not sure I want to."

John gripped the wheel. "This man? You were with him the whole time you were gone?"

"Like I had a choice. He was a pedophile. Do you know what that means?"

Sarah swallowed heavily. She felt sickened by the truth. Of course that's what happened to Danny. If he hadn't drowned, there really was no other answer. Sheriff Toohey had hinted at the possibility, too bleak to even consider, and yet here it was, the foul truth, revealed.

Danny nervously toyed with his cuff. "I don't know how he got me off this place, I might have still been in his trunk. But when I came to, I was in a wire cage in his basement." He used a knuckle to draw a random design on the fogged window. "That went on for a long, long time. I was a different person then. I had to be. Just to survive. Day after day, nothing changed. And then, one day, a lot later, Cahill brought another boy down. By then I was too big for the cage and he had me chained to the wall. I watched him put this other boy in my cage, and then he looked at me and I knew Cahill was done with me, I could tell it by the look in his eyes. He was a monster, and he was going to kill me. It wasn't even personal. It was like I was his dog."

Danny sighed. "This other boy, his name was Brian, and when he woke up he wouldn't stop crying, I told him it didn't matter, crying wouldn't help, it would just make Cahill mad, but he kept crying and begging me to help. So when Cahill came back downstairs to play with the new boy, he turned his back on me and I slugged him with a golf club and I kept slugging him until Cahill stopped making noise. And then we ran upstairs and got outside and ran – Jesus Fucking Christ! – we ran. We ran until the new boy made us stop at the brightest lights we could find. It was a convenience store. At first the clerk didn't believe us but we made her call the cops anyway."

"How old were you when this happened?" John whispered. "How old were you when you got away?"

"I don't know, I was down there for a long time. How old was I when I left?"

"Seven," John replied. "You were seven."

"Okay. The cops picked us up on June 2, 1983. Hey, wait a minute, you would know this. When's my birthday?"

"April 11," John answered slowly. "1972."

"So I was eleven." Danny tasted the word: "Eleven. That's good to know. See? I knew coming back here was the right thing to do. I'm filling in the blanks already. Anyway," he turned in his seat. "The cops came, and they tried to help, they really did, but in the end they stuck me in Juvie. They didn't know what else to do. I couldn't remember anything, I couldn't even remember my name. They took my fingerprints, but that was a dead-end. I couldn't even lead them back to Cahill's house; we got turned around when we were running and I didn't know where it was anymore. So, finally, they did what they had to do: they fed me to the system." He sniffed. "But that turned out okay, I ended up with a pretty good foster family, the Sumners. They were nice people. Kerri Sumners home-schooled me; she taught me to read and write and helped me with Math. She got me to where I could go to school with the regular kids. I was with them seven years, and then I got my GED and I was on my own. And that was okay, too; I got a job in the food court at Klemps and a crib of my own. So you see, I did okay. And then I visited my friend Tony in Florida and started having the dreams, and here I am." He blinked rapidly. "I still can't believe I'm here! And you don't have to do anything for me. I just want to see Jenny."

"And she wants to see you, too." John parked the minivan and stepped outside, taking in a lungful of fresh salt air. Ahead of him, the Cottage Hospital exuded its incorruptible aura of competence and strength. He was struck by the dichotomy of what he was seeing and the story he had just heard. How could two such experiences exist within the same moment of time?

Sarah took his arm, her eyebrows furrowed with concern. "John? Sweetheart? Are you alright?"

"I'm fine." He shook off his thoughts. He knew it was better to live in the world as it was, accepting its ugly side, than to pretend that the ugliness did not exist. They crossed the sidewalk to the automatic door. The reception desk was occupied by a young aide.

"Can I help you?" she asked brightly.

Micah stepped forward. "We'd like to see Jenny Jarad?"

"One moment." The aide consulted a chart and her watch. "She's in Room 210. Visiting hour is only until four. That leaves you about twenty minutes."

"Have they updated Jenny's condition?" Sarah asked.

"It says here she's stabilized. We think she's doing very well."

"I'll go first." Micah stepped ahead of the group. "She's expecting me. If she looks like she's doing as well as they say, then we can spring Danny on her."

Danny breathed nervously. "I'm going to be a surprise, there's no way around that."

Micah pushed on the chrome handle and entered the room. Jenny was resting peacefully, and Micah smiled. Her color looked good and he sighed with relief. As he did, Jenny slowly opened her eyes and smiled, hampered by the oxygen tube that branched up her nose. "Micah?"

"Hi, Mom." He leaned forward and kissed her forehead. "I'm glad to see you. The doctor says you're much better. That's good."

Jenny tried to smile again, and this time her smile reached her eyes. "See you. S'better."

"Mom, I'm staying home until you're all better. I took an extended shore leave." He patted her hand. "It's okay. You just take it easy."

Jenny squeezed back. "I am. I will. I'm better."

"That's good." Micah released her hand. "Now, Mom, there's someone else here to see you, but I don't want you to get too upset about it."

Jenny gazed at her son, her question obvious in her eyes. "He's here? Danny's here?"

"Yes, Mom, he's in the hall. But you have to take it easy." Micah stepped back, making room along her bedside. "I guess you guys can come on in."

Danny stepped through the doorway to the edge of Jenny's bed. "Hi, uhm, Mom?"

Jenny struggled to focus her eyes. "Micah? Micah? It's Danny?"

"Yes, Mom. It's him."

"I knew." Jenny's smile illuminated the room. "Oh sweet Jesus, I knew."

Tentatively, Danny reached out to touch her skin, his fingers brushing and stroking her arm. "I can't believe I'm seeing you, Mom. I never thought I'd see you again."

Trembling, Jenny reached out both arms and hugged him close. She ran her hands over his shoulders, along his back, then lifted Danny's face in her hands. "My baby. My little boy is home. My little caboose."

"Mom, just get better, that's all I want. You just have to get better."

"Home. Stay home." She released him and blinked at Micah.

"He's staying at the house, Mom. And he'll stay there until you come home, too."

The door reopened to admit the stern nurse. "Excuse me people, but your mother is better, not well. I have to ask you all to leave. Visiting hours are over for the day and she does need her rest."

Danny patted Jenny's hand. "Okay, Mom, we're going. But we'll be back, first thing in the morning."

"Yes, we will," Sarah agreed. "Jenny, do you need us to bring you anything?"

"What more...do I need?" Jenny lay back on her pillow, smiling. "My baby...is home."

Chapter Ten

The winter sky was blue like an old china plate, the sand so cold it crunched beneath their boots. Sarah and Danny trudged through the dunes toward the shoreline of Dionis beach, Danny wrapped in a borrowed coat and muffled up to his ears in a green plaid scarf.

"That was some wind last night," he remarked. "Is it usually so loud?"

"No, that was exceptional." Sarah inhaled deeply. "But don't you love how fresh the air is after a storm? It's like there's some special new ingredient in it."

"Sure, but it makes it hard to sleep. Especially when you're in a strange house and you're not sure what the noises are anyway. I was jumping all night." He clasped his hands behind his back. "Thanks for asking me to come to the beach. I needed to get out of the house."

"I'm glad you could make it. I like the company."

As she spoke, Sarah felt a twinge of guilty conscience. Inviting Danny to the beach had not been entirely unmotivated by self-interest. After hearing his story in the minivan, John and Micah seemed reasonably satisfied, but Sarah wasn't convinced. A few hours alone with him might help erase her doubts.

Danny stooped and picked up a beach pebble, slinging it underhand into the sea. "You know, it's funny. I spent so much time thinking about getting here I didn't think of what I was going to do when I did."

Sarah plucked a scrap of driftwood. "You can start by carrying this. I warned you I was going to put you to work."

"Okay by me. I know how to work, and I want to help. Especially since you people won't let me pay for my room. I asked Micah again this morning and he said: 'Forget it'. I'm not used to being treated this good."

"The whole family is pretty much like that." A gust of wind caught her long hair, and Sarah struggled to tuck it back under her hat. "Islanders are very generous, in their way, once you get to know them."

Danny glanced over, curious. "You're not from Nantucket?"

"No, I'm from Pittsburgh. I just came here to work."

"So how did you and John hook up?"

Sarah smiled at the memory. "My sister and I came here to waitress, but then I found out that the tips were better working behind the bar, so I went over. That's why they still tease me about being a barmaid. But I never was; not really. I'm an artist. Working tables was just how I earned my living." She stooped to disentangle a stick from a clump of eel-grass. "Then Joan – she's my sister – started dating Cook, he was the sous chef at Captain Tobey's, and John was Cook's best friend. And that's how we met."

"So you've only been here yourself for what? Seven months?"

"No, nine. Nine months." Sarah contemplated the number. "Wow. It has been only nine months. That's hard to believe. So much has happened it seems like a lot longer."

"You and John must've got married right away."

"We did, there's no getting around that. But it was September and Joan and I had to decide what we were going to do because our housing contract expired October first. Originally, we were going back home to get 'real jobs', but when the time came, and I thought about leaving John, I couldn't go. And by then, Joan couldn't leave Cook, so there we were." Sarah laughed. "Stuck!"

"Where's your sister now?"

"Last I heard she was in Jamaica, lucky dog. They're working together on a private yacht. Cook's the chef and Joan went with him as a personal assistant. They're getting married this September, after season, and they promised to come back to Nantucket for the ceremony." Sarah patted her stomach. "I should look like a cow by then."

Danny stopped short. "You're...pregnant?"

"Um-hum. We just found out. The baby's due the end of September."

"Jesus! You're something else. When you make up your mind to go after something, you get it."

"I can't take credit for all of it; the baby was a surprise." Sarah waved her stick at an inquisitive seagull and decided it was time to bait her hook. If Danny was a con-man after John's inheritance, it was time to find out. "But like all good things it only brings more work. Now John and I only have seven months to build our house and get it ready for the baby."

"You're building a house, too? Where? Here on the island?"

"Um-hum," Sarah nodded. "In Quammock. It's beachfront property, with a beautiful view of the ocean."

"Wow. Cops must make good money. Or is it yours?"

"Neither; we both make a decent living but it's nothing huge. We couldn't do it now except John got an inheritance from his great-uncle. That's what's paying for the house."

"His great-uncle? Which one?"

"Ethan Jarad. Do you remember him?"

"No. No, I don't. But it's like I said. Most of my memory is blank." He stared out to sea. "But maybe there is something, I'm feeling some resistance. I don't know, maybe it'll come to me later, when I've had more time to think about it."

"Let's hope." Using her boot, Sarah dug out a driftwood branch and shook it free of damp clinging sand. She handed the branch to Danny, who wedged it awkwardly under his arm. "No, not like that," she gestured. "You need to cradle and stack it. Like this."

"Okay, I get you." Danny rearranged his driftwood cargo. "Step back. You've been doing this longer than I have."

"Sorry! But I love doing this, it's my excuse to get outside. I can't paint all the time. That makes painting too much like work. I don't want to ever get bored with it."

"You're the first artist I've ever known. And earning a living as a painter, that's something different. If I'm going to stay here, I'll need to get a job soon. Do you know of any restaurants that might be looking for help?"

"Are you kidding? You can take your pick. They can't get enough help on this island." They moved toward an eroded, pebbly headland. "But they'll want references."

"Not a problem. I have a couple of them from back in Brooklyn."

"That's where you're from? Brooklyn, New York?"

"I like to think I'm from here. It's like you said with being a barmaid; Brooklyn's where I lived, but it's not who I am."

"Of course not, Danny. I was just asking if that's where you've been."

"Brooklyn, New York. God bless America. But I'm not going back. I'm going to stay here with my family, and build my future here."

"Didn't you leave anyone behind? Back in Brooklyn?"

"There's nobody there. I had a girlfriend, Donna, but we split up. I can't blame her for it. She wanted to get married; it was important to her, and she wanted to start a family. But I couldn't see it." He shook his head. "I have a few friends from work, and the Sumners, but they retired and moved to North Carolina." His voice dropped to a whisper. "No, there's no reason for me to go back to Brooklyn."

"What about your things? Did you leave your car in Hyannis?"

Danny laughed. "I can tell you've never lived in Brooklyn! I don't have a car. I couldn't afford the insurance. I do have a TV and some more clothes, but I'll call my friend Louis and he can have them. My apartment is month-to-month so that's not a problem. The landlord won't care, I'm paid up." Danny shrugged and stopped, raising his free hand to shield his eyes from the sun. "Who's that?"

Sarah followed his glance and noticed a flame-red pickup parked in the shelter of the sandy bluff. Working near the truck, a lone man struggled with a length of chain, winching a large driftwood log out of deep water. "I'm not sure," she admitted. "It looks like Eddie Farrar. But that's not his truck."

Noting their approach, the man stopped his work, locking his winch and digging into his shirt pocket for a cigarette. He flicked a match against his thumbnail and nodded a greeting. "Hello, Sarah Jarad. Haven't seen you in awhile. Thought maybe you'd given up on our driftwood competition."

"You cheat, Eddie, using a chainsaw. If it's too big to carry it's not ready yet to take."

The ruddy man crooked a smile at their long-standing contention. "That's your rule, missy, not mine. I've got a permit here, nice and legal, that says I've got as much right to timber washed up on public land as any man." He ran a possessive hand over the fender of the red truck. "Notice anything new?"

"As a matter of fact I did, Eddie. Who's is it?"

"Mine, of course." Pride of ownership overcame Eddie's natural peevishness. "Brand-spanking new. First new truck I ever owned. King cab, and this beauty's got every option available: air conditioning, even got a CD player." He stroked the fender. "I waited a long time for this. Had a little surprise money come by and decided to live a little. Paid cash, too."

"She is a beauty, Eddie. Congratulations."

"Thank you, missy. I'm a proud man, that's no lie." He cocked an eye in her direction. "Aren't you going to introduce me to your boyfriend?"

"Of course, I'm sorry. Daniel Jarad this is Eddie Farrar ..."

As she said Danny's name, the cigarette slipped from Eddie's mouth and fell into the folds of his open jacket. Frantically, Eddie dug into his jacket to retrieve his smoke and danced in the sand, slapping his shirt for embers. "Dammit girl, that's not funny!"

"It's not meant to be funny," Danny stated flatly. "I'm Daniel Jarad."

"Is that right?" Eddie dropped his cigarette in the sand and crushed it beneath his heel. "You're Daniel Jarad? Well, there's only one Daniel Jarad I ever heard about and he disappeared as a boy."

"That's right, I did." Danny affirmed quietly. "But I've come home."

"Somebody's getting taken here and it ain't me!" Eddie Farrar was so upset he looked cross-eyed. "I don't know who you're supposed to be, mister, but Danny Jarad's dead and buried these twenty years!"

Eddie's tone was so confident Sarah blinked. "How do you know that, Eddie? How do you know Danny Jarad is dead and buried?"

"Well of course he's dead – it's plain common sense! No seven-year old child wanders off and survives on his own." Eddie unhooked his chain and began cranking furiously, shouting over his shoulder. "You leave me be! I've already told everything I know about Danny Jarad and I'm not going to be pestered about it now!" He hoisted and tossed his chainsaw, producing the first ding in the bed of his new pickup. Giving them one final glare, Eddie climbed into his truck and peeled away, spewing sand, the final insult.

"What's up with him?" Danny observed. "I think we hit a nerve."

"No kidding." Sarah shivered. "That was some reaction."

Danny pointed to the sodden, hundred-pound log bobbing in the shallows. "Do you want me to get that, too? I think you won it."

Sarah recognized Danny's tease for what it was. "No, let's save it for later. When we get back, though, remind me to ask John if the police ever questioned Eddie about your disappearance…"

"You know what? Let's head back," Danny suggested. "I'd like to get some rest before the party tonight."

She shivered again and realized she was chilled to the bone. The breeze had freshened, and they were going to have to walk back facing the wind to get to the minivan. "That sounds like a good idea."

"You know? I'm not nervous at all about tonight. Actually, I'm looking forward to meeting the rest of the family. It's going to be a big night, no doubt about it."

"It shouldn't be too bad. Aunt Al only asked the immediate family; she didn't want you to feel overwhelmed."

"So how big is my 'immediate family' anyway?"

Sarah numbered the bloodline in her head. "Sixteen, and that's not counting kids. Tonight will be for grown-ups only. You can meet your nieces and nephews later."

"It blows me away that I have brothers and sisters, and nieces and nephews." He sighed. "I can't get a grip on the fact I'm not alone anymore. Sarah, you talk like you're close with your sister. Do you know what I mean?"

"Yes." Sarah stuffed her hands in her pockets for warmth and felt something hard tucked into one corner. Fumbling through her gloves, she withdrew the pebble and rediscovered Addie's magic jewel. "Hey. I forgot about this."

"What is it?"

"It's sea-glass. Broken bottles get worn soft by the water. When the pieces come ashore, Addie collects them. She calls them jewels. See?"

"I'm meeting everyone today. Who's Addie? Another relative?"

"No, she's a woman I see on the beach every once in awhile. I'm surprised she's not here today." Sarah rubbed the sea-glass between her finger and thumb. "She looks for treasure and finds things like this."

"Addie. Addie." Danny tasted the name and tunelessly began to sing: " 'Addie, Addie, got no Daddy.' Sarah, I think I remember Addie. The kids used to make fun of her. Oh-mi-God. I wonder if she remembers me?"

"I know she does, Danny. She still talks about you!"

"Oh-mi-God, I'm right." Danny placed both hands on his chest. "I'm right! I remember Addie. I remember her! Sarah, I remember her, I remember here!" He capered across the wet sand like a lunatic, waving his scarf in delight. "I remember her! I remember here!"

Sarah laughed at his exuberant display. Danny danced himself breathless, then bent over and placed his hands on his knees, gulping great lungfuls of air and waving a conciliatory hand. "Don't mind me. I'm okay. Really. I'm okay." He straightened up and stumbled back up the beach. "I'm not nuts, I swear. It's just I wasn't really sure before, and now, I am." Danny stretched his arms skyward and yelled. "Now I am!"

"You're not nuts. Here." Sarah extended Addie's magic jewel. "I think you should have this."

Danny paused, reaching forward and accepting the gift. "Thanks, I think. What do I do with it?"

"You make a wish and throw it back into the sea. Then your wish comes true."

Danny studied the small square of emerald glass. "Is that guaranteed?"

"Or your money back."

"What the hell. What can it hurt?" He closed his eyes and made a fist, drawing back and pitching Addie's jewel out into the water. The green glass skipped across a frothy incoming wave and vanished into the surf.

"What did you wish for?"

"I can't tell you that! Then my wish won't come true."

"That's only birthday wishes. You can tell sea wishes."

"It's not hard." Danny answered softly, staring at a seagull skimming the breaking waves. "I just want my life back. I just want to move on with my new life. Sarah? Do you think I have a chance?"

"I think you've already started. Now you just have to keep trying until you get there."

"Well," Danny replied. "That's why I'm here."

Chapter Eleven

One hundred and sixty years ago, during the height of Nantucket's prosperity, whaling captains spiked fresh pineapples on either side of their front gate to publicly announce their safe return from a perilous sea voyage. The gesture grew to mean that anyone passing by was welcome to stop in and visit, and friends and family would sit by the fire and listen enraptured to tales of harpooned whales, speeding Nantucket sleigh rides, and the valiant struggle to round Cape Horn and trade in distant, exotic China.

The sea-captain who built Aunt Alexandra Hussey's house had married one of the congenitally social Folger sisters and, tiring of the perpetual expense of real fruit, had surrendered and simply carved a pineapple into his front door. As Sarah and John crossed the threshold and stepped into the paneled hallway, they were met by the sharp yapping bark of Aunt Alexandra's pet pug dog, Sir Regence of Dunmoyle.

John draped Sarah's coat across a needlepoint bench stationed next to the stairs. "Hello, Rug-Rat," he pointed toward the living room. "Go tell your mother we're here."

He caught his reflection in an ornate rococo mirror and paused to straighten his tie. Sarah stepped up behind him and placed her arms around his waist, resting her chin on his shoulder. "You look dapper, as always."

"We make a handsome couple."

"Vanity, all is vanity." Sarah quoted, nevertheless retrieving a lipstick from her purse. "I wonder if Micah and Danny are here yet?"

John cocked one ear toward the undercurrent of voices coming from the living room. "I don't hear them. They might have stopped at the Club Car for a quick one on the way over. When I think of what Danny's up against, I can't say I blame him."

"So you think his story is true?"

"I don't think he's told us the whole truth yet. That story about amnesia – it strikes me as convenient."

"This morning at the beach he said he remembered Addie Simpson."

"He did? What did he say?"

"He remembered a rhyme about her: 'Addie, Addie, got no Daddy.' And he said he remembered the other kids were mean to her."

"That's pretty much common knowledge, but it does prove my point. He may remember more than he's telling and just not want to talk about it, if his story is true. I checked with the Brooklyn Social Services division and they do have a case file for 'Kevin Sumners'. Unfortunately, it's sealed as part of his juvenile record." He turned as Aunt Alexandra Hussey entered the hall, splendidly arrayed in a mauve silk pantsuit. "Good evening, Aunt Al."

"Hello, John. Hello, Sarah." Perfectly coifed and perfumed, Aunt Alexandra bypassed both of them to peer through the glass side-panes surrounding the front door. "Isn't he here yet?"

"He's riding in with Micah. They were right behind us. They should be here any minute."

"Isn't this thrilling?" Aunt Al kissed Sarah cheek-to-cheek. "It's truly a banner day for the Jarad family! I couldn't believe the news when I heard it. And John, how is your mother? Jenny's doing well?"

"Her doctor wants her to stay in the hospital for observation," John explained. "But if she keeps doing as well as she is, he said she can come home in a few days."

"I agree with that prognosis wholeheartedly. I know your mother, John. Jenny will mend better under her own roof." Aunt Al paused and tapped her teeth with her fingernail. "I hope I did the right thing restricting the guest list tonight. I wasn't sure how to approach this evening. I'm sure Daniel will want to meet the entire family, but I thought it would be harrowing enough without entertaining a roomful of children, too."

"He's planning on staying on Nantucket, Aunt Al. He can meet the kids later."

Vindicated in her decision, Aunt Alexandra beamed. "Splendid! Let's join the others, shall we?"

John offered Sarah his arm and they followed Aunt Alexandra across a parquet floor into the living room. As ostentatious as it was, Sarah loved every inch of the old house. The living room ran the entire length of the first floor and French doors framed a subtly-lit limestone terrace. A log fire crackled in the veined marble fireplace that was tucked between floor-to-ceiling shelves packed with regiments of leather-bound books. Overstuffed couches and brightly-patterned chairs were scattered in conversational groupings around the room. The couches and chairs were occupied by Jarad relatives, and for the first time in her island experience, Sarah recognized every single person in the room.

Mary Rose stood to join them and gestured at the ambiance. "Gathering ideas for your new house? Quite a palace, isn't it?"

"I love this house," Sarah confessed. "But the style is a little grand, for me."

"Good God, I hope so." John rolled his eyes. "Or we'll need to call T.B. May and start over."

"Where's Danny? Didn't he come with you?"

"He's with Micah. We think they might have stopped along the way."

Uncle Jim Starbuck strolled by, doing duty with a silver tray. "John? Sarah? Can I get you a beverage?"

"I'll take a whiskey, Uncle Jim," John stated. "Honey, what will you have?'

"Whiskey? John, you don't drink whiskey."

"Tonight, honey, I'd like a whiskey. Is that a problem?"

"No," Sarah's tone voiced her doubt; if anything, John normally drank beer. "I'll have ginger-ale, Uncle Jim. Thank you."

Mary Rose sipped her wine. "So, how are the house plans coming? Have you two decided anything yet?"

"T.B. May is drawing up the blueprints for us, if that's what you mean."

Mary Rose placed one hand on her hip. "Yes, Mr. Snappy, that is what I meant. As long as we're being direct, I guess I also wanted to know if you've decided to sell the property?"

"We're going with George's offer. No one else comes near it."

"That's so great! I'm so happy for you! John, you're rich!"

"Mary Rose, keep it down, will you? We haven't told anyone else and tonight's not the night to announce it."

"Oh, yeah, right. Shhhh. Don't worry. I won't tell a soul."

Uncle Jim returned, bearing drinks. "Here we go. A gingerale for the young lady, and John, this is for you. Sarah, I heard you have some news for us. Let me offer my congratulations."

"Thank you, Uncle Jim."

"You two have been busy," he winked roguishly. "Ah, how well I remember the pursuits of youth."

"I'm surprised you can remember that far back." Aunt Peggy, Uncle Jim's wife, joined in. "Sarah, let me add my congratulations, too. It's wonderful to have more children in the family. There's really nothing quite like their energy to keep you feeling young. As a matter of fact, personally, I think it's a shame Alexandra didn't invite the children tonight. This was supposed to be a family gathering."

"My dear," Uncle Jim remonstrated. "Alexandra's concerned about her antiques."

"Things, Jim, they're just things." Aunt Peggy airily waved her hand. "Things can be replaced but family is priceless."

"You might feel differently if some of these 'things' were yours."

"I'm sorry, dear. Did you say something?"

"Nothing." Uncle Jim wiped the corners of his mouth and studied the ceiling. "Nothing."

Aunt Peggy turned her focus to her nephew. "John, you're quite the fortunate young man. We also heard about Uncle Ethan's bequest. Tell me, will you continue to work for the police?"

"My dear," Uncle Jim interrupted. "That is John's job."

"I know that, Jim, I know that. I just thought, you know, that with Ethan's inheritance and all, John might want to retire from that particular line of work."

"I'm a little young yet to retire, Aunt Peg."

"Well, you know, John, now might be a good time to get out. This island's certainly not as safe as it used to be, especially with all these foreigners moving here. You heard they robbed Mindy Butterfield's house and stole her silver?" Aunt Peggy quivered with indignation. "Some of it was heirloom! She'll never be able to replace it."

John swirled his drink. "We'll find out who did it, Aunt Peg. Chances are it was someone local."

"Local's not much better." Uncle Jim reached for his pipe pulled a bag of tobacco from his waistcoat pocket. "I don't know what's come over this island lately. People have changed. They've forgotten the fundamental values behind brotherhood and community."

"Maybe, John," Sarah made a suggestion. "Maybe you should see what Eddie Farrar's been up to lately."

Mary Rose glanced over, curious. "Why pick on Eddie?"

"Because he was driving a brand-new truck and he told me the money was unexpected. It was the strangest thing, really. He was like, crowing about it."

"It wouldn't surprise me a bit to catch that man out a thief," Aunt Peggy stated. "His family's been a disgrace for three generations."

John frowned. "That is odd. Eddie's never had money before."

"Does Eddie have a record?"

"Honey, now you are digging. I do remember something from years ago, but I don't think it was burglary…"

"Don't you remember?" Mary Rose replied. "Eddie got busted for possession of marijuana."

Aunt Peg gasped. "I never heard that!"

"Well, I did; it was the talk of my senior class. And it wasn't a dime bag, either; I heard they found a five-hundred pound bale in the shed behind Eddie's house. And Richard Robey was walking around school looking green for a week, too, petrified the police were coming for him next. Word was he and Eddie found the bale floating in the Sound and they fished it out together."

"Is that why Richard left Nantucket?" Sarah asked.

"No, that came later when he wasn't just selling pot, he was pushing heroin."

"Mary Rose!"

"Well, it's true. Heroin is what got Sheriff Toohey's attention." Mary Rose turned toward the door. "Wait a second. I think they're here."

"Excuse me, people." Aunt Alexandra sang, sailing across the floor. "I'll go greet our guest."

"Quick, John," Uncle Jim removed his pipe from his teeth. "You're the investigator. Are you convinced this guy really is your brother?"

"It looks pretty good so far, Uncle Jim, but I'm going to ask for testing. There's dental records, DNA. But we haven't had time to do anything yet."

"I heard Jenny recognized him in the hospital yesterday," Aunt Peggy countered.

"She did, Aunt Peg, but Mom's on some heavy medication; she may not be thinking clearly. Personally, I'm waiting to see the test results."

Aunt Alexandra's heels warned the family of her approach. Everyone stood, as if to greet a royal presence. Sarah glanced around and noticed that curiosity and anticipation were apparent on every face.

"Tommy!" Great-Aunt Tindy grappled with her cane. "Help me with this thing. I want to stand where I can see him."

Danny entered the room, standing between his aunt and his brother. He looked pale but resolute. "Hello, uhm, everyone. I can't tell you how happy I am to be here."

"My dear." Aunt Alexandra patted his arm. "These are your adult relatives; you can meet the children later. Ladies and gentlemen, allow me to re-introduce – Daniel Carrick Jarad."

Standing among the roomful of Jarad relatives, Sarah noticed that Danny's physical resemblance was remarkable. From across the room, she heard Great-Aunt Daisy draw the same conclusion. "He certainly looks right," the elderly woman acknowledged. "He has the Jarad eyes."

"He's short," Great-Aunt Tindy noted. "Looks like improper feeding to me."

Aunt Alexandra nudged Danny forward and began to work him around the room. "You've already met some members of this group, Daniel. John and his wife Sarah, your sister Mary Rose, and your Aunt Peggy and Uncle Jim Starbuck."

Danny smiled shyly. "John, Sarah, it's good to see you again."

"Welcome back," John took his brother's hand. "You'll get quizzed on our names later."

"I should take notes. Sarah, you look gorgeous as always."

"You've got the Jarad charm," she smiled. "Welcome home. This is your older sister, Mary Rose."

"Don't rub it in. Hello, Danny." Mary Rose reached to shake her brother's hand and stopped herself. "Oh to hell with it." She wrapped Danny in an embrace. "I'm so glad to see you! My husband Matt is at home with our three boys, but I want you to come over and meet us all, once you feel more settled."

"Thank you. I'll do that."

"I'm your Aunt Peggy." The plump older woman almost curtsied. "Your father Jack was my older brother. And this is my husband, Jim."

"Jim Starbuck," the older man stepped forward. "Call me Uncle Jim."

"Thank you, Uncle Jim, Aunt Peggy. It's nice to see you both."

Aunt Alexandra led Danny toward the two Jarad great-aunts who were waiting expectantly. Uncle Tommy stood unbending behind his mother.

"Daniel," Aunt Alexandra gestured. "These two ladies are your grandfather Ike's sisters. Daisy Jarad and Lucinda Jarad. And this is Daisy's son, Tom."

Danny gently took Aunt Daisy's knuckled hand. He smiled winningly. "Can I call you Aunt Daisy?"

"My dear, dear boy." The elderly woman's resolve visibly melted. "I insist on it. You were a great favorite of our brother Ethan, you know. It's a shame he isn't here to see this day."

"Well, send him over, Daisy," Great-Aunt Tindy stirred restlessly. "Let me have a look at him. My eyes aren't what they used to be."

"One moment more, Sister." Great-aunt Daisy patted his hand. "Daniel, this is my son, Tom. Tom is your father's first cousin. That makes you two second cousins."

"Tom is our only double Jarad," Aunt Alexandra offered. "Both his mother and father shared the Jarad surname. They were only distantly related, of course."

"Distant, very distant." Uncle Tommy repeated, reaching to shake Danny's hand. "Tom Jarad. Nice to meet you."

"It's nice to meet you, too." Danny nodded pleasantly. He turned and bowed. "And Great-aunt ... Tindy? I've been wanting to meet you."

Great-aunt Tindy's eyes narrowed. "You have the right look, young man, I'll grant you that. But don't try to work your charm on me. I'll make up my own mind, in my own time, thank you very much."

"I wouldn't want it any other way."

Aunt Alexandra took Danny's arm and steered him toward the last familial group. "And last but not least, your sister Jackie, your brother Pete and his wife Anne, and your Uncles George and Edward."

"I've got a lot of family." Danny smiled. "Jackie? It's nice to meet you."

"Danny?" Jackie's smile wobbled. "I want to believe it's you, I really do, but I'm having a hard time. You were gone for so long."

"I know it." Danny's eyes teared up. "Jackie, this is hard for me, too. We'll just have to give it some time. Okay?"

"But where were you?" Jackie insisted. "Where did you go?"

"I'll explain it all in a minute, I promise. Let me say hello to everyone, first." He turned to greet the remaining family members. "Pete, right? Micah said you'd be here."

"Hello, uhm, Danny." Pete blinked rapidly. "It's good to have you home. This is my wife, Anne."

Anne, a petite blonde, smiled. "Nice to meet you. Welcome home."

"George Jarad." A distinguished older man stepped forward and took Danny's hand. "Your father Jack was my brother. And this is your other uncle, Tristram."

"Ed. Call me Ed. Danny, welcome home. Glad you're back among the fold."

Aunt Alexandra breathed an exaggerated sigh of relief. "Well, that's everyone. You probably never thought you'd get through them all!"

"I am feeling overwhelmed," Danny admitted. "But I'm happy to meet everyone. Of course, right now, I'm just praying Mom gets better and maybe later, when everything calms down a little, I can get to know everyone better."

"Plenty of time for that," Aunt Alexandra nodded. "Jim, perhaps you could check on drinks?"

"Of course." Uncle Jim rubbed his hands. "Danny? I'll bet you could use something. Name your poison."

"Actually, um, Uncle Jim, I am a little dry. Got a beer?"

"Coming up. Anyone else need a splash while I'm up?"

Formalities over, the group relaxed. Micah crossed over to join John and Sarah by the fire. "I think that went well, all things considered."

"At least he's holding up." Mary Rose studied Danny as he chatted with his uncles. "You have to give him credit. It took a lot of nerve to walk into this room."

"He said he wasn't nervous," Sarah said. "I talked to him this morning. He said all he wants to do is get back with the family. Well, here he is; he got his wish."

"Great-aunt Daisy was on the mark," Mary Rose admitted. "Look at him. He fits right in."

Overhearing the remark, Great-aunt Tindy leaned forward. "Looks are all very well, my girl, but I'd like to see some proof."

"Hear, hear." Uncle Tommy agreed. "I'm glad to see I'm not the only one who doubts this young man's veracity."

"I'm not saying I doubt him, Tom," Great-Aunt Tindy frowned. "I'm saying I'd like to see some proof."

"Well, I'm not buying any of it." Uncle Tommy harrumphed, swirling his drink. "This person shows up here, no proof, no nothing, and we're just supposed to believe he's Jack's boy?"

"Tom, lower your voice," his mother hissed. "This isn't a town meeting."

"No, he's right." Danny moved back to the center of the group. "He has a right to doubt me; you all do. I know my story sounds unbelievable. I can hardly believe it myself, especially what's happened to me the last few days."

"So what did happen to you?" Uncle Tommy challenged. "Why don't you tell us that."

"Sure, I'll tell you what I can. I'll tell you what I remember." Danny shrugged. "But I have to warn you, there are gaps. I don't remember everything. My therapist said I probably never will. You have to understand, when you get trapped in a place like I was, a place where you're helpless, where you lose all track of time, reality goes blank. When I try to remember some things, all I get is static. It's like listening to a bad radio."

Jackie spoke up. "So you've seen a therapist?"

"Oh, sure. I had to go; the Court ordered it. It was a condition of my foster care, to help me sort through my uhm, fear. And rage. I have a lot of rage. But the last time I went voluntarily because I started having these dreams. My therapist tried regression hypnosis and that's what brought me here."

"Hypnosis?" Uncle Tommy plunked his drink on an end-table. "What kind of dog and pony show is this?"

"Tom!" Aunt Alexandra glared. "Would you please be quiet? I'd like to hear what Daniel has to say."

"So what did happen?" This time it was Pete. "How'd you get off-island?"

Danny swallowed heavily. "I was kidnapped."

"We never got a note," Uncle Tommy argued. "We never heard one peep about ransom."

"I wasn't kidnapped for ransom." Danny clenched his fists. "The man who took me didn't want money. He wanted…me."

The roomful of Jarads fell silent until Jackie whispered: "No one tried to help you?"

"There wasn't anyone. And Cahill, he was the kidnapper, said he'd kill me if I tried to get away. He would have, too, I know he would have. He could have done it. He beat me pretty bad when he felt like it anyway." Danny stared at the floor. "We figured out that I was with him for about four years. All I know is it was a long time. It was day, after day, after day, after day."

"Sweet Lord Jesus," Aunt Peggy breathed.

"Then one day, Cahill brought another kid downstairs. That's when I knew he was going to kill me. I wasn't even scared anymore; it was like I was waiting for it to happen, for it to be over with. But he ignored me; he was only interested in the new boy." Danny wiped his eyes. "The new kid, his name was Brian, and he said I could go live with him if I helped him get out of the cage. That's what finally got me mad enough to try to do something. You see, Brian could still remember who he was, he could still remember his family, and I couldn't remember anything anymore. My memory was gone. Everything was blank." Danny shifted uneasily. "So the next time Cahill came downstairs, I hit him and we got out of there. Brian and me, we ran. We ran until the cops picked us up. They let Brian call his family in Philadelphia. He wanted me to go with him, but I couldn't. I didn't want to go to his house, I wanted to go back to mine. But I couldn't remember where my house was. I couldn't remember my name. I had nothing to give them. So the cops stuck me in Juvenile Detention until Social Services found me a foster home, and then I went to live with a family in Brooklyn, New York, and that's where I've been ever since."

The room was silent. Everyone jumped when Uncle Tommy slowly began to applaud. "Now that's a great story! No doubt about it. What a work of fiction! But I still say there is no proof that this young man is Daniel Jarad."

"For the love of God, Uncle Tommy, will you leave him alone?!" Jackie trembled with anger. "Hasn't Danny been through enough?"

John gestured for silence. "Wait one minute. We can get proof. I have the original dental records." He glanced at his brother. "Would you be willing to do that? To see a dentist to prove who you are?"

"I already know who I am." Danny's angry eyes challenged the group. "I know it. But I'll do whatever it takes to prove it to you."

"Then that's where it stands for now." John's sternness overrode Uncle Tommy's protest. "I'll make an appointment with the dentist first thing tomorrow, and we'll settle this for sure."

"I'm ready now," Danny replied.

CHAPTER TWELVE

Over the years, Sarah had seen her share of hangovers, and the two men slumped at the kitchen table were exhibiting all the classic symptoms. She noted Danny's pallor and John's bloodshot eyes and deliberately lowered her voice. "How late did you two stay out last night? I didn't hear you come in."

"I don't remember looking at the clock," John groaned.

"Might have been three, maybe four." Danny used both hands to slide a can of tomato juice from the fridge. "Thanks for letting me sleep on your couch, man. I appreciate it."

"Thank you for driving me home."

Sarah stopped munching on her toast. "Danny was driving? John, where were you?"

Danny sniggered. "Hanging his head out the window singing 'Born to Run'©."

"Oh my God, I hoped that was you." John rubbed his face. "Please, honey, don't yell. Handing him the keys was the last sensible thing I remember doing. Did Micah get home okay?"

"I think so. He left at midnight. Said he wanted to go running this morning." Danny rummaged through a drawer. "Is there a can opener somewhere?"

"It's electric. On the counter next to the toaster." Sarah moved to his side. "Here. Do you want me to make you a bloody?"

"You read my mind." Danny relinquished the can of juice. "Thank you. You're a doll."

Both men cringed as Sarah used the blender to mix tomato juice and vodka, hot sauce, black pepper, a teaspoonful of horseradish, a splash of bottled clam juice, and a squirt of fresh lemon. She poured the drink into a tall glass with ice and handed it to Danny with an apology. "We're out of celery, so you won't get your salad, but that should work."

"It looks great." He took a tentative sip. Sipping it again, he held it to one side and gave a low, appreciative whistle. "You know what? That's terrific."

"Don't be so surprised." John rose unsteadily to refill his coffee mug. "I met her in a bar."

"Speaking of work," Sarah asked. "Are you going in today?"

"Not like this," John stated flatly. "First coffee, then shower. Big shower."

"When you go into town I'd like to go with you. Can I borrow your truck? I want to pick up a few things for your Mom before she gets home; milk, bread, juice, you know. Maybe we should think about dinner, too. How about steak and salad?"

"I can't think about food right now," he groaned.

Danny raised the pitcher. "John? Can I pour you one of these? It's helping."

"Shoot me first." He stood slowly. "I'd better go get ready. This is going to take awhile. Oh, and honey, call Mark Scanlon, will you? And see if he has time for us this morning?"

"Sure thing."

"Thank you. I'll be back."

Sarah watched her husband shuffle toward the stairs and experienced a vision of John as an old man. She pushed the vision to imagine him fat and bald and stifled a giggle.

Danny sipped his drink, holding it with both hands. "I feel sorry for the dentist. He may not like my breath this morning. We'll need to go by the house first so I can get cleaned up before we go."

"Okay. Let me see what time Mark has available." She looked up the number in her address book and reached across the counter for the phone. Missy Scanlon, Mark's wife and dental hygienist, answered on the second ring, and Sarah explained their request.

"You need Mark to do what?" Missy marveled.

"We need to see if he can confirm an identification for us based on a dental record."

"Well, I guess he could do that. Let me go him. Mark?" Missy put Sarah on hold and muzak filled her ear. "Sarah? Mark says that's fine although I've never heard of such a thing. Let me check his book. How's ten-thirty? We can fit you in then. Does that work for you?"

"Ten-thirty sounds great. We'll see you then." Sarah hung up the phone and returned to her tea. It was cold.

"I am so ready to get this done," Danny leaned forward on his elbows. "Maybe it's just me, but I don't think everyone was convinced by what I said last night."

"You were gone a long time, Danny. It's a leap for some people to make."

"I wish they'd get over it." He rotated his glass on the tabletop. "It's not like I'm asking them for anything."

"Seeing Mark will help. If he can give you a positive I.D. maybe that will convince the doubters."

"Will it convince you?" He looked up. "Will you accept my dental record as proof?"

Caught by the direct nature of his question, Sarah blushed. She had spent a considerable amount of time pondering the uncertainty of Danny's identity, and had finally decided that choosing not to decide until after the dental check was enough of a decision to make. But now, put on the spot, she realized she wasn't being fair. Danny had mustered the courage to step forward and claim his family, and he deserved the courage of a straight answer from her.

She reconsidered the facts. Danny's horrible story seemed plausible and physically he fit in with the rest of the family. If Mark Scanlon introduced positive dental evidence into the mix, what would her answer be?

"Yes," Sarah decided. "I will accept the dental evidence as proof."

"Thank you!" Danny slapped the tabletop. "I'm going to win every member of this family one vote at a time if I have to!"

The shower squeaked off and they heard John pad across the loft upstairs. "In case anyone's wondering," he announced. "I'm feeling better."

"Rehydration is the key." Danny tipped back and emptied his glass.

"Do you want some food to go with that? We have cold cereal or I could fix you some eggs, if you like."

"No, thanks. I'm all set. This'll do me." He emptied the pitcher. "Sarah, let me ask you a question. You've been to the Jarad house. Have you ever stayed there overnight?"

"Sure we did. Last September. John and I stayed there until we found this rental. Why?"

"This is going to sound stupid, but there was more to me staying here last night than driving home alone." Danny picked his cuticle. "If I'm going to stay here, I'm going to have to find my own place pretty quick. I know it's free, but that house creeps me out. Yesterday, when I was shaving, the bathroom door swung open by itself. I jumped out in the hallway so fast I dropped my towel."

Sarah laughed. "Don't take it personally. That house was put together in so many different pieces nothing is plumb. If you forgot to latch the door, a truck rumbling by outside could have made it swing open."

"I'd buy that except for one thing." Danny narrowed his eyes. "When I was standing in the hallway it swung shut. I was wet, and naked. If there was a draft, I would've felt it."

"Micah was there. Did he notice anything?"

"He was downstairs, and when I told him about it he said 'odd things happen in old houses'. You know Micah. He told me not to worry. You know, I've noticed he doesn't have a lot of imagination. But I do, and Sarah, before I jumped I swear I saw something standing behind me in the mirror."

Sarah shivered. She had experienced enough psychic episodes of her own to understand the conviction in Danny's tone. "I believe you, but think about it this way. If it is a spook, it has to be someone related to you. Seven generations of Jarads have lived in that house. Maybe it was a relative trying to welcome you home."

"Maybe." Danny laughed nervously. "Anyway, don't tell John. It sounds stupid in the daytime. He'll think I'm wacked."

"He's heard worse. He lives with me." Sarah collected the dirty coffee mugs, placed them in the sink and filled them with tap water. "I guess I'm next." She passed John on the narrow staircase. "You look sharp. I won't be a minute."

"She's the only woman I know who really means that," John remarked, disconcerted by his missing coffee mug. He opened the cupboard, selected a clean mug, and finished the coffee. "I heard you say just now you wanted to stay on island. Do you mean it?"

"Yeah, there's nothing for me to go back to. If this is where my family is then this is where I want to stay."

"You should tell Mom that when you see her today. That's just the kind of news that could help her recovery."

"Sure. Do you think she'll be getting out soon?"

"In a day or two. Dr. Nyugen said her prognosis is good." John fell silent. He had spent a considerable amount of time lately contemplating his new responsibilities: the baby, and Uncle Ethan's bequest, and the time frame required to build their new home. A fresh item had recently moved foremost into his mind.

If Danny was determined to make Nantucket his home, he would need money to live on until he got back on his feet. Just this morning, in the shower, John had made a decision. If Mark Scanlon could prove Danny's identity beyond a reasonable doubt, he would sell the Lost Forest property and give his brother half.

Even as he had formed the idea in his mind, John had felt a weight lift from his shoulders. The rightness of the decision was indisputable. Danny had been Uncle Ethan's favorite, not he, and this was the most sensible, equitable interpretation of Uncle Ethan's Will that he could come up with. It was possible that the property had originally been meant as Danny's birthright. John relaxed. He would not knowingly play Isaac to his brother's Esau.

"Ready when you are," Sarah announced, trooping down the narrow stairs. She collected her purse and her parka and stood in the hallway, looking expectantly between the two slow-moving brothers. "Are we going anytime soon?"

"I'm ready," John nodded, finishing his coffee and absent-mindedly patting his pockets.

Danny dangled the keys. "Oh, John? I've still got them."

"I'll drive," John growled, grabbing the keychain and leading them both outside.

They crossed the driveway and Danny gave Sarah a nudge. "On the way over, John, are you going to offer another selection of classic rock for our listening pleasure?"

John adjusted his sunglasses. "Let's get one thing straight. I'm a little hard-pressed to appreciate humor this morning." He opened his wife's door and left his brother to fend for himself.

"Jesus!" Danny muttered. "You sure are grumpy."

"He's not usually this bad," Sarah confided, leaning back between the passenger seats. "You're a bad influence. He doesn't usually drink hard liquor."

"I'm thinking about taking it up." John started the minivan. "I'm feeling a sudden need. I'm under a lot of pressure."

Sarah settled in. "If you're serious about that, John, we need to talk. And if you want to talk about pressure, in seven months I'm going to experience a pressure so big they call it a contraction."

"She wins." Danny laughed as they drove through town. "I can't wait to get this over with. It'll be nice to have proof to show everyone. And I appreciate staying at the house, but I need to start looking for my own place. Will that be hard, do you think?"

"You're going to have sticker shock when you see our rents," Sarah warned.

John maneuvered the minivan onto Milestone Road. "I think the best idea would be to find a caretaker position. They usually come with an apartment, and if you did want to get another job, at a restaurant like you were saying, you could walk to work."

"That sounds great. Do you know of anyone?"

"We'll put the word out. Sometimes I hear about those openings at the station, but the best answer will be going through Mom's friends. Don't worry. Once Mom gets back on her feet, stand back. She'll organize your life like you won't believe."

"It's her gift," Sarah agreed. "Jenny loves making sure everyone is happy."

The asphalt pavement of Milestone Road cut through a thick pine forest, leading them across the flat sandy width of the island. The hour was early, and the morning sun telegraphed a band of blinding gold directly into their eyes. John adjusted his sunglasses. Sarah noted the wispy gray puddles of fog that floated in the low, boggy hollows among the wind-warped trees. She also noticed a beaded row of individual glittering specks flying along the horizon and recognized them as incoming planes, lining up to land at Ackerman Field to tackle the practical business of supplying an island with goods for the day already begun. She turned in her seat and caught Danny admiring the scenery. "This is the only place in the world where you can order fresh bagels and they fly them in from the mainland, still warm. Or order Chinese takeout from Hyannis and they'll fly it in for lunch."

"It's another world," Danny breathed. "I don't know how you guys can afford this."

"Island economics," John offered. "Tourists come here with spendable income."

"It's a balance, Danny, you'll see," Sarah explained. "You pay more for everything, but you get paid more. Back home you would never pay a hundred dollars for dinner, but here it's understood that's what a dinner costs. Granted, your hundred bucks will get you a meal you'll remember for the rest of your life, but you add that kind of spending up and the profit multiplies geometrically."

"I don't see how that could work," Danny sounded doubtful. "Someone's got to pay."

"Well, you won't be enjoying a lot of hundred dollar meals," Sarah smiled. "You'll eat at home for five. But if you do get work in a restaurant, you'll earn tips, and when a table of eight tips for dinner, that's a hundred bucks right there. And that's just one table. You may have as many as ten tables in a night."

"A thousand bucks? Cash? A night?"

"Not every night," John nodded. "But it is why we attract such a transient population. The kids can work, and play, all summer long and take home some real money."

"What about now? In the winter?"

"It's a little slow right now. But John's right; wait and watch. By the middle of August, even the waitresses will be wearing eighteen-carat gold jewelry."

They passed a black cylindrical water tower as the minivan continued into 'Sconset proper. Slowing, John turned left on Chapel Lane and pulled into the crushed oyster shell driveway of the Jarad house.

Sited in the center of a quarter acre and made private by a tall boxwood hedge, the Jarad house possessed a graciousness that few island homes could rival. As they climbed the wide front steps and entered, they found Micah dressed in his running gear busily preparing his breakfast. Jenny's three-legged cat Ahab was keeping him company, perched on the counter and watching him stir the eggs. Micah squinted in John's direction. "Hey, buddy. How are you feeling? You were quite the wild man last night."

"I'm feeling better, now. Something sure got into me. Must've been a wild hare."

"It was funny to see that side of you again, 'Bro. It's been awhile." Micah carried his plate to the table. "Sarah, Danny, there's coffee and juice. Help yourself."

"I'm fine." Sarah slid along the wooden bench next to her husband, clearing a space on the table to rest her elbows. "I had breakfast. Thanks."

Danny hesitated, peering down the dark hallway. "I think I'll go jump in the shower…"

"Go ahead. It's okay," Micah grinned. "I haven't heard anything unusual this morning, if that's what you're worried about. Take Ahab with you – he'll let you know if there's someone flitting about."

"Micah, don't tease," Sarah said. "This house is enough to scare anybody. Danny, why don't you hang a towel across the mirror? That might help."

"I guess I could try that." Danny squared his shoulders. "But it'll make it tough to shave. Wish me luck."

The phone rang, and Micah reached across the counter to answer. "Hello? Hey, Mary Rose." He gave a wide smile. "That is so great. Tell her we can't wait to get her home. No, no, he just stepped in the shower, but I'll be sure to tell him. John and Sarah are here. Sure, we could do that. Let me ask." He lowered the receiver. "Mary Rose says the doctor is releasing Mom later today. We can pick her up anytime after one o'clock. Can you two be there?"

"You know we will be," John nodded.

Micah raised a finger. "Oh? Really? Are you sure? Okay, well, if that's what she wants. Okay. Bye." He replaced the phone. "Mom doesn't want us to broadcast the news. She's still feeling tired and she wants to just come home and rest. She must really be tired if she's passing on a party." He drummed his fingers on the tabletop. "So you're following through on that I.D., then? Not that I have any doubt, mind you, but call me later and let me know what you find out. It'll be nice to get things on an even keel around here again. I can take more time if I need to, but since Mom's okay I should be getting back to my ship. It's early yet in the year to use all my leave."

Danny padded back into the kitchen barefoot, dressed in jeans and a Go Navy sweatshirt. A white towel was draped around his neck and his hair was still damp.

Micah took one look at him and cocked a sarcastic eyebrow. "All clear?"

"Don't know what you mean," Danny ducked under the towel and rubbed his scalp vigorously. "Thought I would finish getting dressed in here with you guys so I could hear what you were saying."

"Where's Ahab? Wasn't he with you?"

"He hissed and took off, and I wasn't waiting around to see why." Danny draped the damp towel on a doorknob. "There. That's clean enough. Your dentist friend is going to have to take me like this."

"Mary Rose called," Micah reported. "Mom's being released later today."

"Today? Oh my God, that's terrific! Will we be done in time to meet her?"

"I don't see why not. The dental check shouldn't take more than an hour."

"I'll meet you at the hospital." Micah rose and added his plate to the stack of dirty dishes in the sink. "I should straighten up around here first. Mom is definitely not healthy enough for my version of bachelor living."

Sarah took a look at Jenny's normally immaculate kitchen and agreed. "No kidding. This mess will put her back in the hospital."

"Never fear," Micah clapped his large hands together. "Ship shape and Bristol fashion by one o'clock, guaranteed. I'll see you guys later."

As they trooped back outside, John looked at the sky and frowned. "I don't know. That looks like snow to me."

Danny shivered and turned up his collar. "Have I told you how much I'm enjoying Nantucket? The wonderful climate, and all the friendly people?"

John started the truck. "Then you're in for a treat. You're about to meet our friendly dentist."

As they drove back to town, John peered through the windshield and kept a weather eye on the sky. The wind had turned gusty, whipping the pines and pushing a line of banked gray cloud inland from the sea. A lone in-line skater, wearing black- and red-striped gear raced home along the paved bike path, arms pumping a rhythmic two-count beat.

"I hope he makes it home," Sarah noted. "He took a chance, coming out on a day like this."

"Joey Sousa," John replied. "He's that dedicated. I've seen him skating in a Force Three gale."

John circled the rotary and followed the road right onto Orange Street. In this corner of the island the development had a commercial strip-mall flavor to it, housing as it did a lawn and garden center (shuttered for the season) and a Szechwan/Korean restaurant struggling under its promise of an all-you-can-eat luncheon buffet. A two-bay brick fire station perched caty-corner at the intersection, housing a pair of classic hook-and-ladder fire engines suitable for any children's birthday party or Independence Day parade.

John slowed and turned left into a small parking lot. He parked and reached under his seat to retrieve Danny's case file. "Ready?"

"As ready as I'll ever be."

The weak winter sun hadn't put a dent in the sidewalk's icy surface, and they crunched across gritty rock salt before reaching the double glass doors. As they entered the dentist's sterile waiting room, Sarah wrinkled her nose at the metallic smell. Dentistry was a science nowadays, with no real pain anymore, but that coppery tinge still made her break out in a sweat. Maybe it was disinfectant, but it smelled like fear to her.

Mark Scanlon, the dentist, stood behind the reception counter. He peered over the top of his glasses. "There you are, John. Your phone call sounded interesting. Is this the young man in question?"

Danny reached out his hand. "Yes. Nice to meet you."

"No need to be nervous. This is a simple yes or no proposition." The dentist tapped a pen against one palm and handed Danny a clipboard. "Before we get started, I need you to sign a Release of Information and Indemnification Form."

"What's this for?"

"It's a legal release protecting my practice if I make an unpopular determination."

"Unpopular determination?" Danny grinned and scribbled his signature. "Is that a nice way of saying so I don't sue you if I don't like what you say?"

"Close enough." Mark checked the signature and returned the clipboard to the countertop. "John, did you bring the dental record?"

"Right here," John nodded, handing over the file.

"Then come on back." The dentist led them down a corridor into a side room, scanning the file as he went. "Here we are. Young man, take a seat."

Danny eased himself into the chair. "I hope you can help us with this. It's important that we know for sure."

"I can imagine." Mark rifled through the folder. "That's odd. Halliday usually included X-rays with his patient files. John, do you have them?"

"No, those notes are all we have. Why? Is that a problem?"

"Not to worry. Halliday was a thorough old buzzard. I can use his notes." The dentist peered at the mint-green document. "The only difficulty will be that the Daniel Jarad from this chart and the Danny Jarad sitting in my chair right now only share twelve permanent teeth. The upper front four, lower front four, and each of the upper and lower permanent molars. But there are two fillings indicated on the chart I can check."

"But will it be proof?" Danny gripped the armrests. "We need real proof."

"They've identified Vietnam veterans with less." The dentist snapped on a pair of membranous latex gloves. "Let me see. I need to look for one large amalgam filling, lower right first permanent, and a smaller amalgam filling in the first permanent, upper left. That larger filling is odd, especially in a child. Indicates a congenital defect to me. However," Mark adjusted a protective mask and flicked on an overhead light. "We shall see what we shall see."

Sarah heard a metal probe ping a filling and gooseflesh crawled across her forearms. Seated in the chair, Danny looked resolute, his eyes closed and his nostrils flaring as he breathed through his nose.

"This looks promising. Both fillings are here." Mark stepped back and tugged down his mask. "Let me see if I can explain this. Each permanent tooth has five surfaces, four sides and a top. Halliday's chart indicated a large filling in the first permanent involving three of those five surfaces. The mesial, occlusal and distal. The smaller filling, the upper left first permanent involved only the distal and occlusal. Are you following me?"

"Sure." His patient squirmed. "But is it proof?"

The dentist tapped the chart. "Your teeth certainly fit the description. But I'm a little confused about the tarnish. Those fillings look new to me."

"They are. My dentist back in Brooklyn had to drill them out last summer. He said the fillings were so old they were beginning to leak, and if I didn't replace them I would need root canals. I wasn't going to go through that shit if I didn't have to."

"That's certainly justifiable in fillings this old. I've recommended the same procedure myself. John, can you guarantee that these dental records have never left your hands?"

"They've been in the police archive for the last twenty years. I was the first person to ask for them."

"Then, according to these records, I'd have to say this is indeed Daniel Jarad."

"Yes!" Danny slipped from the chair and stood. "I'd like to see anyone deny me now! John, man, I never doubted it for a second. When I saw you standing on that pier, I knew! I knew I was home."

The dentist removed his gloves. "I wish more of my cases were like this. This has been the most gratifying appointment I've had in years."

"I'll bet." Danny laughed, and reached over to shake Mark's hand. "Thank you, man. I mean it. Thank you. I owe you more than you'll ever know."

"Glad I could help. And thank you. You've given me something to talk about at the dinner table. This story should be worth a couple of outside invitations. My wife will be pleased."

John felt his spirits lift, imagining his mother's delight when she heard the news. What better gift could he ever offer her than the news that her missing son was home? Never before had he realized what a burden the unknowing had been. Even when he hadn't been aware of it, the weight had been there, pressing on him. Now, suddenly, it was gone. It was a miracle. He felt thirty pounds lighter. "We have an answer," he whispered. "We finally have an answer."

"I know, I know," Danny smiled. "I feel like I've been set free."

John laughed, hearing the relief in his brother's voice. Everything was going to be alright. Of course they would have to give Danny time to adjust, but things would work out. They all just needed to give it some time. He led the way back to the truck, and drove to the hospital in a haze of bright imagination. John parked next to an ambulance, and Danny was the first one out of the truck, dancing toward the entrance. "I've got proof, I've got proof," he sang. "I can't wait to tell Mom!"

Sarah laughed at the pantomime. "Go on, then," she urged. "We'll meet you inside."

"No, I'll wait for you. I want all of us to be together to tell Mom the news."

They encountered a receptionist in the front hall, who looked up, surprised to see them enter. "I'm sorry. Your mother isn't ready yet. She won't be released until one."

"We know we're early, and we'll come back," John explained. "But we have some news for her that just can't wait."

"How many of you people are there? I've never seen so many family members in my life."

"We'll get out of your hair today," Sarah added sympathetically, following the two brothers down the hall. John reached Jenny's room first and knocked softly on the hollow door. "Mom?" He repeated his tap. "Hello?"

They entered and caught Jenny sitting up in bed, holding a small hand mirror and trying to comb her hair. "John? I thought that was you."

"Mom? I brought a visitor."

"Just a moment." Jenny groped along a side table. "Let me get my lipstick."

"You don't need it," Danny smiled. "You look fine to me."

"Mom, we just came from the dentist, and Mark confirmed the dental record. It's a positive I.D., Mom. Danny's home."

"Thank God," Jenny raised her arms to her youngest son. "My baby boy. It's about time!"

"Mom, there's more." John cleared his throat. "Danny says he wants to stay here, and make Nantucket his home…"

"Is that true? You've decided to stay?"

"Yes," Danny nodded. "I want to stay here and start a new life."

"Oh, son, I'm so happy. I couldn't ask for more. You'll love it here, I promise. Just wait and see."

"I already love it here, Mom. There's something about this place that already feels like home."

"You know, I've been thinking," John interrupted. "Danny, you don't know this, but recently I inherited some property. It hasn't made sense to me why Uncle Ethan left the property to me, but now I think I can find a purpose in what he did. Sarah and I have already decided to sell the property, and once we do, I'd like to give you enough money to help you get a fresh start."

"That's very generous, John, but if you do, it would have to be a loan. I'd pay you back, every penny."

"I don't think you could pay me back even if you wanted to, because I want to give you half – and half of it is nine million dollars."

"John!" Sarah gasped.

"Son!" Jenny echoed Sarah's surprise. "Have you thought this through?"

"I swear to God it's all I have been thinking about! I've been going over and over this in my head – and I decided that if Mark Scanlon could find proof, real proof, then this was what I was going to do."

Danny looked dazed. "You can't do that, I mean, can you? It's your property."

"That's exactly right, it is my property, and this is what I'm going to do with it." John ran his fingers through his hair. "I can't stop thinking that the property was meant for you, Danny, not me. But Uncle Ethan isn't here to ask, and I have to decide what is right. And I think sharing the property with you is the right decision to make."

"Son," Jenny cautioned from her bed. "I'm afraid you're going to hear about this one."

"I'm sure I will," John crossed his arms, resolute. "So be it."

Chapter Thirteen

John stood outside the South Water Street station, checked his watch, and sighed. Eleven-thirty, half the day gone, and he hadn't even started 'working' yet. He crossed the sidewalk, wondering if he had spent too much time with his family lately. Was that why it felt so damn good to get back to work?

His home life lately seemed to be one continuing crisis. He found himself looking forward to the chance to dig in and get some real police work done. At least with his job he knew what to expect; the phone rang, he interpreted the emergency and reacted with what he believed was a level of professional competence. It took an extreme situation to pitch him off his feet, and he felt some small pride in that fact. Not to mention the relief he felt when his shift was done and he could hand the responsibilities over to a trusted fellow officer and simply walk away.

He paused in front of the plexiglass safety barrier, waiting for Tina Bradley to notice him. The morning shift was ending, and the room behind the barrier was still crowded with an assorted half-dozen of his favorite compatriot grumblers. Earning the right to work the day shift required at least eight years seniority, and that substantial amount of time had honed these police veterans into paragons of individual eccentricity. He caught Tina's eye and she buzzed him in.

"Morning, Lieutenant." Sergeant Jim Parsons nodded, standing next to the coffeemaker and struggling with a sealed gold-foil packet. "Damn and blast. How are you supposed to open these fool things?"

Tina hovered protectively over her console, communicating through body language her desire to intercept the impending ground coffee explosion. "Here, Jim, let me do that. Please. I said I'd get to it."

"Why does this have to be so difficult?" The sergeant doggedly refused to surrender, punching the packet's seams with his thick forefinger. "I survived the evacuation of Saigon, I should be able to make a damn pot of coffee."

"Morning, John," C.J. Allamand, their most recent daytime recruit, covered her yogurt container with one hand. "Prepare to take cover. This could get ugly."

Her remark was met by a short, barking laugh from Joe Curly, the eldest and most revered member of the Nantucket police force. Joe Curly was responsible for recordkeeping, and it was the commonly-held belief that if Curly couldn't find something then it could truly be considered lost. He was a bald, spare, weather-beaten old man with a face full of wrinkles and surprisingly sharp periwinkle-blue eyes. He had recently achieved national prominence by rediscovering – in his spare time – an early Herman Melville short story misfiled in the Atheneum archives.

John sat down at his desk, retrieved his favorite pen and began to check the duty roster. "C.J., this says Hank went out with Sam Ketchum. Which loop did they take?"

"North, northwest. Out to Madaket." She finished her yogurt and tossed the container in the trash. "Cooper went out to 'Sconset."

"Visiting that girlfriend of his again at public expense," Curly shuffled by. "His Sally ever finds out what he's up to she'll fillet him so fast he won't even feel it."

"Let's try to avoid that scenario for today, Joe. I'm here looking for a little peace and quiet."

C.J. leaned her hip against John's desk and smiled sympathetically. "Things a little hectic at home?"

"Honestly, C.J., I don't know what's going on. But I can't complain; it's all good things. My Mom's coming home from the hospital, and I've got so many family members on island I'm tripping over them." John sighed. "I had to come to work just to find a little sanity."

"Been there," she nodded. "When my mother's on the warpath..."

"You idiot!" Tina shrieked, and everyone automatically covered their eyes.

John relaxed, and dusted the coffee grounds out of his hair. "Ah, it's good to be back. So, what's going on?"

"It's pretty quiet, but that's a good thing. You should take a look at the court report; there's a pre-trial hearing on Tuesday for that cousin of yours. I thought you'd want to be reminded about it."

"Jacob Foulke? Thanks, I do. Jake's a good kid, and it is his first DUI. I'm going to push for six-month's probation. Who's the judge?"

"Tom Coffin."

"Even better. Tom's reasonable." He paused to identify the source of a persistent metallic tapping and looked over to George Robey standing outside the plexiglass barrier. George was using an open hand and his signet ring to draw attention to himself. This day the developer was nattily attired in a camel-hair coat and a matching Tyrolean hat. "Tina," John called. "Buzz George in for me, will you?"

Tina reached across her console for the security release. "Oh, my. He's good-looking. Is he married?"

"Charming security system," the developer purred, dusting snowflakes from his lapel. "And no, my dear, I'm not. There is hope for you yet."

Tina pretended to swoon. "Be still my heart."

"Come on back, George." John indicated a chair and noticed for the first time in his memory that the developer appeared flushed and ill-at-ease. "Glad you stopped by. I was going to call you, later."

"Has someone made an offer?" George removed his hat and smoothed his hair. "I'd appreciate the chance to counter."

"No, George, no, that's not it at all. My Mom's been in the hospital, and we dropped everything to focus on her."

Tina approached and offered George an encouraging smile. "Can I get you some coffee?"

"Yes, thank you. That would be delightful. Black, with two sugars, please." The developer grinned as the dispatcher drifted off in a cloud of fantasy. "Will Jenny be alright?"

"Yes," John clasped his hands over his belt. "She's coming home later today."

"Splendid. And I heard some other news this morning. Apparently, your brother Daniel has reappeared?"

"Yes, it's amazing. We made a positive I.D. this morning." John nodded. "It's been an interesting week."

"I can imagine. I remember what your family went through the day Daniel disappeared."

"That's right, you were a part of the search party."

"Me and every other man on the island," the developer deferred modestly. "I only did what I could. Did he...did Daniel say where he's been all this time?"

"He doesn't remember much. He grew up with a foster family in New York." John tested the explanation that Danny and the family had agreed upon.

"Well, that's extraordinary. I'm very happy for your family. I know you've been through a lot." George placed both hands on his knees and spread his fingers wide. "But enough about the past, John. We need to discuss the future."

"Right. Well, George, Sarah and I have considered your offer and we've decided to take you up on it."

"Really?" The developer leaned forward, his eyes bright. He pulled a handkerchief from his pocket and blotted his upper lip. "John, this is absolutely the right decision to make. I guarantee you will not be sorry. Now, the next order of business would be to order a percolation test, but that shouldn't pose a problem."

"Here you go," Tina reappeared, carrying a styrofoam cup with both hands. "What's a percolation test?"

"A standard procedure," George accepted the cup. "The county agent visits a subject property and bores test holes before a sale to ensure that no island water rights issues are involved."

"That sounds fascinating." The police-band radio crackled and Tina blatantly ignored it. "Tell me more."

"Tina, excuse me?" John interrupted good-naturedly. "Dispatch? Could you get it?"

"Oh, all right. I'll be right back," Tina promised. "Don't go away."

George smiled. "John, I can see you're busy. Why don't you let me arrange the perc. test? The county agent owes me a favor and I'm sure he'd get right on it if I asked him to."

John considered the offer and thought: Why not? If he let George take care of this detail they could get a jump on closing the sale. "Okay, George, that would be helpful. Thank you."

"Consider it done." The developer refolded his handkerchief neatly and tucked it into his breast pocket. "Now, I can cut you a personal check as a security deposit and get a cashier's check for the remainder at closing unless you'd prefer that I wire transfer the funds to your bank."

"George, George, slow down," John chuckled. "Let's order the perc. test and take it from there."

"John... ?" Tina called, standing next to her receiver. "I'm sorry but I think you'd better get this. There's been an accident."

John turned his chair and connected the speakerphone. "Dispatch. John Jarad."

"John, it's Hank. We're in Dionis. We've got a 10-55." The reception bristled with static. "You'd better get out here, John. It's Eddie Farrar."

Unconsciously, John stood. "What happened?"

"Christ Jesus! Cut himself near in half with his chainsaw. You should see the blood."

"Secure the area," John scrabbled for his keys. "Don't let anyone leave."

"I've got two witnesses here now, and I think Addie Simpson saw it happen; she was here when we arrived. I left her with Sam but she took off while he was puking behind the car. Hell, she's back in Eel Point by now."

"I'm on my way." Automatically, John locked his desk, issuing commands over his shoulder. "Tina, find Paul Jenkins and tell him to meet us in Dionis. C.J., Jim, grab your gear. Let's go."

George Robey rose unsteadily to his feet. "Eddie Farrar is dead? What happened?"

In his haste, John had forgotten the developer. "George, I'm sorry, but I've got to go."

"Of course, John. I understand completely. Go do what you need to do."

He grabbed his parka and led the way outside, choosing Unit Three. Putting the car in gear he backed up, followed by his two supporting officers in number Six. They roared northwest through a residential development, taking a left on Main and heading toward the dunes at Dionis. The accident site wasn't difficult to find. Unit Five was parked, white strobe lights flashing, next to a late model Jeep Wagoneer, and Sam Ketchum was standing with to two lanky teenage boys. All three young men looked ready to faint.

John indicated the surrounding dunes. "Jim, no one gets through here. If we know about this, so does anyone listening on police band radio. I do not want spectators disturbing this site."

"You got it, Lieutenant."

"C.J., come with me." John felt adrenaline coursing in his blood, his customary reaction to an act of violence, accidental or not. He prioritized the need to secure his witnesses before any site investigation. Mistakes were made by rushing the scene, and his training had taught him to temper his natural impetuousness and to keep his mind and eyes open to every possibility. Now that they were on site, it was time to do the job right. He moved toward Sam and the two teenagers and nodded. "Sam, you okay?"

"I'm fine now, Lieutenant. I just wasn't prepared for…that."

"Don't see how you could be, Sam." John felt some sympathy for the younger officer's experience. He could still remember his first accidental death investigation. Fisherman Lars Pederson had fallen overboard and then been dredged up in his own net. Even after eleven years, the image of the drowned man enmeshed in nylon filament was perfectly vivid. "Where's Hank?"

"Over there, uhm, with the body." Sam's voice cracked and he cleared his throat. "He told me to wait here."

"That's good. And you two boys saw what happened?"

"No, sir, we didn't." The shorter boy grimaced, gripping a cellphone. "He was like that when we found him."

"It's foul," his companion agreed. "I'm never eating meat again."

"Shut up, Aaron! Do you want to make me puke?"

John held up one hand. "That's enough. Let's start with names, please."

"Aaron Minette." The taller boy cocked a thumb at his companion. "He's Caleb Hussey."

"Caleb Hussey? Who's your father?"

"Big Mike," Caleb swallowed. "And he's going to kill me when he finds out I'm not in school. Does he have to know about this?"

"Yes, he does. And why aren't you in school?"

"It's our lunch break," Aaron explained. "We decided to go for a ride…"

"We're not allowed to smoke on campus," Caleb explained, still nervous.

"I get it. Well, what did you two see?"

"Nothing really," Aaron gestured. "We were driving and this crazy bitch ran out of the dunes and waved us down. I almost hit her."

"She was totally freaked out," Caleb agreed. "Screaming and everything."

C.J. looked up from her notes. "Which crazy bitch?"

"Addie Simpson," Caleb said. "You should have seen her. She was screaming so much she couldn't even talk. She made us stop and follow her over here and then we found…him." He rubbed his arms. "I knew something was wrong by the smell. All the hair on the back of my neck stood straight up."

"We called you right away, as soon as we saw him." Aaron gestured with his cellphone. "We didn't touch anything."

John scanned the surrounding sand. "Where is Addie now?"

"She took off down the beach," Aaron pointed toward Madaket. "I'll tell you what, that old woman can move when she wants to."

"Did you see anyone else?"

"There was another car," Aaron looked to his friend for confirmation. "But it turned around before it got here."

"They looked lost," Caleb nodded sagely. "Tourists, likely."

"What kind of car was it?"

"I don't know. Something big and dark," Aaron shrugged. "Some kind of SUV?"

"Alright." John nodded. "Officer Allamand is going to take your information, and after she does one of these officers will follow you home. I want you to tell your parents what happened, and tell them I will contact them later today."

C.J. stepped forward. "Let's start with addresses, please."

Satisfied that he could move on, John turned and strode through the sand, stepping over a half-buried section of brick red erosion fence. Jim Parsons was rolling out yellow police tape and blocking the path between the two dunes. John forced himself to slow down and really study the terrain, knowing from experience that subtle indications of an event could be effectively erased in the first few panicky minutes. He noticed that the sand above the tide line, although cold, was too dry and soft to have maintained an effective footprint pattern. Reaching the end of the path, he called out: "Hank?"

"Over here, Lieutenant."

The reply came from his right. John turned, and as he left the shelter of the dunes, the breeze picked up, rustling the dried sea-grass and bearing with it the coppery odor of fresh blood.

The first indication of trouble was a damp ruby-colored stain outlined against the normally beige sand. The stain was the size of a child's wading pool, and John knew with certainty that no human being lost that much blood unless they had severed an artery. Unfortunately, he had seen that pattern once before, at the site of a two-car DUI, and that crash had been fatal.

"We got ourselves a big one this time, John." Although Hank's voice was steady, John knew him well enough to detect the underlying agitation in his tone. "Poor, dumb bastard."

John took a deep, steadying breath and surveyed the area. Eddie Farrar's flame-red Dodge 4X4 was parked in the soft sand below the steep, pebbly bluff. An industrial winch was bolted to its long bed and a quarter-inch steel cable snaked from the winch down to the waterline. A creosote-stained telephone pole had been hooked to the cable, reeled in, and was now resting on dry sand. Three two-foot sections of pole had been sawed off and were stacked next to the truck's right rear tire.

Hank put his hands on his hips. "Would you please tell me what the man wanted with an old telephone pole? You can't even burn the damn thing, the creosote will kill you."

"There's no telling." It was time, and John knelt to observe the fatality.

Eddie Farrar lay on his back, pressed up against the tar black pole. Both hands were clenched around his upper left thigh above an appalling, gaping wound and his plaid jacket was saturated with clotting arterial blood. Fighting the pain, Eddie had dug a hollow in the sand with the heel of his right work boot. His hair was plastered to his scalp and his face was a ghastly mask of drying, bloody splatter. Eddie had died leaving the world one final snarl, and John wondered if the snarl indicated the measure of fear the man had felt while dying. He took a deep breath and looked away.

"I know, it got to me too," Hank agreed. "The man did not die happy."

The chainsaw lay where it had fallen, three feet off Eddie's port side, choked into silence by deep sand. Hank pointed to a fresh split in the pole. "Looks to me like he cut into that spike and the chainsaw bounced back on him. I've heard of such a thing but I've never seen it happen before." Hank dropped his voice. "Hope I never have to see it again."

"You and me both." John stood slowly. He scanned the surrounding beach and noted three distinct lines of tracks. The heaviest path ran from the road through the dunes directly to Eddie's truck, the churned sand patent evidence of the presence of two witnesses and two investigative officers. A separate single line of footprints trudged from the winch well to the water and back again. These single prints were interwoven with a carved s-curve from the steel cable and provided corroborative evidence of Eddie's task.

A third single set of footprints slipped down the side of a dune toward Eddie's truck and vanished into the churned communal path. This set wasn't much smaller than Eddie's, but the prints supplied a different tread. The tread reappeared on firmer sand down by the tidal line, and continued away toward Eel Point. John would need to confirm the facts, but Eel Point did suggest the presence of Addie Simpson.

"Damn fool should have known better than work alone like that, scavenging for as long as he did." Hank shook his head. "What a nasty way to die."

"Nothing nice about it," John agreed. He looked up and noticed Jim Parsons waving his arm.

"Lieutenant," Jim pointed. "The M.E.'s here."

Paul Jenkins, the Medical Examiner for Nantucket County, approached, walking stiffly through the sand and carrying an old-fashioned black leather medical bag. "John, Hank. Who have we got?"

"Eddie Farrar, Paul. Looks like he got careless with his chainsaw."

"I'll say he did. Ooh, that's bad." The Medical Examiner paused, then knelt next to the body. He opened his bag and rolled on a pair of latex gloves, reaching forward gently to probe the wound. He shook his head, then reached up and firmly closed Eddie's staring eyes.

"That is what got him?" Hank asked.

"It looks pretty straightforward." Paul stood and removed his gloves. "Judging from the clotting, I'd say he died within the last hour, maybe hour and a half. He may have had a stroke and that's what triggered the accident, but I won't know that for sure until I get him to the morgue. John, I'm afraid accidental death means an autopsy. You'll need to inform the family." Paul frowned. "I'm not sure who's left over there. You know his father died last November?"

"No, I didn't know that."

"Um-hum. Lung cancer. And I think his sister's remarried. The only person left may be his mother."

"I remember her. Thin, blonde?"

"Bottle blonde, now, I'm afraid." Paul ran his hand through his own silvered hair. "Time catches up to us all. When you see Beryl, will you offer her my condolences?"

"Of course." John drew his sunglasses from his pocket. "I'd better get to it. I don't want her to hear about this from anyone else. It's going to be tough enough as it is."

"And John…" Paul Jenkins indicated the gory display. "You don't have to give her a blow-by-blow. She doesn't need to know how bad this was. I'll get Eddie cleaned up before she has to identify the body."

"You're a decent man, Paul Jenkins."

"It's the least I can do. Beryl has not had an easy life."

John checked his watch. Twelve-forty-five. He returned to his car and drove southeast back to town. Informing families of an accidental death was one of the few duties he did not like doing. Each accident carried its own personal implications, and it was impossible to foretell just how family members would react. During his career he had witnessed an emotional spectrum ranging from an hysterical hiccupping breakdown to a surprising display of visible relief.

He turned right off Madaket Street and followed a curving sandy road south toward Ram Pasture and Hummock Pond. All land on Nantucket was worth something, but this low-lying marshy expanse was about as worthless as any you could find. Brackish sea-water had back-flowed into the local water table and poisoned the vegetation. Depending on the happenstance of elevation, the surrounding pine trees had either yellowed or died.

John pulled onto the Farrar's long pot-holed driveway, surprised that he still so vividly remembered the way. One summer many years past, his older brother Pete had spent every free moment hanging out with Eddie Farrar. Pete had even occasionally allowed his little brother John to tag along. The two older boys were busy rebuilding an abandoned Chevy Nova Eddie had hauled home from the dump, and they had spent every penny they earned and hours more in free labor trying to get the wreck up and running. Then, one day, there had been a falling out between the two older boys – John had never learned why – and Eddie Farrar had drifted out of the Jarad orbit.

He slowed as he approached the house. It wasn't as derelict as Uncle Ethan's had been but the Farrar homestead ran a close second. The front porch hid behind a span of rusted wire screen and bushy, untrimmed evergreens. A washing machine stood abandoned next to the front door, piled high with quarter split wood and cheap plastic flower pots. A low, wooden outbuilding ran the entire length of the backyard and was evidently used for storage, housing as it did a decrepit

Farm-all tractor, several lengths of splintered white PVC pipe and a small pyramid of scrap lumber.

Beryl Farrar appeared in the doorway and it stunned John to see the change fifteen years had made on her appearance. He remembered Eddie's mother as possessing a fragile kind of blonde beauty, but the woman in the doorway was thin and haggard, worn out by toil and disappointment.

Beryl pushed the screened door open and stepped out onto the porch. She held a long, smoldering brown-wrapped cigarette in her left hand; her right hand clutched a can of beer. She was wearing a short terrycloth housecoat that exposed her skeletal knees and rag wool socks on feet stuffed into a pair of men's deer-hide moccasins. She appeared indifferent to the cold.

John stepped out of the car and removed his hat as a gesture of courtesy. "Mrs. Farrar, I'm afraid I've brought bad news. There's been an accident."

"Something's happened to my Eddie." The woman inhaled deeply on her cigarette. "Is he dead?"

"Yes, ma'am, I'm afraid so."

Beryl pursed her channeled lips and hissed a lungful of smoke through her nicotine-stained teeth in a slow steady stream. "How'd it happen?"

"He was working alone and his chainsaw slipped. For what it's worth, it was probably pretty quick."

"I see." Beryl sipped the beer. "So what do you need from me?"

"We need you to come identify the body as the next of kin."

"Poor Eddie." She stubbed her cigarette out against the side of the enameled washing machine. "Well, John Jarad, you'd better come in while I run a comb through my hair. I'll be a minute getting ready."

He slowly climbed the front steps. The porch interior was no less cluttered than the outside yard, filled with crates of returnable glass soda bottles, splintered fishing rods, spools of copper cable and a massive plywood console that housed a cracked television screen. He followed Beryl Farrar into the living room. She set the beer can down on the mantelpiece, reached for her cigarettes and tapped a fresh one out of the pack. John noticed the index and middle fingers of her left hand were stained yellow-brown with nicotine.

Beryl repeatedly flicked her lighter with her left hand until she earned a flame. "You want a beer?"

"No. No, thank you."

"You might think this is strange, but I knew this was coming. My dreams have troubled me lately." She plucked a speck of tobacco off her tongue. "It's that Richard Robey. I tell you, that man is evil. Every time he shows up there's some new kind of trouble."

"Were Richard and Eddie working together this morning?" John was puzzled; he hadn't seen any sign of Richard at the site.

"I don't know that. Eddie left before I got up." She waved John toward a chair and retrieved her beer. "Take a seat. I'll be right with you."

She disappeared into the back of the house as John stood over her furniture. The atmosphere in the room was so contaminated he didn't want to touch anything, let alone sit on the soiled upholstery. All the fabric in the room, the couch, the pillows, even the curtains, had taken on the same bruised hue and John well knew why: a ceramic ashtray, filled to overflowing, was displayed on every available horizontal surface.

He was surprised at how calmly Beryl Farrar was reacting to the news of her son's death. He thought it likely that she either didn't understand what had happened, she didn't care what had happened, or the woman was drunk. Considering the beer can in her hand, he decided the third possibility was the most likely. He crossed his arms and nervously tapped one foot. Glancing down, he noted the splendid pegged pine floorboards gleaming dully beneath his feet.

It took a moment for the salient fact to register: he was standing on six-inch wide, pegged, heart-pine boards. He knelt, pulling back a circular rag rug and ran his hand over the smoothly textured wood grain, feeling a sudden exaltation of truth as his rookie failure was finally vanquished.

He had located the missing floorboards from Tom Weston's house in Squantum.

Eddie Farrar had not only been a scavenger, he had also been a thief.

"Is there something about my floor that interests you?" Beryl Farrar stood framed in the doorway. She had changed into a home-sewn wool suit of turquoise blue and her mouth was shakily outlined in vibrant red lipstick.

"Where did you get this floor?"

"It was a Mother's Day present from my son, years ago." Beryl lit another cigarette. "Eddie knew I liked nice things. When he found them he brought them home for me."

The next question slipped out. "Did you know he stole it?"

"So you say. I say prove it." Beryl shrugged and stepped before a mirror, sighing at her ravaged reflection. "You know, I used to be pretty once. Back home some folks even said I was clever. But from the first day I stepped on this godforsaken island I could see right then what you all thought of me. It was written across your sad, stupid faces. Well, that's your loss is all I have to say. Not one of you every gave me a chance to show you who I was, and my poor kids never got a chance neither." She fumbled with an unseasonable black straw hat, using her right hand to hold it in place and her left to bobby-pin it to her hair. "Well, none of that matters anymore. You can have it all back. I am through with this place."

"I can see why you would want to leave this house." John offered. "Unpleasant memories…".

"I mean I have had all I can take of this goddamn island and all you so-called righteous people!" Beryl glared. "Oh, I know you and your kind, John Jarad. You think you're so much better than the rest of us, that the same rules don't apply. Like that brother of yours, so high and mighty when he caught my Eddie shoplifting parts, but he didn't seem to mind helping my son siphon gas when it was Peter Jarad who needed a free tankful." Beryl coughed a short, bitter laugh. "And let's not forget Ethan Jarad neither. Now there's another one!"

"What did Ethan have to do with you?"

"You don't know about him at all, do you?" Beryl sneered, returning to the mirror and pressing her hat firmly to her head. "Well, Ethan Jarad is the man who convinced my Eddie to drop out of high school and help him with his drug-running. They made a trip twice a week to New Bedford until Ethan Jarad lost his nerve and left my son high and dry." Beryl tugged down a small dotted veil. "I begged Eddie not to do it. I begged him to finish high school and earn his diploma. I warned him – God knows I did – that he'd never get a chance in this life without one. But Ethan Jarad kept waving his easy money and God help him, Eddie was weak."

John gripped his hat. He found it hard to believe Beryl's story and yet, he wondered, what if in his mind Uncle Ethan had only been guilty of 'bending' the rules? There was plenty of precedent for that type of thinking within their family. It had taken his Dad to finally stand up and insist on 'no more' and break that pattern of compromising behavior. Had Uncle Ethan bent the rules, and hired Eddie Farrar to help him do it? "I've never heard one word about it…".

"You want proof? Christ Almighty! Where do you think Eddie got the money for his new truck? Go ask Ethan's lawyer why don't you?! She'll tell you Ethan Jarad left my son twenty-five thousand dollars cash – and every penny of it was blood money, blood money pure and simple, for ruining my sons' life." Beryl opened the snap on her purse with her left hand and angrily stuffed a pack of cigarettes inside. "Do you have any more intelligent questions, Officer Jarad?"

"No," John whispered. "No. I don't have any more questions."

"Well, if we have to go do this thing, let's go." Trembling, Beryl Farrar lit a cigarette from the opened pack on the mantle. Inhaling deeply, she coughed, and looked at John through yellowed, bloodshot eyes. "You can have my house, you can have my land. My daughter's gone and now you've taken my son, too." She checked herself in the mirror one last time and grimaced. "I'm so done with this place I don't even care anymore."

Chapter Fourteen

The wind whistled in across Nantucket Sound past the Brant Point lighthouse and the gray-shingled mansions aligned shoulder-to-shoulder along Cliff Road. The minivan slipped a little on the icy cobblestones and Sarah slowed, taking a left while glancing into brick storefronts rich with subtle indirect lighting, gleaming hardwood floors, and window displays featuring crucified hand-knit three-hundred dollar sweaters.

She smiled at one of the few outdoor signs still permitted by strict local zoning. Grandfathered in and ten-feet high, painted on a brick sidewall, an eight-point compass rose cited distant latitudinal bearings, a fading reminder of the island's maritime history. Nantucket to London: 2,856 nautical miles, 52.6° NE; Rio de Janeiro, 4,105 nautical miles, 152.7° S/SE; Hong Kong, the fabled antipode to their world, 7,023 nautical miles, 354.7° N. And then, lastly, and always the reminder: Island Elevation: 30 ft.

Danny followed her glance and noted the elevation measurement. "So what happens if it rains?"

"We swim." She eased the seatbelt off her belly and gave a passing thought to one effect of global warming: a menacing rise in sea-level. If the worst did happen, Sarah wondered, in the end what would they see? A slowly creeping tidal rise, saltwater lapping under the kitchen door? Cliff-sized slabs of eroding sand toppling into the sea? Or would Nantucket finally fall victim to one apocalyptic hurricane, erased off the map in a single day like doomed Port Royal, Jamaica?

Danny leaned forward and pointed through the windshield. "It still freaks me out to see all this water. When I'm at the house, I forget it's an island, and then I see the ocean again and it blows me away. It's so beautiful and it's right there."

"I know what you mean. I never get tired of it."

Nantucket Harbor sparkled in the distance, a sliver of pewter visible through a screen of evergreens frosted with snow like giant cupcakes. Black-banded gulls with yellow beaks and red legs circled a modern concrete pier. Tethered nearby, a wooden dingy sprouted a fully-decorated Christmas tree, up to and including bulbous colored lights and a gold tin-foil star. "When we first came here, my sister and I used to walk this waterfront for hours admiring the view. We were probably trespassing back through some of these little alleys, but nobody seemed to mind." She focused on the shopping chore ahead. "Have you and Micah used anything up since you've been here? We should restock the house before Jenny gets home."

"I don't think so. Toothpaste and shampoo I brought with me."

"I should have asked Micah for a list. Oh, and don't let me forget to buy orange juice. Jenny likes the kind with extra calcium but without the pulp. Your mother is a very particular person."

"I'll try to remember." Danny shut his door and followed Sarah into the store, passing a cork bulletin board plastered with generations of index cards and hand-made tabbed advertisements. A neon orange slip of paper caught his eye and he paused to read: " 'Lazy GrAss Lawn Care.' Come on! Who're they kidding? That's no typo!"

"Nantucketers have a very dry sense of humor." Sarah wheeled a shopping card around. "You'll notice it more the longer you stay."

"Hey, wait a minute. Look at this." Danny unpinned an index card. "WANTED IMMEDIATELY: ON-SITE CARETAKER. Moderate salary, garage apartment included. Call M. Butterfield, 101 Gardner Court, 503-228-9103."

"M. Butterfield? I bet that's Mindy Butterfield, the woman John told us about. Remember? The one who lost her silver?"

Danny snapped the card with his index finger. "What are the chances this is still open? It sounds perfect for me."

"We can call Mindy and ask – and we can drive by Gardner Court on the way home. Then you can see if you like the layout before you call."

"I think I'm going to like the layout no matter what it looks like." Danny folded the note card and secured it inside his pocket. "This is great! I feel like things are starting to come together. Let's get the shopping over with so we can go see the apartment."

"This shouldn't take long," Sarah pushed the cart toward the produce section. "All we need is steak and salad." She reached for some fresh spinach. "Hey, Danny? Do me a favor? Go see if they have any of those little cherry tomatoes?"

"They're over there." Danny pointed. "I'll get them."

"And a purple onion, too, if you find one."

Three teenagers shuffled by, heading for the prepared foods deli. Sarah paused to watch them pass, noting that there was something about East Coast style that even when people tried to look scruffy they still looked good. The boys wore baggy, low-rider jeans and unbuttoned flannel shirts over concert T-shirts; one had a navy blue bandanna wrapped around his head. The girl, slim and distant as a runway model, displayed a Goth predilection with matte finish makeup, black lip liner, a silver brow-ring, and tortoiseshell cats-eye sunglasses.

Sarah smiled and ran her hand across her stomach. Just a year ago, she admitted, that girl might have been me. But not any more. Now she was walking a different path. What a difference twelve months can make!

When she returned her attention to the produce section, Danny had vanished.

She turned a complete circle before relocating him over by the dairy case, talking to a slim brunette in a winter-white business suit. Even from the back, the woman looked vaguely familiar, and as she turned in profile, Sarah recognized Mrs. Witherspoon's legal assistant, and John's former fiancé, Ava Descartes.

Danny and Ava appeared to be sharing quite an animated conversation. As Sarah watched, Ava swung her hair over one shoulder and toyed with her chin. What's up with that? Sarah wondered. Obviously, Ava had never studied body language when she worked for the Nantucket police – she was telegraphing her interest in Danny all over the place.

Ava saw Sarah approach and smiled warmly. "Sarah, how are you? I've just met Danny Jarad. Isn't this the oddest thing? For a minute there, when I first saw him, I thought he was Micah. I've heard everyone's back on the island." Ava tugged her jacket straight, her tanned hand in stark contrast against the nubby white wool. "How's Jenny?"

"She's doing well, thank you. The doctors are releasing her later today."

"What a horrible scare!" Ava returned her attention to Danny. "Your mother was always very gracious to me whenever I visited. You Jarads have such a wonderful home. It has so much potential. You're very lucky to be staying there."

"I know it. But I'm moving out as soon as I can find my own crib. I'm no free-loader."

"You know, my Aunt Estelle is in real estate; she may know of something. I'll ask her. Why don't you give me a call later? I'm in the book."

"Thank you. I'll do that."

Ava tapped her manicure on the plastic handle of her cart. "Nice seeing you again, Sarah. Taa-taa."

"Taa-taa," Sarah replied, watching Ava turn down the next aisle. "I couldn't help but notice, Danny. Before I came over, was she asking you out?"

"You saw that, did you?" Danny scratched his jaw and grinned. "That's one pretty direct ... uh, woman. Came right out and asked me if I liked to party."

"So? Are you going to call her?"

"No. That's not why I'm here. I'm looking for something better, something real." He spun the plastic bag and dropped the tomatoes into the cart. "I want to find a connection like what you have with John. You must know what I mean. Didn't it feel great when you could finally stop all the running around?"

"Yes, it did. When I met John, it was like a load was lifted off of me. And for what it's worth, I think you're heading in the right direction to find something like that for yourself."

"That's what makes me so happy. I think I am, too." Danny commandeered control of the cart. "So, what else do we need? Salad dressing?"

"I'll make some; I have a balsamic vinegar that's really good. All we need now is enough steak for eight people." Sarah followed the cart toward the meat counter, mentally considering her bank balance. For all John's talk of big money lately, she still hadn't seen any of it, and their account was playing the old Limbo tune: 'How Low Can You Go?'

Danny read her mind. "I want to pay for the groceries; please, let me, I insist. I haven't paid for anything yet, and I am staying at the house for free. Oh, and don't let me forget, I want to get Mom some flowers for when she comes home. Do they sell them here?"

"Sure, but they'll be expensive. Don't forget, everything is imported."

"I don't care, I'm going to do it. Mom should have flowers." He stretched his arms wide and wiggled his fingers. "Besides, I want to spend some money; it's burning a hole in my pocket. Why don't you go ahead? I'll meet you over there."

"Alright." Sarah steered the cart toward the butcher shop, impressed by Danny's thoughtfulness. It hadn't even occurred to her that they should buy Jenny a 'welcome home' bouquet. She caught herself liking John's younger brother more and more. Sure, she admitted, Danny was a little rough around the edges, but what else could you expect with his God-awful background? She stopped in front of the meat counter. As on the previous occasion there was no sign of Stan the butcher, but another customer slouched near the chrome scale, impatiently flipping a paper number through his fingers. As Sarah entered his peripheral vision, the stranger glanced over, turned back, and then returned his full attention to her, openly appreciative.

"Hello there," he leered.

"Hi." Sarah felt a blush creep across her cheekbones. Deliberately, she ran her left hand through her hair, displaying her wedding band and hoping it would be obvious enough to discourage him.

It wasn't. The stranger strolled closer, rolling up onto the balls of his feet and running his tongue along the inside of his lower lip. "You live around here?"

Sarah clipped her answer to the polite minimum. "I do."

"I'm Richard. But you can call me Dick. What's your name, pretty lady?"

"Sarah. It's Sarah." She was not going to give him any more information than was absolutely necessary.

"Sar-ahhh," the stranger breathed, moving even closer. "A very pretty name for a very pretty lady."

Sarah readied herself to drop the bomb on this guy. She had learned early on that some men needed to hear a flat 'NO' to get the message and this guy was ignoring all her signals. Subtlety was not working. A blur of movement caught her eye and she saw a different form of relief moving into sight. George Robey, the developer, had noticed her predicament and was trotting over, indignant, his coattails flapping with his long stride.

"Richard!" George demanded. "Richard, what are you doing?"

"Nothing, George, nothing." The stranger stepped back. "We were just talking, that's all."

"Hello, Sarah." George nodded. "It's nice to see you again. Richard, I see you've met Sarah Jarad?"

Richard raised one eyebrow. "She's a Jarad? And how would I know that, George? When have you ever seen a Jarad looking like her?"

"You moron, she's John Jarad's wife." George grabbed his brother's elbow. "Let's go. Outside. Now."

"Fuck off," Richard Robey wrenched himself free. "I'm still waiting for my order."

Stan stepped through the door, swinging a marbled slab of striated beef. "Here we go. One sirloin steak, thick cut two inches." He slapped the meat on the marble countertop and wrapped it in brown paper. "Best piece of beef in the house."

George Robey gaped at his brother. "That's your order? An extra-thick cut of beef?"

"Can't help it, Georgie, I'm hungry," Richard grinned wolfishly, reaching for his package. "Got any money? Come on, 'bro, I know you do. Lend me a twenty."

"Here." The developer dug out his wallet. "Pay for that and go wait in the car. I'll be right out."

"Sure thing, Georgie." Richard winked. "Thanks."

The developer waited for his brother to leave and then turned. "Sarah, please let me apologize for Richard's manners. I'm afraid he is what he is." George sighed. "He served a tour of duty in '73 and Viet Nam changed my brother in ways I can't begin to understand. I hope he didn't upset you."

"No, George, he didn't. I'm fine."

"Thank you for understanding." George buttoned his coat. "I spoke with John this morning about the property. When you see him next, tell him I'll be in touch. Thank you again. Good day."

Stan rested his heavy forearms on the countertop and watched George leave. "You know, I've know them two since they was boys, and you wouldn't know it to look at 'em, but they're alike as two peas in a pod. Trouble once, trouble again, that's what I say."

Sarah was intrigued by Stan's remark; she could easily imagine that Richard Robey was trouble, but George? He was so smooth, so cultivated. Her curious nature gave her a nudge. "How is George Robey trouble?"

"Too smart to get caught; that's where George's trouble lies. There's that money that disappeared from his father's estate; no one every explained that to my liking, and his mother came out of it without a penny to her name." Stan frowned. "George dated my daughter Abby for awhile back in school and she's told me a thing to two about him since. Scared her off, he did, and a good thing, too. Abby's married now, with four kids and never a thought or a wasted look back." Stan clapped his hands and rubbed them together. "Now, Sarah Jarad, what can I get you?"

"I need enough steak for at least, I think, eight people? I'm not sure how many we're going to feed."

"I'm running a special today on New York Strips. They're very nice. You'll be happy with 'em."

"That sounds great, Stan. Thank you."

"Coming right up."

As the butcher wrapped her purchase, Sarah reviewed her introduction Richard Robey. She could see how Richard had earned his bad boy reputation. It had come naturally. And no wonder he so easily got under John's skin; Richard Robey was the antithesis of everything her husband represented.

Danny rounded the corner and returned in triumph, bearing an armload of long-stemmed magenta roses intermixed with sprays of lacy white baby's breath. "Hey, Sarah, look at this. Won't Mom love them?"

Sarah gasped at the extravagant display. "Danny, they're gorgeous! But what did that cost you?"

"Doesn't matter." He waved off her question, placing the bouquet in the wire basket, taking great care that none of the petals got crushed. "What matters is that Mom's coming home. That's the only thing I'm thinking about."

"Those would be for Jenny Jarad then?" Stan interrupted, expertly wrapping the steaks in brown paper and string. "She's coming home from hospital?"

"Yes." Sarah reached for the tidy package. "We're supposed to pick her up at one."

"Good. I'm glad to know she's mending." Stan crossed his arms and narrowed his eyes at Danny. "So you'd be her son that went missing. Daniel Jarad, the one who came home?"

"Yeah," Danny smiled. "I am."

"Hum. Making your home here now? On Nantucket?"

"I hope so. I'm trying."

"Well, good luck to you." The butcher draped a clean towel over his hand and reached across the counter. "Welcome home. It tore your family up when you went missing."

"Thank you." Danny shook the butcher's hand through the nubby cloth. "Thank you very much."

"You send Jenny my best. Ask her to come by and see me once she's up and about." Stan snapped the towel over his shoulder. "Tell her I missed seeing her smile."

"Thanks, Stan. Will do." Sarah steered the cart toward checkout.

Danny reached into the cart and started to unload their purchases. "If we need to pick Mom up by one, will we have enough time? You know, to see that apartment?"

Sarah checked her watch. Twelve-thirty. "Don't worry. We should be okay; nothing's frozen. We can go straight to the hospital from there."

"Great." Danny pulled the bouquet from the cart and protectively cradles the roses, smiling at the cashier while glancing at her plastic nametag. "Hey, uhm, Betty. I'll pay for this separately."

"Yes, you will," Sarah agreed. "I don't have enough money in my bank account to cover what that's going to cost you."

The cashier peeked through the florist paper with glitter-striped nails. "They're beautiful. Who's the lucky girl?"

"My Mom. She's getting out of the hospital. Sarah, why don't you go on ahead? I'll meet you outside."

"You don't want me to see how much that costs, do you?"

"Go on." Danny waved her off. "You don't have to be right every single time, you know."

Sarah lifted her plastic bags and headed out to the parking lot, smiling. Danny certainly was a character. Give him a year and he'd have half the island charmed; give him two and he'd have charmed the half he hadn't met yet. She unlocked the minivan and loaded her groceries in the back as Danny trotted out of the store, looking both ways and holding his bouquet in his arms. Sarah noticed that someone, probably Betty, had fashioned additional wrapping out of two plastic shopping bags to protect the roses from the cold.

"I think you made a hit. Betty seems enamoured."

Danny climbed into the passenger seat as eager as a child. "I can see you like teasing me and I'm not going to play your game." He fastened his seatbelt and pointed due north. "Go."

They pulled out of the lot and turned right, passing a row of small boutiques shuttered for the winter. Sarah turned off into one of the most prestigious island neighborhoods. The homes on Mindy's Butterfield's street were small and plain and gave no visible indication of their surprising market values. Even more desirable, Mindy's home claimed a corner lot. The house was a classic New England saltbox, including a solid central chimney and a glassed-in all-season porch. A circular front gate and a brick sidewalk completed the property and, Sarah knew, at the height of summer Mindy's garden was ablaze with perennial flowers. "I'll turn around. You can see the apartment better from the other side."

A shingled two-car garage sat behind the house, sporting a second floor balcony with a small, private deck. A decorative cupola topped the roof and featured a gleaming copper harpoon weathervane.

Danny breathed softly. "That would be my apartment? That right there?"

"That's it. What do you think?"

"Fuck me. And she would pay me to live there?"

"You'd probably have to take care of her cat when she travels, but I assume that's pretty much the deal."

"Quick!" Danny gripped the dashboard. "Find a phone before someone snags it!"

"I'm on my way." Sarah smiled at his enthusiasm, turning right, crossing Main Street and heading north on Centre. "I don't know what else Mindy might want you to do. 'Caretaker' sounds pretty general. She may want you to do some yard work or help her plant flowers. Are you okay with that?"

"That is not a problem. Man, this is a dream come true! I hope she likes me."

"I'm sure she will." Sarah pulled up to the entrance of The Great White Whale, a two-story Victorian hotel. She reached for her purse and scrabbled for change. "Here. They have a payphone in the lobby. Give her a call."

Danny made a fist around two quarters. "You know, it's funny. But I'm a little nervous."

"I'm sure you are. Now, go on. You'll never know until you try." Sarah gave him a push. Danny opened the door, crossed the sidewalk, and disappeared into the cavernous hotel lobby.

Sarah sat back, remembering how nervous she had been at her first job interview. Fresh out of school, she had walked into the career guidance center and fumbled her purse, spilling the contents across the floor. Mrs. Rigley, the counselor, had asked her to sit, reassuring her repeatedly that she had seen it all before and as long as Sarah didn't vomit or faint, she was already ahead of the game.

She remembered her mounting excitement as Mrs. Rigley mentioned an artists' colony, small but very influential, in a resort town thirty-miles off the coast of Massachusetts, on an island called Nantucket. Mrs. Rigley had warned Sarah that the job actually meant waitressing in a restaurant, but it came with room and board and offered her both an upscale market location and the chance to score some big league East Coast arts scene contacts.

The lobby door reopened and Danny trotted out grinning from ear to ear. He opened the door and slid back in the minivan, excited and happy. "She wants me to come by tonight – for an interview! I'm supposed to meet her at seven-thirty. Can John lend me a tie?"

"I'm sure he can. Oh, Danny, I'm so excited for you!"

"You and me both! I can't believe my luck! But then why not? It could happen." He fastened his seatbelt. "You know, it was kind of strange. When I told her who I was she got really interested. I've never had that before, you know, where people recognized me because of my name."

Sarah smiled wryly. "Get used to it. I'm still trying to."

"She did say one thing that was odd though. She wanted to know if I was serious about the job, about how long I would be willing to work for her. What's up with that?"

"She probably heard about John's inheritance, and thinks that you'll quit working for her, once we get the money."

Danny picked his cuticle. "She shouldn't worry about that with me. I know John's promised me the money, but I'm not counting on it. I've been burned before."

"You don't have to worry about John." Sarah rose to her husband's defense. "He keeps his promises. I know for a fact he's working on the sales agreement right now."

"I trust him," Danny insisted softly. "I do."

Sarah coasted down the hill toward the Cottage Hospital, scanning the parked cars. "Oh, good, he's already here. And so is Mary Rose; that's her car."

Danny reached for his bouquet. "I can't wait to see Mom's face when she gets a load of these."

The automated double door swung open and Mary Rose strolled out of the hospital. She noticed the approaching minivan and waved them over. "Mom'll be right out. You should see her. She's hauling at her ropes, can't wait to get home. Dr. Nyugen wanted to give her one final check-up. He told her to take it easy, but I'm not sure she heard a word he said."

The door opened a second time and disgorged an elderly couple and John, following at a polite distance. He noticed his family clustered on the sidewalk and cocked his head. "Have they already released her?"

"Not yet," Sarah took his hand. "She's due any minute."

Mary Rose narrowed her eyes. "John, where were you? I didn't see you in the waiting room."

"I wasn't in the waiting room; I was in the morgue. We found Eddie Farrar this morning. I had to give his mother a ride in to identify his body. She's in there now."

"Eddie Farrar is dead?" Sarah gasped. "How'd that happen?"

"His chainsaw slipped. The hardest part was telling his mother. She went off on me." He rolled his shoulders. "She said he never finished high school because Uncle Ethan hired him to work a drug-smuggling operation out of New Bedford." He looked at his sister. "Did you ever hear anything about that?"

"I heard rumors." Mary Rose bit her lip. "After Dad sold Jarad Shipping. Remember how mad everyone was when Dad made the announcement? Uncle Ethan said he'd start his own shipping business and there wasn't a damn thing Dad could do to stop him. But I never thought he'd do it."

"Maybe that's why Uncle Ethan got so withdrawn," Sarah suggested. "If he knew he was doing something illegal, maybe he didn't want to involve the family, in case he got caught."

John frowned. "If he was smuggling, he didn't do it for long. Beryl Farrar said he lost his nerve and left Eddie 'high and dry' shortly after they started." He snapped his fingers. "And he sure wasn't smuggling anything after he sold his boat. What year was that, Mary Rose? What year did Uncle Ethan sell his boat?"

"Hold on, let me think. He sold his boat and loaned me the money to buy my Toyota. That would make it July of '79? Isn't that right?"

"Yes. The summer Danny disappeared."

"That's right. That's why he loaned me the money, so I could help drive everyone around. Mom wasn't doing so great, she wouldn't leave the house in case she missed a call…"

Danny cleared his throat. "Well, I've got some good news. Remember the lady whose house got robbed? She's looking for a caretaker and I made an appointment to see her tonight. You never know. This might work out, and you should see the apartment that comes with the job!"

"Mindy's looking for a caretaker?" John asked. "Well, you can stop worrying about burglars. Sam Ketchum stopped the Stimson boys for running a stop sign and found Mindy's silver in the back seat of their car."

"Zack and Brett Stimson?" Mary Rose gasped. "But I know those boys! They're friends with my Dave. They wouldn't do something like that!"

"They confessed to it this morning. Their lawyer said they did it as a prank just to see if they could get away with it." John shook his head. "And, evidently right after the arrest, Ruth Stimson invited Mindy Butterfield over for coffee, and now Mindy is refusing to press charges."

A classic black Mercedes sedan crested the hill, coughing and rattling and streaming blue smoke. The group watched as the sedan rolled into the curb, jolting the driver.

"What's he doing here?" John growled. "Didn't you tell him Mom asked for 'no crowd'?"

"I told him. I told him." Mary Rose set her hands on her hips, indignant. "He just ignored me, as usual."

The car door creaked and Uncle Tommy emerged, nodding politely. "Hello, everyone. I don't see your mother here. I assume Jenny's still scheduled to be released today?"

Mary Rose stepped forward. "Yes, she is, Uncle Tommy. And I specifically told you she didn't want a crowd."

"I'm not a crowd, my dear, I'm family. And there's some business I want to discuss with her. I believe it's a matter of some urgency."

"She's in no shape for business today, Uncle Tommy," John answered. "Let's get Mom home and you can talk to her later in the week."

"I don't believe we have that luxury of time, John." The older man smoothed his tie. "I've heard about your decision concerning your inheritance, and I think you're making a serious mistake. I wanted to discuss it with your mother before you committed yourself to it."

"For chrissakes, Uncle Tommy!" Mary Rose snapped. "I can't believe you would bring this up right now! Mom's getting out of the hospital and this is just the kind of stress that put her in there!"

"Uncle Tommy," John said, "what I do with my inheritance is my business, not yours. My mother has nothing to do with it, and I do not want you bothering her about it."

"Very well then, I'll speak to you directly. John, I have seen my share of shady dealings and I think you're falling for one right now. I believe I'm within my rights as a member of this family to demand a DNA test to ensure that this young man really is Daniel Jarad."

"Uncle Tommy, we've been through this. He's been identified. The dental check was conclusive."

"Not to me." Uncle Tommy set his jaw. "And I assure you there are quite a few family members who side with me on this issue."

"Name one," Mary Rose spat. "Besides your mother."

"For crying out loud," Danny lowered the bouquet. "Do we have to go through this again?"

"John, listen to me. I'm prepared to pay for the test out of my own pocket." Uncle Tommy indicated the hospital entrance. "They can take the blood samples while we're here. It will only take twenty minutes of our time. They'll send the samples to a laboratory in Boston and we can have a truly conclusive answer in three or four days." Uncle Tommy clasped his hands. "John, truly, I have your interest at heart. I'm only doing what's best for the family. Twenty minutes, that's all it will take. Twenty minutes. And we'll know for certain."

John took a deep breath and calmed himself, trying to be reasonable. "What do you think, Danny? Would you go through another test, just to make everyone happy?"

Danny hurled the bouquet onto the sidewalk, scattering magenta petals across the cement. "I don't believe you! I've done everything you asked and you still don't believe I'm your brother! Well, fuck you! And fuck your money!"

"Danny, please!" Sarah pleaded. "It's just a blood test!"

"No fucking way! Not for all the money in the world!" Danny stepped onto the grass and stood, trembling. "I will never have a blood test on this island! Never! Do you hear me? I know just what would happen if anyone found out!"

"Found what out?"

"You're so smart, can't you guess? I'm HIV positive, and I'm not spending what's left of my life walking around this island with everyone acting like I've got the plague." He pointed at John. "I'm not living that way and if that's the gift you're giving, you can keep it!"

"AIDS?" Mary Rose whispered. "You've got AIDS? Jesus, Lord God."

Danny stooped to retrieve the shattered flowers, plucking the torn stems, trying to reform the bouquet. "Don't you get it? That's why I had to find you. I don't have forever anymore." He refolded the florists' paper and then, admitting the hopelessness of his task, stuffed the bouquet headfirst into a nearby trashcan, turning to face his family, his eyes swollen and defiant. "I've seen friends die of AIDS and it's not pretty. And sooner or later I'm going to get sick and it'll be my turn. And when that time comes, I'm not sticking around. I'm going to walk into the ocean and finish it. But when I do, it'll be on my terms, not yours! I am in charge of my life; it's mine. My life belongs to me, not you."

Sarah breathed her sorrow. "Oh, Danny, we had no idea…".

"I just wanted to know what it would have been like, what my life might have been like if I hadn't…gone. I just wanted to know what I lost. And meeting you has made it worse, not better, because now I know what might have been and I won't ever get it back."

"Don't say that," Mary Rose said. "Nothing's over yet."

"Good God Almighty!" Uncle Tommy scoffed. "Don't tell me you're falling for this melodrama!"

"Uncle Tommy, that's enough!" Mary Rose shouted. "Have some compassion, will you?"

"I'm perfectly compassionate, my dear, but I'm also reasonable. Regardless of this emotional outburst, I have yet to see one iota of proof that anything this…this person says has a word of truth in it. God knows your father wasn't the brightest light on the shore, but even Jack Jarad would have had his doubts about this!"

"This discussion is over," John interrupted, his face pale, his tone chipped as flint. "This is my decision, Uncle Tommy, not yours, and I am satisfied that Danny is my brother. We don't need any more tests."

"But John, son, use your head…"

"Uncle Tommy, listen to me. My mother is about to come through that door and I do not want her to find you standing here. If she starts worrying about your doubts it will kill her." John ran his fingers through his hair. "Now get out of here, Uncle Tommy, and I mean it. Get out of here now."

The older man drew himself up. "Very well. I have done my best, I can do no more." He pulled his keys free and walked stiffly to his car, starting up the antique sedan and backing out of the parking space, his eyes directed straight ahead and his chin held high.

"Jesus, John," Mary Rose stammered. "You sure let him have it."

"I am through with this back and forth bullshit. We don't need any more proof." John straightened his coat. "We are done with that. It is time to move on."

The automated door opened again, and Jenny Jarad sallied forth in a wheelchair pushed by a young aide. Jenny looked magnificent with her hair freshly coiffed and her coral lipstick firmly in place.

"I told them I didn't need this silly chair, but they insisted on it." She tapped the armrests, smiling happily. "So? Are we ready to go home?"

CHAPTER FIFTEEN

"Honey?" John paused halfway down the loft stairs, straightening his tie. "What are you doing up? I thought you were going to sleep in."

Sarah turned away from the computer monitor, her face under lit a ghostly luminescent blue. "I couldn't get comfortable so I thought I might as well get up and investigate, instead."

"Investigate what?"

"HIV. I don't know anything about it, John, not really. Just the usual rumors; it only affects gay men and I.V. drug users. I was worried about it and it is our problem now. I mean, how do we deal with this? What do we have to be careful about? The silverware? Sheets, towels? I have no idea."

John glanced at the clock. "And you decided to figure all this out before dawn?"

"It's not that early, and I like being pro-active. You know that."

"I do know that – it's gotten you into trouble before." He squinted over her shoulder at the screen. "We might as well be pro-active together. What did you find?"

"The Web site for The Center for Disease Control." Sarah highlighted the text with the mouse. "Look: 'HIV transmission between family members is extremely rare'; it takes contact between skin or mucous membrane and infected blood. I was thinking about Danny's tears yesterday, but it says here 'contact with saliva, tears or sweat has never been shown to result in a transmission.' "

"That's reassuring." He sat down and admired his wife, who was crossing the kitchen to pour herself more tea. The pregnancy was altering Sarah's posture and he found her new stance entrancing. "What are your plans for later today?"

"I'm going shopping with Danny. He wants to get a few things for his new place. You should see how excited he is. It's like watching a little kid."

"Talk about excited, did you notice my mother last night? I can't remember the last time I saw her looking so happy."

"She was radiant. I watched her all night long; she never took her eyes off him. She's so happy to have him back nothing else comes close."

"I noticed that, too. He even had Jackie laughing and that takes some doing." John finished his coffee and stood, placing his mug in the sink. "I'll call T.B. May today and make sure he's filed our preliminary plans with the Zoning Commission. Let's see if we can speed things up."

"I'd think we'd better." Sarah stretched her flannel pajamas across her abdomen. "But I'm not the one in a hurry."

John laughed. "I promise, once that's done, we'll be good to go."

Sarah followed John out and caught him at the door, wrapping him in a hug. "John, be careful out there."

"What's this? Why the sudden display of concern?"

"I don't know. I have a funny feeling."

He drew back and looked into Sarah's eyes. "Funny ha-ha? Or funny sick?"

"Never mind. It's nothing, don't mind me." She gave him a playful push. "It's the hormones talking again."

"I'll call you later." He paused. "Maybe we should buy you a cellphone."

"No, thank you. I don't want a cellphone. I have enough distractions as it is. Besides, where can I go on this island where there's not a pay phone within a block? It drives me crazy when I see people driving down the road yacking on the phone. The other day I saw a man with a cellphone in his right hand and a coffee in his left. He had a newspaper spread out across his dashboard and I'm thinking, what part of your anatomy are you driving with?"

John chuckled. When Sarah got over-excited her grammar went out the window. "I still think a cellphone is a good idea. What if you have a flat tire on Milestone Road? Especially once the baby gets here?"

"Alright, I'll think about it."

"Fair enough." John nodded. He stepped out the door and was propelled toward his truck by a blast of frigid wind. The atmosphere had a swollen feeling to it and he checked the sky – oppressive gray clouds were rolling in from the north/northeast, not a good indicator for fair weather. John slid into the truck and shivered, blowing on his hands.

While waiting for the engine to warm, he organized his plans for the day. If George Robey had ordered the perc. test as promised and the results were favorable, they could start reviewing the sales agreement. Once that was signed, George had promised to wire transfer the money to the bank, and John toyed with the idea of checking his account balance over the next couple of days just to hear the computerized voice announce: eighteen million, five hundred thousand dollars. Plus change. John smiled to himself. What a suggestion!

As he drove into town the wind continued to surge against the truck. It was still early enough that the roads were deserted, but John found some signs of life: Phillip Macy pumping gas and giving him a mock military salute as he drove by; Mimi Cheswick clutching her red wool coat tight and fighting the wind for the door of the Salon de Beauté. He pulled up at the station, parked, and hustled himself inside. The temperature had dropped at least ten degrees in the few short minutes it had taken him to drive to work. John frowned; it was shaping up to be a raw, nasty day. The security door buzzed and he let himself in.

Tina covered the mouthpiece of her phone with her hand. "Glad you're here. Addie Simpson's mother is on the line and she wants to speak to someone more important than me."

He pointed at his desk. "Send her over."

"Ms. Simpson? One moment. Lieutenant Jarad is here now. I'll transfer your call."

The phone rang as John sat down. He flipped on the speakerphone. "John Jarad."

"John? It's Miranda Simpson." The elderly woman's voice quavered with emotion. "John, I need some help. My girl Addie's gone missing and I want you to find her for me. I've hurt my leg or I'd do it myself."

"The weather's pretty foul today, Ms. Simpson. Maybe Addie found some place dry and decided to hole up until it blows over."

"But she's been missing ever since you sent that officer over here! John, it's been two days! I couldn't sleep last night I was so sick with worry. And this time Addie took her clothes and she cleaned out my canned goods pantry. She's never done that before."

John scrabbled for a pad of paper. "If she were sheltering somewhere, where would she be?"

"Now I don't want to get Addie into any trouble, John, Lord knows we've had enough of that as it is, but once or twice I did find her in one of those nice cottages they've got closed up for the winter along Dionis beach. Bless me if I can find how she gets in them but she does! And she never makes a mess, John, she never does, and I clean everything up just fine, but you might try looking for her there. Like I said, I'd do it myself, if I could."

"Alright, Ms. Simpson, I'll send someone over to take a look. We'll call you as soon as we find her."

"Thank you, John. I appreciate the help."

"Tina?" John called, glancing around the empty stationhouse. "Where is everyone?"

"Roy and Hank are out on a loop, and C.J. took a call that came in about twenty minutes ago. She left you a note – it's on your desk."

He found the pink memo in his in-box and scanned its contents. "Did she say anything about why she was going to Sesachacha Pond?"

"No, only that the county agent called with some kind of problem. Do you want me to page her?"

"Yes, please." John sat at his desk, hoping against hope that the unknown 'problem' was something minor. "Then patch her through over here, will you?"

"You got it." Tina started flipping switches. "Wow, she must be right there. Here she comes."

The phone rang and John picked up. "C.J.? What's going on?"

"John? We've got a Code Two out here. One of the county guys was digging a perc. test and he found some bones."

"It's not Addie Simpson is it?"

"Addie Simpson? No. Why? Is she missing?"

"Her mother just reported it. Evidently she's gone missing for a couple of days."

"Well, this is definitely not Addie Simpson, John. Whoever this was has been here for awhile. And John? I think you'd better come out here."

He frowned, considering what this discovery might mean to their construction schedule. It was common knowledge that many Quaker burials went unmarked, and if the site proved to be an early Wampanoag grave, forget it, all bets were off. Once the federal government got wind of anything Native American and stepped in, the property sale could be delayed for years. "C.J., notify the H.P.C.'s office and tell them you need a state archaeologist. They'll send one out."

The receiver clicked twice before she replied: "John? The guy from the county says we don't need a state archeologist, we need you. And John, I've seen the bones. He's right."

He stood, reaching for his keys. "Alright. I'm on my way. Tina, hold down the fort."

He took the road northeast toward Sesachacha Pond. The morning sun broke through the low clouds, sending shafts of banded sunlight toward the pond's choppy surface. Taking advantage of the rising temperature, gulls soared among the shoreline currents, plying the stiff updraft off their ruffled wings. John lowered his window to test the air; the day had an on-again, off-again quality that he found disconcerting.

He turned onto Hoicks Road and drove past Uncle Ethan's homemade gate, bumping across the rutted, frozen meadowland. C.J. was waiting with the county agent, both of them leaning against the fender of her patrol car. The county agent finished a cigarette and ground the butt under his heel, not even waiting for John to stop the car before walking over, expostulating loudly.

"Morning, John, morning! George didn't tell me I was going to dig up a boneyard."

"He didn't tell you, Randy, because he didn't know. Neither did I." John stepped out of the car. "So where's this grave?"

"Over under the tarp." Randy pointed toward a mound of damp beige sand. "See, I needed three holes three-feet deep for proper testing, so I picked some low ground to save myself some trouble. This spot was sunk so low at first I thought it might be an old well. Then two feet down I started pulling up bone. That's when I shut off my auger."

"And you called us."

"No, John, no, not right away." The shorter man struggled to keep up with John's longer stride. "First I dug it out with my shovel to make sure they weren't old sheep bones, you know, this being a meadow and all."

"It's no sheep," C.J. added darkly.

"Not every grave got a marker," John suggested. "We might have an old Quaker burial, or even an indian mound."

"Ayah. Only one problem with that," Randy pulled back the canvas tarpaulin. "Your Indian's wearing sneakers."

The small skeleton lay on its right side, hands clasped as if in prayer. Splintered ribs mixed with grave dirt, proof of the auger's power. The skull gleamed like worn ivory against the dense yellow sand and exposed a fractured cavity that shattered the smooth white dome of bone.

"See, John, it's like I said," C.J. breathed softly. "Look at the size. Chrissakes. It's just a kid."

"My auger didn't go anywhere near that head," Randy sputtered. "What caused that wound was sommat' besides me."

John crouched next to the grave. The body had been wrapped in some type of weatherproof gear, now decayed; remnants of olive-drab rubberized cloth remained. He reached into the grave and pulled open the protective latex cocoon to find a sub-layer of matted red plaid wool and denim cloth with copper rivets.

"Lieutenant!" C.J. hissed, scandalized by the breach of forensic procedure. "Should you be doing that? This was no accident!"

"I can see that." The sun broke through the clouds and a metallic gleam caught his eye. Reaching down, John flicked clumps of grainy sand away from the skeletal hands and probed between the fragile finger bones. Slowly, he stood, and lifted a gold chain from the grave. "I wanted to see this first."

Randy leaned in. "What is that? What have you got there?"

There is a certainty that is felt after an endlessly repeated succession of doubts and trials, when all the questions fall into perfect concordant place, and the answer comes forth in a rush of undeniable, clairvoyant truth. John rubbed the grave dirt off the gold St. Nicolas' medal in his hand and he knew.

C.J. saw revelation in his face. "Oh my God, John. You know who this is, don't you?"

"Yes. Yes, I do." He turned the medal over and read the inscription on the back: Ethan Hezekiah Jarad. Auld Lang Syne. June 2, 1937. Slowly, John wrapped the gold chain around his fingers. "It's my brother, Danny."

"I knew it!" Randy slapped his thigh. "I knew it the minute I dug him up. No one had to tell me."

"But I thought your brother had come back? Isn't he living at your house?"

"That's not my brother. That's some stranger. This, this is my brother."

"So who's that guy?"

"I don't know that." John stumbled across the frozen ground, moving toward his car. "But I'm sure as hell going to find out."

"John, hold on! Wait a minute!" C.J. trotted to catch up. "You're in no shape to drive."

"I have to go home. I have to find out who he is. I have to find out what he wants."

"Sure, John, sure, of course you do." She pushed him up against his car. "Just give it a minute. Sit down. You're in shock."

"You are looking pale, John, that's a fact," Randy agreed. He looked at C.J. "I've got a half-pint of whiskey in my truck if you think it'd help."

"Get it," she ordered.

Randy returned with his half-pint and John took a pull. The liquor burned his throat all the way down and left him coughing, but the reflex did help clear his head. He leaned forward and rested his elbows on his knees. "C.J., have you told anyone else about this besides me?"

"No, John, no, I didn't."

"Okay. Call Paul Jenkins. Tell him we need an exhumation and an autopsy. I want to know exactly what happened here as quickly as he can get me a report."

"Consider it done."

John stood, tucking the gold chain and medal into his breast pocket and buttoned it tight. "I'm going home now. I want some answers."

"You go do what you need to do, John. I'll cover this end."

"I know you will." He climbed into the unit and pulled a u-turn across the meadow, gunning the engine and speeding toward the gate. His thoughts were spinning. He found it impossible to believe that all his recent hopes, all his hard-won relief in his brother's return had been part of a cunning, deceptive lie, but here it was, the truth; he had seen the terrible proof with his own eyes. His brother Danny was dead and had been for all these long years, and everything John had learned recently to the contrary was either suspect or sham. An impostor, a con-man, had come in to take advantage of his family, and for all his investigative training and skill, he had been as thoroughly fooled as anyone.

He shook his head. Even more disturbing was the evidence that Uncle Ethan had been involved in Danny's death. But he had the proof, Uncle Ethan's gold medal, in his pocket this very moment. His brother's body had been buried on Uncle Ethan's land, and someone had buried Danny with a semblance of Christian decency. The body had been wrapped in a coat and not just shoveled into a grave; the saint's medal had been tucked between his hands. These actions implied some tender concern, not the modus operandi of a panicked, anonymous killer.

Uncle Ethan, did you do it? John agonized over the idea. Did you murder Danny? And in God's name, why?

It must have been an accident, he rationalized, an unintentionally fatal mistake. He found it impossible to believe that Uncle Ethan had been a cold-blooded killer; yet he had seen the evidence of murder with his own eyes. Could Uncle Ethan have knowingly struck Danny down? Knowingly murdered a seven-year old child, his own flesh and blood? He shook fat tears of anger from his eyes. Surely that conclusion was impossible; Uncle Ethan might have been negligent, perhaps, but not evil…

A blaring horn grabbed his attention; he had been weaving across the road's striped centerline. John took a deep breath and refocused on his job. This emotional upheaval was getting him nowhere. What he needed to do was to apply his training and his investigative skills to the situation; he needed to consider the evidence with a rational mind. As hard as it would be, it was time to stop thinking like a brother and start thinking like a cop.

John drew a deep, ragged breath. "Now, what do I know for a fact?"

Fact One: there were other ways to fracture a skull besides the use of blunt force. Explosive impact, for instance. John recalled lab samples from his academy days and straightened up with sudden certainty. He had seen that type of fracture before. "It's an exit wound. Danny was shot."

He also knew for a fact that Uncle Ethan had owned a gun, a souvenir of his Pacific arena war days, a Japanese pistol in a crumbling leather holster. John vividly recalled the pistol's channeled wood grip and odd oriental characters stamped along its blued-steel barrel. His mother had been particularly nervous about the existence of the gun and insisted that Uncle Ethan lock it up whenever any of her children were coming to visit. They hadn't found the gun in Uncle Ethan's house before it burned; would they find it now if they sifted through the ashes?

John shook his head; the facts were too unfathomable. Everything he knew right now was speculative, and speculation often paved the way to error. He would know more once Paul Jenkins finished the autopsy; something might make more sense then. But for now one thing held true: Danny's impostor was walking around, and whoever he was, he would have some answers.

He slowed and glanced at his watch: ten-twenty. Nantucket town was to his right, 'Sconset six miles out Milestone Road to his left. Sarah had said the she and Danny were going shopping 'that morning'. Knowing that the stores in town stayed shuttered until eleven, and also knowing how efficient Sarah liked to be, John guessed that she was already on her way to or at the Jarad house. He turned east, praying that if he was late and he missed them at the house at least he would see the minivan coming toward him on the road back to town.

He accelerated brutally and the patrol car shuddered, fighting the cold front John had noticed that morning. The front had completed its' invasion, shrouding the island in lowering gray cloud. The pine trees lining the road hid among swarming patches of low misting fog. Individual trees loomed out of the gray with a silent, almost sentinel quality. The patrol car sped past the black water tower on the edge of 'Sconset; past shingled cottages shrouded behind twiggy boxwood hedges. He pulled into the crushed shell driveway of the Jarad house and felt the prickling sparkle of panic run up his spine. The minivan wasn't there. The only vehicle parked in front of the house was Jackie's red Jeep.

John ran inside. Using his shoulder for emphasis, he unlatched the front door and entered the slate hallway. Jackie was sitting at the kitchen table, sipping coffee from a mug. Micah looked up from frying sausages on the old gas stove. "Hey, man. What are you doing here?"

"Where's Sarah?"

Micah's smile faded as he reacted to John's tone. He reached down and turned off the gas and slid the cast-iron skillet to a back burner. "She left for town with Danny. Why?"

"Where's Mom?"

"She's in the living room looking at old photo albums." Jackie tilted her head. "John, what's going on?"

"I don't know how to tell you this other than to just say it, so here goes. We were running a perc. test on the property at Sesachacha Pond and we found a grave. We found Danny's body. The real Danny. Our brother, Danny."

The stoneware mug rang as Jackie dropped it on the floor. "What? Danny's dead? Are you sure?"

"Jackie, I saw his body with my own eyes. The guy we think is Danny is not our brother. He's some fake, an imposter."

Micah sat down heavily. "But John, what about the proof? You had proof. That dental stuff."

"I can't explain it. Jim Scanlon made a mistake, that's all. But you have to believe me. Danny is dead. I'm sorry, but I'm sure of it." He unbuttoned his pocket and dangled the gold medallion. "I found this buried in the grave. It was deliberately placed between his hands."

Micah reached for the medal and read the inscription. "Shit. So Uncle Ethan was involved in his death?"

"It looks that way."

"Oh, John," Jackie wept. "I believed him. I believed every bit of his story."

"We all did, Sis. That's what con men do. But I have to find him now because he's with my wife. And my child."

Jackie glanced at the living room. "Oh my God. This is going to kill Mom. How do we tell her?"

"We have to be careful; we can't shock her into another attack. But we have be quick; I have to go find Sarah. She's out there with him."

"I'm going with you," Micah stood. "Procedure be damned. This is personal now."

"I'll stay with Mom," Jackie volunteered. "She shouldn't be left alone, you know, in case something happens."

"Thank you." John turned down the hall and led the way toward the living room. At the top of the short staircase, all three siblings stopped and stood side-by-side. Seated on the couch below, Jenny was wrapped in an afghan, her silvery hair backlit by a halo of light as she bent low to peer at old photographs.

Jenny felt their stare and looked up, delighted. "John! What a surprise! What are you doing home?"

He stepped down and perched one corner of the coffee table. "Mom, I have some hard news and I want you to be prepared for it."

"That sounds serious, son."

"It is serious, Mom," Micah stated. "It's real serious."

"How bad can it be?" Jenny smiled weakly, glancing between her three children. "Everyone's safe, aren't they?"

"Mom." John gently took her hand. "We were running a test this morning out at Uncle Ethan's property, and we found a grave."

"A grave?" Jenny frowned. Her eyes grew vague. "What kind of grave?"

Jackie sat down next to her mother. "Mom, John's pretty sure he found Danny's body today. The real Danny."

Jenny's face contracted with pain. She pushed Jackie's hand away. "That's not possible! Danny went shopping with Sarah."

"That's not Danny, Mom. That's an imposter, a con-man."

"You're wrong!" Jenny stood, trembling. The afghan dropped to the floor and she moved toward the hallway, stumbling over Micah's outstretched legs. "My son returns to me and now you're trying to take him away!" She stopped on the staircase, blind with tears, and turned back to face her children. "I had no idea the three of you could be so cruel."

"Mom, wait," Jackie implored. "We're not being cruel. John's telling the truth."

"It's not the truth! It can't be!" Jenny clutched the banister. "And I won't hear another word! I'm going to my room and when I come down I won't hear one more word! Do you hear me? My son is home and that's the end of it!" She stumbled up the stairs. "My son is home and I don't want to hear any more!"

Jackie turned to face her brothers. "I can handle this. I can. John, go find Sarah. I'll keep an eye on Mom. If there's trouble, I'll call her doctor." She glanced up the stairs. "She just needs some time to think things through. We dropped a bomb on her."

"Did Sarah say where they were going?"

"No, she just said 'shopping'."

"They're in the van," Micah grabbed his coat. "We can drive around until we find it."

He glanced at his watch: eleven-fifteen. "She mentioned an apartment on Gardner Court. Let's check there first."

The two brothers sprinted for the patrol car. Micah opened the passenger side door and wedged himself in, drawing his knees up tight against the dashboard. John slid behind the wheel and shifted the car into gear, reaching for the handset to call in an APB and then stopping himself, pulling up short. He had a sudden, frightening insight into the heart of the imposter's game. Reaching forward, John turned off the police radio. "I'm not calling this one in, Micah. This one has to stay private."

"You don't want backup?"

"I can't." He tightened his lips. "I'm not sure who I can trust anymore."

"You can't trust the police? Why not?"

"Because it just hit me. This imposter? He must have an inside contact, someone local from the island. Think about it. How else would he know to come here? The title transfer was published in the Inky Mirror and he was, what? On the island the next day? If his con was a set-up to get the property, the imposter must have known about the transfer before it made the paper. Sonofabitch. Otherwise he wouldn't have had the time to get his teeth fixed to match the dental record!"

"What are you saying? He's in on this with Mark Scanlon?"

"No, I don't think it was Mark. Mark didn't have access to the dental records until I gave them to him." John struck the wheel with his fist. "Goddammit! Those records are sealed! The contact has to be a cop!"

"So who's in charge of the records?"

"I hate that idea even more, because that's Joe Curley. Christ! I hate this! I hate not knowing who I can trust. But goddammit! Someone knew just what information to feed him to make us believe his story."

"A silent partner on an inside job. Nice, very nice." Micah crossed his arms. "I hate to say this, John, but if there is a contact in your department, the impostor may already know you found Danny's grave and the jig is up."

John glanced at the dashboard clock. "Did you get any phone calls while he was still at the house?"

"Not that I know of. Sarah showed up and they left right away…"

"Then we might still have a chance; we only just found the grave. Let's hope the contact may not know where they are any more than we do."

John cut the lights and slowed as they entered the perimeter of town, braking to circle the rotary. He followed Orange Street passed the frozen glaze of Goose Pond and continued toward Main Street, taking a right onto Gardner Court. He stopped the unit at the curb beside Mindy Butterfield's house and leaned over the wheel. "I don't see them, do you?"

"Looks empty to me."

"Where else could they be?" John muttered, turning the unit around in the Butterfield driveway.

"It's still early," Micah suggested. "Maybe they stopped somewhere for coffee."

"The Coffee Tree." John pulled back onto Orange Street and turned right, crossing the rough cobbles of Main Street onto Centre. The Coffee Tree was a trendy little bistro located half-way along the popular street. John slowed even more and the two brothers scanned the line of parked cars, peering down narrow side streets and back alleys hoping to locate the minivan.

"I didn't see anything, did you?" John glanced at Micah, frowning.

"No."

They circled the block by taking two rights: northeast on Chestnut and southeast on Federal. Both streets were lined with discrete gild-trimmed signboards advertising an assortment of Bed & Breakfast accommodation. They cruised past the parking lot of the only obviously-commercial establishment in the neighborhood, an ornate Victorian hotel, The Great White Whale.

"John, stop! Stop! There it is!"

He pulled into the lot. There could be no doubt they had found the correct vehicle: the minivan's rear bumper was plastered with a collage of expired beach permits and conservancy decals that only Jenny Jarad could have accumulated. He left the patrol car to idle and placed his hand on the minivan's hood. The sheet metal was stone cold. John felt a spasm of doubt. What were Sarah and the imposter doing at a hotel?

Micah unfolded himself and voiced a doubt that very nearly mirrored John's own. "I don't get it, John. Why would they have stopped at the Whale?"

John stood alone in the January air and felt a wave of mistrust wash over him. "Let's go find out, shall we?"

"Okay, 'Bro. I'm with you." Micah shut the door and followed John through the oak doors into the carpeted hotel lobby. The reception area was deserted but a slim, waist-coated maitre d' stood near the restaurant door, glancing up from his clipboard and smiling uncertainly at the two looming Jarad brothers.

"I'm sorry, gentlemen, we're not open for lunch until one."

"We're not here to eat." John removed his gloves. "We're looking for someone and it's very important that we find him." He pointed at Micah. "Looks like him only half his size. Anyone fitting that description been in here this morning?"

The maitre d' calculated the authority of John's uniform and nodded. "Well, yes. He came in with a woman, a brunette, over an hour ago. They're in the Reader's Nook." He pointed his index finger. "It opened at ten."

"Thank you," John moved across the carpet. "Micah, remember what I said. We take him clean. No mistakes. I don't want Sarah or the baby to get hurt."

"You can count on me, John."

The Reader's Nook was an intimate, paneled alcove shielded from the lobby behind the main reception area. Originally designed as the hotel's private library, the cozy room with its crackling hardwood fire and leather reading chairs had been reconstructed into a more profitable early hours coffee bar. The two Jarad brothers entered the alcove, scanning the empty chairs clustered around small Indian teak tables. The alcove was deserted except for a pair of customers seated on a loveseat before the fire.

'Danny' turned, his arm resting easily along the back of the small couch. "John? Micah? Hey, what are you doing here?"

"Who is it?" The brunette flipped back her hair and turned to smile. "Oh, it's John and Micah. How funny. How are you?"

John blinked. "Ava? Where's my wife?"

"I dropped her at the drug store," the imposter replied reasonably, checking his watch. "I'm supposed to meet her at noon. Why, John? What's up?"

"What's up?" Micah reached over the loveseat and hauled the impostor up by his collar. "I'll tell you what's up, you sonofabitch. You're not my brother, that's what's up. We just found his grave. And I don't know who you are, but you're not him."

"John! Stop!" Ava shrieked, standing up and stepping quickly to one side. "Do something!"

"Let me go!" 'Danny' struggled for his footing and weasled out of his leather jacket. "I said, let me go!"

John grasped his brother's arm. "Micah, take it easy – let me charge him. I'll take it from here."

Micah turned his head, distracted by John's request. The imposter wrenched his right arm free, drew back and threw a sucker punch that plowed into the older Jarad brother's midsection.

"Stop!" Ava's shout echoed off the low plaster ceiling. "No! Don't do that!"

Even as he doubled over, Micah retained his grip on the imposter's shirt. He slowly gathered the fabric in his hand and pulled him to floor level. "That was a very bad idea," he breathed. "You just made me mad." Straightening up, Micah returned a staggering blow, sending 'Danny' tumbling up and over the loveseat into a coal scuttle perched on the limestone hearth.

"Micah! Back it down!" John ordered. "That's enough!"

"He hit me first, John. Sonofabitch hit me first."

The impostor crab-backed up against the stones of the chimney, wiping a thread of blood trickling down his chin.

"Jesus Fucking Christ! Alright! Alright! Just don't let him hit me again!"

"What's going on here?" Ava demanded, hands on her hips. "Will someone please tell me what is going on?"

John pointed at the imposter. "He's a fake. He's not my brother. And I'm making an arrest."

"Of course I'm your brother." The impostor pulled a cocktail napkin of a side table and blotted his lip. "Your dentist friend confirmed it for us, remember?"

"I don't know how, yet, but Mark made a mistake. Uncle Tommy was right. I should have insisted on a DNA test. You were very clever to use AIDS to keep me from it."

Slowly, 'Danny' rose. "If this is about the money, you can keep it. I know who I am and that's all I came here for. If I'm not welcome, I'll go back to Brooklyn."

"We're way past that now. I'm arresting you for impersonation with intent to defraud." John began to recite Miranda. "You have the right to remain silent and refuse to answer questions. Anything you do say may be used against you in a court of law. Do you understand this?" He continued. "You have the right to consult an attorney before speaking to the police and to have an attorney present during questioning now or in the future. If you cannot afford an attorney, one will be appointed for you before any questioning if you wish. Do you understand this?"

"Whoa, wait a minute," Ava raised her hands. "I don't know anything about fraud. He asked me to meet him here for coffee. This was just a date."

The imposter scowled. "Oh no you don't, bitch. If I go down for this, so do you."

"Shut up," Ava demanded. "Don't say another word until we see a lawyer."

Micah finally grasped the truth of the situation. "Chrissakes! She's his partner. The inside man."

"Inside woman," John corrected, continuing his recitation. "If you decide to answer questions now without an attorney present you still have the right to stop answering at any time until you do talk to an attorney. Knowing and understanding your rights as I have explained them to you, are you willing to answer my questions without an attorney present?"

"You've got nothing on me," the imposter scoffed, taking one hesitant step toward the door. "I don't see you holding a warrant."

"I don't need a warrant. I've got probable cause."

"I could walk out of here right now."

"Go ahead and try," Micah suggested eagerly, flexing his fists.

"Oh stop it! This is ridiculous!" Ava straightened her jacket. "John, you know as well as I do impersonation is a misdemeanor. He'll get six months, max. Besides, are you sure your family wants to face this kind of scandal? I'd think about it, John, if I were you. I mean, is it really worth it?"

"Hold it, bitch," the impostor spat. "I'm not doing time. We never said nothing about me doing time."

"I told you to shut up," Ava smoothed her hair. "They've got nothing on us if you'd just shut up and let me handle this."

With a sinking feeling, John admitted that Ava was right. He really didn't have anything on them. She was a clever girl and she had certainly done her homework. Impersonation was a misdemeanor under Massachusetts state law. Was it worth spilling this scandal all over the island only to have the imposter released in four to six months? His family would suffer more from the fraud than the two conspirators would. They would end up interviewed on a talk show somewhere. Would it be better to accept knowing the truth and simply cut their losses? Would it be better to let them walk and avoid the resulting turmoil of malevolent gossip?

Micah grimaced. "I don't understand you, Ava. Why did you do this to us? You were like family."

She shrugged indifferently. "Because I could. Because I wanted to. You people don't deserve to have that kind of money. You wouldn't even know what to do with it. My God! Can you imagine how I felt when I read the Will and realized what it meant? I mean, how perfect is that irony?! I only found out about it after I sent John away!" She turned toward John and sneered. "You with your pathetic little nothing police job, your boring little rental apartment. I saw a chance and by God, I took it!" She pointed her index finger at him. "I could have hauled you back in, John, I could have, it would have been easy, but guess what? You were already married! Tell me, John, tell me this. How much did I mean to you that you were married to someone else eight months after we broke up?"

"Ava, I had no idea. You never said anything to me."

"Why tell you anything, Lieutenant Clueless? I mean, really, John, it's so tedious to have to explain everything to you. I mean, really, why bother?"

"Jesus!" The impostor broke off staring at Ava long enough to speak. "Lady, you are whacked."

She waved off his remark. "So, John, Micah? What's it going to be? Do you really want to put your precious family through this? We are only talking six months, after all. I mean, is it worth it? And what about your mother? What if this is the stress that kills her?"

Micah blanched. "You bitch."

"And you're a loser. So, John, I guess it's up to you. What's it going to be?"

He prepared himself to surrender when a different idea began to wiggle slowly in the depths of his mind. He recalled a recent news item Sarah had followed about a dubious Van Gogh painting. Sarah had explained that the attribution was right but the artist's signature was missing from the canvas. After the auction, the new buyer had reneged on the purchase and then sued the auction house trying to prove intent to defraud. The Court had thrown the case out – forgery couldn't be proved without a signature.

And then, he had it. He had them. If he played this new idea right, he would have them both.

"Oh, no," John shook his head, addressing the imposter. "I've changed my mind. I'm not charging you with impersonation – I've got you on forgery. You signed that dental release as 'Daniel Jarad'." And he quoted from memory: "Forgery: 'Intent to injure or defraud; utters or publishes as true a false, forged, or altered record'. I've got you on forgery and that's ten to twelve years, state prison."

"What the fuck? I am not going to prison!"

"Ten to twelve years," John emphasized. "And I'll make sure you get every day of it. She may walk, but I've got you – hard time."

"Fuck that!" The imposter stood slowly. "What if I turn State's? Can we cut a deal?"

"Shut up, you little shit!" Ava hissed. "Don't tell them anything! You're giving it away."

"Screw you, bitch. Look," he raised his hands. "It was all her idea. She's the one who came on to me."

"Where did you meet her?"

"South Beach, Miami, at a party. She kept telling me how much I looked like you. I thought it was a pickup line until she mentioned the money. Then I got interested."

"I should have guessed. It's where you got your tans."

"Smart boy, John." The imposter glanced between the two Jarad brothers. "She sent me three thousand bucks and the dental records to get my teeth fixed. You need proof? I still have the copy of your Uncle's Will; it's in my duffle bag, back at the house."

Ava took one step toward the door, her eyes wary.

Micah stretched both arms wide. "Don't even try."

"I was so close." The imposter whispered, staring out a narrow casement window. "I was almost there. I could almost taste it. That money would have set me up for life. I could'a been a player."

John reached for the handcuffs tucked into his belt. "Okay, player. Let me introduce you to a new game plan."

CHAPTER SIXTEEN

"I can't believe you left me sitting there," Sarah grumbled, stirring brown sugar into her oatmeal. "I miss all the action."

"That is not true and you know it," John countered reasonably. "Everything that happened was because we were trying to find you."

"That does it. I am buying a cellphone. I hate being left out of the loop. I flipped out when I called your Mom and Jackie answered, and she told me what was going on with you and Micah and Danny."

"Honey? Let's not call him that, okay? Danny Jarad was my brother. That guy was a fake, a...fraud."

"Right. Sorry, John, I wasn't thinking." Sarah sat back. "You're sure now who he is?"

"Raymond Wayne Perry of South Miami Beach, Florida. C.J. found his real driver's license when she searched his duffle bag. Metro-Dade DMV faxed us a photo confirm. It's him."

"It's pretty amazing when you stop to think about it. I mean, think of the details he came up with. He even knew about Addie Simpson!"

"Ava fed him pretty much everything he needed." John spooned sugar into his cup. "We searched her apartment, too. It was amazing, the things she had on the family. Cartons of files, newspaper clippings, genealogies, legal records, it was all there. She certainly did her homework. She knew exactly what she was doing. She knew Danny was our blind spot and she deliberately used him to get at the money."

Sarah lowered her spoon into her oatmeal, grown lumpy and cold. "You told her about Danny and you never told me?"

"Don't take it like that, honey. Of course she knew about Danny." He sighed tiredly and stood, pulling the curtain aside and staring out the kitchen window. "She's lived on island her entire life."

Sarah wrestled with her bruised pride, trying to keep her focus onto John's needs. It broke her heart to see him looking so discouraged. "It wasn't all Ava's doing, John. The imposter did his homework, too. That juvenile record from Brooklyn? The story about the other kidnapped little boy? We all fell for that, not just you."

"But I'm supposed to be a professional investigator," he muttered. "I'm supposed to know the difference between the truth and a lie. But I wanted to believe his story so badly I let him slip past me. Kevin Sumners was just some kid he knew growing up in Brooklyn – they went through Juvie together. And when the time came and he needed it, Raymond borrowed his identity, too." He let the curtain drop. "And I swallowed every bit of it, hook, line and sinker."

"You would have figured it out, given enough time. Look at the time they had to plan this! Months! You figured it out in only a few days."

"Only because we found Danny's grave – and that was pure luck. And I still don't know what happened to him."

"John! Will you give yourself some credit?" Sarah stood. "The bottom line is you prevented a fraud. That has to count for something!"

He grinned crookedly. "We did stop them though, didn't we?"

"Yes, you did," Sarah stated. "What we need to do is find our balance again. Forget about Raymond and Ava and everyone else and let's focus on our future." She unrolled a blueprint, borrowing the sugar bowl, the salt and pepper shakers and his coffee mug to anchor the four corners. The stiff paper crackled as Sarah ran her hands over the floor plan outlined in white against the cobalt blue paper. "So, John, now look. Think. How is this going to affect us? Can we still go through with the property sale?"

"I don't see why not. Nothing changed legally. The title is still in my name."

"Great. Then that's where we start." She ran her finger across the blueprint. "Will you call George Robey today and check on the sales agreement? Tell George we need a closing date."

"Okay. I'll call him from the station."

"And call T.B. May, too. Ask him if we can move the garage around to the back of the house or over to one side. Pulling straight off the road into the garage is bad luck."

John blinked. Sarah continued to surprise him with some of her selective superstitions. "And why is that?"

"Come on. Everyone knows a straight line draws bad luck to a house the way a tree draws water."

"Okay," he chuckled. "Anything else?"

"No, other than that, I think it's perfect." Sarah closed her eyes. "Imagine the view from our bedroom with that whole wall of windows. We can fall asleep listening to the surf. Doesn't that sound dreamy?"

"Yes, as long as you remember we'll be facing due east. It's going to get bright early."

"Fine by me, as long as the baby's room is on the west side and we can sleep in a little."

John glanced up at the sound of a car pulling into their driveway. "That's odd; it's Mary Rose. Uh-oh. Batten down the hatches. She's with Mom."

Sarah checked the wall clock. It read eight-thirty. "It's a little early for a social call, don't you think?"

"This is not a social call," he observed as Mary Rose helped Jenny out of the car. Jenny settled her coat and marched sturdily up the sidewalk. "I know that walk," he warned. "Mom's on a mission."

Sarah shuffled toward the door, mustering as much goodwill as she could summon at that early hour. She opened the door wide. "Good morning."

"My dear, I hope we're not too early," Jenny apologized, stopping on the threshold and clutching her leather purse to her chest. "But I wanted to catch John before he left for work. I hope you don't mind."

"Not at all. Please come in. We were just finishing breakfast." Sarah noted that Jenny looked bedraggled. Her silver hair was pinned into an unkempt bun and she had dark circles under her eyes. "Would you like some coffee?"

"No, thank you, none for me," Jenny replied, briskly. "Please don't go to any trouble."

Mary Rose held up both hands. "Don't give me that look. She made me bring her. Besides, you two had it easy. She woke my house at seven-fifteen."

John kissed his mother's cheek. "Mom? How are you feeling today?"

"Fine, John, fine. And I do not want to be coddled in any way." Jenny sat, taking his chair and unbuttoning her coat. "I would just like to say that yesterday was a very difficult day for us all. And John, I couldn't sleep last night worrying that you might think that somehow I had doubted your veracity. I have already apologized to Micah, and Jackie, and I wanted to come here first thing, to tell you how sorry I am for my behavior."

John smiled at his mother's use of formal language, a dead-giveaway that she was embarrassed about the topic under discussion. "Don't worry about it, Mom. Yesterday was a tough day for all of us."

"That is no excuse for my behavior and I won't be happy again until I ask your forgiveness. I doubted you yesterday, son, only because I couldn't believe what it was you were saying. My desire to have Danny back kept me from hearing the truth. I can only hope I didn't hurt your feelings because of my reaction. If I did, son, I am truly sorry."

"You didn't hurt my feelings, Mom. I knew where you were coming from."

"Good. I needed to hear that." Jenny relaxed. "And I have to say I'm so proud of the way you and Micah put a stop to that imposter. That con-man tried to hurt this family and I will not have it. Yesterday, I was not prepared, but I will not be caught out again. So, John, what's going to become of Ava and that imposter?"

"He's been charged with felony forgery. It's up to the jury now. He'll get some prison time, probably MCI/ Plymouth. But Ava? I'm not sure. She's only an accessory, and she was clever – she never actually signed anything. All we have is hearsay: 'he said, she said'. That makes it a tough case to prove. Even if the jury finds her guilty as an accessory, she'll be out in eighteen months, maybe less."

"She'd better not come back here after what she's pulled," Mary Rose growled. "She'd better get out and just keep going."

Jenny frowned. "I still find it hard to believe that Ava cooked up something like this. Why, I knew her mother!"

"She's certainly not the person I thought she was," John frowned. "She had this whole other agenda and we were just a part of it."

"She used us, you can say that," Mary Rose crossed her arms. "She deliberately used us to get what she wanted."

"But where did she meet that imposter? That's what I want to know."

"I was just telling Sarah. His story is they met in Miami last October. Ava was there on vacation. He says she came up and mentioned how much he looked like people she knew back home. He thought it was a pickup line until she mentioned the money." He lifted his coffee mug and one corner of the blueprint curled in response. "Once Ava got back to Nantucket she mailed him a copy of Uncle Ethan's Will, for proof. It's the only mistake she made; he kept the envelope and it does have her return address typed on it."

"So what's going to happen now?"

"They're in the Main Street lockup until Judge Coffin sets a court date. When and if they're convicted, they'll get shipped to facilities on the mainland. This really was Raymond's first offense. He had no priors, not even a traffic ticket. That tells me Ava really was the instigator here."

Jenny Jarad stared at her son. "Has Ava shown any remorse?"

"No." He swallowed. "I tried to talk to her yesterday. I asked her why she did it, to try to understand what was going through her mind. But when she saw it was me, she turned her face to the wall and put a pillow over her head. I think she was crying, but she really and truly is only speaking to her lawyer."

"I knew there was something wrong with her from the beginning," Mary Rose stated. "A tailored size two. It's not natural."

"Not everyone has large bones, dear," Jenny Jarad smiled gently. "Now, John, there's something else I need to ask you. It's the other reason I was up half the night." She firmed her lips. "How did Danny die, John? How did my little boy die?"

"Mom," he tried to answer, but his voice broke low. He struggled to filter out the details of the Medical Examiner's report that his mother did not need to hear. The shattered skull. The rotted red cloth jacket. The thin, splintered ribs. He swallowed hard and tried again. "Mom, Paul Jenkins confirmed it. Danny was shot."

"Murdered? You're saying my little boy was murdered, then?"

"It may have been an accident. It wasn't a...close-contact wound."

"God help us," Jenny whispered, plucking a handful of tissues. "God help me."

"Mom, please, take it easy," Mary Rose leaned forward. "I know this is hard."

"Hard? God, yes, it's hard. What makes it harder is that I knew Danny was dead before John found his grave."

"You knew there was an imposter?" Sarah asked.

"Yes, in my heart, I knew. Even in the hospital, when I said the words, I knew they weren't true. If Danny were alive, I would have felt something." Jenny clenched her fist and pressed it against her chest, rocking slowly. "I just wanted him back. I wanted him back so badly. I wanted it more than I can say."

"Oh, Mom, I know you did. We all did. We all wanted Danny back."

Jenny nodded through her tears. "At least now we know where he is. At least we have that much. When will Paul Jenkins release his body, John? We need to arrange a memorial service and a proper Christian burial."

"It's not up to Paul." He pushed off the counter. "This is still an active investigation. We need to hold all the evidence until the case is closed."

"Who's in charge of the investigation?" Mary Rose wondered. "It's not you, John, is it?"

"Oh, son, do you think that's wise?" Jenny echoed. "Shouldn't you assign it to someone else?"

"No. No, I won't. Danny was my brother. It's my investigation. End of story."

"Now, son," Jenny remonstrated. "I think you should reconsider that decision. Someone less closely involved might be better suited to pursue the case." She twisted her hands. "I would hate to see you obsess over Danny's disappearance the way your father did. You and Jack are so much alike, sometimes I worry."

"I'm not going to obsess over Danny's case, Mom, I'm going to solve it." John rolled the blueprint tight. "Besides, Dad had nothing to go on. I do."

"What more do you have?" Jenny blinked. "What information do you have that your father didn't?"

John handed Sarah the blueprint. "For one thing, I'm pretty sure Uncle Ethan was involved. Dad never knew that."

"Ethan?" Jenny studied at her son. "What makes you say that?"

"The nature of the grave." John rubbed his hands together. "The evidence indicates Uncle Ethan's presence at the grave the day Danny was buried. Dad didn't know that."

"Uncle Ethan had a pistol, too," Mary Rose offered. "I remember seeing it at his house."

"And I've asked the demolition crew to keep an eye out for it. If they find it, we can run it through forensics. That may be a piece of our puzzle."

Jenny sighed. "I just keep wondering if I should have known something. Ethan was acting so oddly around the time Danny disappeared. I put it down to the nature of their relationship, but now that I look back on it, I suppose it could have been guilt." She hunched her shoulders. "What I don't understand is how he could have kept something like that from us? He saw what we were going through. Losing Danny killed your father. How could Ethan have lived with that knowledge, day after day, and not told us about it?"

John cleared his throat. "I think he did it to protect himself, Mom. I think there was some kind of accident and Danny died, and Uncle Ethan had to make a choice – and he didn't have the courage to stand up and tell the truth. I think he decided to hide, and to lie. And even if he didn't actually do it, I think he knew who did. Either way, he's was the one who hid Danny's body. I'm sure of that much."

"But why? What was so important that Ethan could do this terrible thing?"

"I think it had something to do with drugs, and maybe Danny stumbled onto it. I've heard from a few people that

Uncle Ethan was working a smuggling ring off the island about that time."

"And he knowingly exposed Danny to that kind of risk?" Jenny whispered, horrified. "For what? For profit?"

"You know, John," Mary Rose interrupted. "Maybe you should talk to Richard Robey while he's on island. If Uncle Ethan did have anything to do with drugs, Richard would know about it."

"Oh, I'm going to talk to Richard Robey," John glanced at the kitchen clock. It was ten after nine and he was late for work – again. He reached for his coat. "There are a couple of people I'm going to talk to. Sheriff Toohey is one of them, and Beryl Farrar is another. I'm convinced she knows more than she's telling, too."

"Call me later?" Sarah asked.

"Sure." He kissed his wife, mother and sister goodbye and moved out into the cold. The sun was rising over a peach-striped horizon and their small square of front lawn was rimed with frost. John pulled on his leather gloves and breathed in the promise of a fresh start and a new day. And today, he decided, was the day he would get some answers.

Unit Three was still parked in the driveway. After yesterday's confusion, he had neglected to return it to the pound. He opened the patrol car door and slid across the stiff seat, cranking the ignition and rubbing his hands together while waiting for the engine to warm. He gave a moment's thought to actually having a garage to park their vehicles in. John shook his head. What an idea.

As he backed around his sister's car and turned toward town his stomach rumbled. Except for the two cups of black coffee, he was empty, and he decided to make a quick stop along the way and pick up something to eat. Privately, he hoped this work day would be an easy one and he would be able to spend a significant chunk of time going over Danny's case file. If he could just start separating the facts from the deliberate obfuscations Raymond and Ava had constructed, John hoped he might begin to glimpse what had actually happened to his little brother.

He took a left on Sparks Avenue, considering the snarl of motivations he had uncovered. Present events just continued to prove that you never really knew what motivated some people to act. Desperation, betrayal, physical or emotional fear, panic – these were feelings you could understand that might lead some people to violence. But greed? Where did greed fit in? Greed had certainly led Raymond and Ava's into committing fraud – but when John thought of Uncle Ethan, he wondered: could greed lay the foundation for cold-blooded murder? Especially the cold-blooded murder of an innocent child?

John squinted, trying to imagine living a life with that type of secret eating away at you. He tried to imagine knowing the godforsaken truth and never being able to speak it out loud, of never being able to share the burden of truth with anyone up to and beyond the grave. No wonder Uncle Ethan had been such a furious alcoholic! A fifth of vodka a day would certainly dull any normal feelings of remorse – and how else could anyone endure such a hellishly endless deception and stay sane? Even harder to fathom, what would it do to a human spirit to live twenty years with the constant nagging dread of hearing someone speak the unforgivable truth?

John coughed, surprised, caught red-handed in his own moral trap. For while he had been busily judging Uncle Ethan actions, one of his own recent half-truths had snuck up and tapped his shoulder. Because, contrary to what he had told his wife and family, his interview with Ava Descartes had not been entirely wordless.

Before she had turned away, Ava had studied him for a full minute, her face bloodless and pale without makeup. "I'm not sorry for what I did, John. At least I had the guts to try," she announced dully. "Now go home to your little wife and try to make her happy. But don't think you're fooling me. You think you've finally made a commitment, but it's only because your marriage is still so young. Give it time and you'll see. Another year or two – and you'll be tired of her."

"That is not true. I love Sarah."

"Oh, John, I know you better than you know yourself! You only think you love her. Right now she's the exotic animal in the local zoo. Oh, I'll give Sarah credit – she's kept you hopping with that rush wedding and now this pregnancy. But trust me, once she runs out of tricks, you'll be back to the same old thing." Ava laughed bitterly. "Go on. You'll find out I'm right soon enough. You're such a sucker. You've made a bigger mistake than I have."

And that's when his ex-fiancée, a woman John had once loved, sat down on her cot, turned her back to him and placed the thin jail-house pillow over her head.

Blindly, he pulled into a parking space and stopped the car, wondering why he hadn't felt it necessary to share that conversation with his wife? Lord knows they shared everything else! Because, his inner voice reasoned, it had been a part of a private conversation between himself and his ex-fiancée – and nothing Ava had said had a bearing on his case or on any aspect of his married life. He had made his commitment to Sarah standing at the altar before God, and while Ava was certainly entitled to her opinion, she was wrong about him. He had made the commitment to Sarah and their life together. That was it. End of story.

So, John's conscience prickled, that certainly sounds reasonable. But where, he wondered, just where did his version of the truth end and his ability to lie begin?

"Chrissakes!" John unsnapped his seatbelt. "This case is starting to get to me."

He removed his hat and entered the donut shop. The air was warm and rich with the perfume of roasted coffee beans and the thick, sugary vanilla scent of freshly baked goods. The stout manager of the bake shop, Martha Goody, looked up as he entered. "Morning, John. What can I get you?"

"Morning, Martha. A large half decaf, a dozen of the glazed and a copy of the Inky Mirror if you have it."

"Coming up." She plucked a waxed tissue square and began to fill a cardboard box. "I heard about you and that con-man, John. Talk's all over town this morning." She closed the box with her thumbs and nodded toward the tables. "You arrested Ava Descartes, too? She a part of it?"

"Seems to be." John nodded, passing across a ten-dollar bill. "We'll find out more at the trial."

"Won't miss that." Martha counted out his change. "You know, John, I never liked that girl. Always thought she was wrong for you. Too stuck up for words."

"She's surprised us all." He nodded. "You have a nice day."

"I'll try, John. You too."

He carried his purchase back to the car and ripped into the box, filling his mouth with the warm soft dough, wolfing down a donut and a half before starting the unit up and pulling back out onto Sparks Avenue. John chewed and sipped and grinned, feeling better now that he had something solid in his stomach.

Leaning forward, he clicked on his dispatch radio. Instantly, Unit Three was filled with crackling static and then, clearly, the sound of Tina's voice. "John? Are you there? Over."

He reached for the handset and answered around a mouthful of donut. "Yes, Tina. What's up?"

"You need to get to Madaket. Code 2-0, 10-32. They found a floater."

He rotated the steering wheel hard right, pushing the unit toward Main and Madaket road. Madaket harbor was close enough to Eel Point and there was only one missing person's report he was aware of. John flicked on his lights and the siren and raised his voice to be heard over the pounding the unit's suspension system was taking. "Tina? The 10-32? It's not Addie Simpson, is it?"

"No, it's not Addie Simpson. It's an adult white male." The reception bristled again. "Sam Ketchum's already on-site – and I've notified the M.E.'s office, too. Paul Jenkins said he'll meet you there."

"On my way." He floored the accelerator, thankful for the non-existent off-season morning traffic. It was still early – the only pedestrian he startled was a lone jogger jolted fully awake by the patrol car's blaring siren and concussive passage.

He cruised past the dunes of Dionis and the landscape flattened into a low, sandy wasteland. At the fork in the road near Long Pond John turned right into Madaket. The road narrowed and he brought the unit to a skidding halt in a gravel lot at the top of a long, slanting concrete commercial pier. Leaving the car to idle, he trotted down a boat ramp to meet

Paul Jenkins, who was slowly climbing up and away from the oily gray water of Madaket harbor.

"Morning, John." Paul nodded, removing a pair of latex gloves and discarding them in a nearby fifty-gallon oil-drum trashcan. "Not that I'm complaining, but I am seeing a lot of you, lately."

"Who've we got?" John followed the Medical Examiner upwind, keeping one eye on a paramedic loading a black plastic body bag onto a portable gurney.

The older man calmly fished out a briar pipe and a small cotton bag of tobacco. Filling his pipe and tamping the tobacco with his thumb, Paul frowned. "It's Richard Robey, John. Although between the surf and the collateral damage it was hard to tell who we had, at first."

"Richard Robey?" John repeated, stopping short to process this new possibility. "Richard Robey?"

"Can't say I'm surprised. Richard's been asking for something like this for years." The Medical Examiner lit a wooden match and drew repeatedly on his pipe. "I don't know what he's been up to lately, but I know I still hold him responsible for Betsy Ketchum's overdose and I know there's others like me." He pointed his chin toward Sam Ketchum, the dead girl's cousin, who was standing nearby. "Can't honestly say I blame them."

"Betsy Ketchum?" John recalled details of the earlier case. "That was heroin, wasn't it?"

"Yep. Nasty stuff." The older man looked across the ruffled water. "But I'm afraid that's old news, now."

"What killed him?" John fell into step and the two men continued up the ramp. "Did he drown?"

"Nope. Right now it looks like someone emptied a gun into him. I think Richard went into the water after he was dead, but I won't know for sure until after the autopsy."

"Multiple wounds? Sounds like someone wanted to make sure he was dead."

"Maybe so, John, but this was strictly amateur hour. One bullet broke his left femur, I can see that already. The other damage was centered around his chest. If this was a professional hit, your killer made a real mess of it."

"Multiple wounds might also indicate a defensive reaction to a threat."

"Then why try to hide the body in the water? If it were a case of self-defense there'd be no need." Paul tapped his pipe against his palm. "He's been in the water at least one full day, John, maybe two. If I were you, I'd see what the Rip's been up to lately. That might tell you where he went in."

"I'll do that." John sucked in a deep breath. Of course he knew all about the Rip, the strong offshore current that ran along the southern coast of Nantucket like a permanent undertow. Local children were taught in kindergarten that if they were caught by the Rip and carried away from the beach to just float with it – as long as they didn't struggle the Rip would float them around Smith's Point and drop them in Madaket Harbor as easy as catching a bus. Finding Richard's body in Madaket Harbor already told him two things and he needed to consider each item thoroughly. One, Richard Robey had gone into the water somewhere within reach of the Rip, which meant virtually anywhere along the southern coast of the island as far east as 'Sconset; and two, whoever thought they could dispose of Richard's body by rolling it into the water probably wasn't from Nantucket or they would have known enough to avoid the Rip and its well-known predilection.

It wasn't much, John admitted, but it was a place to start.

He heard a warning shout from the group of spectators and glanced up to see a hunter-green Suburban tearing into the graveled parking lot, its driver blatantly ignoring the yellow crime scene tape blocking access to the marina. Stretched to its limit, the tape snapped like a firecracker as the vehicle slid to a halt. The driver's side door popped open, revealing a disheveled George Robey behind the wheel.

"Here comes trouble," Paul Jenkins warned.

"John Jarad! I want to talk to you!" The developer struggled with his seatbelt. "I want to talk to you now!"

John stretched out both arms to intercept the clearly overwrought man. "I don't know what you've heard, George, but you shouldn't be here."

"Chrissakes, yes, I should be here! I'm listening to my scanner and I hear they pull a man's body out of Madaket harbor. My brother hasn't been home in a couple of days. It's not Richard, is it?"

"I'm sorry, George, but yes, I'm afraid it is."

"It can't be! He had no business near the water!" George charged the stretcher and shouldered the paramedics aside. Gripping the zipper on the body bag, George tugged it open. Extended salt-water immersion had not improved his brother's looks. George gagged and stepped aside to vomit into the gravel near his shoes.

"I'll take that as a positive identification," the Medical Examiner remarked softly. "It'll save me some trouble, later."

George pulled a handkerchief from his breast pocket and wiped his mouth. With a look of disgust, he balled up the linen square and tossed it into the trashcan. "I can't believe this," George whispered, wiping his eyes with the heel of his right hand. "This is not right. I can't believe he came back here to drown."

"He didn't drown, George. He was shot."

"Shot?" George's voice quavered near hysteria. "What do you mean shot? Who would've shot my brother?"

"Has Richard mentioned any trouble lately? Maybe something from before? Someone with a grudge?"

"Let me think, let me think." The developer repeated, unconsciously smoothing his hair. "Richard said he ran into a couple of guys at Silky's last Saturday, but he wasn't looking for trouble, so he left."

"Did he mention any names?"

"Sure. Pete Cassard and Rene Peloso." George swallowed heavily. "But they wouldn't do something like this, John, they had no reason to. I'm telling you, Richard came home to get clean. He wasn't looking to start any trouble."

"I'll talk to them," John replied doubtfully. He knew the two men George had mentioned. They were well-established local lobstermen and off-hand he couldn't think of any historic reason they would want to see Richard Robey dead. Plus, both men were familiar with the Rip. Richard's murder looked more like imported trouble. "Did Richard ever mention someone from off island?"

"There was this stranger," George straightened his tie. "Came to the house late on Tuesday night. His name was, what was it? Ah, Tom or Rob, something short like that. I didn't catch a last name. When I told him Richard wasn't home, he walked off into the night. Why? Do you think he might have had something to do with this?"

"What did this stranger look like?"

"Nothing much of anything, really. Five-foot ten, maybe a hundred and forty pounds, brown hair, thin, narrow face. Nothing distinguishing." The developer snapped his fingers. "But he was from the mainland, I do remember that because he had this really annoying nasal accent."

John nodded. The investigation was taking shape. Establishing a timeline was critical. "When was the last time you saw Richard?"

"Me? Well, let me see. We ordered Chinese take-out, what night was that? Monday? Yes, on Monday."

"It's been three days since you saw your brother, and you weren't worried?"

"Chrissakes, John, of course I was worried! But Richard kept odd hours and I work a long day. I wasn't his keeper, you know."

"George, I'm going to have to ask you some tough questions if I'm going to catch his killer," John squinted into the rising sun. "I'm counting on your help with this."

"Of course, John, of course, I'm sorry. I'll help you every way I can." The developer turned his eyes toward the sea. "Just thank God he came ashore, that's all I have to say. At least I can bury him decently." George crossed his arms and shivered. "I know he was trouble, John, but he was my brother. A proper burial is the least I can do for him."

CHAPTER SEVENTEEN

"John, you've been awful quiet this morning." Sarah turned to face her husband. "Is something on your mind?"

"No." His fingers drummed the steering wheel. "Just thinking about my cases. There are a lot of loose ends I'd like to tie up."

"Anything I can do to help?" Sarah offered hopefully.

"No. No, thanks. I just need some time to think about things. Sort them out. You know."

Sarah fell silent and decided to give John some room. She knew he was deeply involved in his multiple investigations just now, but still, she couldn't help but feel slighted by his recent inattention. Just when she needed him the most, Sarah felt her husband growing distant and preoccupied. She rubbed her belly and tried not to feel sorry for herself – but it seemed like lately, whenever she reached out for John, she found herself shut out.

She adjusted her seatbelt and tried to get comfortable. Comfort was another aspect of pregnancy that she found irksome. For one thing, she had trouble sleeping on her stomach, her favorite and usual position; now it gave her indigestion. And anything strapped around her middle felt absolutely too tight and constricting. All in all, she admitted with a small sigh, pregnancy was proving to be a very difficult and irritable time.

She studied the line of slow-moving vehicles directly ahead, part of the procession following a black hearse along a winding crushed-shell lane into an ancient cemetery. Intermittently, her view was interrupted by the truck's windshield wipers as they struggled with icy buildup, packing knobby ridges against the glass. It was rare weather for Nantucket, but a blue norther had blown in during the night and turned drizzle into sleet. As she watched, the defroster softened a slush ball and it melted, sliding slowly down the glass.

John leaned forward and used his cuff to wipe the fogged windshield. "I don't know what George was thinking. He should have known better than to hold a graveside service, this time of year."

"I'm surprised he's even having a service. I mean, Richard was murdered. Aren't you supposed to hold the body until the killer is caught?"

"It wasn't really necessary; Paul took all the samples he needed. And holding the body was upsetting George. If we need to, we can get a Court Order and exhume the body later."

"The killer took an awful chance." Sarah stated, determined to discuss the details of the case and help John whether he wanted her help or not. "I mean, hauling his body down to the water. Someone might have seen him do it."

"I'm counting on it that someone did." John's face reflected a red brake light as the car in front of them slowed. "Did I tell you C.J. found a shower curtain in a dumpster behind the Nantucket Island Bank yesterday? We sent it to the Boston lab for analysis. We think it was used to move Richard's body."

Sarah laced her fingers together and glanced out the side window. No, she frowned, John had not told her about the shower curtain yesterday, and here was another example of neglect to add to her list. She tried, and failed, to keep an aggrieved tone out of her reply. "No, John, no, you didn't tell me that."

"Yes, well," he nodded absently. "We may get lucky, yet."

She pushed past her frustration to consider what John had actually said. "Wait a minute – the NIB? That's the bank where Ava Descartes worked!"

"That's right."

"Well, John, listen to this – what if Richard Robey found out about Ava and Raymond's scam and he tried to blackmail them – and they killed him to shut him up?"

"You're not bad, but you're a day behind." John smoothly pulled over and parked on a grassy verge. "I had them both paraffin tested. Unfortunately, they're clean."

Sarah felt patronized by John's distant tone and voiced her rising exasperation. "So maybe they had another partner! Did you think about that?"

"Yes, honey, I did consider that, but there's no way. Raymond would have told us about it by now. He's spilling his guts at any chance to reduce his sentence." John squinted curiously at his wife. "Sarah, are you okay? You seem a little tense."

She wrestled silently with herself, torn between two competing desires. More than anything she wanted to tell John that she couldn't help feeling she was being left out of his life lately, and that her resentment about it was growing. She knew she would feel so much better if she could just get this pent-up feeling out in the open, but at the same time, she wondered: how could I dump all that on John right now? He didn't need her adding her problems to his burden. He had enough to think about. She decided to keep her feelings to herself. "I'm sorry, John. I'm fine. I guess I'm tired. I didn't sleep very well last night."

"Sweetheart, we don't have to be here, you know. No one will miss us if you'd rather go home."

"No, no, we should be here. Everyone else from the island will be. I want to participate." She took a slow, steadying breath and rallied her wobbling spirit. "I'm okay. Really, I am."

"If you're sure." John peered out into the freezing rain. "This isn't going to clear up anytime soon."

She tried to smile. "I'm sure. C'mon. Let's go."

John opened his door and walked over to her side of the truck, offering Sarah his arm and wrestling the wind for control of the umbrella. Together, they stepped up the hill, dodging oily shallow puddles, the wet crushed shell path crunching like broken teeth beneath their shoes. From all sides, car doors slammed a hollow chorus as fellow mourners left their vehicles and followed a path that led them all into the heart of the graveyard.

Sarah stopped ducking the sleet long enough to glance around, and found herself completely encircled by archaic slate and marble markers: a blank-eyed angel, a huddled sleeping lamb, a limbless tree. She stopped so suddenly she tugged on John's arm and he fumbled the umbrella, releasing a drenching slash of freezing rain that dribbled down the back of his neck. "Aahh, honey!? What's wrong?"

"John, look at how strange this is! These markers – they're not even in rows. Look! They're concentric."

"I should have told you about this place. You're going to like it. It's called the Burgess' Pie. Only Burgess family members get buried here."

"I thought Richard's last name was Robey?"

"It was, but his mother was a Burgess, so he's entitled."

"But look at this place!" She pointed toward a central granite pylon deeply engraved with the name BURGESS. "It's ridiculous – all these stones face the middle!"

"It's their tradition. All Burgess' family members get buried with their feet to the center. That way, on the Day of Judgment, when the angels call, they'll all rise up and face each other – surrounded only by other Burgesses."

"I've never heard of such a thing," Sarah sputtered. "It's…pagan!"

"They've buried them this way from the beginning. The only graves missing are the men who died at sea or died fighting in foreign lands. That's the Burgess' rule: no body, no headstone." John recalled Uncle Ethan's odd disposal and grinned. "Apparently, their tradition is just the opposite of ours."

"Well," Sarah placed both hands on her hips indignantly. "If what you say is true, when the angels call, I'm sure they'll all enjoy rising up and meeting Richard."

"That would be worth hearing," he chuckled. "I've heard some of the old Burgesses were next to the Devil in righteousness." He tightened his grip on the umbrella. "Honey, have you seen enough? Let's get out of this weather."

They tucked their shoulders into the wind and joined the shuffling queue of mourners making their way toward a large stoutly-pegged white canvas tent. Before Sarah's eyes, the humped rain-slick black umbrellas took on the fantastic form of some supernatural sea-creature struggling and sloshing its way through the mortal mud. And, always aware of the needs of her condition, she also noted the thoughtful downwind placement of a teal-blue Port-a-Loo, filing that vital piece of information away for future need. She knew she would need it.

They ducked through a canvas flap and Sarah slowly unbuttoned her coat. She noted the center of attention – a gleaming mahogany coffin resting on four solid wooden battens over an open, sandy grave. "At least it's a closed casket ceremony," she whispered.

"I saw the body." John shook the sleet off their umbrella. "Trust me. It wasn't an option."

The gravesite was framed by overlapping slabs of unseasonably green sod, and the coffin was topped by an extravagant display of imperial lilies. The lush tropical flowers overpowered the warm confined space with their rich, heady scent, and Sarah found herself feeling woozy. She looked around for the source of the interior warmth and located a large portable space heater discretely tucked in one corner. "Holy cow, John. Someone sure went to a lot of trouble over this!"

"Must have been George. There's no one else in their family left."

George Robey spotted them from across his brother's open grave and smiled tightly. Dressed in a slate gray flannel suit with a navy and silver barred tie, the developer stepped delicately across the muddied ground to join them. "John, Sarah. Thank you for coming."

John clasped George's outstretched hand. "Please accept our condolences, George. It's a shame this happened."

"Thank you." He nodded, allowing himself another small, tight smile. "And John, thank you again for easing things with Paul Jenkins. I appreciate your effort. I hated the idea of

Richard locked up in the morgue. He's better off here – resting at peace – with the rest of the family."

Sarah nodded politely. "You have quite a family history here, George. I've never seen anything else like it."

"Yes, I believe our Pie is unique. But I'm afraid it's finished now. Richard completed the final circle – there's no room left. When it comes my turn, I'll need to start a whole new pie."

"Yes, um, well…" Sarah stammered, caught by the awkward nature of George's response. "Ah, let's hope that's a long way off."

"Yes, let's." George smoothed his perfectly groomed hair. "John, I hate to ask, but I need another favor – I hope you won't mind."

"Of course not, George. What more can I do?"

"I hoped we could postpone closing on your property for a few days. I'm not in any shape right now to make a business decision, and this whole thing…" George gestured toward his brother's coffin, "…has me reeling on my pins. My lawyers are reviewing our sales agreement, but I really need a few days to find my bearings." He sighed wearily. "Would that be alright? If I took a few days before we signed?"

Slowly, John blinked. "Of course, George. Take all the time you need."

"Thank you." George winced and reached up to massage his right temple. "I'm leaving for Hilton Head first thing tomorrow morning. I don't plan on being gone for longer than the weekend, but I...I really need some rest." He glanced over toward the funeral director who was waving discreetly to attract his attention. "Excuse me. I believe I'm needed elsewhere. Find yourselves a seat; I'm sure we'll get started soon."

The noise level inside the tent had risen appreciably above a murmur as more mourners filtered in and choose seats from among the rows of folding golden oak chairs. Sarah noted a cluster of familiar faces on the opposite side of the tent and watched Jenny Jarad coordinate the placement of her brood. Mary Rose had decided to sit with her mother (over the silent, arched eyebrow protests of her Quigley in-laws) and she was giving final instructions to her three rambunctious boys. Her husband, Matt, was nowhere in sight.

"Your Mom's over there," Sarah pointed. "Let's sit with them."

"Lead on," John nodded, and clasped her hand.

They snaked through the crowd, jostled on all sides by the steady incoming stream of islanders who stopped and stood, bewildered by the lush spectacle that met their eyes. It was beginning to look like a capacity crowd, Sarah decided; evidently every soul on Nantucket was chancing the weather to pay their last respects to the scion of a prominent local family whether they had actually liked Richard Robey as a person, or not.

The crowd contained the usual mix of island characters: brawny charter fisherman with weathered faces, deeply-lined crows feet the all-too-visible consequence of constant overexposure to glaring sun and parching salt wind. A few of the fishermen had their ponytails tied back with black ribbon, a considerate gesture specific to the occasion. The opposite end of the island population was represented by an assembly of extremely well-groomed men and women in tailored suits who spoke surreptitiously into cellphones – George's business contacts from his real estate and county development connections. Adding the lone splash of color to the event,

Father McNimick sat in his black cassock and white surplice, a plum-colored stole swinging from both shoulders as he comforted an elderly man with a cane.

Sarah ducked to avoid the brim of a woman's hat and solidly nudged the stocky man standing in front of her. The stranger turned and smiled gently. "Excuse me, young lady. I'll be happy to move out of the way as soon as I'm able."

"I'm so sorry," Sarah blushed. "It sure is getting crowded in here."

"Why, hello, John. Didn't see you standing there."

"Honey, this is Sheriff Toohey. I know I've told you about him. He's been helping me with my investigations."

"Of course. It's nice to meet you, Sheriff."

"Well, well, well. And it's nice to finally meet you, young lady." The sheriff cocked one eye at her. "And my wife Rebecca tells me congratulations are in order?"

Sarah blushed even deeper and finally accepted the fact there was simply no privacy to be had on this island. "Yes, we're due the end of September."

"Great! Just what this island needs – another Jarad running around." The big man chuckled and pulled them both aside. "Kidding, I'm kidding. Rebecca says I need to explain myself more; evidently some folks take me the wrong way." The sheriff lowered his voice and rubbed both hands together. "So, John, did you get those lab results back yet?"

"The report came over the fax first thing this morning… "

"And?" Sheriff Toohey interrupted, intrigued. "What news?"

"Someone did use the shower curtain to move Richard's body. It was covered with Type A negative blood."

"That's fine, son," the sheriff cautioned. "But that doesn't necessarily prove the curtain was used to move Richard Robey. Don't forget, twenty percent of the population tests A negative."

"They also matched cotton fibers in the blood to the shirt he was wearing when we pulled him out of Madaket harbor," John continued. "That's pretty conclusive."

"I'll buy that," Sheriff Toohey agreed.

Sarah glanced at her husband, astonished by the conversation. In spite of herself, she could feel her resentment rising. Why hadn't John shared these details with her when they had discussed the shower curtain? And how was she supposed to help him solve his cases if he wasn't going to share his information? Even more infuriating, what else about his cases had he already neglected to share?

"Carpet fibers?" The sheriff pursued. "Hair or skin samples? Fingernail? DNA?"

"The lab I.D.'d a paint sample they scraped off Richard's belt buckle. He may have been moved in a flame-red Dodge car or truck."

"Flame-red?" The sheriff puffed thoughtfully, pulling on his lower lip. "Hummm. Haven't seen too many of them around lately."

"I know where one is," Sarah interjected, looking directly at her husband. "Eddie Farrar had a flame-red Dodge truck. And just because Eddie's dead doesn't mean that someone didn't borrow it. Like the murderer you're looking for, maybe?"

"I know Beryl was unhappy Richard was back on island, she told me so herself." John scanned the tent. "I don't see her here. If she doesn't show up, I'll go out to her place this afternoon. I think maybe it's time she and I had another talk."

"You be careful if you go out there, John." Sheriff Toohey scratched his chin. "I don't like the way this case is shaping up. Paul said Richard was dead before he went into the water. I sincerely doubt Beryl Farrar had the strength to move anything as heavy as Richard's body by herself. If she moved it, she had help. I wouldn't go out there alone." He glanced up as an intricate Mozart prelude began to compete with the soft drumming of the rain on the canvas overhead. "That's our cue. Keep me posted. I'd better go join my wife."

"There you are!" Mary Rose announced their approach. "We lost you at the rotary. Here, Sam," she prodded her son. "Scoot over and make room for your aunt and uncle. Sarah, sit next to me. I feel like I haven't seen you in a month."

"I know what you mean," Sarah dropped into the chair. "And I feel like I've only seen you at funerals lately."

"What a horrible thought! But if nothing else, I have to admit I am getting my money's worth out of this dress. Charlie, stop that! I saw you pinch your brother."

"But Mom, he started it."

"I don't care who started it. I told you to behave. Now, boys, listen to me. I am dead serious. I want company manners from you until we get home."

"When is this going to start? It's taking forever!" Little Dave whined, kicking his heels against his chair. "I have to go to the bathroom!"

Mary Rose slapped her forehead. "I am going to lose my mind. I asked you before we left the house if you needed to go."

"But that was then – I need to go now!"

"There's a Port-a-Loo outside," Sarah suggested. "Down the hill, on the left."

"Thank God someone was thinking ahead. Charlie, did you hear what your Aunt Sarah said? There's a loo down the hill, portside. Take your brother out, will you? Please?"

Spotting a chance at freedom, Charlie jumped. "Sure thing, Mom. C'mon Davey, let's go."

"Now, boys, wait a minute, listen to me. I know it's muddy out there, but please try to keep yourselves clean. This is a funeral, after all." As the three boys bolted for exit, Mary Rose sighed heavily. "I tell you what, it is a never-ending battle. Lord help me, I just do not have the strength."

"You do your best, dear," Jenny leaned forward and patted her daughter's knee. "No one can ask for more."

"How you ever did it with all of us, Mom, I will never know."

"I had help," Jenny replied placidly. "Your father was very good at keeping you kids out of my hair. Speaking of husbands, where's Matthew today?"

"On that job in Cisco. They wanted to finish the roof before the weather hit." Mary Rose glanced uneasily at the undulating canvas overhead. "I hope they made it."

"Don't worry about Matt." John crossed his arms. "He knows how to rig a safety better than anyone I know."

"I know that." Mary Rose looked unconvinced. "Still, I can't help but worry…"

Sarah was distracted by an odd clicking sound and traced it to its source, two elderly ladies sitting in the front row. From their interchangeable appearance, the women must have been close cousins at least, sisters at best. The woman on the right had her mouth set in a severely disapproving frown, and she was tsk-tsking loudly. Her vehement exhalation through her dental plate had made the odd sound Sarah had noticed.

"Gold-plated handles!" The woman muttered. "I ask you, who needs gold-plated handles on their coffin? As if you could buy a ticket into heaven!"

The woman on the left replied softly. "I'm sure George just wanted to do what was best, Rachel. You know, he paid for every bit of this funeral. I consider it an act of pure Christian charity."

"Charity my foot! Throwing good money after bad, if you ask me." Rachel hunched her shoulders and scowled. "All this after he let Althea die in a poorhouse! I tell you what, that George Robey should be ashamed of himself."

"Rachel! It wasn't a poorhouse – Althea was staying with a distant cousin when she passed."

"A cousin who kept a public house and let out rooms for cash money! No, my girl, use a fancy name for a foul subject if you like – and George Robey can put on all the show he wants – but I'm not changing my opinion. George Robey is a crooked skinflint and there's no doubt in my mind he did his mother out of her inheritance."

"Well, he seems to have plenty of money, now."

"And where did he get it, I ask you? Working his little deals and doing honest people out of their homes! Just look at the strangers in this tent, Jane – half of them taking the seats of the good people George Robey helped push off the island!"

"I think it's rather nice to see someone local doing so well," Jane answered spiritedly, settling her purse in her lap. "Especially since the Robey's have suffered such terrible setbacks. First there was Frank, of course, he … died and then Althea left us, and now here's this terrible thing. Personally? I think George Robey deserves our support – and I've decided, when the time comes, that he is getting an exclusive listing on my house."

"Jane!" Her companion turned, gawking. "You can't be serious!"

"I most certainly am."

"Well! Don't say I didn't warn you." Rachel pointed an arthritic finger at the mahogany coffin lying in state. "I wouldn't put it past George Robey to find out he had a hand in what happened to his own brother!"

"Rachel! Please! Lower your voice," Jane replied, sharply. "You shouldn't say things like that! People might think you were serious. George Robey is a fine, upstanding young man, and you have no proof for one thing you've said."

"My instinct is all the proof I need, thank you very much. And my instinct says when I look at that coffin I'm looking at more of George Robey's fine handiwork!"

"I am not here to argue," Jane stood, trembling. "I am here to pay my respects to an island family that has suffered a tragic loss. Now, Rachel, if you will excuse me, I believe I can find more wholesome companionship – elsewhere."

"Fine!" Rachel crossed her arms and turned her scrawny, hunched back. "That's certainly fine by me!"

John leaned over and whispered into Sarah's ear: "Can you tell they're sisters?"

With three sisters of her own and infinite first-hand experience, Sarah had to agree. "I guessed as much."

"And what a sound, logical argument Rachel used, too! Completely ignore the facts and go with gut instinct instead. Ha!" John scoffed. "Amateurs!"

It was his blatantly superior, patronizing tone that finally pushed Sarah over the edge. Her frazzled temper boiled over and she scrambled to her feet. "John, I have to go outside. Now. Will you go with me, please?"

He looked up, startled. "You have to go outside now?"

"Absolutely now. Right this minute. Now."

He fumbled under his chair for the umbrella. "Mom? Save our seats, will you? We'll be right back."

"Certainly, John." Jenny looked worried. "Is something wrong?"

"I'm not sure. I'll find out. We'll be right back." He side-stepping down the narrow row to catch up with Sarah, who was already standing impatiently, arms crossed, next to the side exit. He hurried up, umbrella at the ready. "Honey, you must really need to go."

She turned without a word and stepped outside. The sleet had turned into a misting drizzle, and Sarah held her temper, wanting to get away from public view before exploding. "I don't really need to go. It's just that I'm so furious with you and I don't want to scream at you in front of your whole family."

"Scream at me?" John stopped, his shoes squelching in the frozen mud. "Why? What did I do?"

"I was standing right there when you told Sheriff Toohey everything about those lab results, and it's really starting to piss me off that you're not sharing that kind of information with me, too!"

"But honey, I am sharing everything with you…"

"No, John, no, you're not. First you 'forgot to mention' the shower curtain, and then you 'forgot to mention' the blood work." Sarah gestured angrily. "How am I supposed to help you if you won't keep me in the loop? Dammit, John, we agreed to help each other when we got married, remember?"

"Honey, whoa, wait a minute. I'm not following you. You and I agreed to help each other in our lives. Sheriff Toohey is helping me with my investigation. What's the problem here?"

"Well, excuse me, but it seems like your investigation is your life lately. Have you noticed that? You come home and you're not really there; it's obvious you're still thinking about 'your investigation'. You hardly ever talk to me anymore, we've stopped talking about the house, we've even stopped talking about the baby." She released a long sobbing breath and stood in the rain, miserable and trembling. "John, I never agreed to this. I don't want to live where you cut me out of half your life. It was all or nothing, John. All or nothing. That's what I agreed to!"

"Sarah, honey, take it easy." He felt the sudden need to touch his wife, to physically bridge the gap that had opened between them. He reached out and drew her, unresisting, into his arms. "I had no idea you felt like this; you never said a word to me. What? Am I supposed to guess how you feel? C'mon." He tried to remedy the situation with humor. "I'm a cop, not a mind reader."

"Don't you dare try to be funny." She sniffled into his jacket. "I'm serious about this."

"I can see that. And honey, listen, you do help me – by letting me do my job."

"Don't you dare patronize me!" Sarah pulled back. "I am not the little wife waiting at home for you! Dammit, John, I want to help you solve your cases. Why can't you understand that? I helped you before! This "amateur" saved your life!"

"You don't have to remind me about that," John dropped his arms and stepped back. "I think about what happened last summer almost every day." He firmed his lips. "I know my job is dangerous, I knew that going in. But I am not going to let my job spill over into my life, I can't let that happen. If anything ever happened to you or the baby because of me, I don't know what I'd do." He drew a deep breath. "Sarah, I can't go back to what I was before, I can't do it, I've come too far. I can't go back again. I wouldn't make it."

"John, you goof, I'm not asking to ride in the patrol car! I just want you to share your information with me so that I feel like a part of your whole life – not just the after-hours part."

"Alright, let's try this. In the future, I promise to try to be more 'aware' of what I'm doing and to share my case information with you. But you have to promise me that you'll tell me about the things that are bothering you and not let them build up. Like I said, I am not a mind-reader, and I hate to see you make yourself so unhappy. Will you promise me that?"

"Yes," Sarah smiled through her tears. "I can promise you that."

"Then I promise to do my best." John dipped his scarf into a puddle of rainwater that had collected on the canvas and gently wiped Sarah's face. "Now go visit the loo while we're out here so we can get out of this filthy weather."

He watched Sarah climb into the teal-blue box, leaving him to a thoughtful silence. Sure, he admitted, maybe he had been absorbed in his cases lately, but seriously, who wouldn't have been? Two unsolved murders and one of them a twenty year old mystery involving his own brother? Who wouldn't have been caught up by those situations? But maybe Sarah was right; maybe he had been a little obsessive lately.

His contemplation was interrupted by the sight of a dark green sedan parking on the lane below. A tardy mourner, John decided, watching an individual with a pork-pie hat stretch both legs out of the car while tentatively testing the weather with one upturned palm. As he watched, the stranger left his car, turning his shoulder into the wind and hunching protectively; an odd movement that puzzled John until he saw a lighter's yellow glow. The late arrival was Medical Examiner Paul Jenkins and Paul was enjoying a quick pipe.

The port-a-loo door opened and Sarah reappeared, straightening her coat. "Whew! That was disgusting. Do you need to go?"

"Not right now." John indicated the approaching M.E. with his chin. "Hello, Paul. Come to check on your latest customer?"

"John, Sarah. Pretty good turnout with the weather this bad. Thought it might keep some folks at home. Should've known better; I've lived here long enough." He turned up his collar. "I'm afraid this isn't a social call, John. I knew you'd be here and I have some news. It concerns the skeletal remains you found."

"Paul, listen, do me a favor. Don't be delicate about it, okay? Don't be afraid to say that Danny was my brother."

"Okay, if that's the way you want it, John." Paul nodded. "Something strange is going on, and I don't know what it means. But I swear to God, I triple-checked everything – there's no possibility I made a mistake."

"A mistake about what?"

"The bullet I recovered from…your brother's…skull. It's 8MM; that's not an American caliber. It threw me at first." He toyed nervously with his pipe. "But I did some research this morning. The bullet came from a Japanese pistol, a Type 14 Nambu automatic."

"Jesus," John's mouth went dry. "My uncle had a Japanese pistol. I don't know if it was a Nambu or not."

"Would you recognize it?" The M.E. pulled a color copy from his pocket. "Did the gun look like this?"

John reached for and slowly unfolded the paper. "The grip was different, but yes, that's what it looked like." He dropped his arm, his voice toneless. "Chrissakes. You're telling me Uncle Ethan killed Danny, aren't you?"

"We don't know that yet, John. Where's the gun now? It's important that we know. Is it still in your family?"

"No, it's gone," he shook his head, trying to marshal his thoughts. "It was in Uncle Ethan's house when it burned. We never recovered it."

"Actually, that's a good thing." The M.E. trembled with suppressed excitement. "I think you may never have found the gun because it wasn't there to be found. That's why I came up here to find you. I'm telling you, John – the bullets matched – they all matched."

"What do you mean the bullets matched? How many bullets did you recover?"

"That's what I'm saying. All the bullets matched. The bullet I recovered from your brother and the five I pulled out of Richard Robey – they were fired from the same gun. And that might explain why Richard was shot so many times. The Nambu wasn't a reliable pistol; it liked to misfire when it was new and God knows this one has to be sixty years old. I'm surprised it didn't backfire into your killer's hand."

"Wait a minute," Sarah interrupted, thinking furiously. "You're saying Richard's killer found Uncle Ethan's gun and took it from his house before it burned?"

"That is one of my ideas…".

"The arsonist?" John tapped his lips with his index finger. "The arsonist Matt Prescott kept insisting we had?"

"There's another possibility, John, and I have to bring it up," Paul continued, frowning. "It could also be that Richard's killer is the same person who shot your brother and he's kept the gun all this time." He tapped his pipe against his palm. "Either way, I think you got yourself a problem. It's just my opinion, mind you, but I think whoever killed your brother is still on this island – and always has been."

CHAPTER EIGHTEEN

Rookie Hank Viera ducked his head and glanced out the window at the frosted landscape. "You know what, Lieutenant? Not for nothing, but things look kinda spooky out this-a-way."

"Hank, you've never been down Hummock Pond Road before?"

"Well, not lately." The sandy-haired officer sheepishly scratched his jaw. "I know it sounds funny, but my family, well, we've always lived – and worked – in town."

John adjusted the steering wheel. "More criminal acts get committed outside of town limit than in."

"I can see why," the younger officer shivered. "Jesus! Who's going to see what happens out here?"

The patrol car carrying the two men was heading southwest. Hummock Pond Road bisected one of the few wild acreages left on Nantucket and the low sandy hills were obfuscated by dense thickets of scrub oak and huckleberry, their gnarled lichen-covered branches gray and green and blasted now by February's chill. Carpeted with heather and gorse, Scotch broom and creeping snowberry, the moors sported a lacey cap of new-fallen snow, a feathery, unexpected gift from a northeastern suitor named Winter.

"It's not usually this bleak," John offered. "Come back in October. I've seen it look like an oriental carpet. There are some amazing colors out here, ochre, burgundy, I've even seen aubergine."

"Aubergine?" Hank scoffed, his nervous laughter a loud bray. "What the hell color is that?"

John reddened. "Don't mind me. That's my wife talking."

"Oh, yeah," the younger officer nodded, glancing back out the window. "I've heard of her. The artist."

"That's the one," John agreed.

The landscape darkened as the rutted road dropped down into the lower lands of the salt marsh. Dead barkless trees, dry and white as desiccated bone, lifted shattered branches toward the oppressive sky. Rounding a narrow curve, the patrol car skidded gently as its tires dug for traction against the damp and yielding sand. The car passed under a murder of crows roosting in a large tree and the crows objected loudly to the invasion, flapping their wings and rising en masse while cawing a harsh, primeval protest.

John leaned forward and pulled a clipboard off the dash. He knew that academy training was vital, but he still believed that the most critical part of rookie training took place in the field. Schoolroom knowledge could only take you so far; the reality of an actual situation added the final polish, and John wanted to utilize every opportunity to bring the rookie up to grade. "Here, Hank. Take a look at this before we get there."

"What is that?" Hank wondered before recognizing the document. "Ah, a general consent form."

"We'll need Mrs. Farrar's signature on it before we can search her property."

"Didn't we get a warrant?"

"Yes, but it limits us to searching Eddie's truck and the immediate area." John frowned. "It was all I could get Judge Coffin to agree to; he's a stickler on Fourth Amendment rights. Unless Mrs. Farrar signs that permission for a general search,

Eddie's truck is as far as we can go – for today. I want to be clear on that."

"Sure thing, Lieutenant." Hank lowered the clipboard to his lap. "I read your preliminary report. Just so we are clear on it, are we planning on arresting Mrs. Farrar today?"

"We can't; not on the evidence we have. Everything is still too speculative. All we know for a fact is that the paint sample recovered from Richard Robey's body may have come from Eddie Farrar's truck. That was solid enough for the warrant; now we'll go in and look for corroborative evidence."

"Like what?"

"Well, I'm hoping we find a scratch in the paint somewhere on Eddie's truck. That will link the truck to Richard Robey's murder, and we'll take it from there."

"I don't know, Lieutenant. It seems pretty thin to me."

"And if that was all we had, it would be." John tapped the wheel. "But if Paul Jenkins is right about the caliber of the gun that was used to kill Richard Robey – that my uncle's gun was the murder weapon – then we have to ask, when and how did the Farrars gain possession of it?"

"The Nambu," Hank nodded. "Japanese. 8MM."

"Good. You did your homework," John smiled encouragingly. "Now, I suppose it is possible that there are two Nambu pistols on this island. But personally? I think the chance is slim to none. My best guess is that Eddie Farrar went scavenging through my uncle's house and he found the Nambu, and he carried it home. I know for a fact Eddie had committed B&E before; it's not in his record, he's never been charged with it, but I know he's done it."

"Okay," Hank frowned uncertainly. "But what makes you think Mrs. Farrar used the gun to shoot Richard Robey?"

"Two reasons: one, because she has probable possession, and two, because of the way Richard was killed. The murder wasn't a quick hit; it was a real mess. I've thought it was a revenge killing from the minute we pulled Richard's body out of the harbor. Revenge is the only motive that makes sense."

"But why would she have shot him? That's what I don't understand."

"I think what we have to consider here, Hank, is family history. First there's Beryl Farrar, an off-island Navy wife, married young to a career alcoholic, two children, a boy and a girl; the family scratches out a living for more than thirty years from the edge of this swamp. Things look pretty dismal; from what I hear the Farrar's never owned a bean. The daughter, Tonya, was in my sister's graduating class, and Mary Rose said Tonya split for the mainland the night of their graduation ceremony. Mary Rose said Tonya boarded the mainland ferry still wearing her cap and gown. So we know Tonya Farrar never looked back. And then there's Beryl's husband, Todd, who spent his final years breathing through an oxygen tube until he died – a victim of Beryl's second-hand smoke.

"After her daughter's desertion and her husband's death, Beryl is left with Eddie, her son and from everything I've seen her pride and joy. And who's to say? I don't know, maybe Eddie returned the feeling. I do know Eddie brought home anything he could find to try and make his mother's life a little nicer. And then the day comes and Eddie has his accident and he dies, too." John turned the wheel. "This is where I start guessing. Maybe Eddie did slip and cut himself the way Paul Jenkins says he did. And maybe it was purely accidental. But Hank, here's what I think: I think Richard Robey was with Eddie Farrar on the beach that day, and I think Richard could have saved Eddie's life somehow and he failed to do it. And I think Beryl Farrar found that out. How? I don't know that yet, maybe Richard let something slip. But to my mind that's the only motive that could have pushed Beryl hard enough to murder Richard Robey. I think she found out he could have saved her son's life and he failed to do it – and she killed him for it."

"But you just said Richard and Eddie were friends! Why would he have let Eddie die?"

"That, Hank, is the question we're about to ask Beryl Farrar."

Hank digested John's theory and then nervously cleared his throat. "Lieutenant? What about that off-islander George Robey reported?"

John smiled, glad to see the rookie was challenging his approach. An active, open mind was the key to any successful investigation. "That's a good question, Hank, and I'm going to ask George more about that once he gets back from the mainland. But I'm beginning to have doubts about George's statement, too. We never did find a trace of any stranger asking for his brother – and it's a slow time of year. If there had been someone asking for Richard, we should have found something. And if the stranger stayed on island, he would have had to register at a guest house or hotel."

"Not if he just came over for the day on the ferry," Hank argued. "If he just bought a passenger ticket, there'd be no record. You don't have to register for that – all you need is cash."

"That's a good point, but seriously? If George Robey's 'mysterious stranger' did shoot Richard, then how did he get possession of my uncle's gun? No," John shook his head. "The 'mysterious stranger' doesn't add up. He was only a suspect because Richard's body was dumped in the Rip. But don't forget, Beryl Farrar is from off-island, too. There's no reason to think she'd know enough to steer away from the Rip when she dumped the body." John smiled grimly. "Remember to keep your eye on the odds, Hank. Seven times out of ten, the primary suspect is a family member of the victim. Eddie Farrar was Beryl's son, the only family she had left."

The rookie loudly cleared his throat. "Okay, but what if Mrs. Farrar won't talk to us? What's our plan then?"

"That's where this gets tricky." John nodded, doubly-glad to know Hank was also thinking ahead. Proactive situations, John knew, offered some protection and control; reactive situations were inherently more dangerous. "The warrant allows us to search Eddie's truck; if we find probable cause today – and that is what I'm hoping for – and Beryl comes out to the truck, we could arrest her on the warrant we have. But Hank, listen, we are nowhere near ready to make an arrest; I'd rather just question her today. If she stays in her house and refuses to talk to us, there is nothing more we can do today. We cannot go in and arrest her without another, more specific warrant. Is that clear?"

"Okay, Lieutenant, okay, I remember that much from Academy."

And if Beryl came out of the house voluntarily, John knew, it would be a hostile interview. He still remembered the glaring hatred Beryl had flung at him during their last conversation on the day of Eddie's death. And now, if she was Richard's killer, she would be forewarned; getting an answer out of her would require strategy, something low-key and effective, and John grew even more determined to get at the truth. Not only about what Beryl knew about Richard Robey's murder; he felt certain that she had also held something back during their previous interview, and because he had hesitated that day – constrained as he was by compassion, knowing he was there to announce her son's death – he had not pressed for detail, quite possibly losing the best chance he would ever have at gaining her knowledge of Uncle Ethan's activities and any possible link to his brother Danny's death.

This time, however, he resolved, he would not hold back. Privately, he hoped Beryl did leave her house and come out to the truck, demanding to know their intentions. He particularly wanted to see her reaction when he mentioned the paint sample that scraped off Richard Robey's belt buckle. What would Beryl say once she found out the sample was a dead match to the custom paint job on her son Eddie's truck?

"Hank, listen to me. I want you to be extra careful today. Beryl Farrar may still have my uncle's pistol; she may even have a shotgun or something else inside the house. Under no circumstances do I want you to expose yourself to any kind of risk. That's not why we're here; we're here to investigate Eddie's truck and ask questions only. This situation doesn't warrant an armed response. If it gets confrontational, it's simple, we leave – and come back with backup another day."

"Don't worry about me, Lieutenant. I'm no Jimmy Talbot."

John winced. Jimmy Talbot had been last year's rookie, twenty-one years old, mainland-trained, and as enthusiastic about law enforcement as it was possible for a rookie to be. And last September, as he had responded eagerly to a felony armed and dangerous, Jimmy had taken a .45 slug to the chest. Paul Jenkins had assured John that Jimmy never knew what hit him, but the incident continued to plague John whenever he saw Mercy Talbot crossing the street and averting her eyes when she saw him coming. Some very kind people had explained to him that Jimmy's mother simply couldn't reconcile herself with his responsibility in the death of her son. The explanation hadn't helped.

He turned left and pulled the unit into the Farrar's driveway, considering one final preliminary caution. "One more thing, Hank. If Beryl is our killer, she may have an accomplice. Watch your back."

Hank swallowed heavily. "Any theory on who that might be?"

"I'm thinking one of Eddie's friends? Rusty Craddock, maybe? I saw him with Eddie at my uncle's funeral."

"Rusty might do something like that, if you offered him cash." Hank pointed to a low shed at the rear of the Farrar property. "Hey, Lieutenant, there's the truck."

"I see it." Cautiously, John drove closer to the house, steering the unit around a rotten tree stump that divided the Farrar's side yard into two narrow, overgrown left and right lanes. It surprised John to remember the stump from his childhood visits to the house, although it had been taller then. Halfway between the house and the back lot, he parked the unit and slowly opened his door, deliberately leaving the door open after he stepped from the car, conscious of its limited effectiveness as a shield if that option became necessary. Personally, he hoped that use would not be required this visit. Reaching back in the window he tapped the horn. "Hello? Mrs. Farrar?"

There was no response. If Beryl Farrar was inside the house, she remained indifferent to their presence. John stepped clear of the car and studied the house for signs of life, but there were none to see; no pale smoke rising from the chimney, no glow of electric light illuminating the windows. The house remained silent and dark.

"Mrs. Farrar? Hello?" John repeated, louder. "It's Lieutenant John Jarad and Officer Hank Viera of the Nantucket Island Police Department. We're here to execute a search warrant signed by Judge Thomas Coffin. We're going to search Eddie's truck."

Still no response. Hank Viera whispered: "See anything, Lieutenant?"

"I'm going closer." John unsnapped his holster and drew his revolver, sidestepping so as to present as small a potential target as possible. He quickly scanned the rusted screened-in porch and both the front and kitchen doors, tilting his head and using his peripheral vision to catch any sudden movement from within. "Mrs. Farrar? It's John Jarad. We'd like to talk with you."

At the base of the porch steps he paused. Perhaps Beryl was in town; if so, they would have to catch up with her later. But he had a warrant to search Eddie Farrar's truck now; that much they could accomplish this trip. John returned his gun to its holster. "Hank, I think she's out. Let's search the truck."

As John turned away, a large feathery black object struck the screen next to his head. "Jesus!" John recoiled, dropping to one knee. "Jesus Christ!"

Trapped inside the porch, a large crow fluttered from perch to perch, cawing and eyeing John warily. "You bastard!" He laughed. "You scared the crap out of me!"

"Lieutenant?" Hank worried from his vantage by the car. "You okay?"

"Fine, Hank. I'm fine." He stood, brushing dirt and dead leaves from the knees of his pants. The trapped crow continued to study him, fluttering back and forth as John examined the wire screen for signs of a breach. "You bastard. How did you get in there?"

He walked along the outside of the porch and found a section of screen that had rusted through and fallen in, creating a funnel which had allowed the crow access but had trapped it once inside. Automatically, John noted the grimy glass of the kitchen window and the accumulation of debris housed inside the porch. His inspection stopped at the front door. In the dead of winter, the middle of February, the front door stood half-open to the cold. John took a deep breath and pulled his revolver. "Hank? I think you should come over here."

Breathless with excitement, Hank trotted over. "Lieutenant? What's up?"

"We just found probable cause. Follow me." Slowly, John mounted the porch steps, holding his revolver at the ready. Unsure about their intentions, the crow grew frenzied as the two men drew near, throwing itself frantically against the unyielding screen. John ignored the bird and opened the porch door with his left hand. "I hope I don't get sued for this," he muttered softly. "Mrs. Farrar? Hello?"

He crossed the porch and pushed on the opened front door, motioning Hank to follow. As the two men crossed the hall, John's senses went on high alert and he actually felt the hair on the back of his neck stand up. He rose to the balls of his feet and stood ready for anything. Slowly, John stepped into the living room and his boots squeaked against the floorboards like dry chalk. And then he saw her.

Beryl Farrar sat slumped in an upholstered armchair facing the doorway. She was wearing a faded floral housecoat and slippers and her death was the result of an obvious gunshot wound to the right side of her head. The wall opposite the chair was splattered with a dried plaster of blood, bone splinters and clumped brain tissue, and the greasy stain had long-since separated out, puddling on the floor into a congealed lump that looked to John like nothing less than clotted pink oatmeal.

"Sweet Jesus..." Hank Viera gagged, covering his mouth and lunging for the door.

Automatically, John noted the Nambu pistol resting on the pegged-pine floor next to Beryl's right hand. His mind raced over possibilities. Beryl Farrar a suicide? He found that idea hard to believe. Suicide seemed inconsistent with what he knew of Beryl's tough survivor personality. Beryl Farrar had spend her life fighting long odds; John knew from personal experience that she was a scrapper. And yet, when finally left on her own, had Beryl given up and put an end to it?

Again, John noted the location of the Nambu next to her right hand and his doubt about a suicide theory firmed. He retraced his steps to the patrol car and grabbed the handset, pausing only because he knew his words were going out over a public access bandwidth and there was nothing he could do to prevent it. "Tina? It's John. We've got a possible 10-56 at the Farrar's. Notify Paul Jenkins. We've got more work for him out here."

"Roger that, Lieutenant. Do you need backup?"

"Send Jim and C.J.; make sure they pack a kit."

Hank Viera stepped out of the low scrub, spitting repeatedly to clear his mouth. "Sorry about that, Lieutenant."

"Happens to everyone, Hank." John moved to the back of the unit and opened the trunk, removing a roll of yellow plastic crime scene tape. "Establish an inner perimeter. Mark off this section of driveway from her to say, around that tree, and back again. That will get us started."

"Sure thing, Lieutenant." The rookie took the roll of tape, looking dejected at the routine assignment.

"Establishing a perimeter is critical, Hank. We're going to have to rely on physical evidence on this one." The radio crackled and John returned to the front of the car. "Yes, Tina. I'm here."

"The M.E. is on his way. ETA eighteen minutes. Paul's leaving directly from the hospital."

"Roger that. Thank you."

"Lieutenant?" Hank had completed his task in record time and had returned to the car. "What about the truck? Are we still going to search it?"

"We'll do it now. Grab a flashlight."

Eddie Farrar's red truck had been backed inside the tumbledown shed at the back of the property. As the two officers crossed the tussocky ground of the backyard, a skeletal cat noticed them coming and retreated sullenly, skulking low-slung through a gap in a chicken-wire fence before vanishing into the underbrush. They entered the shed and John flicked on his flashlight, running the bright halogen beam across the softened ground. Both men noticed a great deal of fresh sawdust mixed into the dirt.

"Watch it, Hank, stay clear of those." John pointed out a set of boot prints leading to and from the driver's side door. He knelt, playing the light against the imprint. "Could be Beryl's."

He stood and directed the flashlight into the cab of the truck. The ashtray was full to overflowing, her signature trademark.

They moved to the back of the shed, staying close to the wall. The cobwebby roofline sloped steeply and John ducked into an awkward crouch. The truck bed was fully loaded, and the load was covered with a blue plastic tarpaulin. John reached in and pulled back the tarp, uncovering a load of fresh-cut firewood. The wood had been carelessly tossed into an unformed heap, and John played his flashlight around the outer edges of the load.

"Lieutenant," Hank pointed. "Is that what we're looking for?"

The truck's left tire well held a deep concave dimple, and John realized he was looking at the dent Eddie had put in his truck the day Eddie had thrown his chainsaw after his argument with Sarah and the imposter on Dionis beach. With a shock John realized the incident had occurred less than a month ago, and yet it seemed to him now to be an event from another lifetime. "No," John shook his head. "We're looking for scratch so deep it lifted the paint. I don't know, Hank. We may have to shift this load."

"Let me guess who gets that job," Hank complained.

And then John saw it. A jagged fractured scarring the red paint, the scratch so new the underbody wasn't yet showing any sign of rust. He moved closer and played his flashlight along the scratch. "Wait a minute, Hank. I think we found it."

"That's it?" The rookie nodded eagerly. "That's our proof?"

"It could be." John paused. "So we're supposed to think that Beryl Farrar shot Richard Robey, moved his body in this truck and then shot herself."

Hank blinked. "Supposed to think, Lieutenant? What do you mean supposed to think?"

He moved back to the front of Eddie's truck. "Well, Hank, lately I've learned to distrust the obvious. Let's make sure this truck wasn't hot-wired."

"Why would Mrs. Farrar hot-wire the truck if she had the key?"

"It's all about possibilities, Hank. Check every possibility." He straddled the muddy footprints and opened the driver's door, probing under the dashboard and finding no signs of tampering. John straightened up and tapped his lips with an index finger. "Nothing there. So whoever used the truck had a key."

He considered another possibility and gently lifted the polyester floor mat. Lying flat against the carpet's channeled nap, an ignition key gleamed an inviting welcome. "I should have guessed. Like everyone else on island, Beryl leaves her key under the floor mat. So…what does that tell me?" John stepped clear of the truck and answered his own question. "It means that someone other than Beryl could have used this truck; she may not even have known it was gone."

Hank looked puzzled. "So now you're thinking she didn't shoot Richard Robey?"

"I'm not thinking anything yet, Hank, until I have the facts." John glanced up as a second police unit pulled into the driveway. "C'mon. Let's fill them in."

They left the shed and walked toward the response unit. Jim Parsons opened his door as they drew near. "What have we got, Lieutenant?"

"It's Beryl Farrar, Jim. Looks like a 10-56. We left the scene for the M.E.; suicide is Paul's bailiwick. He's due any minute."

"Has she been dead long?" C.J. wondered.

"Yes," Hank piped up, proud to report a significant item. "You should see her. It's a real horror show inside."

"I need you to establish an outer perimeter along the road," John directed. "Don't let anyone in here except Paul, and I mean anyone. We're going to see the media on this one; news is slow this time of year. I think we can count on them to make an appearance."

"You got it, Lieutenant," Jim nodded. He returned to the car, made a u-turn and passed the M.E.'s green sedan at the crossroad.

Paul Jenkins drove closer and John noticed an unfamiliar face seated in the passenger side of the car. The stranger was a fresh-faced girl with cropped blonde hair and John frowned. Paul should have known better. A crime scene was not the place for any unauthorized interested observers or morbidly curious family members. The M.E. parked and stepped from car, reaching back in for his medical bag. "Well, John. I suppose it's Beryl Farrar?"

"I'm afraid so, Paul."

The M.E. nodded tiredly. "I figured as much, when I heard the address." He gestured toward his passenger who unbuckled her seatbelt to join him. "John, this is my niece, Parian. Parian, this is Lieutenant John Jarad. He'll be heading the investigation once we've released the crime scene."

"Nice to meet you, Lieutenant. My uncle's told me a lot about you."

"Parian is studying to be an evidence recovery technician," Paul explained. "She's interning with me for six weeks this semester. I brought her along today to get some practical field experience."

John considered the grisly scene in the living room and frowned. "This may not be the best introduction to the field. It's not a pretty sight in there."

"It never is." The girl covered her hair with a plastic shower cap. "I'll be alright, Lieutenant Jarad." She reached into the sedan and started testing her camera equipment. "I've been studying Forensic Science at the University of New Haven for almost two years. I believe I have just about seen it all."

"You try stopping her," Paul grimaced. "I can't. She takes after her mother's side of the family."

"Gentlemen?" Parian stepped forward, steadying a tripod spotlight on her shoulder. "Are you ready?"

John led the way back to the house, followed by the M.E. and his new team member.

"Just a minute." Parian fired off three preliminary photographs and then peered into the porch. "Is that a crow in there?"

"Yes," John replied. "He was there when we got here. He may have…ingested…some of the evidence."

"And you thought you'd leave him for me," Paul nodded. "I see. Nice. Very nice. Thanks a lot."

"You're the forensic specialist." John stopped outside the front door. "I'll leave you to it."

The M.E. rolled on a latex gloves, noting that all the light switches were in the 'off' position and then flicking them to 'on'. Even so, the hallway remained dimly illuminated. "First thing, Parian, we'll need better light in here. Set up a secondary source, will you? Use the extension cord, I'll want the light in the other room, as well." He stepped through to the living room, assessing both the situation and the position of the body. "Oh, yes, I see. John? You noticed this pistol is a Nambu?"

"Yes. I noticed that."

"I can see one spent shell casing under the small table to the right. That's consistent with the entry wound." Paul lowered his case to the floor, opened it, and removed a bundle of thin plastic-coated wires, assembling a twelve-inch grid. "Parian? I'll want photographs in a clockwise pattern, working outward from the body. In particular, photograph the scene from two opposite corners, from say, that doorway and from over by the TV. Don't forget to keep a photo log."

"I don't need to anymore, Uncle Paul; it's automatic. I brought my new digital camera." The intern fired off a series of frames and then focused on the impact wall. "Wow. Classic high-velocity splatter. These will look great on my Web site."

"They sure don't make girls the way they used to," the M.E. muttered. "And Parian, don't forget to look up. Crime scenes are three dimensional."

"I get you, Uncle Paul. Okay, I think that does it. She's all yours."

Paul Jenkins moved closer to examine the body. Beryl Farrar's remaining eye was wide-open and bloodshot. After the impact, her body had slumped into the left side of the chair. Her right arm and hand hung free and the fingers of her right hand pointed to the pistol on the floor. Beryl's hands, feet and ankles were discolored bluish-purple with heavy postmortem lividity. Gently, he manipulated Beryl's right arm; it swung freely at his touch. "Rigor's passed," he noted. "She's been dead at least 36 hours, John, maybe more."

"Thirty-six hours is a day and a half. So she died when? You're thinking, sometime Friday night?"

"I can't be specific until I get an inner core temperature." Paul rose slowly. "But Friday night would be my best guess fpr a postmortem interval at this point."

"Then I've got a problem with this setup, Paul. There weren't any lights on when we arrived. It's February; it gets full dark before five o'clock. You're telling me she committed suicide sitting in the dark?"

"John, the woman committed suicide. Maybe she wasn't thinking clearly."

"Bear with me a minute on this. So, what have we got? Richard Robey was killed sometime Thursday; we know that for a fact. Beryl puts his body in the truck and dumps him in the Rip, thinking she's done with him. And then, on Friday, she hears that we found Richard floating in Madaket Harbor and Beryl what? She panics? She comes home and shoots herself, sitting in the dark?"

"Apparently with that pistol."

"Apparently, yes. It's the 'apparently' that's giving me the problem." John knelt next to the armchair and rotated Beryl's left hand. "Look at the nicotine on her fingers. I know for a fact she was left-handed." He indicated the splattered wall. "Now, if you're going to put a bullet through your head, would you trust your weaker hand to pull the trigger? And risk the chance that you might miss?"

"So you're saying this was murder?"

"I'm not saying anything anymore until I have proof." John stood slowly. "I'm tired of getting proved wrong. But I think someone set this up to look like suicide, and whoever did it wanted to pin Richard Robey's murder on her." He rubbed his neck. "Facts. Get me the facts, Paul. I'm going back to the station. There's something else I want to check. And this time,

I'm going to check all my case files. The answer I'm looking for is in there. I know it."

The M.E. looked at John curiously. "What is it you're looking for?"

"I'm not sure yet," John frowned. "But I'll know it when I see it."

CHAPTER NINETEEN

"John, what do you mean you're not coming home? You've got to eat, and I've made dinner already!"

"Just leave me a plate in the oven, honey, will you please?" His tired sigh carried across the phone line. "I'll be home in a little bit. I just want to review my case notes one more time before I leave."

"But you've told me yourself you've got the damn thing memorized! What can't wait until tomorrow?"

"Sarah, I've missed something. I know I have." His voice held an echoing whisper of doubt. "The answer is right here in front of me. I just can't see it."

"Well, John, listen, here's an idea. Why don't you bring your files home and we'll go over them together? A second pair of eyes might help."

"Honey, I can't do that, you know I can't. I need to stay focused. If I come home I'll get distracted." He sighed again. "You can help me most by just letting me do this my way."

Sarah felt washed by anxiety that went all the way through to her bones. She tried another tactic and sang a temptation. "I made a veggie lasagna. It's your favorite."

"Yes, yes, it is. And it'll keep warm. Please, Sarah, just one more hour. I'll be home in an hour, I promise."

"Fine. You do that." She slammed down the phone, trembling with a combination of dread and anger. Sure, they had found Danny's body, but where was the resolution to his case? Even though they knew the truth about his whereabouts, John was no closer to finding peace of mind than before!

She caught herself pacing the galley kitchen, so jumpy and nervous she couldn't sit still. Tension won out and Sarah gave in, grabbing the minivan's keys for a walk along the beach. Still fuming, she slid behind the steering wheel, fastened her seatbelt and considered her options.

Dionis beach was out ever since Eddie Farrar's fatal accident. The absolute last thing she wanted to do was to stumble over Eddie's ghost dredging timber between those lonely dunes. 'Sconset was too far away, over on the other side of the island, and besides, 'Sconset was Jarad Central and she'd had enough of that particular family for right now, thank you very much.

That left Surfside as her best option for neutral territory. Sarah backed out of the driveway and headed the minivan south on Hooper Farm road. It was a calm, clear, beautiful winter's night and she could feel the tension ease out of her neck and shoulders just through the act of movement itself. The moon was full and washed the road with silvery light. Sarah clicked the headlights off as a test, delighted to find the surrounding landscape almost as fully illuminated as during the day. In the friendly semi-darkness, the minivan's interior was filled with a neon green glow, and Sarah reached down and tossed her new cellphone over onto the passenger seat, deciding that she would talk to her husband when she was good and ready and not one minute sooner.

An oncoming car flicked its headlights in warning and Sarah hurriedly turned hers back on. "Oops, sorry," she apologized, and remembered a warning her grandmother had repeated about the treacherous nature of a full moon.

"You kids be careful out there," the old woman had counseled. "Moonlight can be deceptive. You think because of it you can see your shadow in the dark, but don't be surprised when it reveals to you more than what it offers to show."

Sarah shivered at the vividness of the unexpected memory. She hadn't thought about Nanna in months. Briefly, she considered swallowing her pride and returning home to John and the overbaked lasagna. At her side, the phone trilled shrilly and Sarah scrabbled for it, checking the caller I.D. It was John. Her bruised ego stepped forward and she ignored the call, flooring the accelerator and tossing her hair. "Leave me a message," she stated. "You're a grown man. You can take care of yourself."

All around her, the flat, sandy land stretched out into the darkness, the twisted shadowy gray-green scrub punctuated at intervals by silent homes as solitary as moated castles. Occasionally, in one of the upside-down houses, a second-floor window reflected the pulsating blue light of a television set, but other than that reminder of modern technology, the purity of the night belonged to her.

She pulled into a small parking lot near Surfside beach and decided she had done the right thing in leaving the house. Sitting home alone waiting for John to return while planning their consequent argument was not the wisest course for the continued good health of their marriage. A brisk refreshing walk was just what she needed to clear her head and restore her usual sense of humor. Sarah noticed she was not alone in her enjoyment of the night; on the shoreline below, heading west toward Cisco, a female jogger and her dog danced a silhouette against the expansive, mercurial sea.

Sarah adjusted the heater and relaxed into the vinyl seat. Lord knows she felt like she was riding a hormonal roller-coaster lately, what with the stress of planning for the baby and prodding John on the construction of the new house. And of course, dealing with the emotional fallout from Ava Descartes' revelation and the exposure of that imposter Raymond Perry. Sarah could only imagine what all this was doing to her husband, but try as she might, she couldn't help but be irritated by his stubborn refusal to accept her help. They had talked about this very thing! And he had broken his promise!

So, okay, Sarah admitted, maybe she wasn't a 'professional investigator'; maybe she didn't even know what it was that she could do, but at least she wanted to be able to try. Her willingness to try had to count for something. To be continually met by a polite rebuff left her feeling weak and helpless, and she had never enjoyed either of those two emotions.

The phone rang again, and for the second time she ignored it. "Damn the man, he promised he'd let me help."

She turned off the motor and locked the minivan, following a narrow winding path down the steep pebbly bluff toward the shore. Surfside beach was more exposed than familiar Dionis, and the brisk, chill wind plucked Sarah's long hair free and obscured her vision. Halfway down the slope, she paused to pull her wooly cap down closer over her ears and heard the breeze rustling tufts of dried poverty grass like the warning rattle on a snake. When she reached the soft deeper sand, Sarah turned and started trudging due west. Moonlight rippled across the ocean and Sarah noted with satisfaction that as long as she kept her hands stuffed in her pockets, she felt perfectly warm, safe, and content.

After a quarter-mile, she moved toward an old wooden staircase that led up the bluff from the beach to Western Avenue and the abandoned lifesaving station located there.

Ever since Sarah had discovered the antique building with its roofline like an inverted ship's keel, she had loved the stationhouse and its tall matching tower. On clear nights like this, the tower's dramatic shape was delineated against the wide sparkling expanse of the Milky Way and an infinite number of flickering satellites, planets, and stars.

Halfway up the stairs, Sarah felt short of breath and sat down to rest for a moment on a broad wooden step. She leaned into the splintery railing and studied the Lifesaving Station, the building conjuring for her as it did a vision of the gentle past, of ladies in pleated white linen skirts and gentlemen in seersucker jackets struggling with wicker hampers full of cold fried chicken, rich potato salad, deviled eggs, and crisp watermelon pickle.

Her empty stomach gurgled.

"Okay, so I'm hungry," she admitted, thinking of the panful of hot cheesy lasagna waiting back home. Maybe it was time to head back. Slowly, she stood, and as she did a shadowy movement caught her peripheral vision. She paused to watch a stooped figure struggle around the base of the lighthouse tower and move toward the shelter of the abandoned station. Suddenly, recognition registered and Sarah squinted to make sure. "Addie Simpson? What are you doing here?"

Geographically, Sarah knew that Surfside Beach was almost diametrically opposed to Addie's home in Eel Point. And yet, as she continued to watch, Addie reached the shelter of the porch, glancing over her shoulder as she worked to unlock the front door. The door yielded and Addie slipped inside. A half-minute later a small circle of yellow light warmed one of the long, shuttered windows.

Sarah pushed back her hat. This little scenario was certainly odd, if nothing else. As far as she knew, Addie was still listed as a missing person with the Nantucket police, and the older woman's actions just now had appeared nothing less than furtive. What was Addie doing here? Sarah wondered. And if she was hiding, who was Addie hiding from?

Curiosity gave her a nudge and Sarah grasped the railing, climbing the stairs to the street level. Once out of the shelter of the bluff, there was no protection from the wind, and streamers of sand drifted over her boots as she crossed the road toward the Lifesaving Station. She knocked on the door lightly and heard fluttering movements from inside. "Addie? It's me, Sarah Jarad. Let me in. I want to talk to you."

The bolt was drawn back and the missing woman peered through the open door. Addie held a kerosene lantern high and she appeared terrified by her exposure. It occurred to Sarah that confronting Addie this way might not be the smartest thing she had ever done. "Hey, Addie. It sure is cold out. Can I come in?"

"Okay, but hurry up, will you? Don't take all day."

Addie reeked of that sour odor that came from someone needing a full bath. Sarah stepped clear of the doorway and noted that Addie had constructed a snug, safe little harbor for herself inside the Lifesaving Station. A thick pallet of faded quilts and pillows was nestled into one of the warmer inside corners of the high-ceilinged room. Plastic gallon jugs of spring water were neatly stacked next to cartons of pork and beans and canned New England brown bread. A faintly sweet aroma rising from a yellow bucket against the far wall also told Sarah that Addie had been living here for quite some time.

"Are you thirsty?" Addie reached into her supplies. "Here, Sarah. Try one of these. These are good."

It was a can of warm grape soda, but Sarah was touched by Addie's attempted hospitality. Besides which, she was thirsty. She snapped the top and took a sip. Even warm, it wasn't bad. Sipping again, she indicated the room. "Addie, what are you doing here?"

Addie ignored her question and reached for a small hand mirror instead, picking up a black comb and pulling it through her hair. The comb caught on a snarl and the old woman picked the snarl free with dirty fingers. She glanced at Sarah shyly and replied in her strangely sing-song voice. "You have pretty hair. My hair was pretty once, prettier than yours. Mine was yellow. Now it's gray, all gray."

"Addie," Sarah persisted. "There are people looking for you. Your mother is very worried."

"He's back, you know." Addie crawled onto her pallet and drew a blanket around her shoulders. "The brother is back. The one who went away."

Sarah smiled and nodded, explaining gently. "No, Addie, that wasn't Danny Jarad. It was an imposter, a fake. At first we all thought it was Danny, too, but we've found out since then it wasn't really him."

"No, not Danny Jarad, the other brother," Addie frowned at Sarah's incomprehension. "Richard Robey is back. I saw him down on the beach. He hurt Eddie bad. Cut him up and made him bleed."

Richard Robey? The name sounded through Sarah, rattling her bones. The nervous unease she had felt all day was released, and she began to tremble as ripple upon ripple of this new possibility revealed itself. She struggled to get her head around the idea. What if Eddie Farrar's death hadn't been the freak accident John had thought but was instead a deliberate and vicious murder? "Are you sure about that, Addie? You saw Richard Robey hurt Eddie?"

"Um-hum," Addie nodded, twirling her hair around an index finger. "They were fighting. Richard hit Eddie hard and Eddie fell down. He was screaming just like a girl. Oh my, yes. Just like a girl." She adjusted her blanket and began to rock gently. "I ran to get Eddie help but that's when George saw me. He ran to his car but he's older now and I can still run fast when I want to."

Time stopped. Fumbling, Sarah sat down next to the older woman. "Addie, you saw George Robey there, too? You saw George and Richard together on the beach when Eddie got hurt?"

"Um-hum," Addie answered, reaching back and handing Sarah a crocheted afghan. "And George knows my street, he knows my house. So I came here. No one comes here in the wintertime. I can be safe, here."

And just like that, Sarah knew she had found John's missing link. If Addie Simpson could connect George Robey with Eddie Farrar's accidental death, and if Richard Robey and Beryl Farrar both later turned up dead, it was possible that George Robey was a murderer not just once but maybe even all three times.

John needed to hear Addie's story; then he could put out an APB on George Robey and his case would be solved! She reached into her pocket for her cellphone, her fingers blindly searching before she realized she had left the cellphone, unplugged, inside the minivan.

"Shit!" Sarah kicked herself for the oversight, admitting with some shame that if she had not been so pig-headedly angry at John earlier, the cellphone would be in her hand this very second. "Addie, is there a phone here?"

"No, Sarah. I don't even have electricity."

Sarah sighed. There was no help for it. She would have to backtrack to the minivan to make the call. "Addie, I have to go get my phone. Will you come with me? Then we'll call John and tell him about George and Richard."

"NO!" The older woman howled. "Don't you tell! If you tell, he'll know! Sarah, you can't tell! I thought you were my friend!"

"I am your friend, Addie, I swear I am. But you have to listen to me. You don't know this yet, but Richard Robey is dead and George left for the mainland. You're perfectly safe. There's no one left on Nantucket who can hurt you."

Abruptly, Addie stopped howling. "They're gone? Both of them are gone?"

"Yes. So why don't you come with me? It's safe now. I can drive you home to your mother's."

Addie squinted and considered Sarah's idea. "No, I don't think so. It's dark out. I don't like the dark. Sarah, I know. Why don't you call my Mom for me? Tell her I'll come home tomorrow, during the daytime."

Sarah sighed, recognizing an impasse. She needed to get the cellphone to call John, and she certainly couldn't drag Addie back to the minivan. "Alright then, Addie. Here's the deal. I'll go call John and then I'll come back and we can wait for him together. How's that? Is that okay with you?"

"I don't like John Jarad. He's a policeman. Policemen yell."

"Yeah, yeah, I know. We've been through that, remember?" Sarah zipped her jacket. "Now don't worry. I'll be right back."

As Sarah stepped off the porch she heard Addie shut the door firmly behind her and slide the bolt into place. Briskly, she set off, heading back across the road and down the beach steps, seeking the damp sand along the waterline for faster, firmer traction. The beach was deserted and the bright moon played hide and seek behind speeding wisps of cloud. The ocean had gentled, sending rhythmic waves chopping against the shore. Armed with her new knowledge, Sarah felt an adrenaline thrill pumping through her veins, and anticipated John's receipt of her shocking information about George Robey. And best of all, this time John would have to accept her help! She had solved his case for him! Take that, Mr. Professional Investigator!

Sarah climbed the narrow path back to the parking lot, digging for her keys. After she had unlocked the minivan, she slid behind the wheel and felt along the seat for the cellphone. The warning light now glowed like a single accusatory red eye, evidence that the neglected battery was close to extinction. Sarah plugged the phone cord into the dashboard lighter hoping for some extra juice and sent up a silent prayer as she dialed John's line at the station.

Tina Bradley answered on the second ring, not a good sign. "Nantucket Island Police. How can we help?"

"Tina? Hi, it's Sarah. Is John there?"

"No, Sarah, he went out about ten minutes ago. Why? Is something wrong?"

"No, no, I just need to give him a message. It's urgent."

"Well, just a minute. Let me try his pager."

The line clicked as the dispatcher put Sarah on hold. There was an intermittent buzz of static and the line clicked again. "Sarah? I'm sorry. He's not answering. Do you want me to take a message?"

It wasn't the answer she wanted to hear but it was the answer she got. She found herself trembling with suppressed excitement. "Alright. Tina? Tell John that I found Addie Simpson and we're both at the Surfside Lifesaving Station. And please tell John it's very, very important. He needs to hear what she has to say."

And then, just when Sarah needed it most, the cellphone beeped a rapidly repeated sequence and warned her of an imminent power failure.

"Roger that, Sarah. Let me repeat. You found Addie Simpson at the Surfside station and you'll wait for John there. Is that right?

"Yes, and tell him..." was all she managed as the red light faded and the cellphone died in her hands. Fruitlessly, Sarah thumbed a few buttons and rapped the cellphone against the heel of her hand. The marvel of modern technology remained completely unresponsive. She gave it one last hard shake and then threw it back onto the passenger seat. "Dammit! Well, at least John got my message, first."

She put the minivan in gear, deciding to risk the sandy overland trip to the station rather than face the long walk alone in the dark. The adrenaline high Sarah had enjoyed earlier was wearing off, leaving her feeling defenseless and over-tired. She hoped the approaching minivan wouldn't freak Addie out too badly, but her decision at this point was purely defensive. The thought of trudging back to the station through all that cold deep sand simply required more energy than she possessed.

She drove slowly along the top of the bluff until she located a section of the crumbling asphalt that led to the abandoned station. After parking next to the porch, Sarah found Addie waiting for her, holding the half-opened door clenched in both hands.

"I'm glad you're back!" Addie was almost breathless with fear. "I knew it was you, but still, I was scared."

"There's no reason to be scared. I called John, he's on his way," Sarah reported, feeling ill and out of breath. "When he gets here, Addie, I want you to tell him just what you told me, about George and Richard."

"Sure, Sarah, sure, I can do that." Addie indicated a reasonably clean set of striped blankets, folded neatly on the floor. "Here, I made this place for you, so you can keep warm."

"Thank you, Addie." She wrapped a blanket around her shoulders gratefully. Her head was swimming with fatigue. "That was very thoughtful of you."

"And I found this, too." Addie shuffled toward her pallet. "While you were gone."

Sarah heard the sound of wood dragging against wood, but couldn't see past the older woman to make out what it was that Addie was lifting. Addie turned and hefted a splintered harpoon with both hands. Even flaked with rust, the iron flanges looked lethal.

"Ho, ho." The gray-haired woman shook the antique weapon. "Nobody better try to scare us now!"

Sarah smiled at Addie's pantomime. She leaned back against a pillow. "No one's going to hurt us, Addie. John will be here any second. Then we'll tell him about George and Richard, and he'll catch George and put him in jail."

"Bad boys, bad boys, what you going to do?" Addie sang tunelessly. She lowered the harpoon and gave it an affectionate pat. "They were bad boys. They threw stones and called me names."

Sarah took a good hard look at the older woman, looking past the gossip and the myth to truly appreciate the person standing before her, rugged, dirty, and independent, doing the best she could with what she had. "Addie, you're pretty amazing. Do you know that?"

"Um-hum," Addie hugged her knees. "Most folks can't see it. They're too busy being busy to take notice of me."

"Well, I've noticed."

"I know you have, Sarah, that's why you're my friend." Addie tilted her head to listen to the wind and suddenly scrambled to her feet. "I hear a car."

Sarah sat up and dropped her blanket, taking comfort in the knowledge that John had believed in the urgency of her message. Maybe, just maybe, they hadn't grown so far apart after all. Maybe the only thing he needed was a little more time, and a little more room, to think. She decided to try to find more patience for him and his needs in the future, and to try to think less of herself. Sarah smiled gently as she crossed the room. "Take it easy, Addie. He's here to help us."

"Look both ways!" Addie shouted, rigid with terror. "Always look both ways, mother always said!"

Sarah unbolted the door and started her apology. "John, I'm so glad…"

George Robey stood framed in the doorway. He planted his left hand on the half-opened door and pushed it backward, sending Sarah skittering on her heels. "Hello, sweetheart," he gave her his warmest smile. "May I come in?"

"I TOLD YOU!" Addie bellowed, scrambling low across the floor. "I told you he was bad! Now look what you've done!"

"As bad as I want to be," George enunciated carefully, pulling a gleaming new automatic from his pocket. He pointed the gun at Addie and sighted alone the barrel. "Bad to the bone."

Addie shoved Sarah toward a side door. "Go! Go! Move! Up the stairs!"

"Too late for that," George pronounced, aiming the gun at Addie's wide protective back and pulling the trigger.

The gun clicked. Nothing happened.

George Robey looked at the automatic incredulously before laughing softly. "Motherfucker?! Excuse me, ladies, I forgot. This one has a safety." Chuckling, George released the safety and shrugged. "What can I say? I hate reading instruction manuals."

"HAUL YOUR ASS!" Addie screeched, flinging open the side door and shoving Sarah inside. "I said RUN."

Sarah stumbled forward into the dark. She found herself in a small cold room and realized she was actually inside the base of the lighthouse tower. She glanced back for Addie. The older woman stood framed in the doorway, backlit by the kerosene lantern and surrounded by a halo of warm yellow light. Addie pointed her finger up the stairs. "Missy, I said GO!"

The report of the shot echoed off and up the stone walls of the lighthouse tower. Sarah's warning scream joined the booming report that pierced her eardrums. She flinched in pain as Addie collapsed in a heap on the cold stone floor. A pool of dark blood immediately began to puddle under Addie's head.

George Robey stepped through the doorway and stood over Addie Simpson's body. "Stupid cow." Finding Sarah still standing on the staircase, he smiled happily and raised the automatic. "Next one's for you."

Sarah ducked low behind the iron banister and retreated up the staircase. She felt weightless; adrenaline had her feet flying up the steps as her heartbeat pulsed loudly in her deafened ears. She was in big trouble this time and she knew it. She needed to think – think clearly – and find a way out. "Don't panic. Don't panic. Do not panic," she panted, climbing up the circling staircase.

"Sarah? Sarah Jarad?" George Robey crooned, transferring the automatic to his left hand before following her up the staircase. "I just have to ask…where do you think you're going?"

She stopped for breath on the first corrugated steel landing, looking down the long open central stairwell. She was shaking with exertion and fear and there wasn't a defensive weapon in sight. "John knows all about you, George, I told him, and he's on his way. You'd better run."

George Robey chuckled and the low, unpleasant sound echoed up the stairwell. "Oh, I don't think so, do you? I heard him call and check for messages on my scanner. Your husband is still back in town, Sarah, and I do so enjoy your company. I think we can share a bit more time together." George continued up the iron stairs. "Thank you for finding Addie Simpson for me. She was my last threat, you know – my last loose cannon."

"She saw you and your brother kill Eddie Farrar." Sarah clambered up the staircase to the second landing, praying for John's arrival and playing for time. "Why did you do that, George? Why did you kill Eddie? What did he have on you?"

George sighed, and the sigh whispered up the stone wall. "Well, all that was twenty years ago, and I really don't think any of it matters anymore, do you?"

Twenty years ago. Like ripples on a pond, the puzzle fell into place: Danny Jarad's hidden grave on Ethan Jarad's land, George Robey's insistent offer to purchase that piece of property and none other, Eddie Farrar's accidental death and a motive behind the murders of Richard Robey and Beryl Farrar.

"Oh my God," Sarah breathed. "You killed Danny Jarad."

"No, I didn't, actually." George tapped the barrel of the gun repeatedly against the iron handrail, sending up a tinny vibration. "But I was there when it happened." He sighed ruefully. "It was bad luck, that's all it was. We had trouble with the boat; cheap gas and the engine kept stalling because of the rain. We didn't get to shore until after dawn. Christ! You should have seen Ethan Jarad; he was a madman. He was sure we'd get picked up, and he hated leaving Eddie on shore alone; he was convinced Eddie was going through his house while we were gone. And the funny thing was, he was right! Most of the time, Eddie was!" George chuckled again, the sound low and menacing. "We tied off and Ethan ran up to the house, yelling: 'Eddie Farrar, you shrimp-livered bastard, get out of my house!' Eddie ran out the back door and Ethan fired a shot just to scare him. And that's when Eddie came out of the dock house, zipping his pants and asking us what was going on."

Sarah heard the steady clink of metal on metal as the madman below followed her up into the tower. Silently, she retreated to the third level.

"You have to understand something," George whispered. "It was the perfect moment. I knew then, I knew, that if I just had the nerve to control the situation then nothing could stop me. I could have everything I ever wanted." He paused on the landing below, breathing hard. "I only made one mistake. I let Ethan hide that boy's body. I should have done it, I should have buried him myself, but Ethan told me to bring the boat around and I, well, I was young, so I obeyed." George lifted his face and shouted up the stairwell. "And haven't I paid enough? Worrying every goddamn day that someone would find the body and dig him up? And paying that bloodsucker Eddie Farrar every month? Well, I am through with all of that. I took care of Eddie. I took care of Richard. And now, I'm going to take care of you."

Sarah retreated to the top of the lighthouse, circling the stairs until she was dizzy. Reaching the top landing, she opened a rough plywood door and stepped out onto the grated iron catwalk that circled the lighthouse. Sarah tested the catwalk for her weight and felt it jounce beneath her feet. "Oh, Lord, I really don't like this," she moaned.

Lit by the moon, the island spread out below in all its beauty. The ocean shimmered luminously and even at this height Sarah heard the surf rolling against the shore. The landmass was a drift of dark vegetation dotted with stark pockets of pale sand. Over her head, a million stars blazed against the midnight blue sky. Cautiously, Sarah peered over the iron railing, looking down the sheer stone wall hoping for a ladder, a fire escape, toeholds, anything. The smoth wall was plastered and the dark ground sixty feet below looked unforgiving.

"Shit!" Sarah found herself praying as earnestly as she had ever prayed in her life. "Lord, you're going to have to help me. I am really not happy here."

Sarah peered out into the landscape, hoping for a sign of speeding headlights, hoping against hope for John's imminent arrival, but saw nothing. She despaired at the thought of their baby never seeing the light of day, and that decided it; she would fight. Today was simply not a good day to die. She was going to have to make a stand, somehow, without a weapon. She was out of options. There was nowhere to run.

The door slammed behind her, sending a shower of splinters to the ground. Sarah felt the catwalk bounce as George Robey stepped out of the darkness of the tower. She turned to face him as calmly as she could and brushed the hair out of her eyes. "George, you don't have to do this."

"Yes, I'm afraid I do." He cocked his head. "You're my last loose end. Once I kill you no one can touch me. No one." He raised the automatic. "I've been waiting twenty years to finish this."

"George, wait, don't." Sarah begged, raising both hands. "I'm going to have a baby."

"You should have thought of that before you stuck your nose in my business," he snarled.

It was the last thing George Robey ever said. Sarah felt the catwalk bounce a third time and Addie Simpson stepped through the doorway, her eyes fierce and intent in a face masked with blood. Addie hefted the harpoon high above her head and lunged at George Robey with all her weight. George never saw it coming.

He grunted as the metal flange pierced his chest. Slowly, George lowered and dropped the gun, blinking repeatedly. The gun bounced off the metal catwalk and fell into the darkness below. A thick bubble of blood spilled from his lips as he grasped the metal shaft that speared his sternum. George took one step forward and then staggered back into the railing. Slowly, and with a look of infinite surprise, he toppled over the railing, his body pinwheeling around and over the harpoon as he fell into the shadows.

Sarah couldn't watch, but she saw that Addie did. The older woman wiped the streaming blood from her eyes and let Sarah know it was over with a broad, triumphant smile.

Addie cupped one hand and called down to the base of the tower. "Thar she blows!" Then she turned back to Sarah and smiled. "That'll teach him to call me names!"

CHAPTER TWENTY

Sarah heard a soft, muffled cough and cautiously opened her eyes.

Dr. Nguyen was standing at the foot of her hospital bed, scowling. "Good afternoon, Sarah Jarad. I do not recommend running up and down lighthouse stairs in your condition."

She watched the doctor's eyes. They would tell her the truth. "How's the baby, doctor? Is everything alright?"

"You are a lucky woman. The sonogram indicates that everything is fine."

"You got the results?" Sarah sat up. "So you know. Tell me, doctor, is it a boy? Or a girl?"

Dr. Nyugen's dark eyes sparkled. "Yes," he replied.

"Very funny." She relaxed against the pillow. "It has to be a boy or a girl. There are no other choices, right?"

He smiled. "Or it is a boy and a girl."

"Twins? I'm carrying twins? No one in my family ever had twins before!"

"Then you will be the first. And I want you to exercise considerable more caution during the remainder of your pregnancy. Twins can be difficult to carry. The closer you are to full-term, the better."

"This is incredible!" Sarah laughed. "Have you told John yet?"

"No. I only told your husband you were in no danger." Dr. Nyugen smiled. "I felt this additional news should come from you."

There was a tap at the door and John looked in. "It's good to hear you laughing. I guess everything's okay?"

"Get in here," Sarah pointed to the foot of her bed. "Where have you been?"

He displayed a bouquet of yellow popcorn chrysanthemums. "Buying flowers."

"Oh, John! They're beautiful."

Dr. Nguyen retreated, giving Sarah one last pointed look. "Young lady, you will remember what I said?"

"Yes, of course, doctor." Sarah snuggled under the covers, deciding to keep the twins a secret from John until she could spring it on him properly. "Thank you again – for everything."

John sat down gingerly on the edge of the bed. Gently, he reached for Sarah's hand. "Honey? How are you feeling? Really?"

"Actually, John, you know what? I feel great."

"Thank God. You had me worried when I brought you in. You were in and out of it the whole way here."

"John? I'm so sorry. I've acted like a fool. It never entered my mind that George could be back on the island."

"Well, it entered my mind, as soon as Tina gave me your message. You should have seen the cars I blew past on the way to Surfside. Nantucket Towing's still pulling them out of the sand."

"You knew George was the killer?"

"I had suspicions. But never in my dreams did I think he would go after you. And he wouldn't have, now that you mention it, if you hadn't put yourself in his way."

"And if I hadn't put myself in his way, I never would have found Addie Simpson and solved your case for you! You should be thanking me, instead of yelling."

"I am not yelling. I want you to notice that I am using a very moderate tone of voice. But honey, last night I lived through one of my worst nightmares. You can't imagine what went through my mind on the way to Surfside. Why didn't you answer your phone?"

"Because I was so mad I didn't want to talk to you. I know, I know, I promised I would talk to you whenever I got mad, but I didn't. And trust me, John, after last night, I have learned my lesson." She adjusted her pillow and frowned. "So when did you start to suspect George?"

"The day of Richard's funeral, when he asked for more time to close the sale. George Robey never passed on closing a sale in his life. When he did that, it sent up a red flag. And then, when George mentioned he was going off-island, I wondered if he was trying to construct an alibi. For what it's worth, I had Jim Parsons watching George's house. But George slipped by us by using the Island Development van instead of picking up his Suburban at the airport."

"He told me Uncle Ethan shot Danny, but it was an accident. Did I already tell you that?"

"Yes, yes, you did, and I should have suspected it myself." He pulled a photograph from his pocket. "I found this in Danny's case file. The truth was in front of us the whole time."

Sarah pulled the photo from his fingers. It was the picture of the Jarad house the day of Danny's disappearance.

"There they are, all of them, look at it," John pointed. "Uncle Ethan, Eddie Farrar, George and Richard Robey. I'd like to know what they were discussing that day. It took a lot of nerve to volunteer for Danny's search when they knew all the time he was buried in his grave."

"Oh, John. I'm so sorry. Are you okay with this?"

"You know, I think I am. It took awhile, but I think I have my answer. Well, all the answer I'm ever going to get. I guess I'll have to be satisfied with it."

"I'm glad," Sarah stretched. "So how's Addie doing? She saved my life, you know."

"She'll be fine. Got a skull as thick as a stone crab. Ninety stitches and a skull fracture, but they took her off critical when she started demanding more tapioca pudding."

"Hum. And George is dead, isn't he?"

"Yes." John nodded. "His funeral is the day after tomorrow. They're going to re-open Richard's grave and bury the two of them together. You know Nantucket, that'll draw a crowd."

"Poor George. No new pie."

"You must be feeling better. You're getting your twisted sense of humor back."

"John, let me ask you something." Sarah reached for and took both his hands. "I know this is going to sound strange, but what do you think about using the name Daniel if our baby's a boy? Is that too weird for you?"

"Not really, not if you really think about it. Danny, my brother Danny, is the one person who's been pretty much forgotten in this whole thing. Oh, I'm sure we'll shock Uncle Tommy, but I like the idea we're going to remember Danny in our life." He tightened his grip. "I'll tell you what. I'll consider the name Daniel for a boy, if you'll consider the name Jenny, for my mother, if the baby's a girl. How's that?"

"You know what, John Jarad?" Sarah stretched the muscles of her back, stiff from lying in bed for too long. "You've got yourself a deal."

"Why?" John wondered, suddenly alert and suspicious. Sarah had never agreed to any of his other requests so easily before. "Why? What have I said?"

Author's Notes

First off, let me thank you for buying this book. I hope you enjoyed reading it as much as I enjoyed writing it. There's nothing like a good book to keep you company, and I hope you took this one to the beach. If it made you forget you were even on the beach, then I've done my job.

Next, I hope you decide to visit Nantucket! It's a beautiful and mysterious place. Be sure to stop at The Brotherhood of Thieves for a cup of chowder. It's worth the trip.

Now, because I used Print on Demand (POD) to publish, how do you order more copies? (And I hope you do!). It's easy. Simply go to your friendly, local bookstore and have them order *The Nature of the Grave* using the ISBN number off the back cover. You can also go online and order copies directly from Booklocker.com or from another internet book supplier. Copies are available off my Web site www.marthareed.com, and if you buy your copy from me, I'll autograph it for free. There. How's that for a deal?

Stay tuned for more to come! The next John and Sarah Jarad Nantucket Island Mystery – *The Witch of Wauwinet* is in the works. A preview chapter is available on my Web site. Please stop by and take a look, and be sure to sign my guest book and leave comments! I love hearing from other mystery enthusiasts, and I hope you become a John and Sarah Jarad fan.

All the best,

Martha Reed

Printed in the United States
38857LVS00002B/303

9 781591 136385